MW00652685

O'er the Land of the Free

O'er the Land of the Free
Copyright 2015 Beca Sue
All rights reserved

Cover design: Timothy L. Bean

This book is a work of fiction. Names, characters, places and incidents either are the product of the author's imaginations or are used fictitiously. Any resemblance to actual events, locales, organizations, or persons, living or dead, is entirely coincidental.

ISBN: 978-0-9961575-4-4

O'er the Land of the Free

Chapter One

September, 1859

"Virginia! Virginia!"

I could hear my mother calling me from a distance. Slamming my book shut and shoving it into my apron pocket, I scrambled as fast as I could from my lofty perch.

"Virginia Mae Hensley! Where are you at?"

Well, I wasn't about to answer that question if I could avoid it. Holding on tight, I stepped down lower then moved my hands to where my feet had just been.

"Virginia, you better not be to the top of that maple tree again! You know it scares me to death when you get so high in that tree."

No, I'm not at the top; now. I stretched my legs and arms as far and fast as possible. I could tell my mother was getting closer by the loudness of her voice. Maybe I could make it down to what she considered a safe height before she got to the tree.

"Virginia, what am I going to do with you?" Momma asked. "Honey you're thirteen years old. You have to quit spending every spare moment you have at the top of this tree."

I had made it to a limb about three- fourths down the tree. Mother was standing beneath the bottom limbs looking up. At least I wasn't still at the top. "I enjoy reading a book from up here, Momma," I replied. "You should try it sometime. You can see for miles, and it's so peaceful hid among the leaves."

"There would be absolutely nothing peaceful about being at the top of a tree or even on the first limb for me," Momma replied.

3

"You know heights terrify me."

"Don't you ever wonder what the birds see from the top of a tree?" I asked. "I wish I could fly like they do. Imagine the sights they see!"

"If God wanted us to fly, He would have given us wings," Momma replied. "Don't forget, birds sleep outside no matter what the weather. They also feast on bugs and seeds. Would you like that for supper?"

"Of course not," I said. "I just wonder what it would be like soaring through the sky and being able to see the land below. I bet we look like ants to the chicken hawks that get so high in the sky."

"Well, a chicken hawk might look real graceful riding on the wind but when they swoop down and snatch one of our hens or young chicks, I would rather they fly away and never return."

I knew Momma hated when predators killed her chickens, either by air or by land, like the foxes were known to do. I had seen her fire Papa's gun on several occasions at any critter who dared to have chicken for its next meal. Luckily for the attempting thief, Momma had poor aim but the shot usually scared them away for a good long while. No, my momma had no tolerance for any critter trying to make one of her hens its next meal. There would be no point in me continuing to talk about the attributes of being a chicken hawk.

"Well, enough daydreaming," Momma said. "We have supper to fix, so climb down and come help me. It won't be long until your father and brothers are home and they will be hungry."

I climbed the final few feet to the last limb then dropped lightly to the ground. I had practiced the maneuver so many times, I was sure I could perform it in my sleep. Gathering my long skirt up so I could move my legs more freely, I hurried to catch up with Momma's long strides. I knew better than to dawdle after just being found in the maple tree again.

Coming through the back door, I removed my book from my apron and took it upstairs to my room. There was no sense taking a chance of it getting wet while I was helping in the kitchen. Books were few and far between. Sometimes I would read the same book over, when I couldn't get my hands on one I hadn't read yet.

As I entered the kitchen, Momma pointed to the new potatoes I had dug earlier and I took to scrubbing. I would dice the potatoes and fry them, but there would be no need to peel them first. The skin was always thin when potatoes were first dug and they tasted great. After the potatoes were stored in the cellar a while, the skins would thicken and the potato would then have to be peeled.

The thing I hated the most about potatoes was that in late winter they would begin to sprout in the cellar. Then the potatoes had to be dragged outside where you could see and all the sprouts broken off. The potatoes were then put back into the cellar for future use, and later they would be planted in the garden. Each year we had to make sure we grew enough potatoes for us to eat all winter and still have plenty to plant for the next year's crop

I slipped the iron skillet onto the wood cook stove and added some bacon grease. Nothing made fried potatoes taste better than using bacon grease to fry them. Dicing the potatoes small, I added them to the now sizzling grease. Next, I chopped an onion and added it to the potatoes. Sprinkling salt and pepper on the now frying vegetables, the only thing left to do was turn them as they cooked. I added a lid to the skillet to build heat, making the potatoes cook faster. Momma busied herself slicing ham off the large chunk of meat she had brought in from the smokehouse, preparing to fry the meat in another skillet.

With the potatoes cooking, I began to mix the baking powder biscuits. Sifting the flour, salt, and baking powder, I then cut in lard. Milk was added and the dough came together nicely. I turned the dough out on a floured board and kneaded it slightly. Flattening the dough with my hands to about an inch thick, I cut out biscuits and placed them into a pan. I would wait until the potatoes were almost done to put the biscuits into the oven. This would ensure the biscuits would be fresh and piping hot to enjoy with the meal. With some sweet cream butter and strawberry preserves, the biscuits would serve as dessert, too.

Momma and I had picked green beans earlier and strung them on thread to make leather britches. We saved out enough for supper, and they were simmering at the back of the stove. My father and brothers would eat well tonight.

Leather britches were made by poking a threaded needle through the center of the bean and pushing the bean down the length of thread. When the thread was full of beans, it was hung to dry. We had made thirty strings of beans that were three feet long and hung them in the almost empty corn crib. There, they would get plenty of air around them to dry well and not be in direct sunlight. We would add the beans to the crock that contained ones we had preserved earlier in the summer, when they had dried enough. They weren't as good as fresh picked, but it was the only way to keep them over the winter.

I had just finished setting the table when I heard the wagon pull into the yard, the one I called the Curby Thursday wagon, because it was the only day Papa used that particular wagon. The rest of the time, he used the older one we owned. Passing the house, Papa went straight to the barn. Knowing it wouldn't take long for the horses to be unhitched and put into their stalls I grabbed the pan of biscuits and popped them into the oven.

My father owned a general store in the town of Marengo. We lived on a small farm two miles west of town. My two older brothers, Carter and Reuben, worked with Papa when there weren't farm chores to do. During the months that school was in, I would walk to the store when class was dismissed for the day. I was old enough to actually be of help now, instead of just being in the way.

Peering into the oven to check the progress of the biscuits, I heard the back door open. Looking up, I saw Carter smiling at me. "Did you climb to the top of the Maple today?" Carter asked, walking toward me.

"Why would you ask me that?" I replied. "You know Momma and I strung green beans today and dug some of the potatoes. I was quite busy and probably didn't have time to do any climbing."

"Really," Carter chuckled, "then why do you have this maple leaf in the back of your hair here?"

Taking the leaf Carter had removed from my hair, I stuck my tongue out at him. Carter understood me and my need to get close to nature. He even dragged me along sometimes to check his traps during the winter. I didn't like seeing the animals killed but I loved traipsing through the woods behind my brother. Carter, at fifteen, was fun loving and easy going. He could make you laugh on your worst day. Reuben, who was eighteen, was much more serious and didn't enjoy all of Carter's antics. I loved both my brothers, but Carter and I seemed to be kindred spirits. He laughed at all the things about me that made my mother cringe.

As we sat down to eat, Momma asked Papa if he had made the

trip to Curby today. He said yes and a look passed between them that I didn't understand. It was the same thing every other Thursday, which was referred to as Curby Thursday here at home. Momma always asked and Papa would say yes, he had gone to Curby. Then Papa either shook his head yes or no. I knew Papa delivered supplies to a farmer at Curby but I didn't know why Momma always asked Papa every time about the trip. I also didn't understand why the farmer didn't come to Marengo to get his own supplies. It was a confusing thing, to be sure. I had tried asking questions a couple times but Momma always said she was just curious if Papa had gone to Curby. What difference did it make if he hadn't?

When the meal was finished, Momma and I cleaned up the kitchen. With that done, I returned to my book I had been reading earlier. I would have preferred to climb the Maple again but figured I better not make Momma come after me two times in one day. It was very tempting, though, since I could have watched the sun set behind the rolling hills of our southern Indiana farm from a bird's eye view.

I could hear Momma and Papa talking downstairs in the kitchen and then they went outside. Looking out my bedroom window, I could see them headed toward the barn. This was another thing that happened on Curby Thursdays; Momma and Papa went to the barn after the supper dishes were done.

As I watched, I wondered why Momma had the large pan we had put the leftovers in tucked beneath her arm. Momma always insisted we cook way too much food every other Thursday, and throughout Friday, Saturday, and Sunday, too. It was another confusing thing for me to think about. Why did we make the extra food?

Returning to my book, I let the matter drop and got lost in the words. School would start again in three weeks and I wouldn't have much time to read what I wanted to then. When school started, I would have morning chores to do before breakfast. After we all ate, I would help Momma do the dishes then hurry and change out of my old clothes I wore to do chores in and into a nice dress. I would catch a ride to town with Papa as he went to the general store, and he would drop me off at the school. When I returned home with Papa in the evening, there would be more chores to do and supper to help prepare. Then the kitchen would need cleaning, again. Of course, if the store had been busy and I hadn't found time to finish my homework, I would have to complete it before bedtime. No, there certainly wouldn't be much time for book reading or tree climbing once school began.

After reading awhile, I put my book aside and headed downstairs to the kitchen for a drink of water. Scooping water into a hollow gourd from a stone crock, I took a nice long gulp. We were fortunate to have a good spring on our farm that supplied the sweetest water I had ever tasted.

Replacing the gourd, I headed to the living room where I could hear my brothers arguing. As I stepped in, I could see them in a heated game of checkers. Reuben was accusing Carter of moving pieces while his back was turned. Carter was denying it but I could tell by the glint in his eyes that he probably had done just that. Reuben was very serious about his checkers and Carter took advantage of it.

"Carter, I know you moved that checker when I looked up to see where Virginia was headed to," Reuben said pointing at the board.

"You're just surprised I'm actually beating you," Carter said with a smile.

"If you know what's good for you, you will put the pieces back where they were before I looked away," Reuben barked.

"Oh, yeah," Carter said making Reuben's face turn red and his fist clench tight.

"Yeah," Reuben said standing to his feet.

Carter stood, too. "Just what do you plan to do about it, Reuben?"

"I plan to make your eye as black as that checker piece," Reuben threatened.

"I wouldn't be fighting if I were you," I warned both of my brothers.

Carter turned to look at me. He smiled a crooked smile and winked. It was then I knew that he had moved the pieces to get under Reuben's skin, like a sliver of wood or a thorn that could not be pulled out. "Well, come on, Reuben, take the first swing," Carter goaded

Just when I thought Reuben was going to allow his frustration to cause him to give Carter a good wallop, Momma and Papa returned from the barn. My brothers knew it was time to quit fussing with each other. The last time Papa caught them fighting, he had made them move the whole manure pile twenty feet over from its original spot. When they were finished, he made them move it back. My brothers knew there was enough work to do without adding senseless manure moving.

Carter and Reuben sat back down at the checker board and started their game all over, Reuben making sure to keep his eyes glued to the board. Momma and Papa came into the living room and sat down and my brothers looked to them. Momma and Papa nodded their heads and smiled at my brothers. What was that all about? Why was I always the one in the dark around here?

"Why did you carry the leftovers to the barn, Momma?" I asked.

"No reason, Virginia," Momma said. "I just thought I would dump them out for the wild critters."

"Isn't it wasteful when we make all that extra food sometimes just to throw it out?" I asked. "If we had a dog, we could feed the leftovers to him."

"Virginia, dogs kill chickens," Momma said sternly. "We do not need a dog."

"I really wish we had one," I muttered, recalling having this same discussion on other occasions and never being able to persuade Momma that we needed a dog.

"It's late," Papa said ending the conversation. "Time to head up to bed, Virginia."

"Okay, Papa, but I truly don't understand why we make so much extra food and waste it. It doesn't make sense to me."

"Maybe one day it will, Virginia," Papa said quietly, "when it's time."

Trudging up the stairs toward bed, I was more confused than ever. We were not normally people who wasted food, or anything else. As Papa always said, "Waste not, want not". Momma and Papa carried on silent conversations on Curby Thursdays too, when they thought I wasn't watching. And it also seemed Reuben and Carter knew something I didn't. I was certain there was something going on at my own home that everyone knew about but me, but I had no idea what it could be. What was going on and why was it a secret? I fell asleep with the questions still fresh in my mind.

Chapter Two

I crawled out of bed unwillingly. I did not like mornings, especially Monday mornings, but knew the chores were waiting and no one else would be doing them for me. I was responsible for milking the cow each morning.

We actually owned two milk cows, Elsie and Annabelle, but their calving was timed six months apart, allowing one to be fresh while the other was dry. I had to milk in the afternoon, as well as the morning throughout the summer. Momma took care of the chore in the afternoon when school was in, except on the weekend. With me going to the store after school, I arrived home too late for the afternoon milking. School was starting in exactly one week, and I couldn't say I would miss the chore.

I dragged myself to the barn and let Elsie in. Locking her head in the stanchion, I went to work. The stanchion was built in one corner of the barn. There was a feed trough attached to the wall, with boards attached to the outside edge just wide enough for the cow's head to fit through. One of the boards was hinged at the bottom, allowing it to be moved once the cow put her head through the boards and began eating. After the cow slipped her head between the boards to get to the trough, the hinged board was pulled close to her neck and locked in place with a wooden peg. This prevented the cow from being able to walk away or turn around while being milked. However, it didn't prevent her from stepping into the bucket or kicking it over, so I always had to be watching the back hooves.

Plopping down on the stool, I got my rhythm going, squeezing with one hand while releasing with the other. When I finished one side, I hopped off the stool and moved around to the other. Completing the chore, I placed the pail of milk on a shelf to prevent it from being kicked over, and then released Elsie's head. Opening the barn door, I shooed Elsie out to the pasture for the day. Taking the milk into the kitchen, I set it on the counter to wait for the cream to rise. Most of the cream would be taken off and churned into butter.

We kept the milk and butter in the springhouse to keep cool. When we had extra, Papa would sell it at the general store. He also sold any extra eggs we collected.

The springhouse was just a small building made from large stones. It was built over the mouth of our spring. It stayed really cool inside because the water coming out of the spring was very cold. A large hole had been dug out and lined with clay to make a nice well for the water to be held in. After the hole filled with water, the overflow just went out the other side of the springhouse where a nice large exit had been made. The overflow ended up the in the creek that ran through our farm. Along the wall of the springhouse, Papa had built shelves to place the butter and eggs on and the milk can was kept in the cold water.

I helped Momma finish fixing breakfast and we all sat down to eggs, biscuits, sausage, and gravy. When Papa finished blessing the food, he looked to me and cleared his throat. "Um, Virginia, your mother and I need to tell you something. We believe you're old enough now and we need your help come Thursday."

"Okay, Papa," I replied. Finally, I was going to find out what went on around here on Curby Thursday.

"Virginia, have you ever heard of the Underground Railroad?" Momma asked.

"No," I replied. "Is it a train that goes underground?" I had never actually seen a train with my own eyes, but I had seen some pictures of them. As big as they were, I was pretty sure they didn't travel underground, except when they went through tunnels, as pictures had shown them doing.

There was a rumor that there would eventually be tracks laid through our small town of Marengo, but who knew if that was true. The tracks would run all the way from Leavenworth to Indianapolis, the capital of the state of Indiana. There were several people in the county who opposed such a thing, however, claiming the trains would kill their cattle and the tracks would divide their farms.

"No," Papa said, "it's not a real train at all. It's what they call the system used to move slaves to freedom."

Slaves? What would Papa and Momma know about slaves? We lived in a free state. Of course, our county we lived in bordered the Ohio River, with Kentucky being just across the river to the south. I knew slaves were sold at auction in Louisville, Kentucky, but I had never even been to Kentucky. "What do slaves have to do with us?" I asked.

"Well, we don't believe people should be owned by someone and certainly not be mistreated," Papa replied. "The Underground Railroad is a group of people who help the slaves escape their masters and travel to Canada so they can be free."

"Why can't they just move to a northern state to be free?" I asked.

"Because the slaves' owners track them down and take them back," Momma replied. "A lot of times when they are caught, they are brutally beaten or killed in front of the rest of the slaves. The men who own the slaves, called the master, think this will keep the other slaves from trying to run away. A slave is not truly safe until they are in Canada, because slavery is against the law in that country."

"Every other Thursday when I go to Curby, I go to pick up runaway slaves and move them further North," Papa said. "I always take one of your brothers along to watch for anyone approaching while the slaves are being loaded into the wagon. We have a load of items from the general store on the wagon when we go to Curby and so it appears we are making a delivery. We must keep the bottom of the wagon covered at all times, because there's a fake floor in it."

"A fake floor?" I asked.

"Yes," Papa replied. "When I built the wagon, I put the bed on it, then left a two foot space and added another bed. With the sides on the wagon and the wagon full, you can't tell it has the two foot space between the floors."

"Okay," I said. "I don't understand why we would need such a wagon, though."

"Virginia," Momma said, "when your papa and brothers come home from the store on every other Thursday and take the wagon straight to the barn, it's because there are slaves in the wagon. They are hidden between the two floors"

"You mean like people?" I asked. "There are people hidden in the wagon?"

"Yes," Momma replied, "there are people in the wagon. They are slaves trying to reach Canada to be free. We are helping them find that freedom."

"Could we get in trouble for helping them?" I asked.

"Yes, Virginia," Papa replied. "If we're caught, I would possibly be sent to jail and charged an enormous fine. The slaves would be returned to their masters. We believe we need to take the risk, though."

"How long have we been doing this?" I asked.

"Since the summer of 1855," Papa replied. "We didn't tell you because it was safer for you not to know, in case someone asked. You must never tell anyone we do this, not even friends at school or church. Not everyone in the North agrees with helping the runaway slaves, and some people are paid to collect information for the slave hunters."

We had been hiding slaves in our barn for four years and I hadn't had a clue. Well, that's not completely true. I noticed the strange conversation Papa and Momma had on the day the slaves would arrive and that we cooked way too much food for just us. I just never would have guessed my quiet, soft spoken Papa would be breaking the law and hiding slaves in our barn.

"Virginia," Momma said, "we're telling you now because we need your help. The third cutting of hay is ready and we need it for the winter. Carter will mow it today and it will be ready to put in the barn by Thursday. Reuben will have to run the store while Papa goes to Curby. We need you to ride with Papa to Curby to help out. You will need to keep watch while Papa and Mr. Batman load the slaves into the wagon. Mrs. Batman could do it, but if the slave hunters show up, she will look suspicious just standing outside the barn. You could explain that you were there with your Papa making a delivery. Everything needs to look as normal as possible. Do you understand, Virginia?"

"Yes, Momma," I replied. But I didn't understand at all. Why were we risking our lives for slaves? Why would Papa and Momma put our family in danger? I looked across the table to Carter who smiled great big. I knew then that both of my brothers had known all along what was going on in our barn. They had been helping commit the crime, as the law viewed it, and now it was my turn to help, too.

Momma and I cleared the breakfast dishes and cleaned up the kitchen. Carter went to mow hay with our big work horses, Nellie and Clyde. Reuben and Papa headed to the store in a wagon pulled by Stubborn and Ornery, our other two horses. Their names matched their behavior perfectly.

As I washed the dishes, my mind kept going over everything I had been told at the breakfast table. I was scared and excited at the same time. I had always loved an adventure and this was sure to be one. Instead of reading in a book of someone else's exciting life, I would be living one of my own.

****

Thursday dawned sunny and warm. It was a good day to make hay and a good day to go get slaves, I supposed. I hurried through the morning milking and brought the pail in and placed it on a shelf. Momma would skim the cream off later, after it had time to rise.

I helped Momma finish preparing breakfast. As we sat down to eat, Papa gave thanks for the food and asked for a special blessing on the day. I realized as he did so, the special blessing had been part of the Curby Thursday prayer for four years. Today was the first time I knew why Papa would ask for such a thing.

Papa, Reuben, and I headed to town in the special wagon shortly after breakfast. My nerves were on edge thinking about the day that lay ahead. I had never even seen a colored person in real life before. I had seen a picture of a slave in a newspaper one time, though. Underneath the picture a statement "Runaway Slave" was printed and a promise of a reward for any person who could tell the master where to find his missing slave. I guess that's what Papa and Momma meant when they said not to tell anyone. If someone wanted to make some money, they could point the slave hunters in the direction of our farm.

I worked at the store until after noon then Papa and I loaded the wagon with sacks of feed and headed for Curby, which was eight miles south of Marengo. As we bumped along, I asked Papa to explain more about the Underground Railroad.

"Well, Virginia, it doesn't always work the same way every time but usually a "field agent" starts the process. A field agent would be someone working for the Underground Railroad, but pretending to be a preacher, doctor, or maybe a census taker. While pretending to be one of these people, the field agent gains access to the plantations. Sometimes the agent has been sent by a slave who has already made it to freedom. The freed slave sends the field agent to help more of their family or friends find their way through the Underground Railroad."

"The field agent sets up the plan for the slaves to escape from the plantation. After the slaves escape, the field agent hands them off to a "conductor", who guides the slaves to the first "station". Our home is one of the "stations", or safe houses, on the railroad. The slaves we help come across the Ohio River at Alton, where another station is. Crossing the Ohio River is a really dangerous part of the journey, because the slaves can be seen entering and exiting the boat."

"The Alton "station" places a candle in a certain window that is visible to the "conductor" on the Kentucky side of the river. If the candle is not in the window, the "conductor" does not bring the slaves over. All of this activity is done at night, which makes it more difficult."

"It's amazing that so many people would risk their lives to help the slaves. Why do they do it?" I asked Papa.

"I suppose because they believe the way we do, that all men are created equal and in God's image, no matter their skin color. No human should be owned like a piece of property and treated like an animal," Papa answered. "There's even a woman, Harriett Tubman, who lived as a slave and escaped that is now a "conductor" on the Underground Railroad. She works with a Quaker family in Pennsylvania."

"Why do we move the slaves during the day, Papa?"

"We use our business to cover up our activity. If someone saw us on the road after dark, they would ask questions. During the day, it just appears we are doing business as usual."

I thought about what Papa had said the rest of the ride to Curby. I had never really thought about slavery much, because I had never met a slave before. I guess it was out of sight, out of mind. It wasn't my problem, until now.

"Now, Virginia, when we get to Mr. Batman's farm, I want you to get out of the wagon and check out all the farm animals. It will be a natural thing for you to do. Keep a look out for anyone approaching. If you see someone, go to the back of the barn and come in the door to warn us."

"Okay Papa," I replied, my nervousness causing my voice to quiver.

"And Virginia."

"Yes Papa."

"Don't climb any trees in Mr. Batman's yard," Papa said with a big smile.

"I'm shaking so bad I don't think I could make it past the first limb," I replied, conjuring up the best smile I could muster at the moment.

As we pulled into Mr. Batman's farm yard, he came from the barn to greet Papa. I could see the surprise on his face at the sight of me but he didn't ask questions. Papa told me to hop down and do as he instructed. Mr. Batman opened the barn door wide and Papa drove the wagon through and into the barn. The fear made my stomach churn knowing the responsibility I had been entrusted with.

Looking all around, I spotted two small cats. Deciding to see if they were friendly, I walked toward them. When I had covered half the distance, the cats began to come toward me. I knew that was a good sign. Reaching down, I scooped up one of the cats and its purring began to vibrate its whole body, enjoying the attention thoroughly. I sank to the ground and nestled the cat in my lap. Reaching out, I scooped up the other cat and placed it on my lap, too. I stroked their soft fur, keeping my eyes trained toward the road. Suddenly, the cats jumped from my lap, with one leaving a nice big scratch on my hand. Turning to see what had frightened them, I was knocked flat by a huge dog. I had not seen the dog earlier, so it must have come from out in the pasture.

"Hey, buddy, what are you doing?"

The dog barked in reply as I struggled to my feet, dusting myself off the best I could. The dog ran and grabbed a stick and brought it to me. Laying it at my feet, it looked to me expectantly. Not knowing what else to do, I picked up the stick. The dog ran a little distance then looked back at me. Deciding the dog wanted me to throw the stick; I reached back and flung the stick as hard as I could. The dog took off across the yard so fast that he slid past the stick when he attempted to stop. Grabbing the stick up, the dog ran back and placed it at my feet. I knew right then that I must have a dog of my own. I had been missing out all these years. I knew I could eventually convince Papa of the need, but Momma would continue to fret over the chickens and the possibility of the dog killing them. I would just have to figure out a way to get Momma to agree to us getting a dog. I continued to play with the animal, making sure to stay facing the road. I thought the dog would get tired of the game, but it never did.

When the barn door opened, Papa pulled the wagon out with straw in it. I knew the straw was to hide the fact that the wagon wasn't nearly as deep as it should be. Reluctantly, I climbed up on the seat beside Papa for the ride home. The dog whined, laying the stick on the ground beside the wagon.

"Sorry, buddy. I have to go home now," I told the dog.

"I see you met Wilbur," Mr. Batman said, coming up to pet the dog.

"Yes, and I like him very much," I replied. "I would like to have a dog of my own." I turned hopeful eyes to Papa who laughed out loud.

"We will have to convince your mother first."

"I know, but I'm willing to take on the challenge."

"Well, good luck with that," Papa said.

Waving to Mr. Batman, Papa put the horses in motion to start our journey home. As we passed the farm house, Mrs. Batman met us with some homemade cinnamon rolls and a small crock of water for the long ride ahead. It would just be a normal thing for her to do and looking normal was important, according to Momma and Papa. Papa handed her an empty crock and plate from two weeks before.

Why hadn't I ever noticed Papa bringing a crock and plate into the house that didn't belong to us on Curby Thursday? I reasoned that Momma had probably washed them and hid them with the slaves so I wouldn't ask questions.

I was nervous all the way back to Marengo, but Papa just chattered away like a mockingbird. I suppose after four years of being a part of the Underground Railroad, it didn't bother him that we had runaway slaves hidden in our wagon. We passed few people but each time we did, I had to fight down the panic I felt. Of course, Papa knew practically everyone since we owned the store and would wave and holler a greeting each time we passed someone. I hoped in time I would become as relaxed as Papa, as I helped to transport slaves from Curby to our house.

The horses plodded along, taking their own sweet time. At least the trip back was mostly downhill. I had been worried the horses would never get us pulled up the huge hill that we had to climb when we left Marengo. Papa said the hill was called White Oak hill, because of all the White Oaks growing there.

Marengo was nestled in a valley with steep hills to its north and south. There was no way to travel to Curby, or Leavenworth which was farther south, without climbing a huge hill. However, when we started our descent back into Marengo, the view was spectacular. I could see for miles from the top of White Oak hill.

Finally reaching the store, Papa and I helped Reuben close up and we headed for home. Papa went straight to the barn and pulled the wagon inside. Reuben, Papa, and I hopped down from the wagon seat and I looked to Papa to see if we would let the hidden slaves out. He just shook his head no. Reuben and Papa unhitched the horses and turned them out to pasture. I went ahead to the house to see if Momma needed any help.

Momma had supper almost finished and I set the table and began to dip the food into serving bowls. Sitting down, we all joined hands and Papa gave thanks for the food and for the extra blessing on the day. When supper was finished, Papa and Momma headed to the barn with the extra food. They explained that the reason for waiting to let the slaves out was to make sure no one had followed us. They also explained that there was another station in Marengo, and someone from there would try to warn us if they heard that slave hunters were in the area. We would do the same for them. That's why we only went to Curby every other Thursday. The other "station master" went on the Thursday we didn't go.

"Who runs the other station?" I asked.

"We can't tell you," Momma replied. "It's for your safety and theirs, not to mention the safety of the slaves. The fewer people who know the truth, the safer it is for everyone."

"Do Carter and Reuben know?"

"Yes, because one of them has to ride and warn the other station if slave hunters are spotted," Papa said. "Don't try and get the information out of Carter, either, like I know you will. He won't tell you."

I smiled at Papa. He knew me well. If I had realized Carter knew about Curby Thursday, I would have squeezed the whole story out of him long ago. Honestly though, I didn't want to know who ran the other station. I was scared enough about the one we ran.

"There are two stations in Alton, and two in Curby, too," Papa informed me. "If one gets discovered, there has to be another one set up to cover for them. If not, the railroad would shut down temporarily and slaves would be stuck at a station until another location for a station could be found. That wouldn't work very well."

"Where do the slaves go when they leave our house?" I asked.

"Well, you know how Mr. Pierson comes every other Monday to get a load of manure?" Papa asked.

"Yes," I replied.

"He is really picking up slaves and moving them farther North on the railroad," Papa said. "Mr. Pierson is just a "conductor". He doesn't run a safe house. He just moves the slaves from our house to the next "station"."

As we entered the barn with the food, Papa went to a corner stall. Papa had told me he would show me where the slaves were hidden when we brought them back today.

Taking a pitchfork, he moved aside the hay and manure to reveal a trap door. I looked at him with disbelief. How long had that been there? This stall was the one we always kept Nellie in at night. The sound of her big feet thumping must wake the slaves up often.

I would soon realize that a sleepless night was a small price to pay for the slaves. It was much better than being returned to their masters.

How had they arranged all of this without anyone knowing? I considered the next stop for the slaves when they left our house. Mr. Pierson always came every other Monday and cleaned Nellie's stall. He would back his wagon right to the door and Carter or Reuben would help him load the manure. I suppose after everything was shoveled on the wagon, he just opened the trap door and loaded the slaves in the hidden space of his wagon, just like ours. I had wondered why he came and got manure even when it was wet out or during the winter.

Momma had always kept me occupied inside when Mr. Pierson came, telling me not to go get in his way. When I would go to the barn later, there was always a nice, thick layer of fresh straw down in

Nellie's stall that Mr. Pierson had brought on his wagon. I knew now why Mr. Pierson brought the straw with him. It was to hide the fact that his wagon had a fake floor.

When Papa opened the trap door in the floor of the stall, I could see that someone had taken a shovel and dug out a room in the earth. I remembered when Papa had added the floors to the four stalls, about five years ago. He had said it was to make them easier to clean and to keep the horses from pawing the dirt. I knew now the floor had been added to cover up the room used to hide runaway slaves. I had been eight years old when the wooden floor had been added to the horse stalls but did not remember Papa digging a hole under Nellie's stall.

"Papa, Carter was only ten when you and Momma started helping with the Underground Railroad. Has he always known we help slaves escape to freedom?"

"No, Virginia, he has not. Reuben helped dig the room out and your mother tended the store on the Thursdays that I needed to go to Curby. Reuben used to go with me and keep watch for me all the time," Papa said.

"So, how long has Carter known?" I asked.

"About two years," Papa replied.

"Oh, so when he turned the age I am now," I stated, happy to know Carter had not been considered more trustworthy than I.

"Yes, Virginia," Momma said. "I know what we're doing is considered against the law but it truly is the right thing to do. Some slaves are treated very badly by their masters. They need our help so they can escape the abuse."

"I will do my best to help them, too," I promised.

"I know you will, Virginia," Momma said.

Peering into the earthen room, I lowered a lantern into the darkness to get a better look. The room looked to be about eight foot square. A small ladder had been constructed and placed on one wall to make it easier to get in and out of the hole. There were wooden benches along the walls and blankets were folded and placed on one of the benches. A crock of water with a dipper was in a corner of the room and a small table held tin plates and a few forks. In one corner was an area that a sheet had been draped around. I assumed it hid a chamber pot.

I realized then that Momma must get up really early to feed

and care for the slaves so I wouldn't know they were there. She and Papa also had to sneak out after supper to take them food and water. All of the risks my parents had taken and the sacrifices they had made was proof of how important it was to them that the slaves find freedom.

Papa stepped out of the stall where he had just lifted the secret door for me to see the room. Carter had come to the barn and now helped Papa loosen the bolts and lift the back off the wagon. The slaves had crawled into the space feet first, and they looked up at us from their laid out position. The fear in their eyes must have reflected my own. They were as scared of being captured as I was of someone finding out we helped in the Underground Railroad. However, the hope of freedom outweighed their fear of slave hunters.

There were four people stuffed into the small space; two children and two adults. I assumed they were a family. The children were a boy about ten and a girl about eight. It was really hard to guess their age because they were so skinny and frail looking. I could tell food had never been plentiful for them and felt guilty about the abundance we had always enjoyed. I had never gone hungry a day in my life but had never really known what a blessing that was, until now.

Carter reached to help the children out first and they shrank away from him. How could anyone ever think my fun loving brother could hurt them? It was then I fully understood the terror they must have already lived through in their young lives and why we must help them find freedom.

I could see scars on the arms of the adults and the man had a large scar on his face. The children did not appear to have any marks but I was certain they had witnessed the many beatings their parents had endured. Who could blame these people for trying to escape such brutality, hoping to prevent their children from suffering the way they had?

The man reached out his hand and Papa took hold of it to help pull him from the wagon bed. The slave then helped his wife out, and the children were lifted out by their parents. We quickly moved them to the earthen room where Momma had already placed the pan of food. Leaving a lantern burning and matches on the small table so they could light it as needed, Papa closed the trap door and spread the straw out again. Papa then opened the barn door and called

Nellie and Clyde in from the pasture and put them into their stalls. Grabbing a rake, Carter began to smooth out the dirt floor of the barn where indentions of children's bare feet were visible, making the evidence disappear just as the people had vanished from sight moments before.

Being satisfied that things appeared normal, Papa led the way back to the house. I grabbed a book and went to sit close to one of the oil lamps in the living room so I could see the words. Reuben and Carter began a game of checkers, while Papa read the newspaper that was brought from Leavenworth with the mail each week. It was the Louisville Daily Journal, but of course by the time the papers reached us, some were over a week old. The mail wagon also brought several copies of The Crisis, a newspaper printed in Leavenworth. The Crisis provided local news, but the Louisville Daily Journal contained national news. Momma came into the living room to sew on some new pot holders that we were desperately in need of. Looking up from my book, I decided now was as good a time as any to bring up the subject of getting a dog.

"Momma, did you know Mr. Batman has a dog?"

Momma looked up from her sewing and narrowed her eyes at me. "No, Virginia, I was not aware that Mr. Batman has a dog."

"You mean Wilbur?" Carter asked. "I know Wilbur quite well."

"Did you know if you throw a stick, he will bring it back to you?" I asked, turning toward my brother.

"I know if you throw anything he will bring it back to you," Carter said with a chuckle. "One day he brought me a cat!"

"No wonder the cats ran away from me so fast when they saw him coming," I said laughing. "You didn't throw the cat, did you Carter?"

"The temptation was great, but in the end I took the cat from him and turned it loose. Wilbur started to go get the cat again but I called him back and tossed a stick for him."

"Do you think we could get a dog, Momma?" I turned toward my momma with the sweetest smile I could muster. I knew if I could persuade her, Papa would be no problem at all to convince. Papa seemed to like Wilbur and could see the benefits a dog could be on a farm.

"What if a dog eats my chickens?" Momma said.

"We can train it not to, can't we Carter?" I looked to my

brother for help. If the two of us worked together, we could gain more ground with Momma.

"I have never seen Wilbur chase Mr. Batman's chickens," Carter offered.

"But you have seen Wilbur chase cats, catch them, and bring them to you," Momma pointed out.

"Yes, but cats are stupid animals," Carter said having never been fond of the critters.

"And chickens aren't?" I blurted. Clasping my hand over my mouth, I realized I just shot myself in the foot, so to speak.

"I'll think about it, Virginia," Momma said, not making any promises.

"You know, a dog could bark and warn us of strangers approaching. Strangers that might be slave hunters," I added, hoping to plead my case by making Momma and Papa think of the benefits of having a dog.

"Hmm…Virginia does make a good point," Papa said. "Probably should have had a dog all along."

"Stephen, dogs kill chickens," Momma stated. "I just don't know if getting a dog is a good idea."

"Well, maybe we should discuss it a little more," Papa said.

"Yes, maybe," Momma agreed, "when Virginia's not around to sway our decision." Momma turned to look at me and I knew the discussion was finished for tonight. Hopefully Papa could wear Momma down and convince her we needed a good dog.

An hour later I headed upstairs to get ready for bed. As I crawled between my soft clean sheets and sank into my comfortable mattress, I thought about where the slaves were spending their night. I was sure sleeping on the wooden benches with a few blankets did not come close to the comfort I was enjoying right now. I prayed they would make it to Canada and be able to build a new life. What caused anyone to believe it was okay to own people and treat them with cruelty?

<u>Chapter Three</u>

It was Monday morning and the first day of school. I hurried to milk Elsie so I would have extra time to get ready. I wanted to look my best on this special day and make a good first impression. We would have a new teacher at school this year. I hadn't met her yet, but I had heard rumors that she was young, pretty, and very nice; at least according to my best friend, Effie Schultz. Effie had seen the teacher on Saturday when she had arrived, and told me all about her at church Sunday.

The new teacher was boarding with Effie's neighbor, Mrs. George. Effie said Mrs. George was a cranky widow who had absolutely no tolerance for children of any age or sort. Mrs. George's husband had died five years earlier and Effie claimed it was his wife's hateful attitude that caused his death. Effie said Mrs. George had just sucked the life right out of her husband, like a female praying mantis does her mate. She was certain Mrs. George would be a widow the rest of her life, because no one could surely live with her. I wondered how the young new teacher would fare with such a person.

Scurrying through the back door, I plunked the bucket of milk on the counter. Momma had breakfast on the table, so I called to my brothers out the back door to hurry up and finish their chores. A few moments later, we all sat down and Papa said grace. He had hardly said amen before a fork full of scrambled eggs found its way into my mouth.

"Virginia," Momma said sharply, "please quit shoveling your food in and use some manners. You'll choke to death eating that fast, not to mention the indigestion you will suffer later."

"I must hurry, Momma," I replied. "I want to look my best for the first day of school."

"Well, if you choke to death, you won't have to worry with school," Carter said with a laugh.

Carter had completed school the previous year and he would not miss it one bit. School had been a necessary nuisance for Carter and nothing more. Reuben, on the other hand, had enjoyed school and was quite good at math. Papa had placed the responsibility of the store's accounts in Reuben's capable hands a year ago and Reuben was as happy to do the job as Papa was to get rid of the task.

"You're just sad that you won't be attending school this year," I replied, giving Carter a cheeky grin.

"I'd rather work on the farm from dawn to dusk than be confined to that building for seven hours," Carter said. "You just go and do the learning for both of us. You seem to enjoy having your nose in a book."

"I will, and maybe one day I will be a teacher like Momma used to be." I turned to Momma with a smile, knowing it would make her proud if I followed in her footsteps.

Momma had told us all the story several times of how she and Papa came to live in Marengo. Papa had discovered at a young age that he could draw quite well. He grew up in New Albany, a town about forty miles east of Marengo, and just across the Ohio River from Louisville, Kentucky. Papa went to work as a draftsman at the age of sixteen.

People came from all around to have Papa draw up the plans for their big, expensive houses. They would explain how they wanted the house to look and Papa would bring it to life on paper, everything from the outside appearance to the smallest closet on the inside. Papa saved every dime he could as he worked drawing up the fine homes for his wealthy customers. Though he enjoyed the work, Papa had bigger dreams. Living in the city had never appealed to him. He wanted to move to a rural area and have his own farm.

When Papa turned twenty-one, he decided he had enough money saved to pursue his dream. Leaving the small room he rented from an elderly widow, Papa packed all his belongings into a wagon he had purchased. Climbing on the seat, Papa pointed the two work horses he had bought toward the west and never looked back. When Papa came to the village of Marengo, he knew it was the place. He bought the piece of ground where the general store is located and built a two story log structure.

The store was located on the corner of Leavenworth Paoli road, which ran north toward Valeene, and Water Street, which ran parallel to Whiskey Run creek. The building served as a store on the lower level and a place to live in the upper level.

Momma was twenty, and had been the town's school teacher for two years when Papa came to town. They met at church and got to know one another better each time Momma visited the general store. They began to court three months after Papa came to town and were married a year later in 1840. Momma and Papa lived two years in the upstairs of the general store then bought the farm we now lived on.

Our farm was not big, but the eighty acres was plenty for Papa and Momma to take care of, along with the general store. We had some nice fields that ran along the creek which we planted in crops to feed our livestock, such as corn, oats and wheat. The land climbed steeply uphill a quarter mile from each bank of the creek, making a very small valley between the hills. Papa had built our house up the hill a ways on the north side of the creek. The house faced south and there was a perfect view of the creek below. Papa had dug into the bank and made a cellar beneath the house, then added two stories over the cellar. He positioned the house close to the spring, so there would be a water source nearby.

Before building the house, Papa had cut trees from the farm and built a log barn, which was now the one used to hide the slaves. On the top of the hill behind the house the ground leveled off, creating a nice pasture for the livestock.

"Maybe one day you will be a teacher, Virginia," Momma said, "but if you don't learn some manners, you may never be a wife."

I smiled sheepishly at Momma and forced myself to slow down. Finishing my breakfast, I helped Momma clear the dishes from the table.

"Go get ready, Virginia," Momma said with a smile. "I'll take care of these dirty dishes."

"Thank you, Momma." I rushed upstairs to dress for the good first impression I wanted to make at school. I chose the prettiest of the three dresses Momma and I had sewed for me to wear to school. I had outgrown everything over the summer, so we would have to make me some warmer dresses from heavier material for the winter, too.

As I pulled the dress over my head, I couldn't help but think of the young slave girl hidden in our barn. Her clothes were nothing but rags. Before hurrying downstairs, I grabbed three dresses I had outgrown and took them with me. Entering the kitchen, I found Momma preparing breakfast for the slaves to have a meal before Mr. Pierson showed up to get them.

"Momma, do you think the little slave girl could wear these dresses?"

"Yes, Virginia, I believe she could," Momma replied. "Let's just give her one, though. She really can't pack more with her, and there might be other girls later that we could give one to."

"Okay, I think you should give her this one," I said, handing Momma the yellow calico. I knew the color of the dress against her acorn brown skin would be pretty. Too bad I couldn't do anything about the fear in her young eyes or the bones that would surely protrude beneath the new dress. The family was such a sad sight that it brought tears to my eyes to think about their appearance.

I took the other two dresses back upstairs to my room. Rushing back down the stairs and out the back door, I joined Papa and Reuben in the wagon. We headed to town and Papa dropped me off at the school. I would walk the quarter mile to the store when school let out for the day.

Our school had been built the previous year in 1858. It served as the Big Spring's Church, where we attended on Sunday, as well as the local school.

To the back of the school ran the Whiskey Run creek, the same one that flowed through our farm two miles west of town. Whiskey Run eventually collided with Brandy Branch creek just east of Marengo and later with Cider Fork creek. It eventually dumped into Big Blue River near Milltown. There was also a nice spring just down the hill from the school, which is where a good portion of the town got their water to drink.

At the front and off to the right of the school was a graveyard. The grave yard had been there since the town had been founded and held the bodies of some of the first settlers who had come here. The land went straight uphill behind the graveyard for more than a quarter of a mile.

Our town had been called Big Spring until 1851, due to the large spring that was about half way between the school and the general store and came out of a large cave opening. During dry times, Carter and Reuben had taken lanterns and went into the cave. Not far past the opening, the passage narrowed and the only way to go further was to crawl. This had limited much exploring past the opening by most of those who had entered. It was difficult to push a lantern in front of one's self while moving along on your belly. As for myself, I could not abide being confined in such a small space, so I had never attempted to enter the cave.

I had asked Papa one time why the creeks were named after liquor. He said he didn't know anything about where Brandy Branch or Cider Fork got their names, but there was a legend about Whiskey Run creek. The legend states that an Indian named Whiskey shot a man named Run when they met up along the creek one day. The Indian then stole Run's whiskey after he shot him, making the creek become known as Whiskey Run. I thought it was a crazy legend but may have a bit of truth to it.

Marengo used to be located in Whiskey Run Township, just like the creek's name that ran through it. But in 1842 a new township was formed from part of Whiskey Run and Sterling Townships to make Liberty Township, which included Marengo.

When heavy rains came, water would raise high enough to flood the entire opening of the cave where the big spring came out. Sometimes Papa and Reuben would get trapped in town if it rained too much during the day, and Momma, Carter and I would be trapped at the farm.

There was still a bed in the upstairs of the general store, just for this reason. It would be much too dangerous to attempt to cross the swollen creek during these times. However, it usually didn't take very long for the waters to recede and we could resume our daily lives. Papa said it was just the way things were when you chose to live close to a creek.

Entering the school, I spotted Effie putting her lunch pail on the shelf by the back door. She smiled as I came up beside her. Effie was my best friend, and school starting meant that we would see each other six days a week, including Sunday service. It was another reason I liked school so much.

"Hi, Virginia," Effie said. "I think this is going to be the best school year ever. I walked over with Miss Smith and we had a good talk. She has all sorts of fun ways planned to teach us, and she doesn't believe in using the ruler to whack our hands when we misbehave. I made sure to ask."

The fact that Miss Smith would not be using the ruler as a form of discipline was surely wonderful news for Effie. I thought the teacher last year was going to break her fingers off. Effie had a bad habit of saying whatever came to her mind, without thinking it through or raising her hand. No matter how many whacks she received from the ruler, her mouth still got the better of her. I would have thought she could have looked down at her sore hand and just placed it over her mouth to keep it shut. Unfortunately, Effie was slow to learn that the teacher would not tolerate her nonsense.

Maybe Effie's unruly behavior was due to the fact that she was the youngest of four children, and she came along over ten years behind her older siblings. It was like she was an only child and her parents had been worn out from raising the first three. She was allowed to do and say things most parents wouldn't allow. Momma would have taken a forsythia switch to my legs had I acted the way Effie did most of the time. Still, Effie was fun to be around and we found we had a lot in common, even if our upbringing was very different.

Effie's two older brothers were twins, and at age 25, they were married with families of their own. They owned a farm together and had built two houses on their 200 acres of property. They lived near Milltown, along the Big Blue River, and grew corn and wheat that they sold to the mill there. Effie's older sister was 27, and she and her family lived on a farm near Valeene, about six miles north of Marengo. Marengo was in the northern part of Crawford County, and Valeene was located in Orange County.

Effie lived up the hill from the school, and her house could be seen from the school yard. Effie's father cut timber for a living. He had been clearing their acreage for years but still had plenty of trees to cut and sell; especially red cedar which was used to make furniture. The logs were loaded on wagons and taken to Milltown. They were sold at the mill, to be sawed into lumber. The lumber was sold locally, or sent down Big Blue River to Leavenworth. At Leavenworth, the lumber was loaded onto boats and shipped down the Ohio River, being sold along the way.

Our new teacher called the class to attention and instructed Angus to go pull the rope to ring the bell, announcing it was time for school to begin. At fourteen, Angus was one of the oldest boys in the class, and this would more than likely be his last year. His father was the area's leather worker and his shop provided harnesses and halters of all shapes and sizes, along with custom made leather gloves.

Angus and his pa took a wagon around selling leather goods to area farmers. Angus was the only son in his family, though he had two younger sisters, and had been learning the art of leather work the past few years. He would more than likely take over the business from his father one day.

As the bell chimed out its announcement, Effie and I chose seats in the back next to each other. In a one room school, the youngest students sat in the front and the older ones in the back. The older students were expected to help the younger ones with their lessons, when they had finished their own. Last year, the teacher chose me to read to the younger children after recess each day. It was a job I had enjoyed doing as much as the children loved listening to a good story.

Miss Smith introduced herself to the class as the new school teacher. She told us she had seen an advertisement in the Louisville Daily Journal stating the need for a teacher in Marengo. She had mailed her credentials to the address given in the request and had been hired for one year. Her performance would decide if she would be hired back for the next year.

Looking around the room at some of the kids who caused trouble, I thought she might just decide not to come back, whether she was asked to or not. The previous teacher was quick with the ruler, but sometimes it was truly needed, and then some.

Continuing with her introduction, she stated she was from Kentucky, just south of Louisville. As this information sank in, I realized she was from a state that supported slavery. I would have never thought anything about the information before but since I had just found out we are a stop on the Underground Railroad, it made me terribly nervous. I wondered if she would report us if she knew of our involvement. Was she secretly a spy for the slave hunters? Could earning reward money for reporting our illegal activity be something she was interested in? Why would a pretty young woman from Kentucky want to come to our little backwoods town to teach?

"Virginia," Effie whispered, "why are you wringing your hands? You're as white as a fresh bucket of milk."

I looked at Effie and realized I had let my nervousness show on the outside. I was not doing very well at keeping calm when faced with the danger of someone discovering our activity on Curby Thursday. Papa would be disappointed, I was certain. "Um, I guess I'm just nervous about starting the year with a new teacher," I whispered back, which was a true statement, but not for the reasons Effie might think.

"Well, don't be," Effie replied. "I've already told you how great she is and there will be no finger whacking with that awful ruler. What more could you want?"

That she had grew up in a northern state where slavery is not practiced? That she would make an announcement that she was against slavery and supported the views of the northern states? That she had no idea slaves ran away from their masters and she had no knowledge of an Underground Railroad? Those are the things I wanted but knew I could never voice that out loud to anyone, especially my chatty friend Effie. So, in response I whispered back, "Yeah, no sore fingers for you, right?"

To my embarrassment, Miss Smith had quit talking and was watching Effie and me chatting away quietly, when we were clearly supposed to be listening. "Since the two girls in the back are eager to talk, maybe I will start the class introductions with them," Miss Smith said.

My face must have turned four shades of red before finally deciding on the color of the deep red rose in my momma's flower garden. At least I was no longer pale. I clenched my hands tightly at my sides as I thought of punching Effie for starting a conversation with me. What a nice first impression I was making on the new teacher! Slowly rising to our feet, Effie and I introduced ourselves to our new teacher.

"I have already met Effie," Miss Smith said. "I would like to know a little something about you, Virginia. What do you like to do in your free time?"

Well, that was easy to answer. "I love to read, Miss Smith, and I'm really sorry for talking when I was supposed to be listening."

"I like you already, Virginia," Miss Smith said. "You love to read like I do, and you know how to take responsibility for your actions. I believe we will get along just fine."

Sitting down, I vowed to whack Effie's fingers with the ruler myself if she dared try and talk to me during class again. How humiliating to be called out that way! I had always prided myself on the good behavior I had, never once getting into trouble at school. I had even beat down the urge to climb the large oak tree in the school's yard during recess, and that had not been easy.

When school ended, Effie walked with me to the general store. She said she really didn't have anything else to do until it was time to go get their milk cow from the pasture.

With their land being slowly cleared of the timber, the only pasture was at the top of the huge hill that rose up behind the cemetery. At night, the cow was kept in their small barn behind their house. After the morning milking, the cow was led the quarter mile up the hill to pasture. She had to be brought back down each afternoon.

As we reached the general store, I greeted two old timers who were sitting on the porch. The porch stretched all the way across the front, with some wooden chairs placed on it to sit in. It was a nice place to catch a breeze on a hot summer day.

Papa had carved checker boards on two large chunks of wood and men would sit on the porch to talk and play checkers, as the two old men were doing now. The checkers and chairs were moved indoors during the winter, close to the wood stove.

The general store was the place to go if you wanted to find out what was happening around the county. As Papa or my brothers went to Milltown for lumber and sometimes Leavenworth to get supplies, they would bring back news of what was going on in the area. Also, since the general store was also the post office, the mail wagon from Leavenworth stopped once a week to drop off and pick up mail. The mail arrived in Leavenworth by the stagecoach that ran from Indianapolis to Leavenworth and by boats on the Ohio River. The mail was sorted at Leavenworth then taken to all the different post offices within Crawford County.

As I entered the store, Reuben left the counter and allowed me to take over. The store would only be open for another two hours and he had shelves to stock and feed sacks to restack.

We sold a variety of stuff in our store, including dry goods like flour, corn meal, sugar, baking powder, and salt. We also carried livestock feed so that those who did not grow their own could purchase it for their cows, chickens, and horses.

Everyone had a horse for transportation, even if they lived in town. Most people kept a cow or two for milk and raised chickens for eggs and meat. The store stocked buttons, thread, needles, and fabric to make clothing. We sold lumber for small building projects, along with nails, bolts, and hand tools. Papa also stocked ammunition and would get guns for those who requested them.

The flour and animal feed came from the grist mill in Milltown, along with the lumber. Papa, Reuben, or Carter would take the wagon over once a week to pick up the supplies we sold in our store. It saved our customers time if they could come to our store for their flour and feed, instead of traveling all the way to Milltown.

The other supplies were hauled from Leavenworth. There was a button factory in Leavenworth, and the other items came down the Ohio River by skiffs and boats. Papa made a trip once a month to Leavenworth to restock our store and it took a full day to get there and back.

Other items we sold were maple syrup and sorghum that was produced locally. The syrup came from our own tree tapping, while the sorghum came from a farmer who lived just west of Marengo.

As I sat down on the stool behind the counter, our cat, Annie, came to rub on my legs. I scooped her onto my lap and began petting her soft fur. She began to purr, enjoying the attention immensely. Her job was to keep the mice and rats away from all the feed, which was a full time occupation. Each morning there would be at least one mouse or rat by the back door of the store, assuring us that Annie was earning her keep. It's the only reason Papa let her stay because, like Carter, he was not fond of cats at all.

Effie and I talked for about a half hour then she headed home to do the milking. She hated going up the steep hill above her home to bring the cow down. She said the stupid thing would just about run her over as she led it back to their barn. The cow knew there would be feed at the bottom of the hill and couldn't get there soon enough.

I suggested Effie ride the cow down the hill but she said the cow was too bony and ornery for that. She said once she just turned the cow loose to find her own way back to the barn while she followed behind. The stupid beast ran right past the barn and was standing in the middle of the cemetery trimming the grass around headstones when Effie caught up to her. It was the one and only time Effie had tried that tactic.

Papa, Reuben and I headed home a little after six when the store closed. On the way home I told Papa all about our new teacher, even the part about her being from Kentucky and how nervous it had made me to find out she had grown up in a state that supported slavery. Papa assured me that, just because she came from Kentucky, didn't mean she agreed with the practice of owning slaves. I gave that some thought and decided Papa was probably right, but I knew not to breathe a word about our involvement with runaway slaves to anyone. It was a dangerous and illegal activity we were doing, and Papa would surely be sent to jail if the slave hunters discovered our every other Thursday trip to Curby brought back a wagon load of slaves. I would just have to wait and see who Miss Smith really was and with whom her sympathies lay; the slave owners or the slavery opponents.

Chapter Four

As the school year got under way, I fell into a familiar daily rhythm. Get up, milk Elsie, help with fixing breakfast, eat, clean the kitchen with Momma, and then head to town with Papa. It was a lot to get done every morning but no more than most of the kids I went to school with were expected to do. I was just thankful that I could ride to school in the wagon with Papa and not be expected to walk the two miles to and from school.

Effie had been right about our new teacher and I sure hoped Miss Smith would be coming back for next year. She wasn't just pretty and nice, she made learning interesting.

Deciding we would understand and appreciate history more if we were part of the action, Miss Smith chose to teach history class in a "hands on" manner.

We reenacted the "Boston Tea Party" of 1773 during our first history lesson. Pretending to be colonists dressed as Mohawk Indians, we snuck onto an English ship that was in the Boston harbor. We dumped 342 chests of tea overboard and let it float out to sea. The colonists did this because they were furious about the tax that had been placed on tea and other things by the British.

The taxing from England had become enormous and ridiculous. The colonists dumping the tea into the harbor angered the English authorities so much they sent British troops to Boston. This act of defiance by the colonists of Massachusetts would be the beginning of outward showings, making it clear that the colonists were fed up with paying enormous taxes to England and were ready to establish a government of their own.

Miss Smith pointed out that the relationship between the colonies and England continued to deteriorate, until finally the Declaration of Independence was written in 1776 and sent to England, making it official that the colonists were now going to govern their own affairs.

Soon after the "Boston Tea Party" reenactment, Miss Smith planned a history lesson for the great ride of April 18, 1775. We pretended the school house was the place in Concord, Massachusetts, where the colonists were keeping their supply of arms. Angus was allowed to walk home to get a horse and ride back yelling "The British are coming! The British are coming!" which is exactly what Paul Revere, William Dawes, and Samuel Prescott did in 1775.

Miss Smith explained that at the time of the great ride, the British were marching to Concord, Massachusetts to burn the building which housed the weapons of the militiamen, or as they are better known, the minutemen. They also had plans to try and capture rebel leaders Samuel Adams and John Hancock. When Paul Revere and the other men rode through the countryside warning the colonists, it allowed them to get ready to fight the British troops.

Miss Smith pointed out that the colonists were mostly farmers, but it didn't stop them from fighting against the trained British forces. The warning allowed the colonists to move their weapons before the building was set afire and prepare to fight the British as they returned to Boston. They hid along the road that stretched eighteen miles between Concord and Boston and surprised the British with an ambush, shooting at the British Red Coats from behind trees, sheds, rock walls and even houses. The British, surprised by the sudden attack, fled in a disorganized fashion, dodging the bullets of the minutemen all along the way.

Miss Smith told us how the colonist's celebrated this small triumph and an Irishman by the name of Patrick O'Flagharty wrote a song making fun of the British and how they had fled from the minutemen's onslaught. The song had appeared in the Pennsylvania Magazine in May 1775 for all to read and enjoy. Miss Smith had a copy of the song, and to our surprise, she brought her guitar to school and sang it for us. The song was set to the music of an Irish song known as "Irish Washerwoman". All the students danced an Irish jig in the school yard as Miss Smith sang the song. I asked Miss

Smith if I may copy the song to keep for myself. The words to the song were this:

By my faith but I think ye're all makers of bulls,
With your brains in your breeches, your bums in your skulls,
Get home with your muskets and put up your swords,
And look in your books for the meaning of words.
You see, now, my honeys, how much you're mistaken,
For Concord by discord can never be taken.

How brave ye went out with your muskets all bright,
And thought to be-frighten the folks with the sight,
But when you got there how they powdered your pums,
And all the way home how they peppered your bums.
And is it not, honeys, a comical crack,
To be proud in the face, and be shot in the back?

With all of your talkin' and all of your wordin'
And all of your shoutin' and marchin' and swordin'
How come ye to think, now, they did not know how,
To be after their firelocks as smartly as you?
Why, you see, now my honeys, 'tis nothing at all,
But to pull at the trigger, and pop goes the ball.

And what have you got now with all your designing,
But a town without victuals to sit down and dine in,
And to look on the ground like a parcel of noodles,
And sing how the Yankees have beaten the Doodles.
I'm sure if you're wise you'll make peace for a dinner,
For fighting and fasting will soon make ye thinner.

Miss Smith allowed the class to celebrate our pretend victory after we sent the pretend British scurrying back to Boston. She had baked cookies for the occasion and we sat under the oak trees in the school yard to enjoy them.

Effie told me that Mrs. George grumped the whole time Miss Smith made the cookies, saying she was "messing up her kitchen and spoiling us children." Miss Smith had just smiled and continued baking the cookies. Effie's Momma, Lillian, told Miss Smith to come to their house the next time she wanted to bake something.

As we munched on the cookies, Miss Smith went on to tell that the victory of the colonists was short lived. By May 28, 1775, the news of the Minutemen's ambush of the Red Coats reached England, officially starting the American Revolutionary War.

Miss Smith made sure to tell us about the role women had played during the Revolutionary War, too. She told of a woman named Sybil Ludington, who made a midnight ride too, and warned of approaching English soldiers.

Effie wanted to go get their horse and reenact the ride Sybil Ludington had made. Miss Smith agreed, since Effie lived so close to the school. As Effie came back to the school with the horse running full speed, she screamed "The British are coming! The British are coming!" To the horse it must have sounded like Effie wanted him to stop, because that's exactly what he did. Locking his legs the horse came to a complete halt in seconds. However, Effie did not. She just kept going forward; over the horse's shoulders, up the neck, past the ears, down the nose and landing hard on the ground. Her dress was completely over her head, which might have been a blessing because it kept her face from being scratched up.

When we were sure Effie was not hurt, except for her pride of course, we couldn't help laughing at the sight we had just witnessed. Effie's mount just shook his head and trotted back home without a rider. Effie got to her feet and I helped her get her skirt back to her ankles and dusted her off the best I could.

"Goodness, that was quite a ride," Effie said with a laugh.

"Are you sure you're okay?" I asked, not quite being successful in keeping a chuckle from escaping as I asked.

"Oh, yeah, I'm fine," Effie assured me. "I'm just thankful I was riding bareback or my dress may have caught on the saddle horn, leaving me dangling upside down from the horse or ripping my dress off completely!"

And that was Effie. It was why I liked her so much. She had no fear and laughed even when she should be crying. Any other girl would have been completely humiliated from showing her bloomers to God and everybody, but not Effie. She was just embarrassed that she hadn't been able to stay on the horse's back and make the midnight cry successfully.

The next day, Miss Smith allowed us to reenact a battle of the

Revolutionary War. The boys fired the guns and cannons while the girls cooked and tended the wounded. We also carried pitchers of water to the fighting soldiers, which earned us the name "Molly Pitcher".

I got to play a woman by the name of Molly Hays, who took over firing her husband's cannon when he fell wounded at her feet. Angus pretended to be my wounded husband and instructed me on how to fire the cannon as he lay on the ground. It was the most fun I had ever had while being taught a history lesson.

Miss Smith said the Revolutionary War was long and hard, lasting over seven years. Our troops didn't have proper shoes or clothing, not to mention they were untrained to fight battles. They had mostly been farmers up until the time the war began.

A lot of times, they didn't have enough food to eat or proper shelter. It was a true miracle that we won the war at all, especially since England was considered to have one of the world's most powerful military of that time. Miss Smith made sure we understood the sacrifices the colonists had made to create the wonderful country we called home; the United State of America.

I had never learned history in such a way and I knew by actually pretending to be a part of the war, I would remember the lesson well. If I ever became a teacher, I planned to teach history the same way Miss Smith had taught me.

Miss Smith shared some facts about Paul Revere during another history lesson. Paul was actually a silversmith and continued in that trade once the Revolutionary War ended. He began to perfect the art of casting iron, and in 1792, began to make bells. Paul, along with his two sons, Paul Jr. and Joseph, created the first bell of Boston, Massachusetts. After that, they produced hundreds of bells, most being for churches in the Boston area. In 1795, Paul opened North America's first copper mill in Canton, just south of Boston. Paul Revere was not just a fast man on a horse, he was also a huge part of America's start of industry.

Miss Smith also told us that, though history books have always led people to believe Paul and the other men screamed "the British are coming", they probably did not. There would have been a possibility of Red Coats along the roads and in the towns. Also, not everyone living in America was against the British and may have warned the Red Coats that the minutemen knew what they were attempting to do. Paul would have probably just made stops along the way to those he knew supported the cause of the minutemen and allowed the warning to be spread from supporter to supporter in that way. However, it was much more fun to yell "the British are coming" as we learned about the famous battle that started the Revolutionary War.

****

As we pulled into the church yard the first Sunday after school began, Mrs. George hustled over to our wagon before we could even climb down. "Stephen, I just want you to know that new teacher is teaching Virginia and the other children unsavory things."

"Virginia seems to love Miss Smith," Papa responded.

"Well, of course she does," Mrs. George snorted. "What child wouldn't want to run around the school yard all day pretending to shoot someone? The children were even rewarded with fresh baked cookies for their actions."

"I believe they were reenacting the minutemen ambushing the British armed forces while the British were marching from Concord back to Boston, Mrs. George," Papa said quietly. "If you remember your history, you will know that this act was what started the Revolutionary War."

"Of course I know that," Mrs. George huffed. "My grandfather fought in that war."

"Well then, you know how important it is that the children learn how our country won its independence," Papa replied.

"Did you know Effie was allowed to ride a horse like a heathen?" Mrs. George questioned, not ready to give up the fight. "She fell off too, showing her bloomers to anyone and everyone."

"Virginia told us all about it," Momma said laughing.

"I fail to see the humor," Mrs. George fumed. "The same day Effie fell from the horse, the children were in the church yard dancing to a song Miss Smith was playing and singing with a guitar. What do you make of that, Stephen?"

"Well, during the week this yard is where the children play," Stephen said. "The song you're referring to was one an Irishman had written about the British running from the Minutemen as they began to fire on them between Concord and Boston. Virginia has told us all about it. It's the first time I have ever heard my daughter speak of her history lesson."

"You, Stephen, are on the committee to hire schoolmarms," Mrs. George said. "I'm telling you these things out of concern for how the children are being taught."

"Mrs. George," Papa said patiently, "I do not have any reason to believe Miss Smith is not doing her job properly. Should I find her a new place to live for the rest of the school year?"

"Well, uh, no, that won't be necessary," Mrs. George said. "I'll just be keeping an eye on things for you down at the school. I have a very good view from my kitchen window."

"You don't say?" Papa said with a smirk.

Walking past a puffed up Mrs. George, my family made their way into the church. Looking around, I spotted Effie sitting beside Miss Smith. Looking to Momma, she nodded, giving me permission to sit by my best friend and favorite teacher ever. I was glad Papa had not listened to Mrs. George's complaints with any seriousness. If the rest of the year was anything like the first week of school had been, I was going to learn a lot.

****

The slaves continued to come to us through the Underground Railroad and we kept assisting them. Papa and Carter made the Curby Thursday trip while Reuben minded the store. Papa would arrive back just in time to pick Reuben and me up after the store closed.

One Curby Thursday in late December, I went to the barn to help our latest occupants settle in. This time they were all young adults, about Reuben's age. There were two women and two men. It had been a tight fit in the wagon and they were happy to be let out. I realized that slaves with children would probably hold off until warmer weather, since they had hardly anything warm to wear.

Christmas was just a few days away, and arrangements had been made with Mr. Pierson to wait until after the holiday to move the slaves to the next station. Getting a load of manure on Christmas Eve would definitely not be normal activity and would raise suspicions.

On Christmas Eve, we went to the church for a candlelight service and to sing Christmas carols. I always loved this part of celebrating Jesus' birth and looked forward to it each year. As I stood singing with my parents and my brothers, I couldn't help but think of the slaves hidden under our barn. Did they know it was Christmas

Eve? Did they understand the significance of this blessed event? Did they sing carols to celebrate Christ's birth? Surely the slave masters allowed the slaves to have Christmas day off and told the slaves of the importance of Christmas, didn't they?

When we returned home, I decided to take some cookies to the barn for the slaves to have a late night snack. I poured a pitcher of milk, too, and added a gourd dipper for them to drink from. Grabbing a lantern, I headed to the barn. I felt sure that even slave hunters celebrated Christmas and would not be out on this night looking for runaways.

Removing Nellie from the stall so she wouldn't step into the trap door opening, I pushed the straw aside and pulled the door up. It was dark inside, and I lowered the lantern so I could see. Looking up with scared eyes, I realized the slaves were always afraid of being caught and returned to their masters. Seeing it was just me, they reached to take the lantern and placed it on the floor for light. I handed the plate of cookies and pitcher of milk down to their waiting hands. Next, I climbed the ladder down into the hole.

I explained to the slaves that it was Christmas Eve and I wanted to share what a special day it was. To my surprise, they knew exactly what Christmas was all about. They had learned it in a song and from the few slaves who could actually read, though they weren't supposed to know how.

I asked if they would please sing the song for me, and for the first time, I heard "Go Tell It on the Mountain". I had just left church where we had sung lots of songs but none were as heartfelt nor sounded as beautiful as this one. It told of the shepherds and angels and of how Christ was humbly born in a manger, to bring us God's salvation. As I listened to the chorus; "Go, tell it on the mountain, over the hills and everywhere, that Jesus Christ is born;" I knew I wanted to teach others this song one day. I hoped there would come a time when I could sing the song at Christmastime without someone questioning where I had heard it. I made sure to get pencil and paper and write the words down before they left us.

****

Christmas morning of 1859 will be one I will always remember. As I came downstairs to go milk Annabelle, the cow that was fresh now, I could hear Momma and Papa talking in the kitchen, but as I entered, they abruptly stopped. Looking from one to the other, I wondered what was up.

Grabbing the pail, I headed to the barn to get the chore done. The only good thing about milking in the winter was that the cow put off some heat to keep you warm. Finishing up, I hurried to let Annabelle out so I could get back inside the warm house.

After breakfast, Papa announced it was time to open gifts. I couldn't remember a time seeing Papa so excited about the exchange of presents. He and Momma shared a smile and we all went into the living room to see what was wrapped for us. Reuben and Carter each received a new knife that Papa had picked up on his last trip to Leavenworth. Papa then handed Momma a gift wrapped in a burlap sack. Inside was a new cast iron kettle, something Momma really needed. Reuben and Carter each had another present that turned out to be new shirts sewn by Momma. So far, I had not been handed a present but was enjoying watching my family open theirs. Momma handed a gift to Papa, which was also a new shirt he could wear for Sunday worship.

"So, Virginia, what would you really like for Christmas?" Papa asked while sharing a smile with Momma and my brothers.

"Oh, I don't know," I replied thoughtfully. "Anything would be nice."

Carter slipped from the living room and up the stairs. The next sound I heard left no question about what I was getting for Christmas. A sharp bark came from Reuben's bedroom as Carter opened the door. Carter came back down with a wriggling, fluffy puppy of no definite breed. Jumping up, I met Carter at the bottom of the stairs and took the pup from his arms. The pup gave my face a complete washing with its little pink tongue. It had long ears and big feet. Its fur was red, except for the four white socks it appeared to be wearing.

"You're responsible for training him not to kill chickens," Momma reminded me.

"I will, I promise I will!"

"So, what are you going to name him?" Reuben asked.

"I think I will name him Oliver," I decided. Oliver was the best Christmas gift I had ever been given, and I couldn't wait to have the little dog follow me everywhere I went.

Momma and I went to the kitchen to prepare a special Christmas dinner. We would have chicken and dumplings, leather britches cooked with jowl bacon and fluffy yeast rolls. We had made two squash pies the previous day and we would sweeten and whip cold cream from the springhouse into stiff peaks to top the slices of pie. When the meal was almost complete, Papa came to the kitchen.

"You know, Elizabeth, since Virginia knows about the slaves now, maybe we could have them join us for this special Christmas meal?"

Momma considered Papa's words for a moment. "Do you think there is any chance at all of slave hunters showing up?"

"Not on Christmas day. Even slave hunters and slave masters must take a break on this most holy of days."

"Then I believe it would be wonderful," Momma said.

The four slaves were moved from the barn to our kitchen table as Momma pulled the yeast rolls from the oven. Their eyes danced all around, taking in the sights and smells of our home. I knew they had never sat at a table with white folks before, by the stunned expression on their faces when Papa offered chairs at our table. As we all sat down and joined hands for Papa to bless the food, I looked at the dark ebony hands joined with our very white ones. In God's eyes, I knew skin color made absolutely no difference. Just as God wanted Moses to deliver the Hebrew's from slavery in Egypt, He wanted this group of people to be free, too.

When the meal was finished and the dishes had been washed, dried and put away, we all gathered in the living room. The slaves told many sad stories of the plantation they had lived on. Not one of them knew where their parents were, since they had been sold at auction at very young ages. None of the four had been approached by a field agent, but knew of another slave on the plantation who had been. That slave agreed to let them come along when he made his escape. Sadly, the slave who helped them find the Underground Railroad had been older, and when the dogs had been put on the trail of the five runaways, he could not outrun them. He had been captured, but the four sitting in our living room had made it to the conductor and had been moved successfully through the railroad. They were thankful to have made it to a state that was against slavery, but knew they were not going to be safe until they reached Canada.

Before the slaves were taken back to the hidden room under our barn, I asked them to sing "Go Tell It on the Mountain" for the rest of my family. This time, the slaves added a beat to the music by clapping their hands, and we all joined in at the chorus each time. I hated that they must go back to the cold, dark room under Nellie's stall for the rest of their stay but knew it was for their safety.

We didn't have any slaves through January, February and March, because of the cold, and the tracks they would have left should there be snow on the ground. Leaving tracks by the Ohio River would be dangerous. It told of a crossing to the other side and it could be runaway slaves. Snow left no doubt that someone or something had walked over it. It would not take a very experienced tracker to follow footprints in the snow. Even if we sometimes didn't get much snow in southern Indiana, farther north would have plenty on the ground.

In April, the slaves began to return to our little room under Nellie's stall. My nerves tensed at the thought of runaway slaves being hid at the farm, again. I hadn't realized how much I had relaxed the three months we didn't have any moving through our station.

Late the first Saturday night of the month of April, someone rode into our yard, the horse at a run. No sooner had it came to a stop, the rider dismounted and ran to our back door. After knocking hard, the visitor just opened the door and walked into the kitchen. Papa had already started toward the door, because Oliver had taken to barking when the rider came in the drive. I came downstairs to see who would be at our house at this time of night, fearing it was slave hunters. To my surprise, I was looking right at Angus Zink. What was Angus doing at our house at 9:00 at night?

Papa seemed to know exactly why he had showed up. He hollered for Reuben to get some warm clothes on and come to the barn. I had no idea what was going on.

As Papa turned to Angus, he said, "How close are they, Son?"

How close are who? This was as confusing as Curby Thursday, until I found out that secret.

"They crossed the Ohio about three hours ago. I don't know if they will track them to here or not," Angus replied.

Crossed the Ohio? Who would....? Then it dawned on me. The slave hunters had tracked the slaves hidden in our barn to their crossing at the Ohio River. Angus and his family were the other station masters in Marengo! Selling the harnesses and other leather goods was the perfect cover for their involvement in the Underground Railroad.

As I looked at Angus, we realized we both had a family secret, and it was the exact same one. At least I knew someone at school understood the fear I carried with me. Angus didn't want his father arrested any more than I wanted mine arrested.

Papa and Momma sprang into action, and Angus left quickly to get back home before the hunters caught him on the road. He would surely be questioned as to why he was out at such a late hour.

Reuben came down the stairs fully dressed and ready to go. I stood in stunned silence watching the activity all around me.

"Virginia," Momma said firmly, "pull yourself together and come to the barn and help."

I suddenly thought of the poor, scared people under the trap door in our barn and sprang into action, too. As a family, we entered the barn quickly to do what must be done. Carter hitched Clyde to the wagon as Papa led Nellie out of her stall and toward Carter so she could be hitched next to Clyde.

Reuben quickly moved the straw and manure aside and pulled up the trap door. Momma and I were ready with some blankets that the slaves could wrap themselves in for the cold ride. As the slaves exited the hidden room, I could see my fear mirrored in their eyes. We helped them into the small space between the wagon floors and put the back securely in place. At least there were only two this time, a young husband and wife, making the move quick and easy.

Reuben hopped on the seat and put the horses in motion. Since we knew the hunters were coming from the south, the only plan was to go north and hopefully stay ahead of them. There was no time for pretending everything was normal on this night.

With the slaves gone, we pushed the dirty straw back over the trap door. We moved Ornery to Nellie's stall and fed him hay and grain, hoping he would do what horses do best. The plan was to make the stall as nasty as possible so the slave hunters would walk right past it should they come looking.

We could only pray they didn't have bloodhounds with them to sniff out where the slaves had been. Just in case, Momma went to the kitchen for some pepper to sprinkle outside the stall. She continued with the pepper to the place where the slaves had crawled into the wagon. Carter had already raked the dirt floor of the barn to erase the many foot prints.

We all returned to the house to wait for Reuben to come home safely. When he returned, he would leave the wagon in the woods at the edge of our property instead of in the barn. The hunters would know for sure that we acted as a station if they got a close look at the wagon.

If all was quiet at our house, Reuben would ride Clyde back, while leading Nellie behind him, to the barn and place them in stalls. If there was activity at the house, Reuben was to hide in the woods and pray for everyone's safety. This was the plan; however, it had never been put into action until this night.

"Where will Reuben take the slaves?" I asked Papa as we all sat at the kitchen table to catch our breath and try to calm our nerves.

"Well, normally Mr. Pierson takes the slaves from our home to the next station in Chambersburg, which is run by a Quaker family. Reuben will not be going there, though. It would not be safe for the slaves nor the Quaker family in Chambersburg if the slaves showed up there tonight. Reuben will take the slaves to Paddy's Garden, or Little Africa as some call it."

"Where is Paddy's Garden, Papa?"

"It's not too far from Chambersburg. It's a settlement of freed slaves. They own over 1500 acres and are mostly farmers. Mr. Lindley, who is a Quaker too, moved to the Chambersburg area around 1816 from North Carolina. He brought eleven families of freed slaves with him. Of course, there are many more families living there now, since that's been over forty years ago."

"I didn't know there was a whole community of freed slaves living that close to us in Orange County," I said. I had been a little past Valeene once with Papa when he delivered a load of lumber. We had gone through the community of Piersontown on our way there. As we had climbed the hill out of Valeene, Papa had turned right at a Y in the road, and said it led to Chambersburg. We only traveled about a half mile down the road before we reached our destination, so I had never been any closer to Paddy's Garden than that.

"Well, I didn't tell you before because I didn't want you to ask questions," Papa said. "Reuben will take the slave couple to Paddy's Garden and they will blend into the community. If the slave hunters show up there, the Negros will just show them their papers, stating they are free. It will be much easier to hide two colored people among their own skin color."

"Why don't all the slaves just go to Little Africa and live there?

Why do they have to go to Canada?"

"Because the runaway slaves would never be able to get papers documenting their freedom. It would put all the freed slaves living at Paddy's Garden in danger. The two slaves Reuben drops off there tonight will not remain there. When Mr. Pierson comes on Monday, we will tell him that we had to move the slaves for fear of slave hunters closing in on us. Mr. Pierson will then go to Chambersburg to tell the Quaker family. The Quakers will go to Paddy's Garden to retrieve the runaway slaves so they may continue on their journey north."

"Do you think slavery will ever be against the law in every state, Papa? It sure would be a sad life to live as someone's property instead of having the rights of a human being."

"Virginia, I hope one day everyone will be able to sing the "Star-Spangled Banner", even the Negroes, and know the words are true for them; that they live in the land of the free and home of the brave. As of now, only some of us are fortunate enough to sing those words and know they are true."

"Virginia, you and Carter need to go to bed now," Momma said. "If the slave hunters show up, I want you both to pretend you're asleep. Under no circumstances are you to come back down stairs if you hear someone speaking to me or your father."

"Yes, Momma," Carter said speaking for both of us.

Carter and I trudged upstairs to our bedrooms to wait out the long night. I lay in bed shaking from fear of all that could go wrong. Even if the slave hunters didn't show up here, Reuben was still out on the road in the dark with runaway slaves hidden in the wagon he was driving.

Taking slow, deep breaths I tried to get my nerves under control. I knew God loved all of us the same, whether slave or free, and would give protection this night. Now all I needed to do was calm down and put the situation in God's capable hands.

I don't know what time I drifted off to sleep but I awoke to the rooster crowing. I hurried to Reuben's room to see if he had made it back safe. I was relieved to see him in his bed, sound asleep. Hurrying to Carter's room to see if he was awake, I peeked in. Carter was just waking up and he smiled at me as I stood in the doorway. "Quite a scare we had ourselves last night, huh Virginia?" Carter asked.

"Yes, it sure was," I replied.

I headed to the kitchen and found Momma sipping coffee at the table with Papa. From the looks of them, I would guess neither had slept at all.

Momma looked up as I entered. "Go ahead and milk the cow, Virginia. We need to do everything just like we always do. I believe if the hunters had been able to pick up the scent they would have been here already, so we'll probably be okay."

The information calmed me, and I grabbed the pail to do as I was told. With the morning chores done and breakfast eaten, we loaded up and headed to church. I prayed everyone could stay awake through the service, given the long night we had endured.

Entering the church, I spotted Angus and his parents. As our eyes met, I silently told him all was well. We certainly couldn't speak about last night here in the church, or anywhere else for that matter. The Zink's and our family were silent partners on a long line of tracks called an Underground Railroad.

Chapter Five

I awoke April 7, 1860, another year older. As I lay in bed rubbing the sleep from my eyes, I thought back to the year I had just lived. I had learned so much and become responsible in ways I never thought I would have to. Sometimes, I just wanted to climb up the Maple and read, forgetting that our house was a part of illegal activity. However, I knew hiding the slaves was the right thing to do. I prayed that one day all the slaves would be free and able to choose the life they wanted for themselves.

I dragged myself from between the warm covers and got dressed. A good birthday present would be for someone else to milk Annabelle for me, but I knew that wasn't going to happen. Everyone else had their own chores to do.

Trudging downstairs, I stepped into the kitchen to get the milking pail. At that moment, Carter came in the back door with a full pail of milk. Bless his heart!

"Happy birthday, Virginia," Carter said, grinning from ear to ear. "I milked Annabelle this morning to make time for me to give you your present."

"Milking the ornery cow was present enough," I replied with a laugh.

"Maybe so, but I have a better one in mind," Carter said. "I think we have just enough time before breakfast to hit the mushroom patch. They should be plentiful this fine morning."

"Are you going to show me your secret place where you find them by the hundreds, or are you going to drag me all over the woods to find two?"

Carter knew where all the morel mushrooms grew around the area. He would start finding the black ones starting in late March. Through the weeks of April he would find the gray, white, and big yellow honeycomb ones. They were all delicious, no matter what color they were.

Momma would slice the mushrooms in half length- wise, dip them in beaten egg, coat them with a mixture of flour, cornmeal, salt and pepper, and fry them in butter. It was a treat we could only have in the spring because that was the only time they grew in our area. However, finding them was as good as eating them.

"You know, just because it's your birthday, I'm going to take you to one of my best hunting spots," Carter said.

"Let's get going, then. We don't have much time before breakfast and then I have to go to school," I replied.

We headed out the door, each with an empty pail. Carter walked toward the big maple at the edge of our yard then turned north. As I walked under my favorite tree, I looked up to see tiny buds forming on the branches. Soon, it would be full of leaves and I could hide among them with a good book when I had some free time. I couldn't decide which way I liked my favorite tree the best; in the summer with a green canopy of leaves or in the fall when the leaves were a brilliant orange.

We walked about a half mile and Carter stopped and pointed. "See that ash tree right there, Virginia?"

"Yes," I replied.

"In the area around that tree is where we're going to find mushrooms this morning."

I looked at Carter for a moment then smiled and took off running. The contest was always who could find the first mushroom of the hunt, and I was going to win! I ran about twenty steps, caught my foot on a tree root and found myself sprawled on the ground. As I lifted my head to see where Carter was, there was a mushroom right in front of my face. Grabbing it up, I held it up in victory as Carter caught up with me. Carter laughed and snatched it from my hand, saying that it was in his bucket, so he had found the first one. He then reached down and helped me to my feet. We hunted for twenty minutes and found 100 mushrooms. What a great birthday present!

Taking them home, we handed my gift to Momma. She said she would slice them into some salt water and we would eat them for supper. I would receive two gifts from one present; the hunting with Carter and eating the find with my family.

****

Miss Smith pointed out that this was a Presidential election year and she chose to make that part of our history lesson. Of course, none of the boys in the class were old enough to vote and the girls never would be. Women were not allowed to vote in any elections in 1860. Miss Smith wanted us to take notice, though, because she felt that big changes were on the way, depending upon who won the election.

People against slavery, known as abolitionists, were becoming more vocal about the slaves in the South. On the 16th of October the previous year, an abolitionist named John Brown, along with twenty other men, captured the federal armory at Harper's Ferry, Virginia. Among the twenty men were three free black men and a runaway slave. John Brown was attempting to persuade the slaves to take up arms and revolt against the treatment they were receiving. It all ended on October 18th when the US Marines, led by Robert E. Lee, marched to the armory and put a quick end to the situation and the men who had tried to start the revolt. Four of the twenty fled, but John Brown and the rest of the men were put to death.

This event showed how heated the country was over the slave issue. It had been decided that the new territories to the west could own slaves, if they chose to. This angered abolitionists even more and those in Washington DC were divided on the issue.

Miss Smith said the election would take place in November and would be watched very closely. She wanted to keep our class informed, because it was history happening right before our eyes. Miss Smith predicted that the issue of slavery would be the hottest topic among the presidential candidates.

****

School dismissed for the year at the end of April and work on the farm increased. There was ground to plow and disc in preparation to plant the field corn. The early garden things had been planted, and soon the plants that preferred warmer weather would be put into the ground.

In April we had planted the potatoes, peas, and carrots and set out the broccoli and cabbage plants Momma had started from seed. In a few weeks, the beans would be planted and we would set out the tomato plants. Momma had saved seed to start those, too. Come late summer and early fall, there would be plenty of drying and preserving to do.

On the first Curby Thursday in May, a family of four arrived. There was a man and woman and their two children, a boy about ten and a little girl, who appeared to be about six years old. Upon opening the back of the wagon, we could see immediately that the young girl was not well. After helping them unload from the wagon, Momma reached to touch the child. The little girl shrank away toward her mother and I was reminded again that slaves were rarely touched with kindness by white folks in the South.

"How long has your child been sick?" Momma asked the slave woman.

"'Bout three days," the slave woman replied. She cast her eyes to the ground, never looking Momma in the face.

"May I feel her forehead to see if she has fever?" Momma asked.

"Yes'm," the slave woman said, still keeping her face tilted downward.

Momma reached out again to feel the child's forehead. This time the child's mother held her still so Momma could touch her. "She's burning up with fever," Momma said.

"Can you help her?" the slave woman asked, tears pooling in her big brown eyes.

"I will try my best," Momma said. "I will have to use remedies that I have here, though. We cannot go get the doctor because it would reveal our involvement in assisting runaway slaves. Do you understand?"

"Yes'm," the slave woman replied again.

"Please, call me Elizabeth," Momma said. "What is your name?"

"Sadie," the slave woman whispered.

"Virginia, please go draw a bucket of water from the spring and bring it back here with a rag," Momma instructed. "Sadie, I want you and your family to go ahead down the ladder and into the room we have prepared for you. Make your little girl as comfortable as possible and wrap her in the blankets. We will be back shortly."

"Do you want me to leave the trap door up?" Carter asked.

"Yes, Carter, just leave it up, please," Momma said as she and I headed out the barn door.

I went to get the bucket of cold spring water then entered the kitchen to get a rag. Momma was at the stove heating water and adding herbs. "What are you going to give that sick child?" I asked as I looked into the pan of water.

"I added some fever few that we dried last summer along with some dried coneflower leaves," Momma said. "Hopefully, the fever few will bring down her temperature and the coneflower will help her body fight whatever it is she has. With her being ill for three days already, the sickness has had plenty of time to pass through her entire body. I may not be able to help her."

"We will do the best we can, Momma," I said. Grabbing a rag from the ones folded on a shelf, I dropped it into the bucket of cold water.

"Take that bucket out and tell Sadie to bathe the child with the cool water to try and bring her temperature down. I will be out as soon as I have steeped this tea long enough."

I walked back to the barn with the bucket of cool water. Lowering myself down the ladder, I placed the bucket beside Sadie's feet. "Momma said to bathe her with this cool water," I instructed Sadie.

"Yes'm," Sadie said. She reached into the bucket for the rag and wrung it out. Pulling back the cover she had wrapped her little girl in, Sadie began to run the cool rag over the child's hot skin. The child shivered as her fevered little body began to cool.

"Momma will be here in a few minutes with some herbal tea. She's brewing it now," I told Sadie.

"Okay," Sadie said quietly.

Sadie's husband and son had sat down on a bench and watched as Sadie attempted to bring the little girl's fever down with the cool bath. They did not speak a word while I was down in the room. Momma showed up at the trap door and I went up to take the cup she was handing down to me, then she descended the ladder.

"Let's try and get some of this tea in her," Momma told Sadie. "Virginia, please hand the cup to Sadie so she can offer it to....I'm sorry, what's your little girl's name?"

"Rosie," Sadie answered quietly.

I handed the cup to Sadie and Momma helped little Rosie sit up. The child seemed quite listless now. I was afraid she would not be able to swallow the tea that Momma had brewed. When they had first climbed out of the wagon, the child had been much more alert, probably due to the fact that she was frightened.

Sadie held the cup to Rosie's lips as Momma cradled the child to keep her upright. After just a few sips, Rosie pushed the cup away.

"Offer the tea to her every fifteen minutes or so," Momma instructed. "We need to get that whole cup down her."

"Yes'm," Sadie replied softly.

"Elizabeth," Momma said. "My name's Elizabeth."

"Yes'm, Miz Elizabeth," Sadie said, daring to take a small peek up at Momma.

"Virginia and I are going to go fetch your supper," Momma said. "We will be back shortly. Keep offering the tea and bathing Rosie with the cool water." Momma and I climbed up the ladder and went back to the house. Papa was sitting at the kitchen table when we came in.

"How's the child?" Papa asked.

"Not good," Momma said. "She's so weak she can hardly sip the tea I prepared and she's shivering uncontrollably. I know the cool bath is adding to her shivering, but we have to get that fever down."

"We will do the best we can," Papa said.

"I know," Momma said, "but I'm afraid our best won't be enough. The child is very sick and has been for three days."

"We will just have to put the situation into God's hands," Papa said.

Momma and I packed the supper we had prepared earlier to the family hidden in our barn. The sun was sinking very low and darkness would soon be upon us. As we reached the trap door, Sadie's husband stepped on the bottom rung of the ladder and took the container of food from us. Sadie had wrapped Rosie back up in the blanket and she appeared to be asleep.

"Come and eat supper, Sadie," Momma said. "Rosie will be in need of your care all through the night, so you need to take nourishment in order to have strength to tend to her."

"Thank you for your kindness," Sadie's husband said.

"You're welcome. We will leave you to your supper now and be back in a little while to check on Rosie," Momma said. "Normally, we would shut this trap door now until morning, but under the circumstances, I believe we will just leave it open."

Momma went back to the house and I decided to take a walk along the creek. Ollie, the name I had shortened my puppy's name to, tagged along behind me. Ollie was very playful and curious, as most puppies tend to be, and had chased the chickens a few times just to hear them squawk and carry on. Momma had fussed about it, but so far Ollie had never attempted to catch any of the chickens. I had made sure to scold him each time he threatened the flock, just to make sure he understood it was bad behavior.

Carter came outside and shut the door to the chicken coop to keep them safe through the night. Spotting me at the creek, he walked down the hill to join me.

"Hey, Virginia, whatcha doing?"

"Just taking in the last moments of daylight on this warm evening," I replied. I continued to walk downstream to a big rock that Carter and I liked to sit on and dangle our feet in the water on hot summer days. We sat down beside each other and watched as dusk settled on the field of wheat swaying in the soft breeze. The tree frogs began to sing a song, joined by the deep bass of a bull frog. I knew they were perched on the bank of the small pond which was created from the overflow from our spring. Papa and my brothers had dug the pond to provide an easy source of water to use for the garden during dry spells, since the garden was just below the spring. It was much easier than packing water from the creek.

"Do you ever think about how good our life is?" I asked Carter.

"Yes, I do, and when I forget, I'm reminded again on Curby Thursday."

"The little girl is really sick, Carter."

"I know," Carter said. Carter reached down to pick up a handful of rocks and sort through them. Choosing ones that were flat, he placed them beside us on the rock. "Want to have a rock skipping contest?"

"Only if you don't mind losing," I retorted. I looked through the rocks and chose the three I wanted. The object was to get the most skips across the surface of the water before the rock sank. We were allowed three chances to determine the winner.

"You can go first," Carter said with a smile.

Standing to my feet to get a better angle, I drew my arm back, keeping my elbow close to my body and my lower arm extended out. The rock needed to hit the surface of the water fast and flat to get the most skips. Propelling the rock from my hand, it skipped three times before sinking.

"That won't be hard to beat," Carter said as he released one of his rocks. He got five skips before it sank.

"This one will be better," I said. "I was just getting warmed up with that first one." Releasing my second rock, I was delighted to count eight skips before it dropped below the water's surface. I turned to Carter with a smile of victory. "Beat that one, dear brother."

"Not a problem," Carter smirked. Carter wound up for his second throw, but the rock turned out to be a dud. It skipped one time then sank like a lead ball. Carter rolled his eyes at me and laughed.

"So, I'm in the lead with eight skips," I said smugly. Turning my rock just so in my hand, I prepared to seal my win. The rock left my hand and performed two huge skips before disappearing.

"Two skips! Now all I have to do is beat your eight."

"I should get extra points by how high and far those skips were, though," I argued.

"That's not how the game is played," Carter said. Carter turned his last rock over several times, trying to decide the best way to grasp it. Finally, he flung the rock at the water. We both counted aloud as it skipped along. "One, two, three, four, five, six, seven, eight," and I stopped counting.

"Nine!" Carter shouted. "It skipped nine times!"

"It only skipped eight, Carter."

"No, Virginia, it skipped nine. You just couldn't see the last one because it's almost dark."

"You just made up the last one because you thought I couldn't see well enough to know it only skipped eight. It's a tie, Carter. I won't fall for your antics like Reuben. We tied and it's too dark to play again."

"Oh, fine Virginia, it's a tie," Carter agreed. We walked to the house still picking at each other about the rock skipping game. I knew Carter would probably win the next time, because he usually did, but tonight I was going to gloat in the fact that we had tied.

I went with Momma to the barn at nine o'clock that night. As we peered down at Rosie lying limp in Sadie's arms, I knew the situation was not good at all. Sadie's husband and son had fallen asleep, but Sadie was wide awake, the feeling of helplessness evident on her face.

"I got her to drink half the tea," Sadie told Momma.

"That's real good, Sadie," Momma said, reaching to touch the child's brow. "Why don't we try bathing her with cool water again? Virginia, please go get a fresh pail of water."

Picking up the half full bucket, I climbed out of the little room under Nellie's stall. I dumped the water when I got outside and went to get a fresh pail of cold water. I had read between the lines of what Momma was saying: Rosie's temperature was still high and we had to bring it down if she was going to survive. The thought sent a chill down my spine as I carried the water back to the barn.

Momma helped Sadie bathe Rosie's body again, causing the child to shiver uncontrollably. I felt sorry for both the mother and daughter as I watched helplessly. After the cool bath, Rosie was wrapped in the blanket again and offered more tea. She took two small sips before she began to have a seizure. I had never witnessed such a thing and the scene was terrifying. Momma instructed Sadie to help her hold Rosie until the jerking stopped.

"What's wrong with her?" Sadie asked Momma.

"Her fever is so high it's causing her body to react," Momma explained.

Rosie relaxed in her mother's arms and then slipped into unconsciousness. Sadie looked down at her little girl then up at Momma with tears streaming down her face. Neither woman spoke their inner thoughts, but they knew Rosie would probably not live through the night. Even though I was only fourteen, I knew it, too.

"Sadie, I want you to just try and keep her comfortable and if she wakes up, try to get her to drink more tea," Momma said.

"Okay, Miss Elizabeth," Sadie replied. "I thank you for all you're doing for my little Rosie."

"I wish I could do more," Momma said.

Momma and I climbed the ladder out of the earthen room. We lowered the trap door, since Sadie had the lamp lit so she could see to tend Rosie. We decided not to push the straw over the door or put Nellie into the stall. We would just hope and pray no slave hunters tracked this family to our farm tonight.

Making our way slowly to the house, we knew it would be the longest night of Sadie's life as she held her dying child.

"How is the child, Elizabeth?" Papa asked as we entered the house.

"Not good, Stephen; not good at all."

The next morning Momma and I went to the barn together as soon as we awakened. When we opened the trap door, the sight was heartbreaking. Sadie was holding Rosie in her arms while her husband and son stood near her. I could tell the child was no longer breathing and silent tears ran down the faces of her family. I could not bear to watch and turned quickly away. Momma closed the door to allow the family to mourn and went to inform Papa.

"How will we give this child a proper burial?" Momma questioned Papa. "We certainly can't place her in the church's graveyard."

"No, we will not be able to bury her in the graveyard," Papa agreed. "We will dig a hole beneath the big maple at the edge of the woods and bury her there. I'll have Carter pull a large rock down from up on the hill to place on top of the freshly dug earth. Hopefully, no one will stop by the farm and notice the grave."

"This is such a terrible thing," Momma said. "I did everything I knew to do."

"Of course you did, Elizabeth," Papa comforted. "This is not your fault. The child had been sick for three days before she came to us."

"I know, but I just wish I could have helped," Momma said, tears gathering in her eyes.

Grabbing the pail, I went to the barn to milk Annabelle. I tried not to think about the family hidden beneath Nellie's stall; it was just too painful. Bringing the milk back to the house, I helped Momma finish preparing breakfast. After we ate, Papa and Reuben went to open the store. The store needed to open at the regular time in order to not raise questions from the customers.

Carter went to the barn to construct a small coffin for Rosie. When the box was complete, he took Clyde to pull out a large rock from the steep hill that rose up behind our house. The grave would have to be dug after dark and the rock needed to be close by to place over it.

When darkness fell that night, Reuben and Carter both took shovels to the maple and dug as fast as they could. When the hole was finished, we all went to the barn for the funeral.

Sadie was still holding Rosie tightly, refusing to release her all day. Sadie's husband had to pry her hands away to take Rosie. Placing her in the box that Momma had lined with a blanket, Sadie's father wrapped her for the last time. We all stood in the small earthen room as Papa read the 23rd Psalm from our Bible. Afterwards, Papa said a prayer, asking God to bring this family comfort and keep them safe as their journey continued. Carter and Reuben then picked up the small coffin and lifted it through the trap door. They would bury her quickly, hoping no one would ever find the grave.

Momma wrapped Sadie in her arms and the women cried together. Momma promised to mark the grave with Rosie's name, if it ever became safe to do such a thing. The rock would serve as a reminder until then.

Come Monday morning, this family of runaway slaves would continue on the Underground Railroad, but there would only be three. Little Rosie now rested in the arms of Jesus.

Chapter Six

Momma's irises faded away as May became June. Momma and I worked to finish planting the garden. We had planted green beans a few weeks earlier, but put in a second planting, so the work of stringing them would be spread out instead of having so many to do at one time. Momma had started later tomato plants to extend the harvest of those into late September and those were placed in the garden.

Watermelon and cantaloupe loved warm weather, so we waited until June to plant the seed. Momma and I made small mounds in the garden, mixing in generous amounts of rotted manure, and planted the melon seeds in those. The mounds kept the ground warmer and once the seed emerged, we would mulch around them with straw to help keep the soil warm, too. The squash and pumpkin seeds were planted and more sweet corn was put in, which we had planted twice already to provide corn on the cob all summer.

It was Curby Thursday and Papa and my brothers returned home with the usual Curby wagon. Momma and I had almost finished preparing supper and the table was set. Papa came into the summer kitchen where we were cooking, a look of concern on his face. Papa had just built the small one room building that Momma would use to cook in during the warm months, to keep from overheating the house. It was truly a luxury to have such a place as a summer kitchen and Momma was quite delighted with it.

"Elizabeth," Papa said speaking softly to Momma, "we are going to have to unload the slaves now. We can't wait to see if anyone followed us, like we usually do."

"Why is that, Stephen?" Momma asked.

"We have a problem; one that won't wait," Papa replied. "Your skills as a midwife are going to be needed very shortly."

"What?" Momma exclaimed. "Are you telling me one of the slaves is with child and in labor?"

"That's exactly what I'm telling you," Papa replied.

Momma had birthed three children herself and had assisted many women in the area with having their children. She sometimes had to help with farm animal births, too. Momma knew all about helping babies come into the world.

"How did they get into the Underground Railroad?" Momma asked. "You know they try to avoid this happening."

"I don't know," Papa replied. "We will just have to go ask them. We really need to go open the wagon and move them now."

Papa headed toward the door and Momma followed. I hurried and threw the food in the warmer on the top of the stove for later. I followed my parents to the barn, not wanting to miss out on the excitement that was sure to come. I entered just as my brothers removed the back of the wagon and could hear a muffled moan coming from between the wagon floors.

"Help her out of there please, Carter," Momma instructed. "Reuben, get the straw off the trap door. Virginia, go to the house and get more blankets and make sure there is plenty of water heating on the stove. Stephen, please get a lantern filled with fuel; we're going to need it."

Momma was in her midwife mode and was giving orders like a general in the US Army. We all moved to do as she had told us, not questioning why. When the young slave woman was out of the wagon, I could see she was great with child. Before she could reach the trap door, she doubled over in pain. I had already run to the house and filled the water reservoir on the stove and grabbed the extra blankets. I now stood waiting for Momma to tell me what to do with them. Papa returned with a lantern and began to question the young colored man, who was the husband of the very pregnant woman.

"How did you get into the Underground Railroad?" Papa asked. "We don't normally take pregnant women because of the risk it adds. It's almost impossible to keep a baby from crying and that draws attention along the way, not to mention trying to deliver one."

"I'm sorry, sir," the slave replied. "The field agent made contact with me and we wanted freedom so badly. I didn't mention my wife was going to have a baby, because I was afraid no one would help us, then. Once we escaped, there was nothing the conductor could do but move us to the first station."

"Please, call me Stephen," Papa said. "What is your name?"

"My master calls me boy, but my family calls me Henry," the young man replied.

"Okay, Henry, there's nothing we can do now except help deliver this child," Papa said. "My wife, Elizabeth, is a midwife. She has delivered lots of babies and will give your wife the best of care. You will just have to keep the little one quiet the best you can as you continue on the railroad."

"Thank you so much, Sir," Henry replied. "I know we have put your family in extra danger, and I am truly sorry for that."

Momma and Reuben had helped the young woman into the earthen room and Momma climbed down after her. Henry climbed down, too, taking his wife's hand as another pain hit her. I watched as the woman clutched her husband's hand so tight I thought he was going to scream out in pain. I could see the fear on his face, mixed with anticipation.

"My name is Elizabeth," Momma told the laboring woman. "What is yours?"

"Lucy," the slave woman replied, gasping to breathe.

"Okay, Lucy, I'm going to help you have this baby," Momma replied. "I know you're scared, but just do as I tell you and it won't be long before your child is in your arms." Lucy nodded in reply as pain overtook her again.

Looking up through the trap door opening, Momma instructed me to get a pail of warm water and some rags. I headed to the summer kitchen to do as she asked and my father and brothers followed.

Returning to the barn, I told Momma that Papa and my brothers were eating their supper out at the picnic table, where they could catch a cool breeze. They would watch to see if anyone was headed toward the farm, too. With the good view they had of the road, they would have enough time to warn us so the trap door could be closed quickly and covered up before anyone reached our home. Momma said that was the most helpful thing they could do right now. They would be no help at all delivering the baby.

Holding the lantern so Momma could see, I watched a new life come into the world. He was the color of cocoa, with curly hair and big, brown eyes. He squalled as Momma wrapped him in a clean blanket and handed him to his mother, Lucy. Forgetting the pain of just moments ago, Lucy held her son for the first time.

"What will you name him?" I asked, staring in wonder at the little boy who had just made an entrance into the world.

"Joshua," the parents replied at the same time.

"Joshua was the one who led the Hebrews into the land of Canaan, after they had been slaves for four hundred years in Egypt," Henry explained. "We are naming our son after him."

Of course, Momma and I were very familiar with the great exodus of the Hebrew children led by Moses. However, we were a bit surprised to hear the runaway slaves speak of it. Someone among the slaves on the plantation they had come from must have been able to read or someone had shared the story with them.

"How do you know about Joshua and the Hebrew children?" Momma asked.

"Our master allowed us Sundays off, unless you were kitchen help like Lucy was," Henry said. "We would have church service outside when the weather was fit. The story of Moses freeing the slaves from Egypt is a very popular one amongst us slaves. We hope to one day be rescued from the slave masters and live as free people, just as Moses rescued his people from Pharaoh. Because we couldn't see that happening anytime soon, Lucy and I decided to try and escape. We want our child to grow up a free man."

"I can't imagine what it would be like to live as a slave," I chimed in. "To not have the freedom to go where you want, to be told what to do and when to do it. I don't think I could live that way."

"You would not have a choice if your skin was dark and you lived in the south," Lucy said. "I could handle being a slave just fine, but the abuse is what caused us to take a chance and run. Henry has been beaten with a whip on several occasions, and his back has the marks to prove it. I worked in the kitchen, which is much easier work than the fields, but sometimes the master's sons taking a liking to you."

"You mean the boys want you to be their girlfriend?" I asked in disbelief, trying to piece together exactly what Lucy was trying to say.

"Not exactly, Virginia," Momma said. "I'll explain it to you later."

"Sorry, Miss Elizabeth," Lucy murmured. "We learn things at a young age as slave gals."

"It's okay Lucy," Momma said, patting the young girl's arm, "Virginia is old enough to be told about such things. I just have not had the need to tell her of such situations."

Joshua began to fuss; then cry. Momma rubbed her hand over his curly locks and smiled down at him. "I do believe he's ready for his first meal, Lucy. Virginia, please go to the house and gather some of those clean, empty flour sacks we have. Find some pins, too. This little fellow is going to need some diapers. Lucy, would you like me to help you with the first feeding?"

"That would be very kind," Lucy replied looking down at her squalling son and not being real sure how to help him.

Climbing through the trap door, I headed to the house to gather the flour sacks and pins Momma had instructed me to get. Before I closed the barn door on my way out, Joshua's cries were silenced abruptly. I assumed his first meal was now in progress.

Grabbing a burlap sack, I added all the empty flour sacks from the stack Momma had on a kitchen shelf. With that done, I opened the drawer where Momma kept miscellaneous items. I was sure I could find pins there. I attached the pins to the outside of the burlap sack so I wouldn't lose them. With that done, I decided to gather food for the new parent's supper.

Picking up the burlap sack, I went out the kitchen door and took the few steps to the summer kitchen. Momma had prepared fresh green beans with new potatoes mixed in. I had fried eggs to go along with them and made baking powder biscuits, all of which I had placed in the warmer.

Opening the door of the warmer, I found an empty plate where a mound of eggs had been. There were still plenty of biscuits, for which I was grateful. I suppose my father and brothers had devoured every last one of the eggs. Placing the skillet back on the stove to heat up, I prepared to fry more eggs.

With the meal in a pan and the burlap sack slung over my shoulder, I headed back to the barn. As I peered into the earthen room, I could see a content Joshua sound asleep in his mother's arms. Momma reached up to take the sack of diapers from my hand and placed them on a bench. Turning back to me, she took the pan of food and began to dip two plates for Henry and Lucy. Momma always kept clean plates and silverware in the hidden room at all times.

"Virginia, will you please bring a fresh pail of cold spring water so I can fill the crock?" Momma asked before I could even climb down to get another look at Joshua.

"Yes, Momma."

"Lucy, hand that little fellow to me and come eat your supper," I heard Momma say as I headed toward the barn door.

Returning with the pail of fresh water, I descended the ladder carefully. Taking the lid from the crock, I poured it full. I had water left in the pail, so I filled the tin cups that were on the table for Henry and Lucy to drink from. With that done, I turned to look at Momma holding the peacefully sleeping baby.

"Would you like to hold him, Virginia?" Momma asked.

"Do you think it would be okay?" I asked, not being sure since I had never held a baby before.

"You go right on ahead, Miss Virginia," Lucy said.

Momma stood up and I took a seat. Holding my arms out, Momma placed Joshua gently into them. Drawing the baby close to my body, I looked down into his perfectly formed face. I was amazed at this new life I had helped bring into the world. It was truly a wonder of wonders, bringing to my mind part of a Psalm that states "Lord, I praise you, for I am fearfully and wonderfully made."

"I'm going to the house and have Carter get the cradle from the attic," Momma said. "Joshua will need a safe place to sleep while he's here."

"Okay," I said, happy to just sit and hold the baby awhile.

The next few days were a flurry of activity at our home. Momma and I sewed as quickly as we could to make a few outfits for little Joshua. Since the weather was warm, we decided to make lightweight gowns. These could be sewed quickly and easily.

We kept busy washing diapers and hanging them in the corn crib to dry. We were afraid to hang them out on the line. If anyone was to stop by the farm, having diapers hanging on our clothesline would be very hard to explain. No one used that many bags of flour at once to warrant a line full of flour sacks.

I gave Lucy one of my dresses to wear, and we ended up burning Lucy's old one. It was nothing but a rag and when we attempted to wash it after the birthing, it fell to pieces. Tears streamed down Lucy's face as she smoothed the dress over herself and admired the beautiful print. "Miss Virginia, I ain't never owned nothing so beautiful in all my life," Lucy said. "I just don't know how to thank you."

"Just make sure you get little Joshua to Canada," I replied. "That will be all the thanks I need."

"You know, I was sold from my momma when I was twelve," Lucy said. "My Papa had been sold from the plantation when I was a baby, so's I never knew him. I was paraded across the auction block like a fine heifer, that auctioneer talkin' me up all the while. He told the bidders what a good cook my momma was and that I had learnt well during the years I had been helpin' her. At nearly thirteen, I was ready to be sold at top dollar as kitchen help for some other plantation."

"How awful for you," I said. The more I learned about the slave trade, the more I wanted it to end. What kind of heartless, calloused people would strip a mother of her child and sell her like a prized animal?

"That's why we done it," Lucy murmured.

"Done what, Lucy?" I asked.

"Ran away from the plantation," Lucy said. "We knew our baby would be born while we were still traveling to Canada, but we wanted him to be born free. I couldn't bear the thought of having my child or my husband sold, never to see them again."

"I understand why you did it," I replied, knowing I would have attempted to escape too if I had been in Lucy's situation.

"I's just sorry to put your family in more danger by having the baby born here," Lucy whispered.

"Momma knew exactly what to do," I comforted Lucy. "This was probably the best station for your baby to be born. God was watching out for you."

"You think so, Miss Virginia?"

"Yes, Lucy, I sure do."

****

When Mr. Pierson showed up on Monday, he was not happy to see baby Joshua. Carter was home from the store to help shovel the contents from Nellie's stall onto Mr. Pierson's wagon. As soon as Carter told him of the infant who was born in the hidden room on Thursday, Mr. Pierson set his pitchfork aside. "Carter, I will not attempt to move a family who has an infant in broad daylight. It's too risky."

"What will we do with them?" Carter questioned.

"They will have to be transported after dark," Mr. Pierson fumed. "No one can expect to keep a baby from crying for nearly three hours. At least at night there would be a good chance the baby would be asleep. However, I cannot explain hauling a load of manure at ten o'clock at night. Your father will have to figure this one out on his own." With that said, Mr. Pierson tossed his pitchfork into to his nearly empty wagon and left Carter standing in the barn in disbelief.

"Why did Mr. Pierson leave without loading the manure?" Momma asked Carter as she and I entered the barn to say goodbye to Lucy, Henry and Joshua. "I just saw him heading out our driveway as Virginia and I came out of the house. Did he not think it wise to put the manure on the wagon with baby Joshua being hidden under it?"

"Mr. Pierson didn't take manure or slaves," Carter informed us. "He said it was just too dangerous to haul a baby during the day because of the risk Joshua might cry."

"How are we supposed to get Henry, Lucy and Joshua to Chambersburg?" I asked, surprised that Mr. Pierson would halt the progress of the railroad.

"We will just have to take them ourselves after dark," Carter said.

"I suppose I can't blame Mr. Pierson," Momma said. "He's right; keeping Joshua from crying during the ride to Chambersburg would be difficult. Actually, it would be nearly impossible. The road to Chambersburg is a busy one, not to mention Mr. Pierson would have to pass through the small towns of Valeene and Piersontown. The sound of an infant crying from under manure piled on a wagon could not be explained, no matter what story one could think to come up with."

"We will just have to wait for Papa to come home and decide how we will get them to Chambersburg," Carter said pointing to the trap door. At that moment, Joshua began to fuss, reminding us again why Mr. Pierson had left with an empty wagon.

"Stephen, we have a problem," Momma informed Papa the minute he returned home from the store that evening.

"What's wrong, Elizabeth?" Papa asked.

"Mr. Pierson would not move Henry and Lucy today because of the extra risk Joshua posed," Momma said. "He's right, you know. Joshua could definitely draw unwanted attention."

"They will have to moved, though," Papa said. "They cannot live under Nellie's stall until Joshua is old enough to understand he must be quiet."

"Yes, I'm fully aware that we must get them to Chambersburg," Momma said. "Carter suggested we do it after dark, like Reuben moved the couple back in May."

"It's dangerous, especially if someone sees us, but that's probably our only option," Papa said.

"I could ride along, Papa," I said.

"Absolutely not, Virginia," Momma said. "It's much too dangerous."

"But wouldn't it be less suspicious if Papa had his teenage daughter with him?" I asked. "Who would think a father would put his daughter at such risk? But if Papa was out late at night alone, well, that would raise more questions."

"Virginia might be making a good point," Papa said. "The problem is if someone asks where we're headed, I have no idea what to tell them."

"Hopefully you won't see anyone," Momma said. "You're right; there will be no good explanation as to why you're out on the road at such a late hour. I don't know if taking Virginia will help or not, but someone has to go with you. You may need help along the way."

"It's settled then," Papa said. "After the sun sets, Virginia and I will head to Chambersburg. We will have to make it a quick trip, though. It doesn't get dark until after nine and it begins to get light again before five. We are nearing the longest day of the year."

After supper, we all went to the barn to tell Henry and Lucy of our plan. It would be a sad farewell for all of us. Joshua had stolen our hearts with his big brown eyes and dimpled cheeks. If freedom ever came for the slaves in the United States, Lucy promised to send a note telling us how they all were. Of course, Lucy couldn't read nor write, so someone else would have to write the note for her.

Momma told Lucy that our last name was Hensley then wrote our town's name on a piece of paper and placed it in a small burlap pouch she had sewn together. She then sewed the pouch inside the burlap sack that held Joshua's diapers and extra gowns. Unless someone looked closely, they would never know the pouch was there. Of course, if they did find the piece of paper, Marengo, Indiana would not be much to help the slave hunters begin a search.

Lucy and Henry ate their final meal in the little earthen room before they continued on to the next stop along the Underground Railroad. I stayed with them as they ate and cradled Joshua in my arms for the last time. After a while, Momma joined me so she could hold the baby one last time, too. Helping this little life come into the world was making it very difficult to say good bye. Momma and I both knew that we would probably never hear from Henry and Lucy again. The slaves that passed through our station were like fog, just there for a short time before evaporating from our midst, never to be seen again.

As darkness fell, Henry and Lucy climbed into the small space of our special wagon. Momma held Joshua as they slid into the small area feet first. Wrapping the baby in a light blanket, Momma placed a kiss on his forehead then slid him in next to his mother. Lucy looked out at Momma and tears slipped from the corners of her eyes. The future for this family was uncertain, and moving forward was difficult, but they knew they must. They would not be truly safe until they passed over the border into Canada.

Reuben and Carter had filled the wagon with clean straw and they now bolted the back board in place. Papa and I climbed up on the seat. Nellie and Clyde were hitched and ready to go. The horses danced about, knowing this was no ordinary trip. They were normally in their stalls or out in the pasture right now. They did not understand why they were going on a midnight ride.

"Please be careful, Stephen," Momma pleaded.

"We will, Elizabeth," Papa promised. "Just go ahead to bed. Staying up and worrying will do no one any good. Say a prayer and put us in God's hands and leave us there."

"I will try," Momma said.

Papa clicked his tongue to the team of horses and we were off. I felt the panic of what I had volunteered to do come fully upon me. Taking deep breaths, I planted myself firmly on the wagon seat, though my body wanted to leap off and run back to the house. Riding back from Curby with my father ten months earlier carrying slaves had been nothing compared to this. Papa must have known how anxious I was, for he began to sing softly.

Amazing grace! How sweet the sound that saved a wretch like me!
I once was lost, but now am found; Was blind but now I see.
The Lord has promised good to me; His word my hope secures.
He will my shield and portion be As long as life endures.
Thro' many dangers, toils, and snares I have already come
Tis grace hath bro't me safe thus far, And grace will lead me home.

My father had a wonderful singing voice and the strains of the beloved hymn calmed me like nothing else could have. I had sung that song countless times at church but never really let the words sink in. God's grace was always sufficient, and it would be this night, too.

"Virginia, do you know who wrote that song?"

"No, Papa, I don't."

"John Newton."

"I don't believe I have ever heard of him," I said quietly.

"John Newton was once a captain on an English slave ship," Papa said. "One night he faced a terrible storm, one in which he feared he was going to die. It was then that John Newton decided to turn his life around. He eventually became a preacher around England."

"I didn't think England had slaves, Papa."

"They don't anymore, but they used to. Some brave people living in England began to fight against it. William Wilberforce was one of them. Eventually, slavery was made unlawful in England."

"What do you think it will take to make slavery unlawful here?"

"It's going to take a president that is against slavery to make it unlawful here, Virginia."

"Like Abraham Lincoln? He's running in the presidential election. You've read to me about it from the newspaper."

"Yes. Come November there will be a line drawn across the

United States separating the North from the South. Those against slavery will vote for Abraham Lincoln, while those supporting slavery will vote for one of the other three men who are running."

"If Abraham Lincoln is elected, what will happen then, Papa?"

"I don't know, exactly. Hopefully, a law will be passed abolishing slavery and the slaves will be set free, but it probably won't be that easy. I believe the South will fight to keep their slaves."

"Could there be a war, Papa? One like the Revolutionary War Miss Smith taught us about?"

"There could be, Virginia. I honestly don't know what will happen if Mr. Lincoln tries to abolish slavery."

"The Revolutionary War lasted eight years. Do you think it would take that long to free the slaves?"

"I can't see a long war being fought, Virginia. After all, we would be fighting one another. In some cases, it would be family against family. Surely the South would give in before things got too out of hand."

"I hope the slaves are freed, but I don't want a war, Papa."

"I don't want a war, either, Virginia."

We rode along in silence for a while, the only sound being the horses' hooves and the night critters. We had turned right when we came from the farm, toward a very small town called Bacon, instead of left toward Marengo. I wondered if Papa had forgotten where we were going, but within just a few miles he turned right onto a road I had never been on. It did not appear that too many people traveled the road, as it was narrow and grass grew between the wagon tracks.

"I thought we were to travel toward Valeene, Papa."

"We are, Virginia. This road will come out a little south of Piersontown. By taking this road, we will not pass through Marengo. If someone would happen to see us in Marengo, we would definitely be recognized. This is a safer route."

"Oh, okay," I replied, not really liking the narrow road that seemed to go through a forest.

We finally reached Leavenworth-Paoli Road, just about a quarter mile south of Piersontown. Just before we entered Piersontown, Papa stopped at a little spring fed creek to give Nellie and Clyde a drink. As the horses slurped the cool water, I could hear an owl hooting from up in a tree nearby, probably searching for a small rabbit or mouse for his hungry belly. A raccoon had scurried away from the water's edge as we approached. The night was lit up in random places by the blinking of fireflies, and crickets serenaded us from the tall grass along the road. Everything was peaceful, except for the fact that our wagon held a family of runaway slaves.

Starting on our journey again, we crossed the same creek three times, the one the horses had drunk from, before we made it through Piersontown. The little town was named after William Pierson, who owned and ran the only mill powered by a steam engine that any of us knew of. The creek wound around like a snake through the narrow valley. Not far on either side of the road, large hills rose up. The wooden bridges covering the creek sounded very loud under the horses' hooves, so loud I thought it might bring someone out of their house to see who was passing at such a late hour. Holding my breath until we cleared the last bridge, I let out a sigh of relief when we left the small village behind. It appeared no one cared who was on the road tonight. Of course, after listening to the loud steam engine all day, everyone in Piersontown may have just been close to being deaf.

Another mile brought us to the outskirts of Valeene, where the horses crossed another bridge. Under this bridge ran a small river, called Patoka River. The creek we had crossed in Piersontown added to this river at Valeene. The river continued its flow westward, after the small creek merged with it, to places I had never been before.

Papa slowed the horses after crossing the bridge and we rolled through Valeene without speaking a word. We were very aware that if anyone saw us, we would be recognized. The folks that lived in this southern part of Orange County came to our general store for supplies. It was much closer than going to Paoli, which was located in the center of the county.

Pulling the hill out of Valeene, the horses slowed to a snail's pace. Nellie and Clyde were sweating profusely by the time we reached the road to Chambersburg, which turned to the right off Leavenworth-Paoli Road. The turn was about three fourths distance into the long, steep grade.

The horses were relieved that the road went downhill after the turn, giving their muscles some much needed relief. When the road leveled out again, the river we had crossed in Valeene was visible on the right hand side of the road. Papa pulled the team off the road behind a grove of trees, but there was no way to get close enough to the river for the horses to drink.

Reaching into the back of the wagon, Papa grabbed a bucket, and I did the same. Papa had loaded the buckets before we left the farm, just in case we needed to haul water for the horses. Papa stepped down and reached back into the wagon for the lantern.

"Virginia, I hate to do it, but I think we best light this lantern so we can see to get down the river bank. The half-moon is not enough light for us to walk the hundred feet without stumbling, especially when we come back with full buckets."

"Okay, Papa." Stumbling was not the thing I was most afraid of. I knew how water snakes were plentiful in the little creek that ran through our farm, and this river was probably no different.

Trudging through the thick grass toward the river, I stayed right behind Papa, placing my feet in the indentions left by his. I prayed silently that Papa was scaring off any snakes that might be lying in the grass waiting for a field mouse to be his next meal.

As we came to the water's edge, I looked up and down the bank as far as possible, checking the area for any unwanted guests. Papa handed the lantern back to me then dipped his bucket, coming up with it full and overflowing. He placed the full bucket on the bank and reached back for the empty one still clutched in my hand. Just as he bent to fill the second bucket, the unmistakable sound of hooves reached our ears.

"Virginia, blow out that lantern and squat down," Papa instructed, placing the second full bucket on the river bank.

Doing as Papa said, I sank down then lifted the globe and blew out the lantern. The half-moon now seemed way too bright as its beam bounced off the flowing river. I was thankful Papa had pulled the wagon behind the grove of trees before we trekked to the river for water. Listening carefully, we heard the hoof beats get louder before fading away, as whoever was traveling the same road as us this night passed by and kept going toward Valeene.

Breathing a sigh of relief, I stood to my feet again. Papa reached into his pocket to get a match and relight the lantern. As the light flickered to life, it illuminated a pair of eyes just across the river. Taking the lantern, Papa held it toward the water to get a closer look. Staring intently at us was a black panther. We had heard a few customers speak of seeing them when they came to the store, but Papa or I neither one had seen one with our own eyes. Not even Carter, who traipsed all over the countryside trapping, had ever come across one of these big cats.

"Virginia," Papa said at a whisper. "Move very slowly and pick up one of the buckets. Start walking toward the wagon backwards with no sudden movements."

My hands shook as I grasped the handle of the bucket. Lifting it, I started backing up the river bank. Papa picked up his bucket and did the same. The big cat just watched us, never attempting to cross the river. When we had walked backwards for fifty feet, Papa spoke.

"Turn around now, Virginia. Don't run but walk just a bit faster."

Facing forward, I was tempted to fling the bucket of water aside and run for my life. However, I knew from watching our cat at the store that to do that would excite the big cat, causing it to chase us down. Annie would always prowl around looking for mice, and as soon as one ran, the fun began. I did not want to become the panther's fun for the night.

"Take your bucket to Nellie and I'll tend to Clyde," Papa said. "This will be the quickest drink these horses ever had."

"Shouldn't we lead the horses back to the road first?"

"No, we will just spill the water doing that. We will offer the water first. The horses will just have to drink fast."

Reaching the team, I offered the bucket of water to Nellie. Papa blew out the lantern and held his bucket for Clyde. I suppose Papa thought the panther was less likely to know where we were if it didn't have a lantern to guide it, but I was sure the big cat could track our scent just fine in the dark, if it chose to do so. Within minutes, the buckets were emptied and placed back in the wagon. Climbing onto the seat, Papa put the horses in motion. Coming back onto the road, Papa spoke for the first time since extinguishing the lantern.

"Goodness, Virginia, I thought the scariest part of this trip would be the fact we had runaway slaves hid in our wagon. That panther just took five years off my life."

"I was scared I would step on a snake while walking to the river, Papa. I wish I had seen a snake now, instead of that big black cat staring us down from across the river."

"Yes, a snake would have been much less terrifying to see than that panther," Papa agreed.

After a few minutes back on the road, Papa took to singing again, and I joined in. It seemed to calm our nerves after the scare we had just experienced.

Come, Thou Fount of ev'ry blessing, Tune my heart to sing Thy grace.
Streams of mercy, never ceasing, Call for songs of loudest praise.
Teach me some melodious sonnet, Sung by flaming tongues above.
Praise the mount! I'm fixed upon it, Mount of God's unchanging love.

By the time we reached the second verse of "Come, Thou Fount of Every Blessing", there were two voices humming along from the hidden compartment of our wagon. Encouraged by this, Papa sung the whole song through two more times, the humming from inside the wagon turning to words by the third time through. There were no houses along the stretch of road we were on, and I was sure the slaves realized this by the fact that Papa and I had started to sing.

The road remained flat for several miles as we wound our way through the bottom ground where Patoka River cut a path. Papa stopped again to give the horses a drink where the stream crossed the road. The river had become smaller and smaller the farther toward Chambersburg we traveled, as we came closer to the springs that began the flow of Patoka River.

"There's a large hill up ahead," Papa said. "This will be the last opportunity for the horses to drink until we reach Chambersburg."

"Glad we don't have to go fill buckets again," I said.

"Me too," Papa agreed. "On the way back, I will make sure the horses drink from the last crossing the river makes on the road. We will then wait until we reach Valeene to stop for another drink."

"That sounds like a good plan," I replied, relieved we would not have to trek across a field again to get water.

Papa put the horses back in motion and began to sing again to the beat of the horses' hooves. We passed a small church on the left just before we began to climb the first steep hill since turning off Leavenworth Paoli road. There was a sign on the church that read "Danner's Chapel", and the moon beams bounced off a few headstones in a graveyard that was close by. Papa and I quit singing, knowing that where there is a church, there must be homes nearby. Taking our cue, Henry and Lucy fell silent, too. Joshua must have slept soundly the whole trip, for we did not hear a peep from him.

After climbing the large hill after passing the church, the road leveled out for a short distance, giving the horses some much needed relief. We then descended into a valley and the road we were on crossed another road. When we reached the crossroads, Papa turned the horses left. "It's not much farther now," Papa said as we climbed a small grade immediately after turning left.

"Okay," I replied while unsuccessfully attempting to stifle a yawn.

Pulling into the Quaker's yard, we headed straight for the barn. A single candle could be seen in the window, signaling that it was safe to come to the house. The Quakers had been waiting all day for these slaves to arrive and had lit the candle in case they showed up after dark.

Climbing from the wagon seat, I threw open the barn doors and Papa drove the wagon in. Closing the doors behind us, I felt my way through the complete darkness that had enveloped us. Just as I reached out and touched the wagon, Papa lit a match and touched it to the lantern's wick.

"We made it, Virginia," Papa said, a big smile spreading across his face.

"By the grace of God, yes we did," I replied.

Papa climbed from the wagon and headed toward the Quaker's home, leaving the lantern in the barn for me. Looking around, I wondered if they had a stall with an earthen room under it like we did. I began to loosen the bolts holding the back on the wagon, but did not remove it. I did not want to expose the compartment where the slaves were hidden until I was sure it was safe.

"Miss Virginia," Lucy whispered, "is we here?"

"Yes, Lucy, we are in the Quaker's barn. Papa's gone to waken them so you can be moved to safety. There's a candle burning in a window. That's the signal that all is well and it's safe for you to arrive."

"That song you and your Papa sang was beautiful," Henry said. "I can't stop singing it in my head."

"It does have quite a catchy tune," I agreed. "Did you hear Papa sing "Amazing Grace"?

"Oh, yes, and it was quite nice, as well," Henry said. "I had heard that song before, but I didn't know it was written by a preacher who used to be a slave captain. If God can change the heart of a man like John Newton, then changing the heart of a slave master shouldn't be so hard."

"That is true," I said. "If Mr. Lincoln gets elected as President, I feel the issue of slavery will be met head on."

"We don't want anyone to die for our freedom," Lucy said. "We just want to be free."

At that moment, the barn door swung open. I gasped, having not been prepared for the sudden interruption. Framed in the moonlit doorway were Papa and a man with a beard and hat. Papa walked to the back of the wagon and finished removing the bolts. Lucy and Henry peered out at us, glad to finally be released from the small space. Reaching in, I picked up a sleeping Joshua and snuggled him close. Papa helped Henry out first; and Henry helped Lucy.

"You must walk to the house," Papa told Henry. "This station has a hidden space in the cellar."

"Yes'm," Henry replied.

I handed Joshua to Lucy and followed behind everyone as we hurried toward the back door of the Quaker home. Before we even reached the house, the door was opened and a woman stood welcoming us in.

Lucy and Henry were quickly taken to the cellar. I followed so I could say one last goodbye to the family, especially baby Joshua. When I reached the cellar floor, I was amazed with how the Quaker's had concealed the room Lucy and Henry would hide in. A very small section of the wall hinged open from top to bottom, revealing a room behind. When the wall was swung shut, the fact that the wall was not solid showed no evidence.

"We will never forget the kindness your family has shown us," Lucy said as I embraced her.

"I hope you all make it safely to Canada," I replied. Pulling back, I looked down at Joshua who was lying in the crook of Lucy's arm. His big brown eyes were open now, having been awakened by all the moving around. I touched his tight curls and bent to kiss his forehead. This baby would grow up a free man, something his parents had not had the luxury of doing.

I hurried up the stairs to Papa, knowing we had to leave quickly. Daylight would come early, and we needed to be back at our farm when it did. The Quaker man followed us to the barn to close the doors after we passed through. We had been back on the road about an hour when I began to doze off.

"Virginia, crawl into the back of the wagon and lay in the straw," Papa instructed. "You're going to fall asleep and slip off the wagon seat."

"Okay, Papa," I agreed, being too tired to argue. The next thing I knew was Papa shaking me gently.

"Virginia, we're home."

Opening my eyes, I sat up. The wagon was in our barn and I could see the sky beginning to lighten with the coming dawn through the open barn doors. "We made it, Papa," I said groggily.

"Yes, we did," Papa said smiling. "Go to the house and sleep awhile. If your momma is awake, and I'm sure she is, tell her I'll be in shortly."

"Okay, Papa." I trudged to the house, exhaustion heavily upon me. Opening the door, I walked straight for the stairs.

"You're home safe," Momma said from the couch where she had been dozing.

"Yes," I said. "The only scary part about the trip was the black panther."

"The black panther! Where on earth did you see a black panther?"

"Along the river bank when we were hauling water for the horses. I'll tell you all about it in the morning, when I'm fully awake. Carter is going to wish he had ridden along just so he could have seen it. Papa will be in shortly." With that said, I went upstairs to my room. I removed my shoes and curled up on my bed, not even bothering to undress. I did not awaken until nine o'clock.

"Where's Papa?" I asked, entering the kitchen and finding Momma skimming cream from the milk. I assumed she or Carter had done the milking this morning.

"In the barn," Momma said. "He slept about four hours and allowed Reuben to go open the store this morning. He's getting ready to ride into town on Blockhead."

"That should be a fun trip," I said with a laugh. Blockhead was our mule and he pretty much did as he chose, no matter what he was being told to do.

"I'm sure Blockhead will return to the farm tied to the back of the wagon," Momma said with a smile.

Just then Carter came in the back door. Catching sight of me, he smiled that crooked smile of his. "Glad to see you finally dragged yourself out of bed, Virginia."

"It was a long night, Carter."

"I heard you got to see a panther."

"Yes, and I have no desire to see another one," I replied. "Papa said that cat stole five years of his life."

"Sure wish I could have seen it," Carter muttered, sorry he had missed out on the adventure.

"You would have just run scared and that big cat would have pounced on you like the rat you are," I said with a laugh.

"Well, I was going to say I'm glad you made it home safe, but now I changed my mind."

"You love me and you know it, Carter." At this statement, Carter just smiled and pulled a lock of my hair. I smiled back, and without saying another word, we knew we loved each other deeply. He had been worried for Papa and me, and I would have fought that big cat with my bare hands if it was attacking my brother. Of course, I was not about to admit that to Carter.

Chapter Seven

Summer came hot and humid, with a flurry of activity. The green beans were strung to dry into leather britches. When they were completely dry, they were placed in old flour sacks and hung in the cupboard off the kitchen. The peas we had dried in the spring were there, too, in small stone crocks. When the dried beans were ready to shell, they would be added to the cupboard, too.

The cabbage had been turned into sauerkraut and was in stone crocks in our cellar. In mid- August, we dug the potatoes and pulled the carrots. The potatoes were put into a wooden bin in the cellar, and the carrots were packed in crates with sand between the layers and put there, too.

We had a small orchard of peaches, pears and apples. The peaches ripened in August, and we made fresh peach cobblers and dried some for later use. The apples and pears would come ripe in September and October and would be dried, made into pies, and some stored in the cellar to keep for eating fresh later. Any extra fruit would be sold at our store.

August brought a storm that dumped several inches of rain in a short amount of time. The peaceful stream that meandered through our farm became a dangerous, raging river. Papa and Reuben were forced to remain at the store, while Carter, Momma, and I were stuck at the farm. As I looked out the kitchen window, I had a full view of the barn. As I watched the water come off the hill behind the barn, I suddenly realized why Papa, Carter, and Reuben had dug a trench around the back of the barn and built up a large berm.

"The water would flood the earthen room," I muttered.

"What did you say, Virginia?" Carter asked around a mouth full of biscuit he had smothered in butter. He called it a small afternoon snack.

"The trench around the back of the barn prevents water from getting into the barn and flooding the room under Nellie's stall," I said, turning to look at Carter.

"Yes, we learned that lesson the hard way," Carter said. "Two years ago the room flooded from heavy spring rains. Fortunately, there were no slaves staying here at the time. Momma kept you busy in the house while Reuben and I removed the water out of the room by the bucket full. Papa decided to dig the trench after that, to prevent the room from flooding again. Still, if it comes a heavy rain while runaway slaves are here, Papa goes to check on them."

Turning back to the window, I stared out at the pouring rain. How naïve I had been just a short year ago. There had been frightened, mistreated people seeking refuge under our barn, and I hadn't had a clue. I had lived in a world thinking everyone lived as I did, happy and free. I knew there were slaves in the South, but I chose not to think about them or the life they were forced to live.

Now, I knew that slaves were people just like me; people who wanted a home of their own and children who were not stripped from them and sold on an auction block like livestock. Slaves just wanted basic human rights. Why could the slave masters not see that? What could possibly be more important than allowing slaves to live free? The answer came as quickly as the questions formed: greed. The plantations would not be nearly as prosperous if the slave masters didn't have the free labor the slaves provided. Money was worth more than a life.

The rainstorm blew east and the creek went back into its banks. Though they had to wait two days, Papa and Reuben were finally able to cross the creek again. The sun blazed hot and the fields dried out. The August heat and humidity returned, nearly smothering us, as is common in southern Indiana.

Checking the gardens progress one morning in late August, my eyes fell on a watermelon that I thought could possibly be ripe. Stepping into the garden, I carefully picked my way around the vines, being careful not to step on any. I reached the watermelon and knelt beside it. Thumping it with my finger and checking to see how dry the stem had become, I decided it was ripe.

I plucked the melon from the vine and carried it to the springhouse to get cold. That evening after supper, I went to the springhouse and retrieved the cold melon and packed it to the porch of the summer kitchen.

"Cut me a big slice," Carter instructed Momma as she slid a sharp knife through the rind.

"Me, too," I said, watching as the melon split in half revealing bright red flesh.

Momma handed Carter and me generous slices and we sat down on the edge of the porch to enjoy it. After a few minutes, Carter jumped up and went into the summer kitchen. He returned with a tin pie plate. Propping it up on a nearby tree, he turned back to me with a smile on his face. "We get ten chances. Whoever hits the pie tin the most time out of ten seeds wins."

"I'll take that challenge," I replied, propelling the first seed out of my mouth just to watch it fall considerably short of the target.

"You're going to have to spit harder than that!" Carter exclaimed. Taking a bite of watermelon, Carter wallowed the melon around in his mouth a moment then spit all but one seed into his hand. Taking aim Carter shot a seed toward the tin plate, falling just short of the target.

"Looks like you're going to have to spit harder, too," I said laughing. Taking aim again, I spit another seed toward the tin pan, striking it in the center with a ping. At the sound, Momma looked up from her watermelon she had been enjoying.

"Virginia Mae, whatever are you doing?" Momma asked sternly.

"Playing a game with Carter," I replied around a mouthful of watermelon.

"Did you just spit a watermelon seed at that tin pie plate?" Momma asked pointing toward the tree where the pie tin rested.

"Yes, and I hit it, too," I said triumphantly.

At that moment, Carter shot another seed from his mouth, hitting the waiting target. Not to be outdone, I fired one right behind him, gaining another point.

"Virginia, that is most unladylike behavior," Momma scolded. "How do you expect to ever get a husband acting in such a manner?"

"I'm not trying to get a husband," I said, "I'm just trying to beat Carter spitting watermelon seeds."

"Whatever am I going to do with you?" Momma asked shaking her head. "Climbing trees and spitting is no way for a young woman to behave."

"Don't worry, Momma," Carter said, "Virginia will find a fellow who appreciates her talents one day."

"Well, I certainly don't know what man would be looking for such traits in a future wife," Momma muttered.

Carter and I continued our game until we both had spit ten seeds apiece. I had hit the target seven times and Carter eight. Not willing to accept the loss, I challenged Carter to another game. We continued to play until our bellies were so full of watermelon we could hardly stand it. Carter ended up winning by one game as we went back and forth, one winning and then the other. I was certain if I could have fit more melon in my stomach, I could have made the end result a tie, but I just couldn't hold another bite.

The first week of September, Curby Thursday brought us four slaves; one man, two women, and a teenage girl. I was surprised to see the girl be almost as light skinned as me. I thought all slaves were deep brown, but not this one. She was a beautiful golden color, but I knew one of the women was her mother, because the girl called her Mammy.

Papa and my brothers brought fear to the eyes of the women and caused them to cluster in a corner of the earthen room anytime the men were near. For this reason, Momma and I took care of them without any help from the men of our house.

"Momma, why is the slave girl so light skinned?" I asked as we prepared food for the four in our hidden room.

"Remember when Lucy mentioned the slave master's son taking a liking to her?" Momma asked.

"Yes, and I asked if the sons wanted to date her," I said. "She told me that dating was not what the young man had wanted."

"Well, I would guess that the slave master or one of his sons is the father of the light colored girl now staying in our barn."

"Oh," I said, mulling this information over for a moment. "Oh! I understand now, Momma."

"I shall say no more," Momma said.

The realization that some of the slave girls were raped by their overseers added a whole new dislike and disgust to my way of thinking toward the rich plantations owners. The slave masters had to know such things were going on. Nearly white children did not appear from black slaves for no reason at all. If I at nearly fifteen figured this out, then the slave masters and their wives knew the truth, too. To allow such things to go on was just one more reason that slavery needed to be stopped.

When the mail was delivered the last week of August, it contained an envelope addressed to Stephen Hensley, Marengo, Indiana. There was no return address, so we had no idea where the letter had come from. Papa waited until the store was empty then opened the letter. A smile spread across his face as he began to read the letter. My curiosity would not allow me to stay silent.

"Who's it from, Papa?" I asked.

"It's from a station in the northern part of Ohio," Papa said. "The writer states that Lucy, Henry and Joshua crossed the Canadian border safely and that Lucy asked her to write and tell us."

A smile spread across my face. "They made it."

Papa folded the letter and put it back in the envelope. "Yes, they sure did, and Joshua will grow up a free man."

I knew Papa would keep the letter but it would be hidden at our house. Suspicions would be raised if it was found lying around the store. It was nice to finally know for sure that one of the families we had helped actually made it to freedom.

School started again in September, and we were all delighted that Miss Smith was still our teacher. She had remained in Marengo for most of the summer, except for the two weeks she took to visit her family in Kentucky. She opened the school three days a week through the summer for those who were behind in their studies, something no other teacher had ever done before. Also, her guitar had added some nice accompaniment for our Sunday worship services. It was nice that everyone stayed in the same key now. Well, most everyone. There were always a few who couldn't carry a tune if it was thrown to them sealed up in a tin can. For those individuals, there was no instrument around that would help them sing on key.

Mrs. George had complained to Papa all through the previous school year about how Miss Smith was spoiling the children and allowing them to "run around like heathens". Papa finally grew tired of the constant complaining and suggested that a small cabin be built for the teacher to live in. The rest of the committee members agreed and a two room cabin with a loft was erected on the church property.

Mrs. George lost her renter and Miss Smith got a place of her own out of the deal. No one had paid any attention to Mrs. George's grumblings anyway, since they were constant and usually without merit. Miss Smith would continue with her unconventional teaching methods for at least another year.

The first thing Miss Smith brought to our attention when we returned to school was the upcoming Presidential election. There were four men running to be the next president of the United States. They were: John C. Breckinridge, a Southern Democrat from Kentucky, John Bell, a Constitutional Union candidate from Tennessee, Stephen A. Douglas, a Democrat from Illinois and Abraham Lincoln, a Republican from Illinois.

Though Miss Smith had mentioned all the candidates, it was Abraham Lincoln she talked about most. He had been born in Hodgenville, Kentucky, which was Miss Smith's home state. He had lived as a child in southern Indiana, about fifty five miles west of Marengo, which gave us a connection to the man. He finally ended up in Illinois and had studied on his own to become a lawyer.

Mr. Lincoln was running as a Republican, which was a fairly new party. The Kansas-Nebraska Act of 1854 had spurred the formation of the Republican Party, which gave that territory the right to own slaves. Those opposing slavery decided to form their own party so they could elect their own candidates and make changes to abolish slavery.

I could tell by the way Miss Smith talked that if she were allowed to vote, Abraham Lincoln would be her choice. Papa had been right, just because she was from Kentucky didn't mean she agreed with slavery.

I would have looked to Angus to see if he understood the importance of this election, but he was working full time with his father now. Maybe I would walk past the leather shop, on my way to the store after school, and tell him what I had learned today. If Mr. Lincoln became president, the Underground Railroad may become unnecessary, because he would pass a law to free the slaves. The thought of that happening sent a shiver down my spine.

"Are you cold, Virginia?" Effie whispered.

"Huh? It's nearly ninety degrees in here. Why on earth would I be cold?" I whispered back.

"Well, you just shivered. I thought maybe you were cold,"

Effie whispered back.

"No, I'm fine," I said. Looking up, I was surprised to see Miss Smith standing over me.

"Now, this is a familiar scene," Miss Smith said, smiling down at me. "I believe we started the year off in the same fashion last year."

"I'm so sorry, Miss Smith," I said, standing to my feet to face my punishment head on.

"I think I have just the punishment for you, Virginia," Miss Smith said. "I want you to stay after school today and I'll tell you what it is."

"Yes, Miss Smith," I said quietly while taking my seat again. Effie poked my ribs as Miss Smith walked back to the front of the room but I refused to even look at her.

"What do you think Miss Smith's punishment will be?" Effie asked as we ate our lunch together.

"I haven't a clue," I said glumly. "I'm just sorry I disappointed Miss Smith again."

"She knows you're a good student," Effie assured me. "You didn't give her any trouble last year and you achieved the best grades in the school."

"Still, I should not have been talking when she was trying to teach us something," I said. "I deserve whatever punishment Miss Smith has planned for me."

When school dismissed for the day, I remained in my seat. I hung my head in shame as all the other students made their way out the door. Effie leaned down to whisper she would wait for me outside but I shook my head no. I was sure I would want to be alone after facing the humiliation of having to be reprimanded by Miss Smith.

"Virginia, I know Effie spoke to you first," Miss Smith said as she sat in the seat beside me.

"It's no excuse, Miss Smith," I replied. "I know how to ignore Effie."

"Yes, and you usually do it quite well, when you choose to," Miss Smith said with a smile.

"Effie can be quite the chatterbox," I said.

"That's very true," Miss Smith said. "I couldn't just allow you to talk, though, and an idea came to me as I walked toward your desk this morning. You sing quite well, and I believe you could learn to play the guitar."

Looking up at Miss Smith, I tried to figure out where she was going with this. I had been all ready for my punishment and instead she gave me a compliment. "I don't understand, Miss Smith."

"I want to give you lessons," Miss Smith said. "I don't have time to offer this to everyone, but you have talent, Virginia. I know you could learn."

"I would love that," I said, forgetting that I was supposed to be in trouble.

"Good. We will start tomorrow after school. I will give you a lesson every Tuesday and Thursday. Before long, you will be playing chords and singing like you've done it all your life. Do you think you could get your hands on a guitar?"

"I'm sure Papa would know how to get one," I said, my excitement bubbling over.

"Okay. Check with your papa today and let me know tomorrow," Miss Smith said. "You're dismissed now."

Grabbing my books and lunch pail, I floated out the door of the school. I had never been given such an opportunity before in my life.

Heading toward the store, I longed to tell someone my wonderful news, but didn't know who. Maybe Papa would have time to listen when I got to the store. As I walked along, a thought suddenly hit me. Maybe there was someone I could tell, someone who would be as excited about the guitar lessons as I was.

As I stepped into the leather shop, I saw Angus hard at work over a piece of leather. He looked up as I entered, smiling in the way that made his eyes as bright and blue as a clear sky on a winter's day. "Hi, Virginia," Angus said. "What are you doing here?"

"I came to tell you what we learned at school today. Miss Smith told us more about the Presidential election that's going to take place in November," I replied.

"Oh, really," Angus said, putting down his tools and giving me his full attention, "what did Miss Smith have to say?"

"She is pretty excited about Abraham Lincoln being one of the four candidates," I explained. "Mr. Lincoln is running under the Republican party, which makes it clear that he is against slavery."

"Do you think Mr. Lincoln will put an end to slavery if he gets elected?" Angus asked.

"I would think he would at least try to. It sure would be different around here if slavery was abolished," I said quietly, knowing Angus grasped the full meaning of my words.

"Yes, it sure would," Angus said. "Did you have anything else to tell me? You looked awful happy when you came into the shop."

"You know me so well, Angus," I said with a smile. "As a matter of fact, I do have something else I want to tell you. Miss Smith caught me talking during class and made me stay after school."

"And that made you smile?" Angus asked in disbelief.

"Yes, because Miss Smith's punishment is for me to take guitar lessons from her twice a week," I replied.

"You will love that, Virginia," Angus said, beaming at me. "You sing quite well, so learning to play an instrument should come very easy for you."

"I hope so. Now all I need is to find a guitar of my own."

"I wish I knew someone who has one," Angus said. "If I find one, I'll let you know."

"Thanks, Angus. I best get to the store now before Papa sends out a search party."

"Okay," Angus replied. "Stop by anytime, Virginia."

"I will," I promised and stepped out of the leather shop.

Entering the store, I was disappointed to find Reuben at the counter and not Papa. I knew I would have to wait until the ride home to ask Papa about the guitar, which would make it too late to locate one tonight.

"Where have you been, Virginia?" Reuben asked. "I've been waiting for you. I have things I need to get done before closing time."

"Sorry, Reuben," I said, "I had to stay after school and talk with Miss Smith for a few minutes."

"What? It's first day of school and you're already in trouble?" Reuben asked teasingly.

"No, I'm not in trouble," I said, stunned that my too serious brother was actually having some fun. "Maybe Miss Smith was just asking me about my oldest brother."

Reuben's face glowed crimson with my remark. He should have known I was too much like Carter to allow him to tease me and I not have a remark that put him on the spot.

Smiling sweetly, I walked around Reuben and thumped my books on the counter. Placing my lunch pail on the floor, I slipped onto the stool behind the counter and stole a glance in Reuben's direction. I could see he wanted to ask me what Miss Smith had said about him but wasn't sure if he should. The fact that my brother was sweet on Miss Smith had not gone unnoticed by me, as he could hardly keep his eyes off her each Sunday at church and when she stopped by the store to pick up her mail. I wondered now if Reuben would take the bait I had tossed out. Finally deciding to let the matter drop, Reuben walked off to get his work completed.

As we climbed into our wagon and prepared to leave the store a few hours later, Angus rode up. His horse looked to be all done in, like it had been ridden harder than it cared to be. Pulling the horse to a stop Angus held up a burlap sack with something long in it, grinning from ear to ear.

"I remembered someone who had an extra guitar!" Angus exclaimed.

"A guitar?" Papa asked. "Why on earth would you need a guitar, Virginia?"

"To play, Papa."

"You don't know how to play a guitar, Virginia," Papa said.

"Not yet," I replied, "but Miss Smith is going to teach me."

Reuben turned and looked at me, knowing now that Miss Smith had not been discussing him with me at all. I smiled sweetly and winked, making Reuben's face turn red all over again. Carter would be proud of me for making Reuben blush twice in just a few hours. I would be sure to share the story with him later.

"How much do I owe you for the guitar, Angus?" Papa asked.

"It's a gift," Angus said with a smile, "from me to Virginia. She can repay me by learning to play it."

"Thank you, Angus," I said, taking the burlap wrapped instrument. Pulling it out, I was surprised that it looked brand new. I wondered where Angus had found such a nice guitar in such a short amount of time. I was sure it had come from one of his many customers at the leather shop. "It's beautiful."

"I'm glad you like it," Angus said with a smile. "You have to play and sing the first song you learn just for me. You can stop by the leather shop and serenade me."

"It's a deal," I said, running my hand over the wood of the fine instrument.

I told Papa all about Miss Smith's punishment for me talking to Effie during class on the way home from the store. He said he couldn't wait until I could play all his favorite hymns so he would have music to sing with.

Reuben just stared straight ahead, not making any comments at all. I felt just a bit guilty for goading my brother, but not guilty enough not to share the story with Carter at the first opportunity. Reuben clearly liked Miss Smith. I didn't understand why he just didn't tell her. I was pretty sure she liked him, too.

Two weeks after I began taking lessons, I stopped by the leather shop to sing a song for Angus. I had chosen one of Papa's favorites to learn first; "Come, Thou Fount of Every Blessing". My chord changing was still a bit slow and clumsy, but I made it through the whole song in the key of C.

Angus clapped like I had just performed on a stage in New York City, which made me laugh uncontrollably. Encouraged by Angus' enthusiasm, I performed the song again and Angus sang with me. Our voices blended in harmony, and even when I missed the F chord, we just kept right on singing.

"The next song needs to be that little Irish song Miss Smith sang for us last year after the reenactment of the Revolutionary War," Angus told me.

"I'm a long way from being able to move my fingers that fast," I said with a laugh. "Maybe one day, though."

"Of course one day, Virginia," Angus assured me. "In two weeks you have learned to play an entire song. You'll be playing anything you want to within a year. I'm sure of it."

"Thanks for having such confidence in me, Angus," I said. "I have to get to the store now. Reuben gets upset when I'm late."

"Is Reuben ever going to tell Miss Smith how he feels about her?" Angus asked.

I laughed out loud. For goodness sakes, even Angus could see Reuben's feeling written on his face each Sunday. "I don't know, Angus, but if he doesn't soon, Miss Smith might just ask to court him!"

Angus and I laughed long and hard imagining Miss Smith asking Reuben to court her. Effie was the best friend I had, but Angus was sure a close second. Angus and I shared something that

Effie and I never could, though. Our homes were both stations on the Underground Railroad and it made us kindred spirits. After learning the treatment some slaves had been subjected to, Angus and I could not help but hope and pray for their freedom. The question was would the presidential election bring the United States a step closer to that dream becoming a reality?

Chapter Eight

On November 6, 1860, the Presidential election was held. Mr. Lincoln received the votes north of the Mason Dixon line, except for Illinois, which was the only state Stephen Douglas won. The Mason Dixon line was the line that divided slave states from free ones. Lincoln also took California and Oregon, the only two west coast states. John Bell won Kentucky, Tennessee, and Virginia while John Breckinridge took the rest of the southern states. Abraham Lincoln ended up with the most electoral votes, and became the sixteenth president of the United States of America.

It didn't take long for the South's reaction to Mr. Lincoln's victory to be evident. By the time Mr. Lincoln took office in March of 1861, seven southern states had seceded, or separated, from the Union. On April 12, 1861, a battle was fought at Fort Sumter in Charleston Harbor, South Carolina, thus beginning the War Between the States.

"I'm going to enlist in the Union Army," Reuben announced at supper the first week of May.

"No, Reuben, please don't," Momma pleaded. "Surely this war won't last long. Mr. Lincoln will figure out a way to make peace."

"Your mother is right," Papa said. "The war will probably end soon. Give it a little time."

"I will wait a while longer," Reuben agreed, if for no other reason than to please Momma. "The Louisville Daily Journal reported that eleven southern states have separated from the Union now; basically every state below Kentucky and west to Texas."

"President Lincoln has issued a blockade, not allowing any products from the North to be sold to the South. The South will not be able to fight a war without obtaining supplies from the North," Papa said.

"Let's hope the South realizes that and ends this nonsense in a peaceful manner," Momma fretted.

"General Robert E. Lee refused to lead the Union troops," Reuben pointed out. "He has since taken up the cause for the South and is in command of the military forces in Virginia. I fear there will not be a resolution without bloodshed."

"I hope you're wrong, Reuben," Momma said with a sigh.

At church the following Sunday, we all prayed for a quick end to the fighting. Almost everyone who attended the church had a son old enough to join the Union forces. No one wanted to see that happen.

After the service was over, Momma surprised us all by inviting Miss Smith to the farm for Sunday dinner. As she climbed into the wagon with us, I knew what Momma was attempting to do. There was no denying that Reuben was smitten with the pretty young school teacher, and she with him. If Reuben began to court her, maybe he would decide to not join the Union Army.

"So, what are your plans for this summer, Miss Smith?" Momma asked as we ate chicken and dumplings with all the trimmings.

"Please, call me Mary Ellen," Miss Smith said with a smile. "School is out for the year and the only student here is Virginia, and she will be starting her last year come September."

"Okay, Mary Ellen, what are your plans for this summer?" Momma asked, smiling innocently.

"I plan to visit my family in Kentucky for a couple weeks, if it's not too dangerous to do so,"

"Yes, it might become dangerous for you to travel to Kentucky this summer," Papa said. "Kentucky has not seceded from the Union, but it is a slave supporting state."

"I hope my parents remain safe," Mary Ellen fretted. "This war is just crazy. Why can't the plantation owners just allow the slaves to have their freedom?"

"We've wondered that for years," Reuben said, finally joining the conversation. "I will be leaving to fight for the Union if a peaceful solution cannot be reached."

"Oh, Reuben," Mary Ellen gasped, concern very evident in her expression.

"I too believe the slaves should be set free, and I will fight for that cause," Reuben stated.

"Slavery is part of the issue, but the real reason battles have broken out is due to the fact the South has separated itself from the Union," Papa said. "As Mr. Lincoln has pointed out, "A house divided against itself cannot stand", which is a quote made by Jesus and recorded in three of the Gospels. We must pull this country back together to stay strong."

"You're absolutely right, Mr. Hensley," Mary Ellen said. "The conflict is over our country being divided. However, if slavery is abolished along the way, which is the reason for the division, wouldn't that be a nice addition to the outcome?"

"Yes, a very nice addition indeed," Papa said smiling. "And please, call me Stephen."

As we finished the meal, Momma and I got up to clear the table. Mary Ellen jumped up too, in order to help us. Momma allowed Mary Ellen to carry plates to the dishpan, but Momma insisted she sit back down and enjoy dessert as soon as the table was cleared.

"I have a double stack chocolate cake for dessert," Momma announced. "Who would like a piece of that?

"Who would be crazy enough to turn down a piece of your chocolate cake, Momma?" Carter asked. "I'll have two pieces, please."

"You will have one piece, Carter, and you will have it after Mary Ellen gets the first piece," Momma said, shaking the spatula at Carter.

"Of course, Momma," Carter said with a grin, knowing full well that after everyone was served, he would get his second piece of cake.

When we had finished our dessert, I went to add hot water from the stove and soap to the pan of dirty dishes. We had not begun to use the summer kitchen yet, because April had been quite chilly and the first week of May had not heated up enough to warrant the use of the other kitchen.

Mary Ellen came up beside me, bent on assisting. Grabbing a dishtowel, she prepared to dry the dishes after I had washed and rinsed them.

"Mary Ellen, Virginia and I will do these dishes," Momma said as she cleared dessert plates. "Why don't you allow Reuben to show you around the farm?"

"Yes," I chimed in, "Rueben would love to show you around the farm." I turned a cheeky grin toward Reuben who scowled back at me.

"Well, if Reuben doesn't want to show you around, I'll do the honors," Carter chimed in, knowing Reuben would not allow him to move in on the opportunity.

"No, I'll show Miss Smith around the farm," Reuben said, glaring at Carter. "You would probably push her into the creek when she got close enough to it."

"I only push Virginia in the creek, Reuben," Carter said, "but if you want to do the honors, suit yourself."

Reuben knew he had just been goaded into showing Mary Ellen around the farm, but he could not deny he would thoroughly enjoy it. Reuben also knew what Momma had up her sleeve, inviting Mary Ellen for Sunday dinner and all. He hated to tell his family, but not even Mary Ellen Smith would keep him from enlisting in the Union Army come June first.

"Miss Smith, would you like to see our farm?" Reuben asked, offering her his arm.

"Only if you call me Mary Ellen," she replied, taking Reuben's arm.

As the two headed out the kitchen door, a smile spread across Momma's face. I knew Mary Ellen was a pawn Momma was using, but Mary Ellen knew it too, so I suppose it was okay. Would Mary Ellen be enough to keep Reuben home?

When the dishes were finished, I grabbed my guitar and headed for the Maple tree. Ollie followed along behind me, picking up a stick along the way in hopes I would throw it for him.

The leaves of the Maple were small and light green, but in just a few weeks, a full canopy of dark green leaves would shade the area beneath it. The shade would even cover the grave of Rosie, the slave child who had died in our hidden room. Since the South had seceded from the Union and the Confederates attacked Fort Sumter in South

Carolina, the Underground Railroad had stopped on its tracks. Hopefully, it would never be needed again.

Walking to the Maple, I sat down on its gnarly roots and began to play all the songs I knew so far. Mary Ellen had taught me one key of music at a time. She thought it would seem less overwhelming that way. We had started with the key of C, with the three major chords being C, F, and G, and A minor sometimes, because that was the best key for me to sing "Come, Thou Fount of Every Blessings" in. After I had mastered changing those chords smoothly, Mary Ellen taught me the key of G, with the three major chords being G, C, and D, and sometimes E minor. I could now play in four keys, C, G, D and A. We were working on the key of E.

"You have come a long way with that guitar," Carter said, joining me under the tree. He picked up the stick at Ollie's feet and threw it for him. The dog ran as fast as possible and then tried to stop, sliding past the stick. Regaining his feet, Ollie picked up the stick and ran back to Carter so the stick could be thrown again.

"Thanks, Carter," I said smiling at him. "Maybe I could teach you someday."

"I would rather play a fiddle," Carter said.

"Then I suggest you get one," I said. "I have thoroughly enjoyed learning to play the guitar."

"Maybe I will," Carter said smiling. "Want to race to the top of this tree?"

"I should probably say no," I said thoughtfully. "Momma will tan my hide for climbing this tree with Miss Smith here, but you know I never back down from a challenge." Standing up, I leaned my guitar against the rock marking Rosie's grave. Carter got on one side of the big Maple and I got on the other. Ollie looked at us and barked, already knowing what we were getting ready to do. "Ready?"

"Ready," Carter said.

"Go!"

Carter and I began to climb the tree, neither one gaining ground on the other. When we were half way up, we could hear music coming from under the tree. I recognized it as the "Iris Washerwoman" song. Looking down, I could see Miss Smith with my guitar. She was sitting on the rock marking Rosie's grave just playing away and watching Carter and me race our way to the top of the tree.

Carter and I looked at one another from our opposite sides of the tree and laughed. We took off toward the top again, ending the race with a tie. The climb back down was done much slower, our arms and legs tired from the fast climb up.

"I didn't know you were an accomplished tree climber, Virginia," Mary Ellen said laughing.

"It's not a talent I share often," I replied. "It makes Momma cringe if I mention it."

"Hold on and enjoy being young," Mary Ellen said. "All too soon you will have to grow up and act like an adult."

I smiled in reply. Reuben, who had taken a seat at the base of the tree and was now throwing the stick for Ollie, just shook his head at me. "You better hope Momma didn't just see you race Carter to the top of that tree," he said grimly.

"Goodness, Reuben, lighten up," Carter said. "You're just jealous because you can't climb a tree as well as Virginia."

"Yeah, you're probably right," Reuben agreed, surprising us all. "Play us another tune, Mary Ellen. Virginia has a ways to go before she can play as well as you."

"Okay," Mary Ellen agreed and began to make the guitar sing tunes I had no hope of playing. I watched her fingers flow over the strings like the water rippling out of our springhouse and flowing to the small pond below. I couldn't help but wonder what Mary Ellen would say if we told her she was perched on the grave of a runaway slave's child.

Mary Ellen joined us for Sunday dinner all through the months of May and June 1861, but after July 4th, when congress issued a call for 500,000 men, Reuben prepared to enlist in the Union Army.

Other men from the community planned to enlist too, and they would all ride the long distance to New Albany, Indiana, together. One of the men was Kris, Effie's brother. Kris' twin, Kirk, would remain on their farm near Milltown and keep things running. Another was John Line, a young man who, with his parents, attended Big Spring's Church.

A tearful goodbye was said to Reuben as he left to join up with the rest of the enlistees from the Marengo area. Momma hugged him so tight I thought his ribs would be broken. Carter and I took our turns hugging him and pleading with him to be careful.

"Son," Papa said, "I'm proud you are willing to go and fight. Please, come back to us in one piece."

"I will, Papa," Reuben said. "We have worked to help free the slaves for five years through the Underground Railroad, now it's time to finish the job. When this war ends, hopefully all the slaves in the United States will be free forever."

"We will pray that it is so," Papa said, folding Reuben in his embrace.

"Did you tell Mary Ellen goodbye?" Momma asked, tears streaming down her cheeks. I knew Momma was proud of Reuben too, but letting him go without a fight was going to be difficult. She would use Mary Ellen one last time to change his mind.

"I plan to stop by her cabin as I pass through Marengo," Reuben said, "but Momma, I won't be back until this war is over."

"You can't blame a mother for trying," Momma replied, attempting to smile for Reuben's sake.

We all watched from the porch of the house as Reuben rode Blockhead away from the farm and disappeared from sight. Reuben would leave Blockhead in the corral behind the general store and catch a ride in the wagon headed to New Albany. Papa had closed the store for this sad occasion. He knew Momma would need him at home once Reuben left.

For days after Reuben's departure, tears streamed down Momma's face at random times. I knew something had reminded her of Reuben: maybe one of his shirts, or baking a dessert he liked, or his old work boots that still remained in the mud room at the back of the house. Any little thing opened the floodgates and there was nothing Momma could do to control it.

The only comfort Momma had was that Carter would not turn eighteen until December 7, 1861, six months from now, and she prayed the war would be over by then.

With Reuben gone, Papa was forced to make some changes. I started going to the store daily to wait on customers while Papa did the heavy lifting and went to Milltown for supplies once a week. Carter was needed on the farm to keep up with planting, harvesting crops and cutting hay. Sometimes, when the farm work required more than Carter could handle alone, Papa would return home to help him.

Momma took over the afternoon milking and she tended the

garden mostly alone. When I would return in the evening, I would help her preserve what she had picked that day. The summer of 1861 was turning into one of long days and little rest, until a solution came in an unexpected form.

"I have decided not to go home for a visit," Mary Ellen said as she sat at our kitchen table after Sunday dinner, three weeks after Reuben had left to fight in the war.

"That is probably a good choice," Papa said.

"I have a lot of free time since school is out for the summer," Mary Ellen continued. "I could wait on customers at the general store, if that would help you out."

Papa and Momma looked up, surprised at the offer but realized it was a perfect solution. "Would you mind doing that?" Momma asked.

"Not at all," Mary Ellen said. "I enjoy working, and besides, I would be able to get a letter from Reuben as soon as it was delivered."

"So, Reuben writes to you?" Momma asked.

"He said he would," Mary Ellen admitted. "So far, I have not received any letters, though."

"We haven't gotten a letter either, Mary Ellen," Momma assured her. "He's only been gone three weeks, and I'm sure it would take a letter quite some time to get to us."

"So you really wouldn't mind working at the store for the next month?" Papa asked.

"I would love to help out," Mary Ellen said.

"You're a Godsend," Papa said. "If you could work Monday through Thursday, Virginia could stay here on the farm to help Elizabeth. Virginia could work on Friday and Saturday."

"Then it's a plan," Mary Ellen said. "I will be at the store at eight tomorrow morning."

Mary Ellen working at the store helped us out more than words could express. I could stay home and help at the house so Momma wasn't left with all the work of keeping the garden weeded and the bounty of vegetables preserved.

Mary Ellen was a natural working with the public, and before long, the old geezers who sat on the porch and played checkers had several friends joining them. They talked of the war and the battles that were happening between the Union and Confederate troops, pretending that was the only reason they gathered at the store for hours each day. Papa and I knew that Mary Ellen drew the old men to the store, because she was just nice to look at and treated all of them with respect and a sweet smile.

The mail was always delivered on Friday, so Mary Ellen's plan of getting the letters immediately had not gone according to her plan. However, she had showed up at ten on Friday morning to wait for the mail to arrive. I showed her how to sort the mail into the boxes, since she was already there. If Mary Ellen was needed on a Friday, at least she would know what to do with the mail when it arrived. The first Friday in August, her waiting finally paid off.

"I have a letter from Reuben!" Mary Ellen exclaimed.

"That's great news," I said, walking up to look at the long awaited correspondence.

"Do you mind if I go read it?" Mary Ellen asked.

"Of course not, especially since you're just here by your own choice." I laughed softly as Mary Ellen took off like a school girl to the storeroom where we kept extra feed and supplies. Continuing to sort through the mail bag, I found a letter to our family from Reuben, and two more for Mary Ellen. I made a mental note to not tell Momma we received one letter to Mary Ellen's three. I placed our letter on the counter then put Mary Ellen's other two in her box. I wondered how long it would take her to discover she had more mail.

Returning from the storeroom, Mary Ellen was all smiles. I would rein in my curiosity and use some of those manners Momma so wanted me to possess, and not ask her what Reuben had to say. The self-control was about to kill me!

"Oh, Reuben sent a letter for all of you, too," Mary Ellen said, picking it up off the counter.

"Yes, we received one letter," I replied with a smile.

"Are you going to open it?" Mary Ellen asked.

"And risk facing Momma with an open letter from her oldest son who has gone to fight in a war? I don't think so," I said with a laugh.

"Your Momma probably would be upset if you read the letter first," Mary Ellen agreed. "Would you like to know what mine said?"

"Which one?" I asked, flashing Mary Ellen a smile.

"Why, this one," Mary Ellen said, pulling the letter from her apron pocket. "What other one could I tell you about?"

"Have you checked your mailbox?"

Mary Ellen whirled around and hurried to the boxes behind the counter. Searching until she found hers, she reached in and pulled out Reuben's other two letters. "Three! I received three letters!"

"Yeah, well I wouldn't be telling Momma that," I said with a smile.

"It would probably hurt her feelings, wouldn't it?"

"Maybe," I said, "considering my brother has probably only written four letters in his life, and we have all four of them here right now."

Mary Ellen smiled and took the other two letters to the storeroom to see what else Reuben had to say. Papa came in from outside, where he had been talking to the old men playing checkers and Thaddeus, the driver of the mail wagon. He had several days' copies of the Louisville Daily Journal stuffed under his arm that I was sure he would read at the first free moment he had.

"Look, Papa," I said holding up the letter.

"Is that from Reuben?"

"Yes! Momma will be so happy to see it."

"She sure will," Papa said, taking the letter from my hand. "It's addressed to all of us."

"I noticed that. Do you think we should open it?"

"The thought surely crossed my mind, but we better allow your mother the honor."

"Mary Ellen received letters, too," I said, smiling at Papa. There was no doubt now that Reuben and Mary Ellen were courting, even if it was by mail.

"Letters? You mean she received more than one?"

"Yes. She got three and is in the storeroom reading them now."

"Might want to just tell your momma that Reuben wrote to Mary Ellen, without saying she received three letters," Papa said thoughtfully.

"That was just what I was thinking."

At that moment, Mary Ellen came back into the main part of the store, a smile covering her pretty face and making her blue eyes shine. "Reuben has been training to fight and feels his company will be leaving for the battlefield soon. He has written a little something every day since he left, like a journal of sorts. He adds information until the page is full then starts another page. It's why there were three letters all at once. He can fit three pieces of paper per envelope, and had filled three envelopes by the time he could mail the letters."

"Sounds like you will have detailed reports of how Reuben is doing, Mary Ellen," Papa said. "It's good that Reuben will have someone special to write to and receive letters from during this time."

"Yes," Mary Ellen agreed, "I just hope the time is short."

"We all are hoping this conflict ends soon," Papa said, picking up the letter from Reuben and turning it in his hands again. Finally, he stuck it in his shirt pocket and walked back outside to show the old men on the porch what he had received in today's mail and to share what the newspapers had to report on the war's progress.

We took the letter home that evening and Momma was thrilled. Tearing it open, she read the entire thing in a few seconds. Folding the letter, she handed it to Papa to read. Carter and I read it together last. Reuben had been training with the 19th Indiana Infantry Regiment in Indianapolis but would soon be joining other Union troops in the Army of the Potomac.

Papa smiled at Momma. "It seems Reuben is well and will soon see parts of the country he has never seen before."

"Yes," Momma agreed. "I honestly didn't expect the letter to be long. You know how Reuben is. He's not much for writing."

"Well, he sure wrote a lot more to Mary Ellen," was the thought that crossed my mind but I made sure it did not escape my mouth.

"He got to ride on a train from New Albany to Indianapolis," Carter said, his eyes dancing just thinking of the adventure.

"Wonder when he will fight his first battle?" I blurted.

"Goodness, Virginia, hopefully there can be a peaceful solution found to the South separating itself," Momma said.

"We would all like to see that," Papa said, "but I doubt that will happen."

Momma took the letter out and read it one more time. Folding it again carefully, she took it to her and Papa's bedroom. I knew she would save every last one of Reuben's letters, because as careful as we all were not to talk about it, the words on that paper could be the last ones my brother ever said to us. No one knew what the future held for our country that had been ripped in half.

Momma penned a letter back to Reuben. Papa, Carter and I added little notes of our own to a piece of paper. Momma had asked Reuben all kinds of questions that I was sure he would not answer. She wanted to know what his uniform looked like and the material it was made from. She asked if his boots were sturdy and if he was being fed enough. I suppose it was things a mother would fret over but Reuben would just think Momma was worrying over him way too much. The letter went out to Reuben the next Friday, along with three from Mary Ellen, and we all waited impatiently for a return correspondence.

Chapter Nine

We had not known it, but when we were reading letters from Reuben, he was engaging in his first battle. On July 21, 1861, the Union and Confederate soldiers faced off at Bull Run, 25 miles southwest of Washington. The news of the battle reached us the next Friday when the Louisville Daily Journal arrived with the mail delivery.

"There's been a battle fought at Bull Run, a place near Washington," Papa said as he perused the newspaper.

"What does it say?" asked one of the old men sitting on the porch.

I could hear the conversation through the screen door of the general store and walked outside to listen. Mary Ellen followed close behind, having come to the store to wait for mail to arrive. She had received a letter from her parents, but no mail had come from Reuben.

"Let's see," Papa said, reading the article quickly but silently, "seems the Union Army under General Irvin McDowell fought against the Confederates under the command of General Thomas Jackson. It did not go well for the North. The Confederates pushed the Union troops all the way back to Washington."

"That's not good at all," Mary Ellen said.

"No, it's not," Papa agreed. "First, the Confederates take Fort Sumter in Charleston, South Carolina, and now they have gotten the upper hand at this Bull Run battle. This war may last longer than we had previously thought."

"They say that confounded bars and stars flag those Rebels

came up with is still flying over Fort Sumter," another old man on the porch chimed in.

"Yeah and that traitor Jefferson Davis, who thinks he's the President of the Confederacy, used to be a United States Army officer," a local farmer added. He had come to buy some supplies and stayed for the war update.

"Mr. Lincoln may have his plate full with this war between the states," Papa said, paging through the newspapers for more information on the war.

"Yes, what started as a disagreement where a peaceful solution was hoped for is turning into something none of us wanted to see happen," Mary Ellen added, making the men on the porch turn toward her and consider whether or not they wanted a woman's opinion on the subject. Mary Ellen was nice to look at, but whether they wanted her to speak out during the porch discussions remained to be seen.

Two more weeks passed before the second Friday of August brought more letters from Reuben. Mary Ellen received two envelopes and us one. Papa didn't wait to take the letter to Momma first this time. He ripped it open immediately to see what Reuben had written. I stood beside him and we read the letter at the same time.

Dear Papa, Momma, Carter, and Virginia,

By now, I'm sure you have read in the Louisville Daily Journal of the battle at Bull Run. It was an embarrassing loss for the Union troops, running as we did like a dog with its tail between its legs. Rain soaked us as we retreated toward Washington, while Rebel fire kept us running. The Rebels blew up a bridge we were crossing during our retreat, which made us scatter like chickens being threatened by a hawk. Since that time, President Lincoln has removed General McDowell from his command and replaced him with General George McClellan. We're hoping our next battle ends differently. I can assure you, if all our battles go as Bull Run did, this war will be short-lived and the Confederates will win.

It was good to hear about the farm and how the store is running smoothly, especially since Mary Ellen stepped in to help. I miss all of you and pray this war ends soon. Please, continue to write to me. I enjoy getting mail from home.

Love,

Reuben

"Short, sweet and to the point," Papa muttered.

"Well, that's Reuben," I said with a smile. "However, the two letters I put in Mary Ellen's box did not feel thin."

"Again, we will not be telling your mother that," Papa said with a grin.

Angus stopped by the store to check and see if his family had received any mail, just as he did every Friday. Handing him the few items, I was glad he was the only one in the store. It gave us time to talk for a while. "We received another letter from Reuben today," I said to start the conversation.

"Really? What did he have to say?"

"That Bull Run was an embarrassment for the Union Army, basically."

"I feel bad for any Union soldier who took part in Bull Run. Their commander should have had them better prepared. It's not entirely their fault they had to turn tail and run."

"Mr. Lincoln has put McClellan in charge of the Department of the Potomac now," I replied. "He must have felt the blame lay with McDowell, too."

Angus smiled, "You're keeping up with the war reports quite well."

"Papa reads them from the Louisville Daily Journal newspapers when they arrive on Friday. That's why he's out on the porch now. He's sharing any new information with the porch sitters."

Angus laughed out loud. "The porch sitters; I like that term. It's much nicer than saying the old men who have nothing better to do."

"I've gotten to know them the last few months. Since Mary Ellen works here now, the numbers have increased quite a bit."

Angus looked at me intently, making me blush just a bit. "Well, Mary Ellen's not here today and the porch is still full."

"Probably because it's Friday and they all want to hear what the newspaper is saying about the war."

Angus looked as if he was going to say more on the subject when the screen door opened and slapped shut. Mary Ellen hurried behind the counter to retrieve her letters. Turning back around holding her letters and all smiles, she seemed to notice Angus for the first time. "Well, hello Angus Zink. What brings you to the store?"

"Um, just getting the mail," Angus replied, holding up his hand that clutched the pieces of mail as proof.

"Have you heard Virginia play that fine guitar you gave her

lately?" Mary Ellen asked.

Angus smiled and shifted his feet. "No, I haven't heard her play for a while. Since Reuben went to fight for the Union Army, Virginia has been quite busy."

A mischievous smile came to Mary Ellen's pretty face. Glancing at me for just a moment, she turned back to Angus. "You know, I give Virginia lessons every Sunday afternoon out at her home. You should come out and listen. She has gotten quite good. Do you know where Virginia's house is?"

Angus looked at me and grinned. We both were thinking of the night he came to warn us that slave hunters were in the area and we needed to move the runaways that we had hidden. "Yes, I've been to Virginia's house a few times."

"Good! You know where it is then," Mary Ellen beamed. "What do you think, Virginia? Should Angus come out Sunday and listen to us play."

"Um, sure." What had just happened? Was Mary Ellen Smith playing matchmaker between Angus and me? We were just really good friends, nothing more.

"I suppose I'll see you Sunday afternoon," Angus said stepping toward the door.

"Yes, Sunday afternoon it is," I replied, suddenly nervous but I had no idea why.

"I'll be heading home to read my letters now," Mary Ellen chirped. "Make sure you practice up for Sunday so Angus can hear just how good that guitar he bought can be made to sound."

"Yeah, Sunday," I muttered.

When church service ended, Angus met me outside. Effie and I were chattering about what all we had done that week that I hardly noticed him waiting patiently. Effie's parents exited the church and they walked toward home.

Angus stepped toward me and nervously licked his lips. What on earth had happened between us? It used to be so easy to just be friends. "What time should I come out today?"

"Um, let me think. We usually start practicing around three. Would that be okay?"

"Yes, three o'clock is fine."

"Three o'clock for what?" Carter interrupted.

"None of your business, Carter," I spouted.

"Now, Virginia, is that any way to treat your favorite brother? What do you and Angus have planned?"

"I'm just going to come out and listen to Virginia and Miss Smith practice guitar," Angus said, trying to keep Carter and me from arguing right there in front of the church.

"Well, just come for dinner," Carter offered. "Momma always cooks enough to feed an army. She won't mind at all."

"What won't I mind, Carter?" Momma asked, coming up behind us.

Carter spun around surprised. "Angus is going to come and listen to Virginia play guitar this afternoon. I told him he should just come for dinner."

"Why, absolutely," Momma agreed. "You just come home with us right now and have Sunday dinner. I don't know why Virginia didn't ask you to do that in the first place."

"Would you like me to bring our wagon?" Angus asked. "I could bring Miss Smith back to town when I come."

"That would be nice of you," Momma said smiling.

"Okay. I'll go home and get it and be out shortly."

"That's fine, Angus. We will just head on home and finish preparing the meal," Momma said as we began to walk toward the wagon.

Reaching home, Momma, Mary Ellen and I finished dinner preparations. Angus showed up about ten minutes behind us. We had cooked the meal in the summer kitchen and decided to eat on the porch of the little building, where it would be cooler.

Papa had constructed a table with benches down the sides for use on the summer kitchen porch. Ollie sat at my feet through the whole meal, waiting for any morsel that might fall to the ground. Angus felt sorry for him and slipped him a taste every now and then. After the meal, we three women cleaned up the kitchen in no time at all.

Grabbing our guitars, Mary Ellen and I sat on the porch of the summer kitchen and began to play. I could keep up with her quite well now, and I had made sure to practice every song I thought we might play today. I didn't want Angus to feel he had wasted a perfectly good Sunday afternoon by coming to listen to me make mistakes.

"You are getting quite good, Virginia," Angus said. "You

should play at church with Miss Smith on Sundays."

"Angus, you may call me Mary Ellen. Virginia, Angus is right. You should start playing with me on Sundays. It would be good practice."

"Are you sure, Mary Ellen?"

"Absolutely," Mary Ellen assured me.

We played a few more songs then put the instruments away. Carter, Angus, and I walked to the creek to wade in the cool water and Mary Ellen joined Momma in the house. Ollie followed after us, not wanting to miss out on any adventure. Slipping off our socks and shoes, Carter and Angus rolled up their pants legs and I held the hem of my dress up. We began to walk in the shallow water, chasing schools of minnows ahead of us. We reached a part of the creek where the bottom was one big smooth rock. I knew it was slick here, but we continued on anyway.

When we had walked about three feet across the smooth bottom, I lost my balance on the slick rock. Before I knew what had happened, I was on my bottom in the water. Ollie was barking wildly from the bank, almost as if he was laughing at me.

"That was a nice fall, Virginia," Carter said laughing.

"Thanks, Carter," I said, trying to get to my feet. Angus finally reached his hand down to help me up. I grasped his hand and pulled myself to my feet, knocking Angus off balance in the process. He hit the water with a splash.

Carter stepped onto the bank and laughed at both of us, now soaking wet. Looking at Angus, we spoke without saying a word. Making it back to his feet, Angus and I walked to the bank and joined Carter. Moving to either side of him, we quickly pushed him into the water. Knowing he had asked for the dunking, Carter just allowed himself to get completely soaked. Ollie jumped in after Carter, thinking now that it was a game we were playing.

"We better get dry before we return to the house," Carter said. "Momma will not be happy if we come back soaking wet."

"We could stand in the sun and skip rocks," I suggested.

"You must like to lose," Carter said.

"We'll see about that," I retorted.

Each of us chose five rocks apiece. Angus took his sweet time, looking all up and down the creek for just the right ones. As the game began, Carter and I had ten skips each with our first rocks while Angus had five.

"You spent an awful long time searching for a rock that only got you five skips," Carter pointed out to Angus.

"The game has only begun," Angus replied.

After each of us had thrown four times, Carter was in the lead with fifteen skips. Angus's best throw only got him ten skips. Carter threw his last rock, scoring sixteen skips. I threw next, surprising myself with eighteen skips. Turning to Angus I smiled sweetly. "It's your turn, Angus. You have to beat eighteen to win."

Angus smiled at me, his blue eyes dancing. I wondered how someone who had chosen his rocks so carefully and was now so far behind could be so happy. My thoughts were answered in a matter of seconds. Angus flipped his last rock from his hand and Carter and I counted out loud in amazement. Angus beat us with twenty-five skips, a number Carter and I had never come close to.

"And that's how it's done," Angus said with a triumphant smile.

"Indeed!" Carter exclaimed.

The three of us sat on a big rock to dry out the rest of the way. The sun blazed hot, so our clothes dried quickly. Ollie chose a shady spot under a tree a few feet away.

When we returned to the house, Mary Ellen announced she was ready to go home for her Sunday afternoon nap. I followed Angus as he went to the corral beside the barn where his horses had been grazing. Angus began to hitch the horses back to the wagon. "I've had fun today, Virginia."

"Me too, Angus, but of course I always have fun with you."

"You're getting quite good playing the guitar. I expect to see you playing at church next Sunday."

"Thank you, Angus, and thanks again for giving it to me. Remind me to never play skip the rock with you again, though."

Angus flashed his dimpled smile. "I'll see you on Friday at the store, Virginia."

"Okay, Angus."

I watched as Mary Ellen climbed onto the wagon seat next to Angus. I waved as they faded into the distance heading back to town. Though I had been a bit nervous at first, it had turned into a really fun day. I would have to invite Angus to Sunday dinner again sometime soon.

School began again in September but without me attending. Mary Ellen spent her days teaching now, so I was needed at the store daily. Carter was keeping up with the farm chores and would make the trip to Milltown for supplies once a week. Papa didn't like to leave me in charge at the store for long periods of time because of the heavy lifting it sometimes required.

Mary Ellen thought it a shame that I could no longer continue my schooling, so she made sure to write out what she taught to the older kids each week and give it to me on Sunday. I would complete the lessons and give them to her when she came to the store after school on Fridays to check her mail. I was so thankful she took the time to do this for me. It made extra work for her but she wanted to see me achieve my dream of teaching at the school one day. To be able to do this, I needed to further my education.

October brought crisp air and bright colors to our area. The trees were decorated in their short-lived splendor for a few weeks then the leaves turned brown and littered the ground.

The Louisville Daily Journal had little to report about the war's progress, since no real battles had been fought since the embarrassing Bull Run incident. When the mail arrived the second week of November, Papa finally found something worth talking about with the men gathered around the wood stove inside the store.

"The newspaper says that Winfield Scott has resigned as general-in-chief of the Union forces," Papa said.

"Who took his place?" Delmar, one of the men, asked.

"Mr. Lincoln gave the position to George McClellan," Papa said, perusing the article for more information. "I would have thought he would have waited until McClellan proved himself as the commander of the Union troops he was already over."

"Maybe he had no one else for the job," another one of the men around the wood stove surmised.

"Perhaps," Papa agreed.

Letters arrived from Reuben on a weekly basis now. With him waiting for orders on how the war effort would proceed, he was able to send his letters every week from the camp, and receive ones from us.

The letters to the family were always one page with basic information of what was happening in the Union camp. Mary Ellen, however, still received two envelopes each week and she sent out two to Reuben each Friday. I couldn't help but be excited with the thought that Mary Ellen might one day be my sister-in-law.

We celebrated Thanksgiving in mid-November. The holiday was not an official one, but we chose to celebrate the day as the country had in 1789, when President Washington suggested it be a day set aside to give thanks.

Carter killed a nice fat turkey for the meal and Momma baked it and used the drippings to make gravy to pour over our mashed potatoes. There were buttered carrots and yeast rolls to add to the feast. Mary Ellen joined us to celebrate this day set aside to stop and give thanks for the many blessings we had enjoyed the past year. She brought two squash pies with her, made from Momma's recipe and the squash we had grown in our garden.

"What are we thankful for this year?" Papa asked as we sat around the table enjoying dessert.

"I'm thankful Reuben is still well and hasn't been injured," Momma said.

"I'm thankful that the slaves may finally have their freedom," I added.

"I'm thankful that Mary Ellen made two squash pies," Carter said, scooping another piece onto his plate.

"I'm thankful to have somewhere to go today," Mary Ellen said. "It feels like home here."

"I'm thankful Mary Ellen helped out at the store when we needed it most," Papa said. "Hopefully, this war will end quickly and Reuben will come home and truly make Mary Ellen part of this family."

"Yes, that would be a true blessing," Momma agreed.

Mary Ellen's face turned red with embarrassment. Speaking softly she said, "Yes, I would love that, too."

****

December 7th, 1861 came and Carter turned 18. He had not made any mention of joining the Union forces, but he could make the choice to do so now. Momma, nor Papa, had brought the subject up, hoping Carter would just remain at home. My curiosity would not allow me to leave well enough alone. I had to know what my brother was planning.

"So Carter, now that you've become an adult, what's your plan?" I asked while we cleaned the horse stalls. Helping him with the chore was my birthday present to him.

"Well, Virginia, I might just go to California and pan for gold," Carter replied.

I had not expected this answer. It actually sounded like something my adventurous brother would do. "You're going to California? The gold rush is over Carter. There's none left for you, I'm afraid."

"Virginia, do you really think I would go to California and leave Papa to do all the farm work and run the store? I know what you're really asking."

I tried to give Carter my most innocent look. "I'm just inquiring as to what you have planned for your life."

"Hogwash! You want to know if I'm going to enlist in the Union Army."

"Okay, I want to know that, too. Will you be leaving us?"

"Not yet. It's been kind of quiet on the war front so far so I feel I'm needed more here at home. If that changes, I will have to seriously consider enlisting."

"I hope things stay quiet," I whispered. I could not stand the thought of both Reuben and Carter in the war.

"Aw, Virginia, you do care about me," Carter teased.

"Of course I do. Who am I going to beat at skipping rocks if you go away to war?"

"Well, it certainly won't be Angus because he beat us both real good."

I scooped up a handful of straw and tossed it at Carter. Carter smiled and brushed the straw from his clothes. We finished cleaning the stalls before I had to leave and go with Papa to the store. It gave me peace knowing Carter planned to remain here at home, for the time being.

****

Winter marched in and the war marched on. The year 1861 became 1862, and still no end to the war was in sight, though there were not any major battles happening at the moment. Papa said both sides were probably busy planning their next move. I sure hoped the Union army was better prepared for the next battle they faced then they had been for Bull Run.

On days Carter could be at the store all day, I would attend school. It was much easier to learn hearing Miss Smith speak the lesson rather than reading it later and trying to figure it out. Effie was delighted on the days I could attend school. She would sometimes visit me at the store after school on the days I couldn't attend, but having me beside her all day was much better.

When Papa was finished with reading his copies of the Louisville Daily Journal, he would give them to Miss Smith to use. Miss Smith would keep the class up to date on what was happening with the war. Most of us knew someone who had gone to fight for the Union troops, so we were all interested in how the North was doing. Miss Smith told us that this war would be talked about in history books for years to come and wanted the older pupils to pay attention to the history in the making.

****

"General Ulysses Grant has had quite a victory in Tennessee," Papa said as he looked through the newspapers the third week of February, 1862.

I had just come from school to help out at the store. Fridays were very busy, due to the fact the mail arrived and people stopped to check and see if they had a delivery. The men sitting around the stove were always anxious for Papa to read any articles of interest from the newspapers. The general store was the hub of information for our little town.

"What did General Grant accomplish?" one of the men sitting around asked. "It's about time somebody did something worth reporting."

"He and his troops captured Fort Henry and Fort Donelson," Papa said.

"Way to go Yankees!" Delmar hollered. "Make them Rebels run like scared rabbits!"

"I fear we still have a long way to go before we can claim any headway," Papa pointed out.

"Well, it's a start," Delmar said, gathering nods from the rest of the men sitting around.

"Yes, Delmar, it's a start," Papa said, smiling at the old fellow who spent so much of his time at the general store.

The next Friday brought sad news from a report in the Louisville Daily Journal. Papa had just begun to read through the paper when he gasped. "Goodness, this is terrible."

"What is it Papa?" I asked stepping closer to the chair he was sitting in close to the wood stove.

"What's the paper say?" Delmar asked impatiently, mainly because he had not the ability to read it on his own.

"President Lincoln's eleven-year-old son, Willie, died from a fever on February 20th," Papa said.

"That's awful," I said.

"That poor family," Delmar said. "President Lincoln had enough troubles without having to bury his child."

"How sad for them," Papa said. "President Lincoln won't even have time to grieve with this war going on."

We all had no idea how he did it, but President Lincoln pushed on. Though we all knew he must be devastated, he did not allow his own child's death to take his focus from the war and what must be done.

The war effort began to move rapidly as warmer weather came with the month of March. Papa plopped down in a chair close to the stove with the newspapers, perusing them for points of interest. "The Confederates Ironclad "Merrimac" sunk two of the Union's wooden ships this week," Papa reported to everyone sitting around the general store waiting for war reports.

"Two ships is quite a loss for the Union," Carter said. "I wonder if any soldiers were killed."

"The report doesn't list casualties," Papa said. "The Union Ironclad "Monitor" fought back against the "Merrimac", and the battle ended in a draw."

"Well, my math is not quite up to snuff, but I'm pretty sure two sunken Union ships makes the Confederates the winner in that battle," Delmar said.

"It would seem so," Papa agreed, continuing to read the paper. "This is interesting. President Lincoln has taken over as general-in-chief. He is now in direct command of the Union Armies."

"So, President Lincoln just up and fired McClellan?" Carter asked.

"No, it doesn't say that," Papa said. "It just says that President Lincoln is general-in-chief, for the time being."

"That's an interesting turn of events," one of the men listening to the reports said.

"Yes, very interesting, indeed," Papa agreed, mulling over this new information.

No letters arrived from Reuben through the month of March, so we could only assume he was moving with the troops. Where the battle would take place remained to be seen.

Mary Ellen continued to mail him letters to the address she had, not knowing if or when he would receive them. She just didn't want him to think she had forgotten about him and hoped the letters would be waiting for him when he returned from the battlefield.

The war reports from the newspaper throughout April were good and bad. April 6th, the day before my 16th birthday, had brought a surprise attack from the Confederates to unprepared Union troops under General Ulysses Grant's command. The Union troops were camped along the Tennessee River at Shiloh. The result of the battle was 13,000 Union soldiers killed or wounded and 10,000 Confederates, more men than all the previous American wars combined. The report brought tears to the eyes of all who listened at the general store.

On April 24th, the North took control of New Orleans, the South's greatest seaport. This brought smiles and whoops from the men gathered at the general store.

The daffodils that had marked the beginning of spring faded and the irises took up blooming. The red bud trees and lilac bushes added beauty to the landscape and fragrance to the air. Our fruit trees broke bud and the bees began to work the blossoms. As far as nature was concerned, all was right with the world. It was hard to imagine there was a war being fought between the states, for there was no evidence of it here in southern Indiana.

The end of May gave us insight as to where Reuben was. We had not received any letters from him since February. The newspaper reported a battle near Richmond on May 31st, which nearly defeated the Union's troops with McClellan in command. The Confederates were led by Joseph Johnston, who was badly wounded during the battle.

The first week of July, when Papa received his copies of the Louisville Daily Journal for the week, the report was that Union troops had remained near Richmond, and Robert E. Lee had been placed in command of the Confederates, since Johnston was too badly wounded to continue. A battle had begun again between McClellan and Lee's troops on June 25th and lasted seven days, resulting in heavy losses for both sides.

"Do you think Reuben is injured?" Mary Ellen fretted as she listened to Papa read the report from the newspaper. She was working through the summer at the store again. Though she hadn't worked on Fridays the previous year, she chose to work this year, because she had nothing else to occupy her time.

"We don't know for sure," Papa said. "Hopefully he is not among the casualties."

"How will we know?" I asked. "Will they send a letter?"

"Virginia, Reuben's name will be printed here in the Louisville Daily Journal," Papa said. Papa opened the newspaper to a special page for names of fallen soldiers who lived in the area. It listed names of the dead, injured and missing. "I have looked for Reuben's name since March and it has not appeared. We can only assume that so far, he is well."

"But these last two battles have wrought heavy losses. Do you think there has been enough time for the paper to receive all the names and print them?" Mary Ellen asked.

"No, Mary Ellen, I don't think they have begun to print those names yet," Papa said. "The list is not very long in this newspaper I have here, and it includes names of soldiers within a fifty mile radius of Louisville, Kentucky. We will keep checking the list the next few weeks. I will start hanging it up here in the store so other families in the area may check for their son's name, too."

"What an impersonal way to find out your child has died," Delmar muttered.

"I agree," Papa said, "but it's not like they have time to find each soldiers family and tell them personally, or send a letter."

As the war continued, I knew that little section of the newspaper would become the most important part. Families from all over the Marengo area would be crowding around it each week until they found their son's name or received a letter from him personally, assuring everyone they were okay. I dreaded the day someone actually found the name of a loved one printed on that page, and I prayed it wasn't Reuben's.

Besides the war report on the two battles near Richmond, the only thing Papa thought worth sharing with those gathered in the general store was the fact President Lincoln had appointed a new general-in-chief. After Lincoln had acted as the general-in-chief for four months, on July 11, 1862, he handed the job over to General

Henry W. Halleck. The newspaper stated his nickname was "Old Brains", which hopefully meant he was old and wise. The Union was definitely in need of an old and wise leader.

Papa did not want to tell Momma the war reports because he knew it would make her worry. However, he knew she would find out on Sunday from someone else and would be very upset that Papa had not told her. Papa did leave the newspapers at the store, though, so he only had to tell part of what he knew.

"Elizabeth, Reuben's company has been involved in combat near Richmond again," Papa said quietly after we had finished eating supper.

"Oh, Stephen, was it bad? Did the newspaper report how many were killed or wounded?"

"The report did not give an exact number of casualties," Papa said, skirting around the fact that the losses had been heavy for both sides.

"We must pray for his safety," Momma said. "We must pray for all the young men fighting in this terrible war, whether they are from the North or South. They are all someone's precious son."

"Yes, Elizabeth, we will pray," Papa said softly.

Chapter Ten

The hot, humid July days were filled with work from dawn to dusk. Momma and I preserved all the vegetables ripening in the garden and Carter kept busy with the farm.

Momma and I also picked blackberries and made cobblers and jam. They grew all along the fields on our farm. When we had picked enough for ourselves, we sent the berries to the store with Papa to sell. As it turned out, blackberries were in high demand, and I ended up picking many more. I could see why someone would buy the berries rather than pick them. Avoiding the scratches from the thorns and the chiggers burrowing under ones skin were reasons enough to pay hard earned money.

Every Friday and Saturday, I joined Mary Ellen and Papa at the store. Papa would post the list of fallen soldiers each week from the Louisville Daily Journal. It was the first place a person went when they entered the store. By the final Friday in July, the list had grown to a full page of names.

"Do we have any mail today?" Angus asked, stepping up to the counter.

"It hasn't been delivered yet, Angus," I replied. "The mail wagon should be here anytime, though."

"I'll stick around and wait awhile," Angus said. "Any news from Reuben, yet?"

"No, not a word," I said. Mary Ellen walked back to the counter just then and I quickly changed the subject. "How's the leather business going?”

“Quite well,” Angus replied, understanding what I was doing.

Grasping for more conversation, I asked, “Would you like to come for Sunday dinner this week?” Angus had been coming to the house once a month for Sunday dinner for a year now. He had just been to the farm two Sunday's ago, but I couldn't think of anything else to say at the moment.

“Sure,” Angus replied.

Just then, the mail wagon rolled up in front of the store. Everyone milling around in the store walked out to the porch to join the group already sitting there.

The mail bag was handed to Papa who reached in to remove the copies of the Louisville Daily Journal. The bag was then handed to me so the mail could be sorted. I thought about staying to hear the reports on battles that had been fought and for Papa to read the list of soldiers who had paid the ultimate price, but I decided to look for a letter from Reuben, instead.

Heading back into the store, I took the bag and dumped its contents on the counter. Angus followed me in and began to help sort the mail. As we neared the bottom of the stack, we found what we had been waiting for. Two letters from Reuben were among the mail, one to Mary Ellen and one to the family. There was also a letter from Effie's brother, Kris.

“Thanks be to God!” I exclaimed, picking up the letters.

“Let's go give that letter to Mary Ellen,” Angus said.

Hurrying outside, our enthusiasm was cut short. The somber look on the faces of everyone gathered on the porch of the general store was enough to tell us something was wrong. Slipping up beside Mary Ellen, who was swiping tears from her face, I whispered, “What's happened?”

“John Line's name is on the list,” she whispered.

Mary Ellen need not explain what list. It was not hard to figure out that John Line was now among the names of the many fallen soldiers. Slipping the letters into my apron pocket, I decided it was not the time or place to share the happy news that Reuben had sent letters. Looking about, I noticed John Line's parents were not at the general store. Someone would have to go inform them of the sad news.

“I'll go get Pastor David and his wife, Linda. We will ride out to the Line farm together," Papa said, taking the responsibility to do the unwanted task.

"May God go with you," Delmar murmured, wiping tears of his own.

Papa stepped into the store and Angus and I followed him. Papa handed me the list of fallen soldiers so I could post it on the wall. Walking to the back room for his hat, Papa prepared to deliver the tragic news. I followed after him so I could speak to him alone.

"Papa?"

"Yes, Virginia," Papa replied wearily.

Pulling Reuben's letter from my pocket, I walked toward my father. "We received a letter from Reuben today."

"That is wonderful news," Papa said, fresh tears coming to his eyes. Reaching out, he started to take the letter then changed his mind. "Just keep a hold of it, Virginia. I believe I will need to read the good news more so later than now."

"I understand, Papa. Mary Ellen received one, too. He must have been hurried when he wrote, or Mary Ellen would have gotten more."

"I assure you, Mary Ellen will be delighted with one," Papa said. "I must go get Pastor David now and head toward Valeene to the Line farm. Carter is out back if you need him."

"Mary Ellen and I will be fine. I'll only bother Carter if it's absolutely necessary."

"Thank you, Virginia. I'll be back as soon as possible."

"Be careful, Papa. I will say a prayer for the Line family."

"They are sure going to need it," Papa said with a sigh. Turning, he walked out the back door to hitch the horses to the wagon. Carter met him at the back door and went to help.

I went back to the counter to retrieve mail for those who were coming in from the front porch. In such a small community, everyone would know shortly that a local boy had paid the ultimate price in a battle to preserve our country's unity.

Angus came to stand beside me. "Did your papa read the letter?" he asked softly.

"No, he thought it best to wait until he returned."

"Your papa is a strong man taking on such a task," Angus said. "I don't believe I could do it."

"You just might surprise yourself Angus, if the need presented itself."

Angus looked at me intently. "I hope I'm never in a position for the need to present itself, Virginia."

"Does this mean when you turn eighteen in a few months, you have no intentions of enlisting?"

"I didn't say that, Virginia. I've been giving it much thought. I know I'm the only son in my family, but I feel I should do something for this war. I think I will join the Indiana home guard."

"That would be much less dangerous than joining the Union forces," I said with relief. Angus and I had not discussed his plans, mainly because I had been afraid to ask. He would turn eighteen on January 25th, 1863, just a short six months from now.

"Yes, and it would give me some training," Angus replied.

Mary Ellen walked back into the store then, along with several other people. She and I began to assist the customers with purchases and retrieving their mail. Angus waved and slipped out the door, taking Kris's letter to his parents. He knew they would be thankful for the letter, letting them know that he was well.

When all the customers left, I remembered the letter to Mary Ellen still in my pocket. She had gone to straighten shelves and I walked up beside her. "Mary Ellen?"

"Yes Virginia."

"I have a letter for you," I said, holding out the envelope that contained Mary Ellen's hopes and dreams for her future.

Mary Ellen grabbed the letter from my hands. Recognizing Reuben's handwriting, her tears fell once more, but for a very different reason. These were tears of joy. "Oh, Virginia, he's alive!"

"Yes, Mary Ellen, he's alive," I said with a smile I had been holding in check since the sad news of John Line's death.

Mary Ellen turned and headed for the store room. "I must go read it."

I laughed out loud. "Of course you must, Mary Ellen."

A few minutes later, Mary Ellen emerged from the store room with a big smile on her pretty face. "Reuben is well. He did not have time to write much, but his commander wanted each soldier to write home so their families knew they were alive. Did you receive a letter, too? He said he had written one."

I reached into my apron pocket and pulled out Reuben's letter. "Yes, I have it right here. I showed it to Papa but he wanted to wait until he returned to read it. He thought it would boost his spirits after delivering the devastating news to John Line's family."

Mary Ellen shook her head sadly. "Such a terrible thing for John's family."

"Yes, and it just as easily could have been ours," I murmured.

"That is so true. I will share with you what Reuben said, so you don't have to wait hours to find out. Reuben was part of both battles that have been fought near Richmond the last two months. After the last battle, Reuben and his company withdrew back toward Washington.

Rueben said soldiers were being added to their troop in preparation of fighting against the Confederates led by Robert E. Lee again. Many lives were lost at Richmond, and McClellan, Reuben's commander, wants a much bigger, stronger force the next time he meets up with the Confederates."

"So, he is preparing to go to battle again soon?"

Mary Ellen sighed. "It appears so, Virginia."

"There will be no quick or easy end to this war, will there, Mary Ellen?"

"I don't believe so. Neither side is willing to give up without a fight. The question is how many lives will be lost in the process?"

"There have been too many already," I whispered, thinking of the Line family and the news Pastor David was delivering right now.

****

The one new and interesting report was that on July 17, 1862, the first freed Negro troop was formed. The North winning the war was very important to them, since it would free all slaves. They were more than willing to step on the battlefield and do their part to help the North's cause.

There were no battles reported in the newspaper through the month of August 1862. The list of deceased soldiers grew smaller but there were a few new names added. Fortunately, none of the names were men from the Marengo area.

September came and Mary Ellen went back to teaching school, making it necessary for me to work at the store daily. The second week of September, the Louisville Daily Journal reported a second battle at Bull Run. The results were just about the same as the first battle of Bull Run. 75,000 Union soldiers, led by General John Pope, were defeated by 55,000 Confederates, under the command of

General Thomas "Stonewall" Jackson. Once again, the Union Army turned tail and retreated back to Washington. President Lincoln relieved General Pope of his position.

"How could ya not stand and fight when ya got 20,000 more men than the feller you're fightin' against?" Delmar bellowed.

"We don't know all the circumstances," Papa said, trying to give the Union soldiers the benefit of doubt.

"Mr. Lincoln fired the commander," Delmar pointed out. "Don't reckon I need more information than that."

"I wonder if Reuben's regiment took part in the Bull Run battle again," I chimed in.

"I don't know," Papa said, "but it is possible. With that victory, there's no telling what the Confederates will try next, though."

"I just hope the Union troops are more prepared for what comes next," Delmar muttered. "So far, with the exception of General Grant taking two forts in Tennessee, the North ain't done so well."

"It does appear that so far the South has proved they are as strong as the North, maybe stronger," Papa agreed. "Hopefully, we can turn the tables on that."

"We'd better do it soon," Delmar huffed, "or we'll all be flying that infernal bars and stars flag."

"If the North loses, I believe we will just become two separate countries," Papa pointed out. "I don't see the Confederates being in control of the entire United States, though you have given me something to mull over."

"I'm heading home," Delmar announced. "It's just about supper time and I haven't won a checker game all day."

"See you tomorrow, Delmar," Papa said as Delmar shuffled off the porch of the general store.

"What makes ya think I'll be back tomorrow?"

"You'll be here, Delmar," Papa stated. "It's one thing I can count on."

Delmar laughed loud and began to walk down the road toward home. He had worked hard as a farmer his entire life and had handed his farm over to his son a few years ago. Delmar's farm was located just east of Marengo, and he claimed walking to town each day kept his old bones from stiffening up. Everyone knew he just came to the store to talk, play checkers, and gather gossip, which he passed along to whoever would listen, along with his opinions.

Papa walked into the store and placed the copies of the Louisville Daily Journal on the counter. He knew Mary Ellen would be by soon to check her mail and gather the newspapers to read and glean progress of the war to share with the older students at the school. He wished Mary Ellen could also pick up a letter from Reuben, but there had been one of those in over a month.

****

The last Friday of September brought war reports that made us worry if Reuben had survived the latest conflict. Papa sat on the porch of the general store as people gathered around. It was the biggest crowd the general store had seen since the war began. Everyone knew the pot was boiling and was anxious to hear what was happening. The Union losing at Bull Run for the second time had made us all a bit nervous. Could the South really overrun the Union troops and take Washington? The threat seemed very real.

Papa cleared his throat and began to speak. He had read the articles and was now prepared to explain what was going on. "It seems General Lee has invaded the North," Papa began. "He made it to Harper's Ferry fifty miles northwest of Washington. McClellan and his Union troops pursued Lee and the Confederates and the Union troops stopped the Confederates at Sharpsburg, Maryland, near Antietam Creek. A fierce battle broke out in a cornfield and the area woodlands. When all was said and done, Lee withdrew back to Virginia, but the casualties were great." Papa paused for a moment to gain his composer. With his next words, we all understood why. "The South suffered 13,000 and the North over 12,000. The Union is claiming victory because Lee retreated, but I can't see a win for either side. This battle will result in great mourning all across our country."

"Lord have mercy," Delmar muttered, taking the words off all our tongues.

"President Lincoln has issued a preliminary Emancipation Proclamation. As of January 1, 1863, all slaves will be free," Papa stated. "This war has gone way beyond what I ever dreamed it would. Over 26,000 young men have lost their lives or been injured and unable to continue to fight in just one battle. I can't even imagine that number. Excuse me," Papa whispered and disappeared inside the general store.

The shock of the news finally registered with those standing around on the porch of the general store. Reuben would have fought in that battle, and maybe other men from the area. Slowly, the crowd dispersed.

I turned and walked back into the general store, still shocked with the latest war report. I found Papa in the store room sitting on feed sacks with his face buried in his hands. Turning away quietly, I went back to the counter.

A few people who had been listening outside came in to get their mail but most just went home. Waiting for the list to appear in the Louisville Daily Journal of the latest fallen soldiers would be agonizing.

Mary Ellen stopped by the store after school and picked up the newspaper. Papa was still in the store room, so I decided to allow Mary Ellen to take the newspaper home and read it for herself. I knew she would be terribly upset, and if she was home, she could cry with no one watching her. At least that is what I told myself, but maybe I just didn't want to accept the sad news as truth and chose to avoid the subject. I felt guilty after she left but knew there was really nothing I could have said to soften the blow.

Angus walked in a few minutes after Mary Ellen left. "Were there any new reports in the paper today?"

Looking up I started to speak but nothing came out. Closing my mouth, my eyes filled with tears for the first time since hearing the news. It seemed it suddenly dawned on me the unbelievable number of young men who had fallen, and one of them could certainly be Reuben.

Angus hurried around the counter and wrapped me in his arms. "Virginia, what's happened?"

I slowly told him about the battle at Sharpsburg between sobs. Angus just let me cry and talk without saying a word. When I finished talking, he looked down at me. "Virginia, you do not know for certain that Reuben is among the casualties."

"I know, but even if he's not, there are thousands of families who are going to be touched by this one battle," I replied. "It's just so sad, Angus."

"Yes, it's very sad, Virginia," Angus agreed. Turning me loose, Angus stepped back. I wiped my tears and tried to gain control. When I looked up again, Angus whispered, "I'm so sorry, Virginia, but until we see Reuben's name in print, we have hope he survived."

"Hope," I repeated. It was the one thing I would cling to in the coming weeks.

When Papa and I returned home that night, Carter met us at the barn. He had made the final cutting of hay for the summer that day, to be loaded on wagons and put in the barn come Monday. "Any news about recent battles?" Carter asked as he entered the barn.

"It's not good, Carter," I spoke, sparing Papa from having to tell it twice. I knew Momma would ask him as soon as we entered the house.

The three of us walked to the summer kitchen together, since the weather was still quite warm for the end of September. Carter and I waited on the porch as Papa entered, allowing Papa and Momma time alone as Papa gave her the bad news.

I could hear my mother's sobs as Papa told her about the battle near Antietam Creek. I knew the sounds of mourning would soon be echoing all across the eastern half of the United States, as the names of young men began to appear on the list of fallen soldiers in newspapers across the United States.

I told Carter what the newspaper said about the battle and the mass number of casualties. We both shuddered when we thought about how close the Confederates had come to taking Washington.

Was Delmar right? Would there be bars and stars flags hanging in the North if the Confederates won? Then another sobering thought crossed my mind. If the South won, would slavery become legal in every state, including Indiana and the other slave-free states? The thought sent a shiver down my spine.

Chapter Eleven

September became October, ushering in autumn of 1862. Our family and Mary Ellen held our breath waiting for a letter from Reuben. Friday afternoons found the general store packed, as families came to peruse the list in the Louisville Daily Journal, hoping not to find a familiar name.

There had been no more reports of battles since Sharpsburg, which was a blessing. Everyone needed a break from the devastating news the war reports would bring.

The leaves turned their brilliant colors the third week of October but we hardly noticed. It seemed time was standing still. We kept busy at the store and with the late garden vegetables, filling our time with work so our minds did not have time to dwell on the fact that Reuben was still unaccounted for. His name had not appeared on the list of deceased soldiers, but a letter confirming he was alive and well had not arrived either.

"Mary Ellen, you're worrying yourself sick," I pointed out as she came to the store after school had let out for the day. I could tell the stress of not knowing if Reuben had survived the last conflict was taking a toll on her.

"I know," she admitted, "but I can't seem to put Reuben in God's hands. I know that's what I need to do, but it's so hard."

"I agree it's hard, but you need to find some way to do that. You've lost weight and the dark circles beneath your eyes say you're not sleeping well."

"Virginia, when I close my eyes, I see Reuben. I don't mean the quiet, handsome Reuben we all love; I see a mutilated Reuben struck down in the heat of battle. It's the same nightmare over and over. I'm so scared it means something."

I looked at Mary Ellen's tormented face. I sure hoped she was wrong; that what she was experiencing was just her fears coming to life in her dreams. "We still have hope, Mary Ellen. Reuben's name has not appeared on the casualty list."

"But there's been no letter," Mary Ellen pointed out. "The battle at Sharpsburg, Maryland happened over a month ago, and still Reuben has not sent word assuring us he's okay."

I reached out and gently put an arm around Mary Ellen's shoulders. "Maybe tomorrow a letter will come, Mary Ellen."

"Yes, tomorrow," Mary Ellen whispered.

When the mail arrived the next day, I hurried to dump it out and sort through it. Slowly picking up each piece of mail and placing it in the proper box, I prayed silently that there would be a letter from Reuben.

I noticed a letter addressed to Effie's parents but did not recognize the handwriting. It did not appear to be from Kris, for the script was too neat. When I was down to the last few pieces of mail, I picked up an envelope and gasped. Papa, who had been sitting around the table that held two checkerboards looking through the list of fallen soldiers, glanced up.

"What is it, Virginia?" Papa asked.

I held up the envelope I had just found. "You have a letter in today's mail, but it's not from Reuben."

Papa jumped up from his chair and came to the counter. Taking the envelope from my hand, he looked at the neatly flowing handwriting on the front. Tearing it open, he pulled one sheet of paper out and began to read. Tears gathered in his eyes as I watched him scan the short missive.

"Papa, what's it say?"

"Thank God, Virginia, your brother is alive!" The crowd in the general store turned in Papa's direction. A single clap began, joined by others, until a loud thumping of hands filled the room.

"Let's hear what the boy has to say," Delmar hollered. "Read the letter to us, Stephen."

Papa cleared his throat and began to read:

Dear Momma, Papa, Carter, Virginia, and Mary Ellen,

I am in a hospital in Maryland recovering from injuries I received while fighting at Sharpsburg. I'm sure you have read about the many soldiers who were killed and how close the Confederates came to invading Washington during this conflict. This was the first battle of the war fought on Northern soil, and hopefully the last.

One of the nurses has been so kind to pen this letter for me. I have received injury to my right hand and arm, along with a blow to the head. I was knocked unconscious, but thank God my fellow comrades did not leave me for dead. When the battle was over, they walked among the fallen soldiers looking for survivors. I was found and taken to the hospital, which is where I woke up. Things were confusing for a few days, but I have now regained full consciousness and realized I needed to get a letter home as quickly as possible.

I expect to recover enough to be of some use to the Union Army. I do not believe I will be able to hold and fire a weapon, but I'm sure there is something I can assist with. I have been spared for the time being and will continue to be of service to my country.

I love you all and ask that you continue to pray for me and all the soldiers who are wounded or fighting on the battlefield. Especially remember the families of the soldiers who will never again go home.

Love,

Reuben

Postscript: Mary Ellen, I will write to you personally, as soon as I'm able to do so.

Papa folded the letter and placed it back in the envelope. Words could not express the gratitude he felt. God had spared Reuben.

"Thank you all for keeping us in your prayers," Papa said to all the men gathered near the tables with the checkerboards on them. "Now, if you will excuse me, I must go share this good news with a young teacher, and then my wife and son, Carter. They have been waiting long enough."

"School will be out in ten minutes, Papa," I said.

"Perfect. I will be waiting outside when the time comes. Hold down the fort, Virginia!"

"Yes, Papa, go share the good news."

As Papa walked out the door, Angus and Effie walked in. They both came to check their mail and look for any new names added to the casualty list. I reached into the mailbox and retrieved the letter that had come for Effie's family. "Hi Effie, you have a letter today."

Effie walked to the counter and took the letter from my hand. "Well, it's certainly not from Kris. His handwriting is sloppy. This is very neat."

Peering down at the envelope now in Effie's hands, I gasped. "Effie, that handwriting looks the same as the script Reuben's letter was written in."

"You received a letter from Reuben?" Angus asked.

"Yes, just today," I answered. "He was injured in the battle at Sharpsburg and is recovering in a Maryland hospital."

Angus considered what I told him for a second. Suddenly, a smile spread across his face. "Will he be coming home?"

"No," I replied. "He will be going back to the Union forces when he has healed. His right arm and hand are injured, and he doesn't believe he will be able to hold and fire a gun, but he feels he can still help in some capacity."

"Where was your papa headed to?" Angus asked.

"He was headed to the school to share the letter with Mary Ellen; then home to tell Momma and Carter."

"For the first time since school started this year, I wish I was still a student," Effie said. "I would love to see Miss Smith's face when she hears the good news."

I laughed softly at Effie. "I thought maybe you would continue to go to school even after your sixteenth birthday since there was no threat of being whacked with a ruler."

Effie shook her head, "Goodness no, Virginia. Not everyone loves books like you do."

"I don't have time to attend school this year, but Mary Ellen is continuing to teach me some things. I still dream of one day being a teacher," I replied.

Angus winked and smiled. "And one day you will."

Effie stared down at the letter in her hand. "So, who wrote Reuben's letter?"

"A nurse at the hospital he is in. Maybe that letter is from Kris after all."

"I would just open it and find out, but Mother would be upset with me," Effie said. "I better hurry home with this. I'll see you later, Virginia."

Waving to my friend's retreating form, I hollered. "Bye Effie!"

Angus leaned on the counter and smiled. "Any mail for me today, Miss Virginia?"

Flashing Angus what my momma would call a flirty smile, I replied, "Why, yes there is, Mr. Zink." Reaching into the Zink family mailbox I pulled out several letters.

Angus sifted through the envelopes. "They appear to be orders for leather goods. Pa and I have been keeping quite busy for several months."

"That's a good thing, right?"

"Yes, a very good thing," Angus said, smiling. Leaning close he whispered near my ear. "It keeps my mind on work and my plans to join the Indiana home guard in January; and off the pretty girl at the general store."

Blushing crimson red, I turned to see if the men gathered around the table in the middle of the store had heard Angus. I knew Papa would know about Angus flirting with me by the next day if they had. Delmar would make sure of it. Thankfully, one of them had picked up the newspaper and was telling the rest of them points of interest he found there.

Angus straightened his mail and then his hat. With a wink and a wave, he sauntered toward the door. I watched him leave, wanting to call him back, but too embarrassed to do so.

January 25th, 1863 was three short months away. Angus would turn eighteen and would go to do his part for the war. I dreaded the day the closer it came.

On Sunday, Effie told me that the letter her family received had indeed been from Kris. Kris informed them he had also been injured at Sharpsburg. He had been part of the cavalry and had taken a tumble when his horse was shot from beneath him. The horse fell, crushing his left leg.

He would be coming home as soon as he was well enough to travel. He would be no good for the Union Army now, being he would never march or run again. Thankfully, the doctors believed he would be able to walk, but with a permanent limp.

After church on Sunday, Mary Ellen and Angus joined us for dinner. The talk was of Reuben, and Momma could not say enough times how thankful she was that he was alive.

I noticed Mary Ellen not saying much on the subject and

became concerned. When the dishes were washed, dried, and put away, Mary Ellen and I grabbed our guitars and headed to the summer kitchen's porch to sit and play for a while. Carter and Angus were close by taking turns swinging on the rope swing Papa had hung years ago from the big oak tree in the yard.

After we had played a few songs, I turned to face Mary Ellen. "Mary Ellen, are you not happy with the news about Reuben?"

"Goodness, yes Virginia. Why do you ask?"

"You didn't join in the conversation much at the dinner table. I just thought something was bothering you where Reuben is concerned."

"You are quite perceptive, Miss Virginia. Honestly, I'm so thankful he's alive I can't find words to express it, but there is one thing that bothers me. Why doesn't he just come home now?"

Looking at the hurt and confusion on Mary Ellen's face, I knew there were no words to explain why Reuben felt he must continue to be a part of the war. I would just have to show her.

Carter had just cleaned the horse stalls the day before, so it would not be too much of a chore to do what must be done. "Come with me, Mary Ellen," I said, placing my guitar on the table that was on the porch.

"Okay," Mary Ellen agreed, placing her guitar beside mine.

I walked to the barn and opened both doors to allow light in. Once inside the barn, I walked to Nellie's empty stall. Grabbing a pitchfork, I raked the fresh straw to the edges of the stall, revealing the trap door. I could see shock and confusion on Mary Ellen's face.

"What are you ladies up to?" Angus asked, stepping into the barn.

"I'm showing Mary Ellen why Reuben would choose to continue fighting with the Union Army, even after he was injured and could probably come home," I replied.

"Here, let me help you," Angus said, stepping into the stall. Reaching down, Angus yanked the heavy door up with one swift pull.

Looking into the earthen room, a flood of memories washed over me. A child dying, a baby named Joshua being born, scared slave women who had been raped by white owners, a new Christmas song, and countless others. Descending the ladder, I picked up the lantern that had been left in the room. Opening the tin box that contained matches, I struck one and lit the lantern, illuminating the small interior.

"What is this?" Mary Ellen asked.

"It's a station on the Underground Railroad," I explained.

Descending the ladder, Mary Ellen looked all around the room. "Your family hid runaway slaves here?"

"Yes, we did," I replied. "Angus and his family also ran a station."

"This is unbelievable," Mary Ellen whispered. "Were you ever caught?"

"No, thankfully we were not," Angus said, joining us in the room. "We had a few scares, but our involvement was never discovered."

"This is what Reuben meant when he wrote that he must complete the task," Mary Ellen said. "He had been helping to free the slaves long before this war broke out."

"Yes, he had," I whispered. "Do you understand why Reuben would choose to rejoin the Union Army when he heals?"

"Well, it's certainly much clearer," Mary Ellen said, still staring all around the room in amazement.

Carter came into the barn and peered through the trap door. "Are you all having a party down there without me?"

"No, we're just helping Mary Ellen understand Reuben's decision to continue fighting the war."

"He's just stubborn, plain and simple," Carter said.

I laughed, thankful that Carter could always lighten a mood. "Well, we all know that's true."

Blowing out the lantern, the three of us climbed out of the hidden room. Angus lowered the door and he and Carter raked the straw back over the floor. Walking back out into the sunshine filled fall day, I could see an understanding settle on Mary Ellen's face. I knew she respected and understood Reuben more now than ever before.

`✻✻✻✻✻✻✻✻✻✻✻✻✻✻✻✻✻✻✻✻✻✻✻✻✻✻✻✻✻✻✻

"President Lincoln has replaced McClellan as the Commander of the Army of the Potomac," Papa said as he perused the newspaper the third Friday of November. He was sitting in a chair near the woodstove that was in the center of the store, close to the table holding the checker boards.

"Who did he appoint commander this time?" Delmar asked

while studying the checker board for his next move.

"General Ambrose Burnside," Papa said.

"Ain't that the fourth commander since the war began?" the old man playing against Delmar asked.

"Well, let me think," Papa said. "First there was General McDowell, who was replaced after the embarrassing first battle at Bull Run. George McClellan took his place. So, General Burnside will make the third commander since the war began."

"You're gettin' senile," Delmar told his opponent.

"Maybe so, but I can still beat you at checkers," the opponent said, jumping Delmar's last three checkers in one move.

"You got me sidetracked talking about how many commanders had been in charge of the Army of the Potomac," Delmar objected.

The old man who had just beat Delmar rolled his eyes. "Delmar, you got more excuses than a woman. No offense, Virginia."

Looking over at the group of old men, I just laughed and continued to straighten shelves. "None taken," I replied.

****

The first Friday in December brought the piece of mail Mary Ellen had been waiting for. "Hey, Papa, look at this," I held up an envelope with Mary Ellen's name scrawled on it. It looked as though it had been written by a small child.

"Goodness, do you think that is from Reuben?" Papa asked, taking the envelope from my hand.

"That would be my guess," I replied. "I thought his handwriting was bad before, but that is appalling."

"There ya go, using a five dollar word," Delmar grumbled as he huddled close to the wood stove.

"Okay, it's hideous," I said, trying to hide my smile.

"Why can't ya just say it looks ugly?" Delmar asked. "It ain't that hard and then everyone would know what ya meant."

"You knew what I meant or you wouldn't have come up with a synonym for the word," I pointed out.

"Syno...snyo..syno what?" Delmar fumed.

"Synonym; it's a different word with the same meaning, like grumpy, grouchy, disagreeable; those are all synonyms that explain a person who is in a bad mood."

Delmar looked at Virginia trying to decide if she was taking a jab at him. "Anyone ever tell you you're wordy?"

I laughed out loud. In the past two years, Delmar had become the grandfather I didn't have. "Only you, Delmar, but you know you love me anyway."

Delmar harrumphed and turned back to the important conversation he had been having with the other old men; if the topic of moles and how to get rid of them could be considered important.

Papa handed the envelope back to me and I placed it in Mary Ellen's box. If the letter itself was as sloppy as the envelope, Mary Ellen had her work cut out for her.

When school was out for the day, Mary Ellen came to the store. I reached into her mailbox and withdrew the envelope as soon as she breezed through the door. "I have something for you," I said, holding up the envelope.

Mary Ellen rushed to the counter and took the proffered envelope. "Is it from Reuben? Goodness, this handwriting is appalling."

"That five dollar word has already been used today," Delmar informed Mary Ellen. "You'll have to dig up another."

Mary Ellen looked at me and raised her eyebrows. "What's with Delmar?"

"I used the exact same word to describe the handwriting. Just ignore him."

Mary Ellen laughed and headed to the store room to read her sloppy letter. "This handwriting is ghastly," she said loud enough for Delmar to hear as she passed through the door.

"And there it is," Delmar complained. "It's still just plain ol' ugly, no matter what word ya try to stick on it."

"I sure hope you win a checker game soon, Delmar," I said, "so you can quit being such a grump."

"Well, come and play a game with me, Virginia, and I'm sure my losing streak will end," Delmar said with a smile.

"I'm way too busy to play checkers, Delmar," I replied.

"Actually, your strategy is not nearly as good as your vocabulary."

"I will not deny that, Delmar," I said with a smile. "If I were a commander for the Union Army, I would be replaced, too."

This remark brought a laugh from all the men sitting around the general store. If there was one thing they all loved to discuss, it was how they would command the Union forces. They were all too old to fight in the war, but each had an opinion on how the war effort should be progressing.

Mary Ellen came out of the storeroom shaking her head. "That was very hard to read and I still don't know some of the words that were written. Reuben wrote it with his left hand because his right hand has not healed enough to be of much use. He is out of the hospital and will be preparing food for the Union Army of the Potomac as he continues to heal."

"Reuben is going to cook?" I asked in disbelief. "I hope they're not expecting much."

"At least he won't be on the front line fighting now," Mary Ellen said. "I'm thankful for that."

"Yes, me too," I agreed.

December turned cold and the discussion around the general store was whether or not battles would be fought through the cold months of winter. The previous winter had been pretty quiet, with few conflicts. However, the Louisville Daily Journal we received the third week of December reported a battle that had happened on December 13[th, 1862].

"The Army of the Potomac fought a battle in Fredericksburg, Virginia," Papa said as he glanced through the newspaper.

"How did that turn out?" Delmar asked.

"Not well," Papa said. "It states here that the Union lost over 12,000 men to death and injuries. The Confederates have claimed the battle a Southern victory."

"It appears General Burnside is not President Lincoln's man for the job, either," Delmar remarked.

"Maybe General Burnside will get another chance to prove himself," Papa said.

"With that many losses, President Lincoln can't wait for Burnside to prove himself," Delmar said. "The North needs to win some battles and soon."

"I can't say I disagree," Papa said. "This war has turned very ugly."

"Very ugly, indeed," Delmar added.

We celebrated Christmas Eve night by going to the church and lighting candles in remembrance of the fallen soldiers in our area. Effie and her whole family was in attendance, including her brother,

Kris.

Kris limped to the front with a lit candle and placed it among the others. Everyone knew that one of those candles could have easily represented him, and were thankful that he had been spared. How many young men would lay down their lives before the conflict ended? The numbers were already more than we could have ever fathomed.

After the service, Angus pulled me aside outside the church. "Walk down to the creek with me, Virginia. I have something I want to give you."

Walking the short distance, Angus stopped in front of me. Reaching into his pocket, he removed a small package. "Here, open it."

Tearing the brown paper from the small box, I lifted the lid to find a leather heart. "Angus, it's beautiful. Thank you so much."

"It has something written on it. You can read it when you get somewhere where there's light."

"What does is say?"

"It says "Please wait for me", Angus whispered. "I will join the home guard in one month. It would mean the world to me if I knew you are at home waiting for the war to end; and for my return."

"Of course, Angus, I will wait," I whispered.

Angus dipped his head and kissed my cheek. The only thing I wanted this Christmas was for the war to end. I did not want Angus to join the fighting, even if it was just the home guard. I knew the likelihood of any conflict taking place on Indiana soil was slim at best, but I wanted it all to end and the slaves to be set free. Would it really drag on much longer?

Chapter Twelve

The year 1863 blew in cold and blustery. The United States was no closer to being mended back together than it had been a year ago. The only significant change that came with the New Year was that President Lincoln made the Great Emancipation official. All slaves living in Confederate states were now free. The only problem was the slaves had no way of finding out they had been set free, unless one overheard it among their white owners.

The second week of January, Papa had a bit of good news to report to the men hunkered close to the wood stove in the general store. "The Louisville Daily Journal reported a Union victory," Papa announced.

"That's good news," Delmar said. "Where did the battle take place?"

"The battle was at Stone's River near Murfreesboro, Tennessee," Papa said. "The paper reports a fierce battle for three days with mass casualties for both sides. It seems neither side would back down until the Union, commanded by General Rosecrans, received supplies and reinforcements on January 3rd by train, causing General Bragg and the Confederates to retreat south. The Union now has control of middle Tennessee."

"Does the paper give the number of casualties or just state that they were mass?" Pastor David asked, leaning toward the stove to warm his hands after just entering the store only moments ago.

"Yes, the paper lists an approximate number of casualties. The Union lost over 12,000 men and the Confederates over 11,000."

"Goodness, how can anyone claim a victory after so many innocent young men were injured or their lives cut short?" Pastor David said, shaking his head in disbelief.

"Well, there was certainly not any winner," Delmar said, "but at least the Union now controls a good portion of Tennessee."

"Hopefully General Rosecrans can hold that position and push the Confederates further south," Papa said. "However, until the Union takes Richmond, the Confederates capital, this war will not end."

"Yes, or God forbid, the Confederates capture Washington," Delmar muttered.

The discussion of the war continued around the wood stove and each man had a solution to end the fighting. They all talked of strategy and how they would lead the Union troops to victory. I couldn't help but think that maybe Mr. Lincoln needed to visit our general store in the small town of Marengo to find his next commander of the Union forces. Of course, not a one of those men had ever shot anything other than a deer or small game. I would think looking into the eyes of a young man and pulling a trigger would be a difficult task, to say the least.

January 25th came, and two days later Angus left for Leavenworth to train for the Indiana Legion, which was what the home guard was called. Each county took care of their own guard and patrolled the southern Indiana border between Kentucky and Indiana. The only action that had been seen on the border so far was a small incident at Newburgh, Indiana, which was located several miles west of Leavenworth. I knew Angus was not far away, but it was disappointing that he would not be stopping in at the store every Friday. He would seek employment in Leavenworth so he could remain close to the southern border of the state.

****

"Well, now there has been four commanders of the Army of the Potomac," Papa said as he read the newspaper the first Friday of February.

"Who's the latest choice?" Delmar asked.

"General Joseph Hooker is replacing General Burnside," Papa said. "General Grant has been put in charge of the Army of the

West."

"Let's hope those two men can get the job done," Delmar said.

"I can't believe so many have failed to lead the Union army up until now," Pastor David added. "The Union always has more men in each battle, but still the Confederates seem to have the upper hand."

"I don't understand it either," Papa said. "Hopefully, General Hooker will prove to be the one the North has been waiting for."

The men gathered at the store continued to discuss the many leaders the Army of the Potomac had already had and what might have caused their downfall. There was really not much else to do on a frigid Friday in January in southern Indiana.

After a while, the conversation changed to the best way to keep chickens laying eggs through the winter, with everyone telling something they had tried. Delmar told of firing a gun over the chicken coop after the hens had roosted for the night, claiming it would scare the eggs out of the chickens. Another farmer claimed that hanging a lantern in the coop at four every morning until sunrise to provide more hours of light would encourage the birds to continue to lay. Adding black pepper to the feed seemed to be the most used technique and the one that required the least effort.

The month of February kept my family and me very busy. The maple trees were tapped the end of January and the sap was collected all through February. Papa had constructed a little building he referred to as the sugar shack, and that is where we cooked the sap into syrup. It was quite a chore keeping the fire going and the sap moving so it wouldn't scorch.

The store was slow due to the cold winter months, so Papa just ran it by himself throughout February. I helped Carter haul the buckets of sap from the trees to the shack and Momma took care of the rest. She had the cooking down of the sap to perfection. The syrup created on our farm was sold all year at the store, and on really productive years, Papa even took some to Leavenworth to sell when the weather was fit for travel again.

March found me back in the general store, as the area residents turned their mind toward gardening. Seed potatoes were purchased at the store, and the date to "plant root crops" was noted in the almanac. Every farmer knew that if one wasn't going to pay attention to the signs the Good Lord gave him, one should not be gardening. There was a time and a season for everything and the phases of the moon helped determine them.

I had looked for a letter from Angus since he had left, but so far none had come. On the second Friday of March I eagerly awaited the mail wagon, hoping this would be the day I received that first letter.

Thaddeus pulled up in front of the store at his usual time and I rushed out to hand him the outgoing mail as he handed me the mailbag for Marengo. As I began to sort the mail I nearly squealed with excitement. I was glad I had refrained, for I knew it would have sent Delmar off on one of his many rants. Stuffing the letter with my name on it written in Angus's familiar script into my apron pocket, where I always kept the leather heart he had given me, I continued to sort the mail.

Papa was seated at the checker board table, flanked by the regulars who hung out at the general store, reporting all the latest happenings from the newspaper. Carter, who had come to help at the store because there was nothing to do on the farm, was in a heated game of checkers against Delmar.

Delmar pointed to the right side of the checker board. "Boy, did you move your checker while I turned my head? Don't ya know it's not polite to move your checker when your opponent's head is turned?"

Carter just laughed at the puffed up old man. "I can't help it if you have to be gandering all about to see who is coming in and out of the store, Delmar."

"You're a cheater, Carter," Delmar fumed.

"It's your move, Delmar," Carter replied.

"Oh, this is something that's never happened before," Papa said.

"Your son cheating while he's playing checkers?" Delmar asked.

"No, not that," Papa said. "Carter used to cheat Reuben all the time just to see how riled up he could get him. I'm talking about what's in the newspaper. President Lincoln has issued a draft.

"A draft?" Delmar bellowed. "What do you mean a draft?"

"President Lincoln is requiring all young men in the North ages 20 to 45 to sign up and be a part of a draft. Single men will be selected first, and then married ones. The men who are picked will have to join the Union forces."

"Oh my," Delmar said. "How old are you, Carter?"

"I'll turn 20 December 7th," Carter replied.

"So I still have nearly a year to put up with your cheating," Delmar grumped.

Carter laughed loud and moved another checker when Delmar turned to look at Papa. "So, every man between the age of 20 and 45 has to sign up?" Delmar asked.

"Yes, but there are exceptions if someone is chosen," Papa said.

"Exceptions?" Carter asked. "What kind of exceptions?"

"A man could pay three hundred dollars and get someone else to go in his place," Papa said.

"Three hundred dollars!" Delmar exclaimed. "Who on earth has three hundred dollars to buy themselves out of the draft?"

"Rich people," Carter said.

"So, now this is a war to be fought by the poor young men of our country?" Delmar asked, pounding his fist on the table for emphasis. "And why would anyone step in and go to the war in someone else's place?"

"Maybe because the one they are stepping in for has offered them a large sum of money," Carter pointed out.

"Well, I have heard it all," Delmar continued. "Does this sound unfair to anyone else?" The heads around the general store bobbed in agreement with Delmar. To do anything else would result in being singled out. "By the way, how old are you, Stephen?"

"Forty-six," Papa replied. "I can't imagine how Elizabeth would take this news if she thought she might lose two sons and her husband to this war."

"You just made it under the wire," Pastor David remarked. "I turned forty-eight in January, which I thought was a bad thing, until now."

"I suppose my son will be signing up for this draft," Delmar said. "Glad they will choose from the single men before the married ones, though. I would hate to see my two granddaughters lose their daddy and me my only son."

"Yes, there have been enough families torn apart with sending single young men," Pastor David said. "I don't even want to think about delivering the devastating news that someone's husband and the father of their children have been killed."

"This war has certainly gone on too long and caused much more destruction than I could ever have imagined," Papa remarked.

"Any other news in that newspaper?" Delmar asked.

"Nothing else about the war," Papa replied.

"I shall finish this checker game then," Delmar announced, turning his attention back to the board. "What in tarnation is this? Carter, there is no way you have five kings!"

Carter smiled broadly and rose from the table. "I must go get some work done, now. We'll play again another day, Delmar."

"I wouldn't play another game of checkers with you if you were the last person left on the face of the earth, Carter Hensley!" Delmar bellowed.

"Same time tomorrow?" Carter asked as he headed to the store room.

"If you find the time," Delmar muttered.

When we returned home that night, I went to my room to store Angus' letter until I had time to read it. Entering the kitchen, I began to help Momma with supper preparations. As we sat down to eat, Papa blessed the food and we began to fill our plates. Papa cleared his throat to speak then changed his mind. I knew he was trying to find the courage to tell Momma about the draft but had obviously decided to wait a bit longer.

Finishing supper, I stood and cleared the table while Momma cut the vanilla custard pie she made for dessert. Placing the dirty dishes in the dishpan, I added hot water and soap so they could be soaking while I ate my dessert. Taking my place at the table, I savored the smooth, creamy pie. No one could make a custard pie like Momma. When everyone was finished, I gathered the dessert plates and began to wash the dishes.

Papa cleared his throat again. "That was a wonderful meal and the custard pie was even better than usual, Elizabeth."

"Why, thank you, Stephen. Now, please tell me what it is you're having such a hard time spitting out."

Papa smiled and shook his head. "I should know by now that I cannot hide anything from you.

"Yes, you should," Momma said. "Now, what is it?"

"The newspaper stated that President Lincoln has issued a draft order," Papa said

"A draft order?" Momma asked. "What do you mean?"

"Every man age 20 to 45 must register to have their name put into a pool of names," Papa explained. "The names of the single men will be drawn first. If they still need more men to fight, names of married men will be drawn next. They desperately need men to fight for the North."

"Oh, Stephen, how awful," Momma said. "Young men will be forced to go to war, whether they want to help the cause or not?"

"Yes, they will have to go," Papa said.

"We can only hope this war ends before December," Momma said, already thinking about Carter's twentieth birthday.

"I would like to see this war end tomorrow," Papa said wearily. "Too many young men have died already, in the North and the South."

Finishing the dishes, I went to my room, leaving Papa and Momma discussing the draft. There was not enough daylight left to read my letter from Angus, so I lit a lamp. Settling close to the light, I opened the long awaited correspondence. It had been over a month since I had seen or heard from Angus.

Dear Virginia,

I have been accepted into the Indiana Legion for Crawford County and am now learning my duties. It seems each county has their own set of rules and uniforms. Governor Morton chooses who is in charge, but other positions are voted on within the militia after that.

One rule that every Indiana Legion must follow is there must be at least forty-five members. As far as weapons are concerned, I have not been issued one. It seems there is a shortage of guns, which you are already aware of since your father has not been able to obtain any to sell at the store for quite some time. I have constructed a leather whip for myself to use if necessary. I don't know if it will ever be of any use, but at least I have something.

I miss seeing you every Friday at the store and our once-a-month Sunday dinners. I hope you're learning some new songs on the guitar while I am gone. I will expect to hear them when I am able to return.

I must be honest with you, Virginia. I feel strongly that I should join the actual Union Army. I know I'm my parents only son, and you would prefer I not, but I believe it's something I must do. I will give the war until July 4th, four months from now, to end. If it continues, I will enlist and proudly go to fight for the cause. Please, understand my desire to do this, just as Reuben feels it's his duty to continue to help the cause, even though he has suffered a debilitating injury.

You may write to me using the town name of Fredonia. I am working in the lumber yard in Leavenworth, but have rented a room from an elderly couple in Fredonia. I will anxiously wait to hear from.

Love,

Angus

Folding the letter and wiping my tears, I placed it back in its envelope. In one day I had been forced to accept the possibility that both Carter and Angus would be joining Reuben in the fight to mend the dividing line that now cut across our country, known as the Mason-Dixon Line. Angus would join the Union forces after July 4th, and Carter would be forced to sign up for the draft in December. The chances of Carter's name not being drawn were slim, at best. I placed the letter in my top dresser drawer, hoping to add more as time went on.

March, after coming in like a lamb, went out like a lion. Fifteen inches of snow fell in one night. Papa decided to not even go to town and open the store. No one in their right mind would be out in such terrible weather. Delmar would probably be the only one who came to the store all day, and we all knew he wasn't in his right mind.

The only good thing about a March snowstorm was that it didn't stay on the ground long. The temperature warmed rapidly, and two days later everything was beginning to green up. The snow made an abundance of mushrooms pop up and Carter and I found the most we ever had through the month of April.

Mary Ellen had continued to receive letters weekly from Reuben since there were no battles in progress throughout the winter and into early spring of 1863. Each letter was a bit more legible, as Reuben grew accustomed to writing with his left hand.

I assumed the Army of the Potomac, which Reuben's regiment usually fought with, were preparing for the next move under the fourth commander since the war began, Joseph Hooker. The fact that President Lincoln had not been able to find the right man to lead the Army of the Potomac surely added to the duration of the war.

Angus and I wrote to each other each week, keeping one another informed about what was happening. I told him all about the store and anything I thought he might find of interest from around Marengo. He told me all about Leavenworth and the Ohio River.

I had never been to Leavenworth, though Papa made a few trips there each year. From what Angus wrote, it must be a busy place. There were boats coming and going, some hauling supplies while others brought passengers. Zebulun Leavenworth ran a stagecoach line that would take people from the docks at Leavenworth all the way to Indianapolis. Of course, I had seen the stagecoach pass through Marengo on its way north.

There were several businesses in Leavenworth, including a button factory that used shells from the Ohio River to create the buttons, and a skiff building shop. Angus also told of a giant hay press where hay was pounded into huge bales then put on boats and sent down the Ohio River. The more he wrote about the area, the more I desired to see this riverfront town.

The third Friday in May brought news of the first major battle of 1863. Papa took a seat out on the porch of the general store and everyone gathered around to hear the results. Mary Ellen and I went to listen, too, because there would be no one buying anything until they heard the war report, nor were they interested in retrieving their mail.

"The battle took place at Chancellorsville in Virginia on May 1st through the 4th," Papa began as he scanned the article. "Oh, my, this is not good."

"Well, just spit it out, Stephen," Delmar fussed. "We're packed on this porch like a pig in a poke. I miss the old days when only the regulars came here to discuss important topics."

Papa glared at Delmar for a moment, then continued reading the article so he could give all the statistics. "Seems the North had 130,000 soldiers and the South had about 60,000."

"Lands sakes a living, please tell me the North won," Delmar bellowed. "Going to battle with twice the man power would certainly give you the upper hand. How could you possibly lose if you had 70,000 more men than the enemy?"

"Delmar, do you want to hear the report or not?" Papa asked curtly. Papa was very slow to anger but Delmar had struck a nerve, and he knew it.

"Sorry, Stephen," Delmar muttered. "Please, tell us what the article says."

Papa cleared his throat and began again. "The Confederates suffered 13,000 casualties in the battle and the Union had 17,000. The newspaper reports General Hooker retreated, which made the battle a victory for the Confederates."

"Can President Lincoln not find a commander who will stand and fight?" one of the men listening to the report commented.

"It appears not," Papa said. "The Confederate General Stonewall Jackson was mortally wounded during the battle and later died on May 10th, but it appears enemy fire is not to blame. Somehow one of his own soldiers injured him."

"Well, if the North is going to win this war, we may have to depend on the poor aim of the Confederate soldiers. Maybe one of the soldiers will take out Robert E. Lee the next time," Delmar said, disgusted that the Union could lose a battle with the odds so clearly in their favor.

"They managed to kill or injure 17,000 Union soldiers in this battle," Papa pointed out. "I believe their aim is just fine."

"You make a good point," Delmar muttered.

The porch began to clear as those gathered headed into the store to check their mailboxes, discussing the Chancellorsville battle as they went. I hurried in to sort through the mail bag, stuffing a letter to me from Angus in my apron pocket to read later.

I could not help but feel anxious about the way the war was progressing. If the Union didn't get it together soon, the United States just might become the Confederate States of America, as the southern government was named.

"The report on the latest battle was terrible," Mary Ellen said, "but I can't help but feel relieved that Reuben was not on the front line. Is it wrong to hope his right hand never heals enough for him to grasp a gun with it again?"

Handing Mary Ellen Reuben's latest correspondence, I replied, "No, I don't think it's wrong to hope for that. Until the Army of the Potomac gets a commander who can come up with a good strategy and stand and fight, the Union troops have no hope of victory. Besides, Reuben made it clear that his injuries would prevent him from ever being of use on the battlefield."

"At least his handwriting is improving," Mary Ellen said, holding up the envelope. "He can almost write as well with his left hand as he did with his right."

"That's not saying much," I replied with a smile.

When we returned home that evening, we ate a simple supper of fried zucchini, ham slices, and baked potatoes. Momma had been busy in the garden all day. Carter had spent the day planting the field corn. Papa gave the report again on the battle at Chancellorsville as we ate on the porch of the summer kitchen.

"We don't need a draft," Carter said. "We need a good commander for the Army of the Potomac. The Union had over twice as many men for that battle, and General Hooker still retreated."

"I would venture to say commander number five is on the way," Papa replied wryly.

"Why has it been so hard to find a good commander for the Army of the Potomac?" Momma asked.

"I have absolutely no idea," Papa said. "One thing I do know, if the right commander is not found, the North could very well lose this war. What then?"

"The South will keep their slaves and our country will be divided," Carter said, "or worse, the North will fall under the power of the Confederacy."

"That's a very scary thought," Momma said with a sigh.

When the meal was finished, I hurried to wash the dishes in record time. Papa and Momma had walked to the garden to mark its progress. Knowing this would be my only chance, I headed toward the maple tree as quickly as possible. With its full canopy of leaves, I would be hidden once I made it past the first few branches. I knew at the age of seventeen, which I had become last month, I should really put such childish acts aside, but I couldn't. I loved that tree, and the letter from Angus was burning a hole in my pocket. I wanted to read it perched in the maple tree. Reaching my favorite high limb, I settled in and pulled the letter from my pocket.

Dear Virginia,

May has brought beauty to Leavenworth, as I'm sure it has to Marengo. The most beautiful thing is to sit on the cliff above the river near Fredonia and watch the fields take shape in Kentucky. The farms there are beautiful. I can see the wheat heading out in some of the fields while the earth has just been turned in others. I'm sure corn will begin to appear in those newly plowed fields in just about a week. The scene is making me homesick.

I will be returning to Marengo at the end of June. At this point, I'm sure the war will still be on and Union soldiers will be needed. If it weren't so, President Lincoln would not have gone to the drastic measure of issuing a draft for the first time in our country's history. I know I am not of the age required to sign up for the draft, but I am of the age to choose on my own. I will spend the 4th of July with you and leave a few days later. I have already informed the Indiana

Legion of my choice so they can be looking for a replacement.

I must hurry and finish this letter for I have been so busy with my job and the Indiana Legion that I have had little time for anything else. The mail coach will leave from Leavenworth shortly and I want this letter to be on it. I will see you in just a little over a month. Please, take care.

Love,

Angus

Postscript: While I was dropping off this letter, I saw the report on the battle at Chancellorsville, Virginia. I'm sure your Papa will read it aloud at the general store. The Union has to get better plans for battle if they hope to win this war.

I read the letter one more time then put it back in my apron pocket. Looking out over our farm, I could see Momma and Papa walking along the creek in deep conversation. I could not see Carter anywhere and assumed he was in the barn. The sun was dipping below the ridge as evening settled over our southern Indiana farm. Soon, the frogs would start their nightly song as the fireflies danced to the music. I knew I lived in a very small place on the map, and some might call it a backwoods town, but it was home; and I loved it here.

"If I climb to the limb you're on, will you let me rest a minute before we race back down?" Carter hollered from the ground under the Maple.

"Come on up," I hollered back down.

Carter ascended the tree with the smoothness and agility of a cat. When he reached the limb I was on he smiled and asked, "You ready to lose?"

"Catch your breath, Carter," I replied. "I don't want to hear any excuses about being tired after the climb up causing you to lose."

"The view is really spectacular from up here," Carter said, looking out over the farm.

"The best place on earth," I replied with a smile.

Carter sat on the limb below me and we watched the last rays of light dance across the farm, throwing shadows near the woods that bordered the fields. Deer emerged at the edge of the hayfield and began to graze. An owl hooted from a nearby tree, nearly startling us from our perch. The chickens slowly entered their house for the night and began to fuss over which roost would be theirs. When the first firefly lit the late evening sky, Carter got to his feet.

"Ready to go, Virginia?"

"Yep, it's time," I replied.

"Let's just enjoy the climb down," Carter suggested. "Who knows when we will get to do this again?"

And there it was. Carter was telling me something without saying the words. He would not be waiting until December to see if he was drafted. I wanted to ask when he would enlist, but I could not get the words past the lump in my throat. Slowly, and maybe for the last time, Carter and I climbed down out of the maple tree together.

Chapter Thirteen

June of 1863 came, and it grew very busy on the farm and at the general store. Mary Ellen could be found at the counter of the general store assisting customers and adding up their purchases six days a week. I helped Momma at home as needed, and at the store on days Momma and I had the gardening caught up.

Carter laid down the first cutting of hay on June 5th, a few weeks later than normal. The late snow had stunted the growth of the grasses and clover just a bit. Papa kept the shelves stocked and made the weekly trip to Milltown for supplies.

There had been no more reports of battles since the Confederate victory at Chancellorsville. Everyone wondered what move Mr. Lincoln would make next, and if would he appoint another commander.

"I sure thought President Lincoln would have found a new commander by now," Delmar said as Papa looked through the paper the second Friday in June. There were several men gathered on the porch, but most had left after they discovered there were no new reports on the war.

"I did, too," Papa admitted.

"Well, look who it is," Delmar said, pointing to the two young men riding up to the hitching post at the general store.

I walked to the screen door to look out and see who had arrived. All porch conversations could be heard throughout the warm months if you wanted to take the time to listen. Peering out the door,

I recognized Kris and Kirk, Effie's brothers. Kirk quickly dismounted, but it took Kris more time, due to his injured leg.

"What brings you young men to Marengo?" Papa asked.

"Came over to help Pa cut some cedar trees into post," Kirk said. "He's planning to build some fence around the acreage he cleared last winter."

"Thought we would stop and beat Delmar in a game of checkers before heading home," Kris added.

"You couldn't beat me at checkers if I allowed you to start the game with all kings," Delmar huffed.

"Well, set'em up, old man," Kris said. "Let's just see who wins. Don't give me the benefit of starting with kings, either."

Delmar and Kris began their game of checkers, and Kirk sat down to talk with Papa. I heard Kirk ask if there were any new reports in the newspaper Papa was holding before I went back to help Mary Ellen. She was assisting a woman customer with some fabric for a new dress. There would be buttons and thread to buy, too. I offered to cut the fabric while Mary Ellen matched the thread and buttons to the chosen piece of cloth.

"You just get back on that horse and leave!" I heard Kirk holler. "You're not welcome here."

Mary Ellen and I rushed to look out the screen door to see who Kirk was hollering at, leaving the customer at the counter. A man I had never seen before was tying his horse to the hitching post. Ignoring Kirk's commands, the man sauntered onto the porch. Kirk and Kris both rose to their feet, their faces daring the man to come closer.

"Mister, I can see from the pin you're wearing that you are a supporter of the South," Papa began. "This young man has recently returned from the war injured. He will never walk without a limp the rest of his life." Papa placed a hand on Kris's shoulder, whether to calm him or show support I did not know.

"It's a free country," the man replied. "I reckon I can go wherever I want."

"You best get back on your horse and move on down the road," Kirk said through clenched teeth.

"I'm going into this store to look around," the man replied, taking another step toward the door.

Papa stepped between the man and the door of the general

store. Mary Ellen and I took a step back and bumped into the woman we thought was still standing at the counter. She had come up behind us to see what was happening. "I own this general store, and I will not be selling anything to you, so there's no point in looking around."

"Like I said before, it's a free country," the man said, taking another step.

In one swift move, Kirk stepped in front of the man, picked him up by his shirt and threw him from the porch. The man jumped to his feet and came at Kirk, mad as a wet hen. The two men began to throw punches, Papa hollering for them to stop while Delmar and Kris cheered Kirk on.

When blood began to mix with the dirt on the road, Papa knew the fight had gone on long enough. Opening the door to the general store and pushing past us, he stormed to the counter and reached under it, coming up with a gun. I stared in shock as Papa bolted back out the door, stepped off the porch, and fired the gun in the air. The fighting stopped abruptly.

"Get on your horse now," Papa said to the man. "The next shot will not be in the air and there is not a soul here who would even take the time to bury you."

The man staggered to his horse and untied it. Leading the horse a few feet down the road, the man finally mounted it and road away. Papa lowered the gun and looked around.

The first sound that broke the silence was Delmar clapping his hands, which was quickly joined by everyone else. Papa had just become a hero.

Papa bent down and picked up the copper penny badge that had been torn from the man's shirt during the fight. Looking at it, he decided to take it into the store. Placing the gun back under the counter and laying the pin beside it, Papa went back out on the porch.

"Way to run that Copperhead off," Delmar said.

Stepping out onto the porch, I asked, "What's a Copperhead, besides being a poisonous snake?"

"A Copperhead is someone who lives in the North but supports the South," Papa said. "They wear that copper penny badge so everyone knows their position on the war. If they support the South, they need to move there. They're venomous, just like the snake they are named for."

"Couldn't have said it better myself," Kris said. "Delmar, it's your turn to move."

"I'm so shook up I don't know if I can think straight to finish this game," Delmar said.

"No excuses. Make your move so I can continue to beat you," Kris said.

"Seems you didn't strike your head when you fell from the horse," Delmar muttered. "You still play a mean game of checkers."

"Why, thank you, Delmar," Kris said. "I think you almost gave me a compliment."

"Well, I sure didn't mean to," Delmar grumped, studying the board for his next move.

Delmar and Kris finished their checker game, with Kris turning out to be the winner. The two young men said their good-byes and headed home, Kirk proudly sporting a swollen lip and black eye.

I watched out the screen door the rest of the day, afraid the Copperhead might return. When we returned home that night, Carter was upset that he hadn't been at the store to see the action.

All was quiet around Marengo the next day and even into the next week, until Thursday. A young man came to the general store and rushed onto the porch. "Have any of you seen Union soldiers?" he asked.

"Union soldiers?" Delmar asked. "Here in Marengo?"

"Yes," the young man replied. "I'm part of the Indiana Legion for Crawford County. We have received word that a Confederate spy by the name of Thomas Hines came across the Ohio River with over 60 men dressed as Union soldiers. Hines is looking for southern sympathizers. We don't know exactly what his plans are, but we know he traveled north from near Derby, Indiana. Some of the men from the Indiana Legion have spread out searching for Hines and his men, while the rest remain in groups along the Ohio River, in case he tries to cross back into Kentucky from a Crawford County shore."

"We haven't seen any Union soldiers around here," Papa said. "If we do, I'll make sure to get word to the Indiana Legion."

"Thank you," the young man replied. "I need to keep searching. Be careful if you see this group of men."

"We will," Papa said, "and thanks for warning us."

"Confederate soldiers; right here amongst us!" Delmar exclaimed.

"Yes," Papa said. "Everyone should go home and warn your family and neighbors. Sixty Confederate soldiers is quite a threat."

The store and porch cleared faster than I could have imagined. Mary Ellen had left at noon because we had been slow. Carter had returned from Milltown at noon and could help out in Mary Ellen's place if we got busy. "I'm going to go tell Mary Ellen and your mother of the danger," Papa said. "Carter, please keep a close watch. If those Confederates show up, bolt the door and you and Virginia hide. Tell everyone who comes in about this Thomas Hines and his men."

"Okay Papa," Carter said.

Papa left the store riding Nellie and I turned to Carter. "Do you think the Confederates will come through Marengo?"

"I have no idea," Carter said.

Twenty minutes after Papa left, Effie's nephew, Charles, came running into the store. He was out of breath and so excited he could hardly talk. I could not imagine why Charles, who lived in Valeene, was at the general store alone. He was only twelve years old.

"They're here. I mean they're coming there. I mean they're there and coming here. Momma told me to come here first then go to Grandmother's house. You need to warn the town!" Charles hollered, not making any sense. After he spoke, he turned to run from the store.

"Whoa, Charles," Carter said, stepping in front of him. "Now, slow down and try again. Who's coming?"

Charles took a big gulp of air. "The Confederates are in Valeene. They are in Union uniforms, but we know they're Confederates. Someone from the Indiana Legion stopped early this morning to warn us about them. Momma seen them up the road at Jack's house and sent me to tell you all. The poor horse I rode here is all done in."

"Okay, Charles," Carter said. "Are they heading this way?"

"Yes," Charles said.

"They are probably going to cross back into Kentucky and know the Indiana Legion is on their trail," Carter said, mostly to himself.

"I must go to Grandmother's and warn her, Grandfather and Aunt Effie," Charles said.

"Charles, that horse can't take another step," Carter said,

gazing out the door of the general store at the poor beast. "Let's put him in the corral out back and I'll take you to Aunt Effie's on my horse."

"Okay, but please hurry," Charles said.

Carter went outside and led the horse Charles had ridden to Marengo to the corral. Putting a bridle on Clyde, Carter led him back to the front of the store. Entering the store, he looked into Charles's scared face, "Go ahead out and stand by the horse. I'll be there in just a minute." Turning to me, Carter said, "Virginia, bolt the door behind us."

"Okay, Carter," I replied.

When Carter reached the door, he stopped abruptly. Turning around, he came back to the counter and reached beneath it. Thinking he was going to take the gun, I came up behind him. To my surprise, the only thing in Carter's hand was the badge the Copperhead had lost the day he and Kirk fought.

"Carter, what are you planning to do with that pin?" I asked.

"I'm going to help the Confederates get back across the Ohio River, Virginia. Remember; bolt the door behind me, though I don't believe the Confederates will be stopping here, unless my plan fails."

With that, Carter ran out the door. In one smooth, fluid move, he mounted Clyde bareback. Reaching down, he grabbed Charles's hand and pulled him up behind him. All that was left was a cloud of dust as Carter urged his horse into a run. Staring after them, the question I had in my mind never got past my lips. What was my brother up to?

An hour later, Papa returned to the store, Momma in tow. Momma had ridden behind Papa on Nellie to the store. Momma got off Nellie at the front door while Papa went around back to put the horse in the corral behind the store. "Where's Carter?" Momma asked as I unbolted the door and let her in.

"He took Charles to Effie's house," I replied.

"What was Charles doing here?"

"He came to warn us that Thomas Hines and over 60 Confederate soldiers, dressed as Union soldiers, are in Valeene."

"Goodness, that's not far away at all. Were they headed this way?" Momma asked.

"Yes," I replied.

Just then the door opened and Papa came in. "Whose horse is

in our corral and where is Clyde?"

"Charles, Effie's nephew, rode the horse to the store. He came to warn us that Thomas Hines is in Valeene," I repeated.

"So, where is Charles?" Papa asked, looking around. "And where is Carter?"

"Carter took Charles to Effie's house on Clyde. The horse in the corral couldn't take another step when Charles got here on it. Carter grabbed the Copperhead badge and told me he had a plan," I explained.

"What on earth is he going to do with that badge?" Momma fretted.

"I have no idea," Papa said. "I'm sure he has some kind of plan. I just hope it doesn't get him killed."

"You should try to catch up with him, Stephen," Momma suggested.

"Elizabeth, I have no idea where he is at."

"Carter said he was going to help the Confederates get back across the Ohio River," I said. "Why would Carter help the Confederates, Papa?"

Papa looked confused for a minute then chuckled quietly. "Carter is not really going to help them, Virginia. Wait until he comes back. I believe he will have quite a story to tell."

"You could ride toward Leavenworth, Stephen. That is probably where Carter's taking Hines and the Confederate soldiers and he might need your help."

"Elizabeth, it would be best if I stay right here. If I was to find Carter, it would put him in more danger. Hopefully, he has convinced Thomas Hines and his men that he truly is a Copperhead. If they find out he's lied to them, they will surely kill him."

"Maybe you should warn the Indiana Legion at Leavenworth," Momma said, not giving up on the idea of Papa going after Carter.

"Okay, Elizabeth, I will ride to Leavenworth. We will close the store and I will take you and Virginia home, first," Papa finally agreed.

"There is no time to waste taking us home," Momma said. "Take the horse Charles rode here to Effie's house and make sure Carter got the child there safely. They may have heard more information about Hines and the Confederate soldiers by now."

"Okay," Papa said. "Bolt the door when I leave."

"Be careful, Stephen," Momma said, embracing him quickly.

Papa left the store again riding Clyde and leading the horse Charles had ridden. Momma bolted the door and she and I went upstairs to watch out the windows. I had never thought the threat of Confederate soldiers marching through our little rural Indiana town would ever become a reality, but now Momma and I had locked ourselves in the general store and were watching for their approach. I knew now I had only had a false sense of security.

Five minutes later, we watched Papa pass the store again and head up Water Street. He would cross the bridge across Whiskey Run creek and head south toward Leavenworth.

Fifteen minutes after Papa left Marengo, a cavalry of Confederate soldiers, dressed in Union uniforms, came trotting down the Leavenworth Paoli road from Valeene. They turned left on Water Street and continued in the same direction as Papa.

Momma and I could see Carter riding in the front of the group next to a man I could only assume was Thomas Hines. Momma gasped and I could see from her expression that she wanted to run out and rescue Carter, but knew it would not be a wise thing to do. Instead we just watched them ride by and prayed for Carter's safety.

As darkness fell, Momma and I realized that Carter and Papa would not be returning soon. We fried eggs that we had brought to sell at the store, for our supper. The wood cook stove was still in the upstairs from when Momma and Papa had lived above the store, providing a place to cook our supper.

By the next morning, Carter and Papa were still not home. Mary Ellen and Effie showed up at the store together to check on Carter and share the latest news.

"Thomas Hines and his men burned a house to the ground in Valeene," Effie announced as she bounded into the store.

Momma gasped and turned pale. Effie still had not learned how to start a conversation with any tact whatsoever. "How do you know this, Effie?"

"When my brother-in-law came to get Charles last night, he told us all about it," Effie informed us. "It seems Hines and his men were hungry and demanded food from someone in Valeene. The woman of the house refused to feed the men and they set her house afire."

"Did she escape?" I asked, thinking what a ruthless man

Thomas Hines must be.

"Yes, she ran out the back door to a neighbor's," Effie said. "After that, the Confederates continued south down the Leavenworth-Paoli Road. We have no idea where they are now. Have you heard from Carter?"

"We watched the Confederates pass the store yesterday with Carter riding in the lead with Thomas Hines. Neither Carter or Papa has returned," I said.

"I hope they're okay," Mary Ellen said.

"We pray they are, too," Momma replied.

"I'll stay and help you run the store until they get back," Mary Ellen offered.

"Thank you, Mary Ellen, that will be quite helpful," Momma said.

"I'll stay and wait for Carter," Effie chimed in then smiled sheepishly and added, "and of course help out with the store."

I looked good and hard at Effie. Had I been missing something? Thinking back, I realized that when Effie came to get her family's mail on Friday, she always asked if Carter was there. On several occasions, Effie had gone to talk to Carter before leaving, if he happened to be at the store. "What knowledge do you have about this store?" I asked Effie.

"None, but I know how to sew and I can match thread and fabric better than most," Effie pointed out. "I will help if someone comes in wanting to buy those things."

"Oh," I said, smiling big at my best friend. "You do realize Carter is nothing but a pest, don't you, Effie?"

"You've said the same about me," Effie replied with a smile.

I smiled back. "Yes, so I have."

Papa and Carter returned to the store about noon. By that time, the porch of the general store was overflowing with townsfolk waiting to get an update on Hines and his men. The story had spread quickly about Carter planning to trick the Confederates with the Copperhead badge and that Papa had went to Leavenworth to inform the Indiana Legion of what he knew. As Carter and Papa stepped onto the porch, Momma hugged them both at the same time, tears of joy streaming down her cheeks.

"I'm so thankful you are both safe," Momma cried.

"What did you do?!" I asked Carter, wanting to smack him

instead of hug him.

"I told you, Virginia, I went to help Thomas Hines cross the Ohio River," Carter said with a smile. "Hines was more than happy to have assistance from a Copperhead."

"So, you convinced the Confederates you were on their side with that Copperhead badge?" I asked. "Momma and I watched you pass the store riding next to Thomas Hines."

"Yep," Carter said smiling. "I took them to the deepest part of the Ohio River to cross; a place called Little Blue Island. The Indiana Legion had caught up with the Confederates and as they entered the deepest part of the river, the men from the Legion began to fire on them. Three Confederates were killed and several were taken prisoner. The only disappointing fact is that Thomas Hines escaped. The Indiana Legion is concerned the Confederates will come back for the prisoners."

"I reached Leavenworth and warned the Indiana Legion that Hines and his men were headed toward Leavenworth. They didn't have much time to prepare before the Confederates showed up. Some local men jumped in to help fight against them. The Indiana Legion is using the Methodist church as a prison, until the Confederates can be moved to Indianapolis where a prisoner of war camp is," Papa said, supplying us with the part he played in the capture of the Confederates.

"Carter, how did you know about Little Blue Island?" Effie asked.

"I heard someone talking about it when Papa and I were at Leavenworth picking up supplies one time," Carter replied. "Papa and I went to look at it that day and I remembered exactly where it was located."

"Well, Carter, I almost forgive you for cheating at checkers," Delmar said. "Your devious ways paid off this time."

"I knew it had to come in handy at least once in my life," Carter said, smiling at Delmar. Reaching into his shirt pocket, I thought Carter was going to pull out the Copperhead badge. Instead, he removed a small, folded piece of paper. "Here, Virginia, this is for you."

Extending my hand, Carter placed the piece of paper in my palm and winked. Unfolding the paper, I recognized Angus' handwriting immediately. All it said was *"See you in a week. Love,*

Angus." I refolded the paper and put it in my apron pocket. I would add the short missive to the stack of letters in my dresser drawer. Next week could not come soon enough.

****

Angus returned to Marengo in late afternoon on Friday, June 26th. The first place he stopped was the general store. We were busy, so I did not get to talk to him, except for a few words shared while I handed him the mail out of his family's mailbox.

"Please, come to dinner on Sunday," I said. "We will have time to talk then."

"I will," Angus replied. "I must go tell my parents and younger sisters of my decision to enlist in the Union Army. I hope it goes well."

"They will be upset," I replied. "There is no good way to share such heartbreaking news."

"I know," Angus said, gathering the mail, "but I must do this."

"I understand," I whispered. "See you on Sunday."

Angus walked out of the general store and I wanted to run after him, drop to my knees, and beg him to stay. There had been so many young men killed already and the war did not appear to have resolved anything to this point. I was even beginning to question if President Lincoln could come up with a plan and a commander to turn the war in the Union's favor.

Refusing to give in to tears, I turned to gather mail from a box for another customer. I wished I could take comfort in the fact that Carter would remain safe at home, but I knew that he too would soon announce he was joining the Union army. This war was snatching away ones I held dear to my heart and there was not one thing I could do to stop it.

****

As we finished dessert after Sunday dinner, Angus made his announcement to my family. "I will be enlisting in the Union Army on July 6th. I feel it's time I go and help the cause."

"Oh, Angus, your mother must be devastated," Momma said.

"She is sad, yes, but she understands," Angus replied.

Carter cleared his throat. I looked up, knowing what he was getting ready to say. The urge to run outside and climb to the top of the maple tree where I could not hear this discussion was great. Instead, I looked deep into his eyes and nodded. He should just get this over with.

"Would you like some company when you go to enlist?" Carter asked Angus.

Angus looked at Carter with surprise. "You would ride all the way to New Albany with me?"

"I mean, I will enlist with you," Carter said.

Momma gasped and Papa took her hand. "Carter, you won't be twenty until December. Please, just wait for the draft," Momma pleaded.

"Momma, you know I will be chosen immediately when I register," Carter said. "If I do it this way, I will already have my training in before winter. It's what I feel I must do."

"Elizabeth, this has to be Carter's choice," Papa said. "He's a man now. We cannot keep him from doing this."

Silent tears streamed down Momma's face. Mary Ellen and I dabbed at the ones forming in our own eyes. Two more fine young men would lay their lives on the Mason-Dixon Line. That Line was not just dividing our country; it was dividing families, separating them sometimes forever. At that moment, I hated slavery more than I had ever hated anything in my entire life.

"I think we should have a special celebration for July 4th," Papa announced, attempting to lighten the moment. "Let's all take a trip to Paoli for the occasion. I hear they have the most magnificent courthouse. They will probably even have fireworks."

"That sounds really fun," Carter said, jumping at the chance to change the subject. "None of us has ever made the trip to Paoli. Have you ever been to Paoli, Angus?"

"No, I sure haven't," Angus said. "I would love to see the courthouse I have heard so much about and a fireworks demonstration."

"Then it's settled," Papa said. "We will leave next Saturday morning at six. We should reach Paoli by nine or ten, if all goes well. We will make a day of it."

I could see what Papa was trying to do. He would use our country's Independence Day to take our minds off the fact that Carter and Angus would be leaving two days later. It would also help remind all of us what the war was being fought for. The slaves wanted their independence from slave owners just as the colonists had wanted independence from England.

When Friday, July 3rd, brought the usual mail delivery, it was no surprise to anyone that the Louisville Daily Journal reported that President Lincoln had appointed yet another new commander for the Army of the Potomac. Papa settled on the porch to share the latest news with anyone who wanted to listen.

"Commander number five is now in position," Papa said, his face buried behind the newspaper.

"That's no surprise," Delmar said. "Who is it this time?"

"General George Meade," Papa stated.

"Ah, another George," Delmar said. "Let's pray he can get the job done. Anything else of interest in that paper?"

"Not really," Papa said, scanning the pages. "Oh, wait, here's something interesting. West Virginia has officially become a state after separating from Virginia at the beginning of the war. They have become state number thirty-five."

"I don't think that star will be sewn on the flag just yet," Delmar said.

"No, you're probably right," Papa agreed. "The outcome of the war will have to be determined first."

"So, you're going to Paoli tomorrow to celebrate the 4th of July?" Delmar asked, suddenly changing the subject.

"Yep. I haven't been there before, but I hear they have what's called a square around the courthouse," Papa said, laying the newspaper aside.

"What's the square for?" Delmar asked. "Does it mark some kind of boundaries?"

"No, businesses are placed around the courthouse to form a square," Papa said. "I've been told four roads lead away from the courthouse heading north, south, east and west."

"Sounds like quite the place," Delmar said. "Of course, a city slicker like you from New Albany probably won't be impressed much."

"I still want to see that courthouse," Papa said.

"When do Carter and Angus leave to enlist?" the man playing Delmar in checkers asked.

"Monday," Papa said. "It's not what I want to see happen, and it will make it tough trying to keep up with the farm and store, but Carter is a grown man. He has the right to make his own decisions."

"They will put that boy on a horse," Delmar said. "I don't

know anyone who can ride like Carter."

"Maybe," Papa said, "if that's where he's needed. Hey Delmar, would you mind going to our farm and milk the cow tomorrow afternoon? I've been thinking who to ask and I thought maybe you would go do that for us."

"Is the cow well behaved?" Delmar asked. "I don't like milking all that well and I sure don't want to milk an ornery cow."

"Oh, Elsie won't give you much trouble," Papa assured Delmar. "Elizabeth and Virginia milk her all the time. I'm sure you can handle anything two women are capable of."

"All right," Delmar agreed. "Anything else you need done?"

Papa thought a minute. "Well, I suppose you could collect the eggs. Just take the milk and eggs home with you when you're done. I'll leave a milk can in the barn."

"'Bout what time do I need to milk the cow?" Delmar asked.

"Four or five o'clock would be fine," Papa said.

"And you're sure she won't give me any trouble?" Delmar asked again.

"Nah, just open the barn door and she will take herself to the stanchion. Once you lock her head, she should be fine. I'll leave the bucket of grain and the milking pail in the barn, along with the milk can."

I listened to the conversation from inside the store. I noticed Papa didn't mention that Elsie much preferred women to men, but I supposed Delmar would find that out. To warn him might cause him to refuse to do the chore, so I chose to not say anything, either.

Delmar was right about one thing though; Carter could ride a horse like no other. He could certainly be chosen for the cavalry. I wondered what job Angus would be given. He would be beneficial for mending the harnesses and saddles, since he had grown up learning to do such things. Maybe that ability would keep him in the camp instead of on the front line. I hoped that would be the case.

Chapter Fourteen

Chores began extra early the next morning, July 4th, so we could get on the road toward Paoli. I could not deny my excitement as I milked the cow. Carter fed the hogs and chickens and made sure they had plenty of water. Papa hitched up the team while Momma prepared an easy breakfast of oatmeal.

Returning to the house, I poured the milk from the pail into a milk can and hauled it to the springhouse to keep cool. We all gathered on the summer kitchen porch by five and Papa blessed the food. When we had finished eating, Momma began to pack a picnic basket while I washed the dishes. By 6:00, we were leaving the farm. We would pick up Mary Ellen and Angus when we reached Marengo.

"This is so exciting," Mary Ellen exclaimed as she crawled into the back of the wagon.

"I know," I replied. "Today we will make memories to last a lifetime." As the words came from my mouth, I suddenly grasped the full meaning of that term. I prayed that today would not be the last time I made new memories with Carter or Angus for that matter. Many lives had been lost on the battlefield of the war and I could not ignore the fact that Carter or Angus could be added to that long list of names.

Papa stopped at Angus's house next, since he lived just a bit north of the general store on the Leavenworth-Paoli road. Everyone talked excitedly about all we would see and do this day. None of us had ever seen fireworks before, not even Mary Ellen, only read about them in the Louisville Daily Journal.

As the horses pulled us north toward Paoli, I thought about the last time Papa and I had traveled this road. It had been the night we took Henry, Lucy, and baby Joshua to Chambersburg.

About three miles out of Marengo, we came to the first hill. Up until that point, the road had been mostly flat, following along a creek that was fed by springs along the way. The creek flowed south, eventually dumping into Whiskey Run creek when it reached Marengo.

Papa stopped and allowed the horses to get a drink before he climbed that first hill. Carter suggested that he and Angus walk up the hill, to take some of the weight off the horses. Mary Ellen and I decided to walk, too. As we started off again, only Momma and Papa road in the wagon.

It was not difficult to keep up with the horses, because Papa kept them at a walk. Poor Nellie and Clyde would have to pull twenty miles to Paoli and twenty miles back. Papa needed to conserve every ounce of strength the beasts had.

When we topped the hill, everyone loaded back into the wagon. Looking to my left, I recognized the barely traveled road that Papa and I had taken the night we moved Henry, Lucy, and Joshua. I had fallen asleep on the ride home, but I was sure Papa took the same road on our return trip.

We began to descend a grade until we reached Piersontown, then the road leveled out again and would remain that way until we reached the outskirts of Valeene. Papa slowed the horses to a crawl as we neared the bridge over Patoka River on the south side of Valeene.

"There's a new grave up on the hill," Momma remarked, pointing to the graveyard that sat up on the steep hill above the river.

"That church sits on quite a steep bank," Mary Ellen said.

The horses came to the bridge and Papa pulled them to a halt. "See that cave in the bank of the river?" Papa asked.

We all craned our necks to see where Papa was pointing to on the right side of the road. "The folks around here claim that the first settlers of Orange County lived in that cave in 1807, before building a cabin up on the hill near where the graveyard is now."

"That's interesting," Carter said. "Do you know their names?"

"The last name was Hollowell," Papa said.

"Wasn't Henry Hollowell the first person to live in Big Spring?" Momma asked.

"Yes, in 1811" Papa said.

"Do you think Henry Hollowell was related to the family who lived in that cave?" I asked.

"I suppose it's very possible," Papa replied, "but of course I don't know for sure." Papa put the horses in motion again and we entered Valeene. About half-way through the small town, Papa pointed to a road that took off to the right.

"There's a large hill about a half mile up that road and at the top of the hill is a church called Rock Springs. I have been past it once, and you can see for miles around from the graveyard beside the church. I'm sure it would be a sight to behold when the leaves are fully changed in the fall."

Continuing through the town, we waved to residents who were out in their yards and visiting with neighbors. As we approached a pile of charred wood, Papa pointed and said, "That's probably the home Thomas Hines and his men burned down."

"Goodness, that's awful," Momma said. "I can't believe anyone could be so heartless."

"I suppose anything is acceptable during war time," Carter said.

"Well, it shouldn't be," Momma replied.

We all stared at the remains of what was once someone's home. "At least some of the men who set the fire were captured," I said.

"Yes and are right now spending the rest of the war in a camp in Indianapolis," Papa added. Continuing out of Valeene, we came to the large hill on the northern edge of town and Papa stopped the horses.

"Time to get out and walk again," Carter announced.

This time, even Momma decided to walk up the hill. I was sure glad it was still early morning. The heat and humidity that came with July in southern Indiana would increase as the day wore on. At least it was still bearable at the moment.

The sun was fully up and the sky was clear, but we did not count on it remaining so all day. We all knew how fast a thunderstorm could pop-up, as the heat and humidity climbed.

Half-way up the hill, the road made a Y. I knew that if we traveled to the right, we would be heading toward Chambersburg, the direction Papa and I had went the night we moved Lucy, Henry and Joshua. Today, Papa veered left at the Y and continued to climb the hill.

Once we topped the hill, the road made a hard bend to the right. Everyone loaded back into the wagon and the road was mostly flat until we reached another Y several miles later. We went right at the Y, still heading north.

"If we turned left at this Y, we would eventually end up in Hartford," Papa said. We all knew Hartford was another small Crawford County town six miles west of Marengo.

After turning north at the Y, there were a few hills and another sharp curve to the left. We then came to a steep hill that dropped an eighth of a mile straight down with a curve at the bottom. I dreaded walking back up that hill late tonight.

A few miles later, we began to descend into a valley. Paoli was nestled below, and we could see the top of the courthouse from the hilltop. Reaching the bottom of the hill, we turned right. A half mile later, we crossed a bridge with a small creek beneath it. The courthouse was just ahead.

"That is quite a building," Papa said as we neared the town's square. "Of all the huge houses I drafted when I was a young man in New Albany, none were nearly as grand as this structure."

I stared in awe at the huge, beautiful building. A fifteen foot clock tower protruded above the roof and chimed out the time by the hour. It had large columns in the front that stretched from the ground to the roof. There was a staircase on the outside made of iron that went from the basement to the second floor. A huge American Flag, with its 34 stars and 13 red and white stripes, hung from the railing that enclosed a balcony on the second floor of the courthouse. I had never seen a building so large in my life.

"It is quite grand," Angus said.

"Makes me eager to see all the sites when we leave Indiana to fight in the war," Carter said. "I've heard there are lots of huge buildings in Louisville, Kentucky."

"Yes, there are some big buildings, as well as houses, in New Albany and Louisville," Papa said, "but this building has character. I hope it's standing here long after we are dead and gone, because it's worth preserving."

I looked all around the courthouse lawn. Adults had spread blankets and were enjoying watching the children play games of tag. As I scanned the surroundings, I was surprised to see Negro families among those who had come out to celebrate Independence Day. Crawford County, to my knowledge, did not have any freed Negros living there. I assumed the ones I saw now lived at Paddy's Garden, the place Reuben had taken the runaway slaves the night the slave hunters had been spotted.

Since the war had begun, the freed slaves did not have to fear being picked up by slave hunters. Papa had told me that sometimes the slave hunters would kidnap freed slaves, if they couldn't find the runaway slaves they were hunting. The kidnapped Negros were taken and sold at auction, not given the chance to prove that they were legally free.

Papa dropped all of us off on the square then took the horses and wagon to a nearby field where other horses were tethered. There was a trough for the horses to get a drink before being tied and Papa had brought some hay and feed for them to munch on throughout the day.

As we waited for Papa to return, we all gazed at the different businesses around the Paoli town square. Though our general store offered a variety of things in small selection, Paoli offered all those things and more in individual stores.

The store that drew the attention of Momma and me was a store that sold just fabric, thread, and buttons. Peering in the window, Momma and I could see more bolts of fabric in an assortment of colors and patterns than we had ever seen in our lives. Mary Ellen, who had grown up near Louisville, Kentucky, had seen larger fabric stores but not since coming to Marengo.

"Go ahead in and look around," Carter urged us women. "Angus and I will wait here for Papa. I'm sure we will find something of interest to look at while you women finger and feel everything in that store."

"Okay," Momma replied. "Just tell your father where we are."

"Will do," Carter said.

Entering the fabric store, the three of us did exactly what Carter said we would. "Look at the pattern on this fabric," Momma said, pointing to a bolt of fabric with a yellow and blue design.

Reaching out, I smoothed my hand over the surface. "It's so soft. That fabric would create a shirtwaist I would never want to take off."

"Let's purchase enough to make a skirt and shirtwaist for each of us," Mary Ellen suggested.

"That's a wonderful idea," Momma said.

For the next thirty minutes, the three of us busied ourselves with matching the thread and buttons we would like for our new outfits. When we finally exited the store, our purchase wrapped in paper, we began to search for the men. Staring around the square at the many stores, we tried to decide where to begin.

"There's a barber shop," Momma pointed out, "but I don't believe that is where they would be."

"No, you trimmed Papa and Carter's hair last week, so I don't think they would be there. How about the newspaper office?" I suggested as I pointed at the small building nestled in one of the corners of the square. "You know how Papa loves the newspaper."

Momma scanned the square deep in thought. "Your father does indeed love the newspaper, but I don't believe that is where he is. Carter and Angus would not be nearly as interested in that as your father."

"Do you think they went to look inside the courthouse?" Mary Ellen asked.

"Not without us," Momma said. "They would know we want to see that, too."

Scanning the many options the men had, my eyes finally settled on the general store. "There, that's where they are," I said, pointing toward the building on the opposite side of the square.

"The general store?" Mary Ellen asked. "They see one of those nearly every day. Why would they go into that store when there are so many others to choose from?"

"To get ideas on new items to carry in our store," I said. "Trust me, that's where they are."

"You're probably right, Virginia," Momma agreed. "Let's start there."

Walking uphill to the northeast corner of the square, we picked our way toward the general store. There was so much traffic we found it difficult to move quickly, not to mention having to pay close attention to where we placed our feet. Not one of us wanted to spend the rest of the day with horse manure coating our shoes. Finally reaching the entrance to the general store, we peered in the window.

"Yes, you were right, Virginia," Mary Ellen said. "There the three of them are looking at the same products your father handles every day. Goodness, he didn't have to drive twenty miles to pick up a hammer."

Momma laughed, watching Papa pick up one hammer after another, checking the handle and weight of each one. "Let's sit here on this bench and wait for them. I have no desire to look around a general store."

Plopping down on the bench outside the store, I muttered, "Goodness, I can't believe I came to Paoli to pretend I'm Delmar."

Mary Ellen laughed and asked, "Do you want to play checkers?"

"Speaking of Delmar, I sure hope everything goes well between him and Elsie today," Momma fretted.

"Papa did not mention that she prefers women to men," I said. "I also did not hear Papa tell Delmar to make sure and dump the feed in the trough before he lets Elsie in the barn."

"Oh, goodness, that cow is liable to run him down," Momma said.

"Surely Delmar can handle milking a cow one afternoon," Mary Ellen said. "I could even milk a cow."

"Did your Papa warn Delmar about Romeo?" Momma asked.

"Who's Romeo?" Mary Ellen asked.

"The rooster," I replied. "That's the name Momma gave him, and no, Papa did not warn Delmar about Romeo."

"What was your father thinking? Poor Delmar may be flogged and stampeded. He will never do a favor for us again."

"Well, everyone should know not to turn your back on a rooster," I replied. "They can never be trusted. I just hope Ollie isn't too protective and allows Delmar in the barn."

"I never even considered the dog," Momma said. "He does not like strangers coming to the house, for sure."

"It will all be fine," Mary Ellen assured us. "Delmar will handle it all well."

"I sure hope so," Momma said, continuing to fret about the

situation.

"We're here to have a fun day," I said. "No more talk of the farm and what might or might not happen. Mary Ellen is right. Delmar has been a farmer his whole life. He can handle a protective dog, ornery cow, and flogging rooster."

"Of course, you're right," Momma agreed. "I just don't want Delmar to get injured."

Papa, Carter, and Angus exited the general store at that moment. We decided to take our purchase to the wagon and eat our picnic lunch.

After we finished, we all went to look at the magnificent courthouse. All the offices were closed within the structure, but we were allowed to walk from floor to floor checking everything out.

When we exited, Momma pointed to a spot on the lawn surrounding the courthouse. There was a line of people waiting to get their picture taken. "Oh, Stephen, let's get our picture taken. It would be something we could keep forever to remember the day."

"That's a good idea, Elizabeth," Papa agreed. "We don't have any pictures and with Carter and Angus leaving….well, a picture would be nice."

I knew what Papa had left unsaid. We may never see Carter or Angus again. To have a picture of them would mean a lot, if the unthinkable happened.

We joined the line to wait our turn and had a group photograph taken. Papa gave the man our address so the picture could be mailed to us after it was developed.

After posing for a group picture, Angus suggested, "Let's have one taken of just you and me, Virginia."

"Okay," I agreed. I knew it would be something I would cherish forever. I just prayed it would not be the only way I would ever get to see his face again.

We spent the rest of the day enjoying all the sights around Paoli. Carter and Angus teamed up to play in a horseshoe pitching tournament and came in second place. When it was almost nightfall, Carter and Angus hitched the horses back to the wagon. We traveled about a mile south, toward home. When we reached the top of the hill out of Paoli, Papa stopped and we watched the fireworks from there. This gave us a birds-eye view, and we would be able to start for home as soon as the display ended. It would be at least one in the morning before we reached home as it was.

As I watched the explosions of color, I thought of the song "The Star-Spangled Banner", written as the British attacked Fort McHenry during the war of 1812; a war where the United States fought together for the cause and not against one another. The writer, Frances Scott Key, viewed the scene from one of the British ships where he had gone to negotiate the release of an American prisoner, Doctor Beanes. Each time the night sky lit up with artillery fire, Key would look for the American flag at the fort. If the flag was still there, he knew the Americans were still in control of the fort. *"And the rocket's red glare, the bombs bursting in air, gave proof through the night that our flag was still there."*

I now questioned how much longer the stars and stripes would be a symbol for the United States of America. If the South won the war our country was now engaged in, what would be the outcome? For certain slavery would continue, for the rich plantations needed the manpower. I understood the need, but why couldn't the plantation owners just hire men for the work? Of course, if the North won, the bitterness between some of the slaves and their owners would last a lifetime, maybe for generations. There would be no easy or immediate solution to the slavery issue, no matter who won the war.

Angus leaned down to whisper in my ear. "You're awful quiet, Virginia."

"Just thinking about what the outcome of the war could lead to," I replied.

"The North will win and slavery will be abolished," Angus stated.

"Yes, that is what I pray happens," I admitted. "But the bitterness will last for years, not only between the North and the South, but between the slaves and their former owners. I fear that even if the North wins, the violence will not."

"You may be right, Virginia, but we have to start somewhere to end slavery and the mistreatment of Negros."

"I just wish a peaceful solution could have been found."

"As do I," Angus whispered, knowing that in just a few days he would be training to fight in a war that had gotten totally out of hand.

The ride home from Paoli was easier than the ride there. We

only had one large hill to climb, and it was just a few miles out of Paoli. After topping that first big hill, everyone relaxed and enjoyed the ride for the first two hours. As we neared Valeene, we could see lightening in the distance, making a fireworks show of its own.

"I believe we're going to get wet," Papa said.

"We should have packed a tarp," Momma replied. "At least it would have kept some of the rain off us."

"Maybe we will beat the storm," Carter said.

Papa looked up at the sky and counted the seconds between flashes of lightening. "Not likely, unless we can cover the miles between Valeene and Marengo in twenty minutes."

"Maybe it will be a small storm," I chimed in, hoping I would be correct.

"We can only hope," Mary Ellen said.

The wind picked up and the first raindrops began to pelt us just as we passed through Piersontown. Within five minutes, a downpour was upon us. Mary Ellen grabbed the empty picnic basket and Momma held the package from the fabric store over her head. Carter, Angus, and I huddled under one of the two blankets we had brought to spread on the lawn at Paoli while Papa held the other one tightly around him with one hand, the reins in his other hand. In no time we were all soaked, no matter what we had used for cover.

"I'm going to take the road up here on the right toward Bacon," Papa hollered above the storm. "Mary Ellen and Angus can just spend the night at our house and go to church with us in the morning."

Momma leaned toward Papa, hollering back. "That sounds like a good plan, Stephen. The faster we get home, the better."

Turning right, Papa urged the team as fast as he dared on the increasing slick road. The dirt road had become a muddy mess with the mass amount of rain. The only good thing was we would be home quicker by going this way.

As we entered the narrow road that lead through a forest, the leaves overhead helped keep some of the rain off of us. Within another ten minutes, the summer storm blew over.

"Well, we've all had our Saturday night bath now," Carter joked. "Too bad we didn't have a bar of soap to do the job right."

Momma turned to look at Carter. "Yes, with a bar of soap we could have done our laundry and taken a bath at the same time."

When we reached home, Carter hopped out of the wagon to open the barn doors. Papa drove the wagon in while Carter lit a lantern. Angus, Carter and Papa had the horses unhitched and in their stalls in no time. Momma, Mary Ellen and I couldn't get to the house fast enough to find some dry clothes.

As we passed the milking stanchion on our way out of the barn, I noticed the milk can still sitting there. Walking over to the can, I could see a scrap of paper tucked under the lid. Opening the lid and removing the paper, I walked toward the light of the lantern. There was a note scribbled on it that I read out loud.

Don't worry. The cow got milked. Just didn't keep it in the pail. I'll explain later.

Delmar

By the way, you have a mean rooster!

"I guess we should have warned Delmar about Romeo and to watch out for Elsie's quick hooves," I said.

Carter laughed and said, "Well, no use crying over spilt milk."

"I just hope Delmar is okay," Momma fretted.

"He's fine, Elizabeth," Papa assured her. "It would take more than Elsie to get Delmar down."

"Let's go find something dry to put on," Mary Ellen suggested. "We'll see Delmar at church tomorrow and I'm sure he will tell us all about it."

"Mary Ellen's right," Papa agreed. "Delmar will never allow us to forget it if that cow gave him trouble."

The next morning, Delmar met us outside of church. I could tell by the look on his face he had an exaggerated story to tell. "Stephen, did you have a nice time in Paoli?"

"We certainly did, Delmar," Papa said.

Delmar stood looking at Papa for a moment, waiting for him to say more. When it was clear Papa was done speaking, Delmar asked, "Aren't you curious as to why I didn't come home with some rich Jersey milk?"

"Maybe," Papa said not sure if he really wanted to hear about Delmar's misfortune.

"Now, don't go to thinking I couldn't handle that cow, because I did," Delmar began. "It was Ollie who caused all my problems. He was nowhere to be seen when I arrived but when I had just finished milking, he showed up. Ran right into the barn and scared the wits out of that cow, and me, too."

"I suppose I should have penned Ollie up," Papa admitted.

"I had myself a nice milk bath," Delmar said. "All that rich milk just spilled on the ground; wasted. What a shame. My wife was heartbroken."

"I'll send some milk with Stephen tomorrow," Momma promised. "A whole can full."

"Then there was the rooster," Delmar began.

"We really should have warned you about Romeo," Momma said.

"Romeo? You named that hateful rooster Romeo?"

"Well, he does love those hens," Momma replied.

"And hates intruders," Delmar said. "I nearly had chicken for supper last night, if I could have gotten my hands on him."

"Did he flog you?" Papa asked.

"Tore my good shirt half off me," Delmar replied.

"Goodness," Momma said. "I'll sew you a new shirt, too."

"You could use that pretty fabric you bought yesterday," Carter said, grinning mischievously at Delmar. "The color would bring out the blue in Delmar's eyes."

Delmar glared at Carter then stomped toward the church, hollering back to us as he went. "I'll be heading into the church now. The last thing I want is to have someone sit in my usual pew while I'm outside dawdling. My wife is probably still cackling with the other "hens" and won't make sure no one takes our seat. We'll talk about that new shirt later, Elizabeth."

We watched as Delmar stomped off, knowing if he didn't sit in his normal spot he would believe the whole service had been ruined. Papa shook his head and smiled. "Shall we enter the church?" Papa asked, holding his hand out toward the front doors.

We made our way into the church and sat in our usual pew, preparing for weekly worship.

Chapter Fifteen

Monday morning, July 6, 1863, arrived overcast and gloomy; which was the perfect match to my mood. Carter joined me as I milked Elsie, squatting on the opposite side. Peering at me from under the cow's belly, he smiled and said, "Two teats for me and two for you. We'll race to see who gets done first."

"You know I won't back down from a challenge, even if you are leaving in just a few hours."

"Virginia, that's the thing I love most about you."

Tears came to my eyes and streamed down my cheeks as Carter and I raced to finish milking first. It slowed me down having to wipe my face so I could see to hit the pail. What was I going to do without Carter to goad me and make everything we did a competition? Why couldn't the war just end? In that moment I realized something. I wanted slavery to end, but not as much as I wanted Reuben, Carter, and Angus to be safe. Was I being selfish for such a thought? Was this a question that haunted President Lincoln daily? How many sons, brothers, and husbands would give up their lives for the cause?

"Virginia, I think she's dry," Carter said, touching my shoulder.

Looking up, I realized I had been so distraught that I hadn't realized Elsie had been pumped dry. Grasping the pail handle, I moved it safely away from Elsie's reach. Turning back, Carter wrapped me in a hug, shedding a few tears of his own. "You better stay safe, and keep Angus safe, too," I muttered into Carter's shoulder.

"I will do my best, Virginia," Carter said. "Keep things running smoothly here while we're away."

"The farm and store will be fine," I said. "What are most important are you, Reuben and Angus. Go bring an end to the madness, Carter."

"I know I never tell you this Virginia, but today I will. I love you, little sister."

"I love you too, Carter. I will pray unceasingly until you return."

Papa, Momma, Carter, and I rode together to the general store. Angus and his father planned to meet Carter at the store, and they would leave together. Angus's father was planning to drive them in his wagon. They would go to New Albany to enlist, then to Indianapolis for training.

I would have gotten on my knees and begged them both to stay, but I knew it would do no good. The choice had been made and the time had come. We all said a tearful good-bye, and then Carter and Angus climbed into the wagon and headed toward the rising sun.

Deciding what to do about the farm and the store now came to the forefront. We finally decided Mary Ellen and I would run the store by ourselves on days Papa was needed at the farm. Hay had to be cut two more times throughout the summer and the crops would need tending.

Carter, Papa and Angus had bundled the wheat the week before. The corn Carter had planted in May was growing nicely. The oats had headed out and would need harvesting in a few weeks. Papa would be working on the farm more than at the store, since the farm's workload had become his full responsibility.

Momma would take care of the garden and the preserving, and I would help all I could in the evenings. Overnight, the store had now become my responsibility.

We gathered around the kitchen table for supper the night Carter and Angus left, and the realization was full force. Carter and Reuben's chairs sat empty, a stark reminder of their absence. Papa ate in silence then looked up at me. "Virginia, I'm really sorry you've had to grow up at seventeen. This is not the life I wanted for you."

"Papa, right now no one I know is living the life they dreamed of. We are all making sacrifices. I will do what I must, just as Carter,

Reuben, and Angus are doing what they must."

"I don't know what we will do when Mary Ellen has to teach school in September," Momma said.

"We'll cross that bridge when there's water under it," Papa said.

The rest of the week, I went to town and opened the store. With the help of Mary Ellen, I kept things running smoothly. Most of the men who came to purchase bags of feed lifted the bags themselves, saving mine and Mary Ellen's backs.

Everything seemed to be going according to Papa's plan, until late afternoon on Thursday. The screen door opened and in walked a soldier with the Indiana Legion. I recognized the uniform immediately, since Angus had worn one just like it, not to mention the man who had warned us two weeks earlier of Thomas Hines being in the area wore the same uniform. "We need to spread the word around Marengo to be on high alert," the man said, not bothering with introductions.

"What's happened?" I asked.

"Confederate soldiers, led by General John Hunt Morgan, have crossed the Ohio River into Harrison County," the man said. "A telegram came from Corydon to our headquarters at Leavenworth warning us of a possible attack."

"Do they have any idea where Morgan and his men are headed?" I asked.

"No, but they could be going to Indianapolis to force the release of Confederate prisoners of war being held there. The Harrison County Indiana Legion attempted to hold them back near Mauckport, but failed. All we know for sure is that the Confederate Army is on Indiana soil and is headed north."

"Thank you for stopping to tell us," I replied. "We will spread the word here and send a messenger to Valeene."

"Thanks for the help. I will continue to Milltown and warn folks there. The Indiana Legion spared just a few men to warn local towns, while the rest of the troop left Leavenworth and headed toward Corydon to assist if necessary. We fear we will not arrive in time to be of any help."

As the soldier turned to leave, I followed him outside. I gave the report to the men who were sitting around playing checkers and discussing the weather. As the news sank in, the men sprang into action.

"I'll take care of spreading the word to Valeene," one of the farmers said. "I live out that way anyway."

"Thank you," I replied.

"I'll get started here in Marengo," Delmar offered. "We should probably get our guns loaded and ready, just in case."

"I honestly don't think we have a chance of stopping the Confederates, Delmar," I replied, "but if it makes you feel safer, load your gun."

The porch of the general store cleared as quickly as it had two weeks earlier when Thomas Hines was heading toward Marengo. Looking up at Mary Ellen, I shrugged my shoulders. "Maybe we should check and see if the gun under the counter is loaded."

"I would, if I knew how," Mary Ellen confessed.

"Why don't we just close the store and go to my house," I suggested. "We would be of no use if the Confederates showed up here, and Papa will want to know what's happening."

"That's a better idea than loading the gun," Mary Ellen agreed.

I had ridden Knucklehead to the store that morning to save hitching up the team. The mule was cantankerous with one rider and I honestly didn't know how he would react with two people on his back. Not taking time to put the saddle back on, I slipped the bridle over his ears and lead him from the corral in back to the front of the store.

"I'll get on his back then help you up," I told Mary Ellen.

Looking at me skeptically, Mary Ellen murmured, "Okay."

Leaping up, I hooked my elbow on Knucklehead's whither bone and struggled up on his back. Carter always made that maneuver look so easy and I was glad he was not here at the moment to be entertained by my clumsy mount. Scooting forward as far as possible, I reached down my arm for Mary Ellen to grasp. "Just grab my arm and I'll pull you up," I said. Carter had pulled me up behind him on Clyde or Nellie countless times. How hard could it possibly be?

Mary Ellen grasped my arm and pulled. Before I knew what had happened, my body spun sideways and I landed on top of Mary Ellen. Knucklehead, seeing he had the upper hand, kicked his back feet straight out and took off toward home, braying all the way. All that was left of him was a cloud of dust in mine and Mary Ellen's face. Standing to my feet and offering a hand to Mary Ellen I said, "Well, that didn't go as planned."

Laughing and refusing my hand, Mary Ellen replied, "I believe I'll help my own self up this time, thank you very much."

"And that's why we call him Knucklehead," I said, pointing to the stupid beast fading in the distance.

Standing up and dusting herself off, Mary Ellen asked, "Now what do we do?"

"We walk," I said. "It's our only option. We shouldn't have to go too far, though."

"Why is that?" Mary Ellen asked.

"Because when Knucklehead shows up at home without a rider, Papa will come looking for me."

Mary Ellen laughed again. "Ah, I see."

We began to walk toward the farm, having conversation we had been too busy all week to have. There had been so many customers to assist every day that all we could say when the store closed was, "See you tomorrow."

"I wrote to Reuben and told him Carter was enlisting," Mary Ellen said.

"I believe Momma told him, too," I replied. "Has he mentioned his injury in his letters lately?"

"Not a word," Mary Ellen said. "He's never even explained what happened. All I know is he suffered injury to his right arm."

"He's never given us details, either. At least his penmanship has improved."

"For a while there, I was only able to read about every third word," Mary Ellen chuckled. "His letters were like a hidden puzzle."

"With no instructions on how to solve it," I added.

"Do you think the Confederates will come this way?" Mary Ellen suddenly asked.

"I honestly don't know. Thomas Hines was definitely scouting for something when he crossed the Ohio River with his men two weeks ago. He might encourage Morgan to head this way, since the area is a little familiar to him."

"The goal could certainly be to free the Confederate prisoners of war in Indianapolis," Mary Ellen said thoughtfully. "Those men could be added back into the Confederate troops where they are so desperately needed."

"Now that I think about it, what else would cause Morgan to cross into Indiana?"

"Do you think the Indiana Legion was able to stop them?" Mary Ellen asked.

"According to Angus, there were never enough weapons and the Indiana Legion soldiers were forced to get their own or do without. That would mean each man is also responsible for his own ammunition. Those two things alone would hinder their success, not to mention the Indiana Legion would not be trained to fight like the Confederates are. Up until now, Harrison County has seen no action and Crawford County has only recently taken part in tracking down Hines and capturing a few Confederate soldiers."

"The odds are definitely stacked against the Indiana Legion," Mary Ellen said.

We had walked about a mile and I could now hear a wagon coming toward us. Stopping, I waited to see who it might be. As soon as the team of horses came into sight, I knew it was Clyde and Nellie. Papa was driving them faster than I had ever seen him do. As the team came closer, Papa spotted us and began to slow. Pulling alongside us, Papa halted the team. "Virginia, what on earth happened? Knucklehead came home with a bridle and nothing else."

"He ditched me and Mary Ellen at the store," I said. "We had plans of riding him home."

Papa looked at me confused. "But it's not time for the store to close yet."

"Yes, I know, but something has happened. I'll tell you about it on our way home."

Mary Ellen and I climbed onto the back of the wagon, allowing our feet to hang down. I found it to be the most comfortable place to ride, even more comfortable than riding on the seat. Papa turned the team around and headed back home. During the ride, Mary Ellen and I told him what we knew so far about the Confederates crossing the Ohio into Harrison County.

"Closing the store and coming home was the right choice," Papa said. "I can't say that attempting to ride Knucklehead double was wise, though." Papa turned to look at Mary Ellen and me, then burst out laughing. "Sure wish I could have seen that!"

"Stupid, ornery animal," I muttered.

The next morning, Papa drove Mary Ellen and me to the

general store with the wagon. He wanted to gather information about General Morgan and the Confederate attack, if there was any available. We had no way of knowing if the Confederates had passed through Marengo and were now traveling toward Indianapolis. If that had happened, we would know within minutes of entering the general store, or maybe even before that.

"At least if the Confederates plan to go to Indianapolis, there are Union troops training there," Mary Ellen said as we rode along.

"Yes, there would be a way to defend the prison and the town," Papa agreed. "Here in our small town, we would have no choice but to allow the Confederates to march in and take what they wanted."

The thought of the Confederates coming through Marengo and doing what they wanted caused a shiver to pass down my spine. Thomas Hines had already burned a house in Valeene two weeks ago, just because his demands weren't met. If this was considered acceptable behavior by the South's leaders, there was no telling what they were capable of doing.

When we reached Marengo, everything appeared fine. As we turned on the road leading to Valeene, Papa slowed to examine it. There was not a mass amount of boot or hoof prints, so no army had passed through.

Of course, the Confederates could have continued north on another route out of Harrison County. Thomas Hines could have certainly got his hands on a map while in Indiana the last time, allowing the Confederates to chart out the best possible route to Indianapolis from Corydon.

As turned on the street of the general store, we could see several men gathered on the porch already. The fact that Indiana had just become a state involved in combat was something to talk about. I knew that not one of those men would be leaving until the mail was delivered. The copy of the Louisville Daily Journal with the reports of the event wouldn't be delivered today, but Thaddeus, the driver of the mail wagon, would be overflowing with information.

"It appears that crazy Thomas Hines was able to get information back to his commander," Delmar said as we stepped onto the porch.

"The Confederates have definitely brought terror to Indiana," Papa agreed. "I just wonder what they want here, other than the prisoners of war at Indianapolis. I honestly don't see how they could get that far into Northern territory without being captured, though."

"Wherever they are going, they didn't come through Marengo again," Delmar said.

"For which I am thankful," Papa added, opening the door to the store.

The porch became crowded as the morning pressed on. Finally, at eleven o'clock the mail wagon arrived. Thaddeus was mobbed by people and pelted with questions until Papa took control. "Please, allow the poor man to speak. I'm sure he will tell us everything he knows."

Handing the mail bag to Papa, Thaddeus said, "The Louisville Daily Journal printed a special edition copy yesterday about Morgan and his men raiding Corydon. It came by boat to Leavenworth this morning. The Crisis also printed an article about it. I have included both in the mailbag. Those two papers will tell everything there is to know about the Confederates crossing the Ohio River into Indiana."

Papa took the bag. "Thank you. I'll take care of reporting what the paper has printed."

"You're welcome. I have a long day ahead, so I'll just be on my way." Thaddeus put the reins to the horses' backs, and with a whoop he was on his way again.

"So, Morgan must have made it to Corydon," Delmar said, picking up on what Thaddeus had said.

Papa reached into the mail bag and removed the bundle of newspapers from the previous week. He then handed the mail bag to me so Mary Ellen and I could sort the mail. I took the bag into the store and placed it on the counter, then returned to listen to the report Papa was about to give. Mary Ellen had been straightening shelves, but joined me at the screen door to hear the latest news.

Papa unfolded the special edition and scanned the article. "General John Hunt Morgan seized two steamboats, the *John B. McCombs* and the *Alice Dean*, at Brandenburg, Kentucky. He and 1800 cavalry strong crossed the Ohio River and disembarked near Mauckport, Indiana."

"So, they're on horses," one of the men interjected.

"Yes, it appears so," Papa said. "The *Alice Dean* was set afire, but the other steamboat was sent downriver. The Indiana Legion attempted to stop them as they entered Harrison County but failed.

Morgan and his men continued north, stealing horses and killing a Lutheran minister along the way. A telegram had been sent to Corydon from Governor Morton, encouraging the town of Corydon to fight."

"Well, at least they knew the Confederates were coming," Delmar said.

"Yes, and it states that Union troops were coming from the South, chasing after Morgan and his men. The job of the militia at Corydon was to hold Morgan and the Confederate cavalry until Union troops arrived."

"How'd they do?" someone asked.

Papa continued to scan the story. "Not too good. 450 men from Corydon, led by Colonel Lewis Jordan, set up a log barricade just south of town. The battle lasted less than an hour. Colonel Jordan surrendered the town to prevent any more loss of life. There were four men killed and ten wounded. Morgan and his men looted the town, stealing supplies and money."

"How many Confederates were killed?" Delmar asked.

"It states eleven killed and forty wounded," Papa said.

"Well, now that ain't too bad for a thrown-together militia," another man said. "Them Corydon fellers must have pretty good aim."

"Where's Morgan now?" Delmar asked.

"The Union troops blocked the Confederates from returning to the South, so they went north. The last report the newspaper had was that Morgan and his men went by Beck's Mill and into Salem. Once they entered Salem, Morgan and his men burned the train depot, all the railcars on the tracks, and the railroad bridges on each end of town."

"Them Confederates sure like to burn things up," a man among the crowd said.

"Does the paper say anything more?" Delmar asked.

"No, that's all there was to report, except that Morgan and his men left Salem and headed northeast," Papa said.

"Glad they're traveling in the opposite direction of us," Delmar said. "The Confederates could burn our little town to the ground in less than an hour."

"Any reports on the war in those other newspapers?" another onlooker asked, pointing to the stack Papa had laid on the checker board table.

Picking up the newspapers, the first article Papa saw was about the battle at Gettysburg, Pennsylvania. The headline read "Victory for the North". "It seems the North has won a battle at Gettysburg, Pennsylvania," Papa said.

"It's about time!" Delmar hollered.

"The battle was fought July 1st through the 3rd." Papa scanned the article for more details. "Oh, my, 51,000 young men were injured or lost their lives during the conflict. The newspaper states that as Robert E. Lee retreated with his men, there was a line of wounded soldiers stretching fourteen miles behind him."

"Lord, have mercy," Delmar muttered. "What a sad thing this war has turned into. I know them southern boys are the enemy now, but they didn't used to be. Just a few years ago, they were fellow countrymen."

"How much longer will this death and destruction last?" Pastor David wondered aloud as he stood among the men on the porch of the general store.

"I suppose until we are no longer a divided nation," Papa said. "I just pray President Lincoln figures out a way to make that happen soon. The tears flowing from the eyes of all the families of the dead and wounded is certainly forming a river by now."

The celebration by our little town of the North's victory had been cut short by the mass number of casualties. Who could rejoice when so many young men had lost their lives or suffered life-changing injuries.

Papa went on, though with little excitement, to tell of another victory for the North on July 4th. General Grant had finally gained the stronghold on the Mississippi River. The Confederacy would no longer have support from its western allies. This news was good, especially if it caused a quicker surrender from the South and ended this bloody war. To think about Carter and Angus preparing to step into the midst of the destruction caused my stomach to churn.

I turned back into the store to sort the mail and Papa handed me the list of fallen soldiers to post on the wall. I would have never dreamed when this war began we would still be fighting two years later. It seemed a lot of blood had been shed and yet neither side had gotten anywhere.

Concentrating on the task at hand, I began to read names on

the newly arrived mail and place the articles in the appropriate box.

Leaving the shelf she had returned to organizing, Mary Ellen came to the counter. "Was there a letter for me today?"

"No, not today," I said. "The battle at Gettysburg might have prevented Reuben from getting a letter sent."

"That's true," Mary Ellen said. Mary Ellen looked down for a moment. When she looked back up, tears glistened in her eyes. "I just wish this war would end. So many young men have lost their lives and more are added daily."

"I wish the war would end, too," I said, tears gathering in my own eyes. "How much longer do you think it will last, Mary Ellen?"

"I don't know, Virginia," Mary Ellen said, swiping at her tears. "I honestly don't know."

The next week went by quickly, the general store requiring all the energy Mary Ellen and I could muster. Papa made the trip to Milltown on Tuesday for needed supplies and spent Monday and Thursday working on the farm.

In the evenings, I helped Momma preserve what she had harvested from the garden that day. Mary Ellen moved in with us at the farm to help Momma, too. She took over the chore of feeding the chickens morning and night and collecting the eggs. There was really no reason for her to live in the little cabin by the school during the summer months, anyway.

On Friday, Papa came to the store with Mary Ellen and me. He said it was to help with the heavy lifting, since lots of feed was sold on Fridays, but I also knew he wanted to be at the store when the mail arrived. Not only would there be the latest happenings of the war, there just might be a letter from Carter or Reuben.

A crowd began to gather on the porch by mid-morning, though not quite as large as the previous Friday. Morgan and his raiders must have continued toward Ohio, for we had not heard any more about them. Since the immediate threat had left the area, the need-to-know wasn't as pressing.

The men talked of the weather and crops and played checkers, biding their time. I could hear Delmar telling of the enormous catfish he had caught the previous night from his pond.

"I caught it with chicken liver," Delmar said. "I had killed a chicken for dinner last Sunday, so the meat was good and ripe."

"How big did you say it was?" one of the men on the porch

asked.

"It was three feet long and weighed thirty pounds," Delmar said with pride.

"How did you get it pulled to the bank?" the same man asked.

"I just kept my pole low to the ground and walked backwards," Delmar replied.

"It was awful hot yesterday. Maybe you got overheated and it made you crazy or just plain forgetful. Either way, you did not catch a three foot, thirty pound catfish from your pond," the man argued.

"I did too," Delmar defended. "I would show it to you, if I hadn't turned it loose."

"Why would you turn such a catch loose?" the man playing checkers against Delmar asked.

"It was too big," Delmar replied. "It would have been too much for my wife and me to eat at one time."

"You could have shared it with us," Delmar's opponent pointed out.

"Well, I reckon I could have," Delmar said thoughtfully. "I'll remember that next time."

"Well, next time, while you're remembering you have friends to share your huge catfish with, try to remember its correct size. Thirty pounds and three feet long; of all the tall tales," another man lounging on the porch complained.

Just then, the mail wagon appeared at the end of the street. Papa was in the back of the store and I hollered to tell him. I knew if Papa wasn't out there to protect the poor driver, the group of men on the porch would talk his ear off and make him late the rest of the day. Papa grabbed the bag of outgoing mail and headed toward the door. As Papa stepped onto the porch, the mail wagon came to a stop.

"Good morning," Papa said, taking the bag Thaddeus handed him and placing the outgoing mail in the wagon. "Heard any more about Morgan and his raiders?"

"It's all there in the newspaper," Thaddeus replied, "along with the riots that broke out in New York City."

"Riots?" Papa asked. "Why would there be riots in New York City?"

"Something about protesting the draft," Thaddeus said. "The craziness is never-ending." With that, Thaddeus clicked his tongue, and the horses were off again.

Papa reached into the bag and grabbed the bundle of newspapers. Dropping the bag to the ground, he unfolded the pages, searching for the report on the riots. Gathering articles from several daily papers, Papa began to scan the reports. I picked up the mailbag and set it inside the store, but Mary Ellen and I stayed within hearing distance to learn of the riots Thaddeus had spoken of.

"How many reports are there about the riots?" Delmar asked. "You have a whole handful of papers there."

"It seems to have been going on for several days," Papa said. "The first report was in the Tuesday edition, on July 14th, and the last I have is in yesterday's edition."

As Papa read the articles to himself, I wondered again why the crowd gathered at the general store to hear Papa give the reports. Most of them could just take turns reading the newspaper when Papa was finished with it. There were probably a few who couldn't read; but certainly not everyone who gathered on the porch every Friday was illiterate.

I looked around at the expectant faces and the truth finally dawned on me. The crowd did not want to read the articles; they wanted a friend to tell them the news, good or bad. They would rejoice together, or take comfort from one another. Papa delivered the news the way they wanted to hear it, adding the touches of empathy that the newspapers rarely portrayed.

Waiting until Papa looked up again, Delmar asked, "Where did the riots take place?"

"New York City," Papa said, shaking his head and looking as if he didn't know where or how to begin. "The draft was enforced on Monday, and the poor people living in New York City were upset with the fact that the rich could pay $300 and purchase a substitute."

"The poor people here should be upset by that, too," Delmar said. "Rich or poor, if your name comes up, you should answer the call."

"That might be true," Papa said, "but the way some people, mostly poor Irish immigrants according to the paper, have chosen to show their dislike is, well despicable."

"What have they done?" Pastor David asked. He had joined the crowd after he saw the mail wagon pass his home. After the death of young John Line, Pastor David had made sure to be on hand every

Friday, in case he was needed to comfort a grieving family.

"As of Thursday, which would have been a report of things that had transpired on Wednesday, there have been nearly 120 people killed due to the rioting," Papa stated.

"120 civilians? Just innocent people?" Pastor David asked.

"Yes, and that's not all. The rioters have set fire to two churches, some public buildings, and destroyed homes of known abolitionists, along with the homes of Negro families."

"Why are Negroes being targeted?" Delmar asked. "Most of them probably don't have $300 to buy a substitute for the draft. Truth be known, they are probably becoming substitutes."

"The Irish immigrants blame the Negroes for taking jobs and adding to their own miserable living conditions," Papa said.

"It seems that the rioters are using the excuse of the draft to act out in violence against anyone they have decided has wronged them," Pastor David said.

"Yes, it seems so," Papa agreed. "There's more, though. The rioters have slain Negro men, hanged them and set them afire, and set fire to an orphanage where over two hundred Negro children lived."

"What?!" I exclaimed, not able to keep quiet any longer. "What kind of evil would cause a person to set fire to an orphanage for innocent children, no matter what skin color they had?"

"The evil one who walks to and fro, looking for those to devour," Pastor David said quietly.

"Thankfully, all of the children made it out alive, but it still leaves them with no roof over their heads," Papa said.

"Is anything being done to stop the riots?" Delmar asked.

"The police are trying to restore order but haven't been very successful. The Police Superintendent, John Kennedy, was beaten unconscious. The last thing the newspaper stated was Union soldiers, returning from Gettysburg, were being called upon to help restore order," Papa said.

"What a shame," Delmar said. "Those poor soldiers have just left a bloody battlefield and now will have to deal with this mess. I don't agree with being able to buy out of the draft, but destroying property and killing innocent people is no way to show disapproval."

"Any reports on Brigadier Morgan and his raiders?" someone sitting on the porch listening asked.

"Just that Morgan and his men crossed into Ohio and have been running hither and yon, leading the Union Army on a wild goose chase," Papa said.

"I'm sure those Union soldiers are needed somewhere else, too," Delmar said. "That could be part of Morgan's plan, to distract a portion of Union soldiers."

"It most certainly could be, Delmar," Papa agreed. "I know Morgan is trying to get back across the Mason-Dixon Line, but I believe he will be captured before he can accomplish it."

"I hope so," Delmar said. "That crazy critter needs to be caged."

The discussion of the riots and General Morgan's raiders continued while I went to sort the mail. I had not made a dent in the mail bag when I spotted familiar handwriting. The envelope was addressed to me. Tucking the letter into my apron pocket, I continued to sort, hoping to find a few minutes to read the letter when I got home tonight.

There was also a letter to my family from Carter, and one for Effie that also appeared to be from Carter. The thing that surprised me was there was no letter from Reuben to Mary Ellen again this Friday.

Mary Ellen sauntered over to the counter, a look of assurance on her face. Looking on the counter and not seeing what she was sure would be there, she asked, "Any mail for me?"

"Actually, no there isn't, Mary Ellen," I replied.

"I wonder why Reuben didn't write," Mary Ellen said thoughtfully.

"Maybe the letter got misplaced along the way," I said cheerfully. "That means you will have two next Friday."

"Perhaps you're right," Mary Ellen replied. "I was just sure I would have one this week."

Glancing down, my eyes fell on the portion of the newspaper I had yet to hang. It was the extremely long list of fallen soldiers in the area. Looking back up, Mary Ellen and I communicated without words. Each of us grabbed a section of newspaper and began to scan the pages. When every name had been read, we were relieved not to find Reuben's name among the fallen.

Taking the paper I went to hang it on the wall, where I was sure it would be thoroughly scanned by every person who came into the store throughout the week.

Removing the previous week's list, Mary Ellen and I again perused each name. Satisfied that Reuben's name was not on either list, I folded the old list and placed it on the stack under the counter with the others. Papa saved each one, just in case someone needed to reference one later.

"Reuben is fine," I told Mary Ellen, trying to convince myself with my own words.

"Yes, no news is good news, right?"

"Yes, Mary Ellen, no news is good news."

Mary Ellen went to the storeroom for a few supplies to restock the shelves. Effie entered the store a moment later. It was then I remembered the letter she had received. As she walked up to the counter, her smile told me she was expecting mail. "Did that bag have anything in it for me, perhaps?" she asked, patting the now empty mail bag.

Deciding to have a little fun, I smiled and affixed a most innocent face. "Are you expecting a letter from someone?"

"Maybe," Effie replied, blushing slightly.

"My family received a letter from Carter," I said, watching Effie's reaction.

"Really? What did he have to say?" Effie asked, not able to contain her enthusiasm.

"I haven't opened it yet."

"Oh," Effie said, the joy leaving her eyes.

Reaching back into Effie's mailbox, I retrieved the letter I was sure had been written by Carter. "Why don't you see what he has to say?"

Effie snatched the letter from my hand and headed for the door. Just before she walked out, she turned back. "Thanks, Virginia! I'll talk to you later."

"Have I just been pushed aside for my annoying brother?"

"I'll come back later and chat," Effie promised.

Effie walked through the screen door, allowing it to slap shut. Watching her go, I had to admit that I liked Carter's choice. Effie had spunk, and that is exactly the kind of woman Carter needed. One that could take his teasing but be able to give back whatever Carter dished out. The two of them just might work out.

"Didn't I just hear Effie?" Mary Ellen asked, coming from the store room.

Smiling at Mary Ellen, I replied, "Yes, but she didn't have time to talk. She just stopped by to pick up her letter from Carter."

"I thought I had seen a spark there," Mary Ellen said with a chuckle.

"It's good Carter has someone special to write to," I said. "I'm sure he will get lonely so far from home."

"Yes, I'm sure he will, too," Mary Ellen agreed.

That evening after the supper dishes were washed, dried, and put away, I slipped out of the summer kitchen to visit my old friend. Thankfully, Momma didn't have work she needed me to do and she and Mary Ellen were busy sewing on a new outfit, using the fabric we had bought at Paoli. I would have been forced to read my letter from Angus by the light of the lamp in my bedroom if she had, since it would have been dark by the time we finished.

Looking around and seeing no one, I headed toward the Maple as quickly as possible. Climbing only half way up, because I could stand the suspense no longer, I settled in to read the letter that had been burning a hole in my apron pocket all day.

Dear Virginia,   *July 13th, 1863*

I have nearly completed my training here in Indianapolis. Soldiers are needed desperately, so the training is done as quickly as possible. We have been taught how to swiftly load our guns and fire in unison with other soldiers. We practice marching and staying in formation daily, though I don't yet know how that will help us on the battlefield. For now, Carter and I will both be foot soldiers, but I believe Carter will eventually be made part of the cavalry, due to his way with horses.

I assume by now you have heard all about John Hunt Morgan and his men. We were put on high alert in Indianapolis, for we feared he would end up here. I thought we might fight a battle before ever leaving Indiana. Morgan is still on the rampage in Ohio, but I believe his days of raiding are numbered. The Union troops are blocking his every attempt at crossing back into Kentucky, capturing groups of his men along the way. The last count I heard, Morgan was down to 400 men, after crossing the Ohio River at Mauckport with 1800.

The battle of Gettysburg brought a victory for the North, but the death toll was tremendous. I'm sure your papa has read all about it on the porch of the general store. I honestly don't know how many soldiers the Confederates can lose before they surrender. The Union has more manpower at each battle, but still the

Confederates stand strong. One has to respect their zeal to fight and persevere.

I do not know how often I will get to write, since my company will soon be traveling south to join forces under the command of General Rosecrans in Tennessee. I suppose if you write to the Indianapolis address I have included at the bottom, I might receive it before I leave. Once I'm in the South, I do not know how I will get any mail. I will have to ask other soldiers when I get to Tennessee how letters are sent and received.

Please, write as often as you can and tell me about home. It's the one thing I will look forward to. I already dream of returning and I haven't even left the state, yet. Hopefully, the war will end soon and I won't be gone but a short while.

Love,

Angus

Folding the letter, I stuffed it back into my apron pocket with plans of adding it with the others already in my dresser drawer. Looking out over the farm from my lofty perch, I watched the sun sink behind the western hill and the night sounds begin. A cricket began the percussion as the frogs croaked the melody. A katydid joined in to add its unique cadence. Finally, a whippoorwill began its night song, a sound all its own, stating its name over and over. The first star appeared faintly in the sky as the full moon rose large and luminous on the eastern horizon. The only thing missing in this moment was Carter's voice. I could hear it in my mind, though. "Come on, Virginia, race you to the ground."

Chapter Sixteen

The third week of July, 1863 brought typical summer weather for southern Indiana. The heat was nearly unbearable and the humidity made skin feel as if it had been misted with water. The uncomfortable conditions made tempers flare quickly, and a bit of shade and a cool glass of water became a priority in the late afternoon. The hope was there would be a cooling, pop-up rain shower, but that just made the humidity worse afterwards. The fact of the matter, it was just too hot for man or beast.

"Goodness, Virginia, it's too hot to even play checkers," Delmar complained as he sat on the porch fanning himself on Tuesday.

Mary Ellen and I fanned ourselves with old newspapers, trying to catch a breeze on the porch of the general store while there were no customers. "I never thought I would hear you admit that, Delmar. Sweat would probably just cause the checkers to slip right through your fingers."

"I think you might be right," Effie's father, Joe, said. He had stopped by to play a game of checkers since it was too hot to do any work. He ended up fanning himself on the porch and making meaningless conversation.

"Maybe you and Mary Ellen should go get those guitars you keep in the back and play us a tune," Delmar suggested.

Mary Ellen laughed, fanning all the harder. "Our fingers would slide right off the strings."

"Maybe if it cools down later in the week we'll play something for you, Delmar," I said.

"I should bring my banjo down and join in sometime," Joe said.

"I didn't know you played banjo, Joe," Mary Ellen said.

"I haven't played for a while, but I'm certain it would come back to me if I practiced a bit," Joe replied. "I assume it's just like riding a horse, once you learn how, you never forget. I do need some new strings, though."

"That sounds fun," I said, getting excited about the idea. "Mary Ellen orders our guitar strings from a music store in Louisville. I'm sure they sell banjo strings, too. We'll send an order in Friday's mail, and they should be here by the next Friday."

"Why don't you just kill some varmint and make your own strings from its guts?" Delmar asked.

"I'll let someone else do the killing and drying of varmint's guts," Mary Ellen said with disgust.

A customer pulled up in front of the store, so Mary Ellen and I left our fans to go assist him. It turned out he was in no hurry on this hot afternoon and plopped down in a chair on the porch to complain about the weather and rest a bit. Mary Ellen and I returned to the porch and commenced fanning again, hoping for a breeze to blow our way.

When Mary Ellen and I returned home from the store that evening, we found Momma in the summer kitchen turning blackberries into jam and jelly. She had saved enough of the juicy berries to make blackberry dumplings for dessert after supper. The stifling heat of the summer kitchen nearly took my breath as the steam rose from the blackberry juice mixed with sugar boiling rapidly to reach gel stage. "I say it's too hot to eat and we just have blackberry dumplings with whipped cream over them and call it a meal," I announced.

"I plan to just have ham sandwiches for supper," Momma said. "I've been in this hot kitchen too long already, especially after spending a hot morning in the berry patch."

"Why don't we get up extra early in the morning and go to the blackberry patch together?" Mary Ellen suggested. "It would be much cooler and the three of us could pick the berries in no time. We can do that, can't we, Virginia?"

It took everything in me not to stomp Mary Ellen's foot for

making such an offer. Had she ever picked blackberries? Did she know what she had just gotten us into? I could not imagine she had spent much time in a blackberry patch, or she would have had more sense than to tell Momma we would help her the next morning before we went to the store. Plastering a smile on my face that had rivulets of sweat racing down it, I replied, "Sure, Mary Ellen, why not?"

"That is so nice of you girls to offer to help me," Momma said. "We will start at dawn and should have the patch finished before you have to leave for the store. I picked half of the patch today."

I savored every bite of the blackberry dumplings later, reminding myself that to get such a treat, you must first fight the thorns. I felt guilty for wanting to leave Momma to pick the berries alone, but it was an awful job. I had been doing it every July for as long as I could remember, and I was hoping to have a year of reprieve. Thanks to Mary Ellen and her thoughtfulness, I would again be forced to fight the briars, chiggers, and heat.

The next morning, Mary Ellen was knocking on my bedroom door as the first rays of the rising sun lightened the sky. I really just wanted to tell her to go away but knew it wasn't an option. Dragging myself out of bed, I dressed in my old clothes and trudged downstairs.

"Mary Ellen, is that the oldest dress you own?" I asked. "You will probably have berry stains on anything you wear, so make sure that's a dress you have no plans of wearing anywhere again, except on the farm."

"This dress is old enough," Mary Ellen assured me. "Your momma is already in the summer kitchen gathering the pails."

"Well, let's get to it, then," I replied.

When Mary Ellen and I reached the summer kitchen, Momma had oatmeal prepared with fresh blackberries to top it with. After filling our bowls, we went outside to sit on the porch. The day hadn't even begun, but the heat and humidity was already in place promising another scorching afternoon. I hadn't wanted to be rude and ask before but my curiosity got the better of me, overriding my manners. "Have you ever picked blackberries, Mary Ellen?"

"Well, no, but all that has to be done is pluck them from the vine, right?" Mary Ellen replied.

"They grow on briars, not vines," I said, "very sharp and mean briars."

"Well, I suppose I will have to be careful not to get pricked," Mary Ellen said.

By the time we had been in the berry patch thirty minutes, Mary Ellen's hands looked as if she had been battling a wild cat. I quit counting how many times she had said ouch when I reached fifty. She was in so much pain; I decided not to mention that she would probably be covered in chigger bites. Momma and I had picked two pails full while Mary Ellen was still on her first one.

"You weren't joking when you said blackberry briars are mean," Mary Ellen said, rubbing another scratch.

"No, I wasn't," I replied. "The more you pick them, the easier it becomes, though. You learn how to avoid the briars."

"Your hands don't have any scratches on them, Elizabeth," Mary Ellen said.

"I have been picking blackberries my whole life," Momma replied. "Virginia is right though, you learn how to avoid the thorns with practice."

We picked for another fifteen minutes and were nearly done when Mary Ellen screamed. Throwing her pail in the air, she ran from the patch. Reaching the grass, she lifted her skirt and looked all around.

"Mary Ellen, what's wrong?" Momma asked, rushing to her side.

"Sn..sn..snake!"

With that one word, I too left the berry patch. If there was one thing I could not tolerate it would be snakes. Coming up beside Mary Ellen and Momma, I looked all around to make sure the slithery creature had not followed Mary Ellen from the patch. "I think we have enough blackberries for today," I announced.

"Yes, I think Mary Ellen has been tortured enough," Momma agreed. Picking up two pails each, we headed toward the house. The pail Mary Ellen had thrown would be retrieved tomorrow, after the snake had time to leave the area.

Reaching the house, I encouraged Mary Ellen to strip all her clothes off and wash her entire body. "You might still get some chiggers, but changing your clothes and washing off will help prevent some from embedding under your skin, making you want to scratch until you bleed. I'll go get some salve to soothe the injuries to your hands."

"I don't think I want to pick any more blackberries," Mary Ellen said before I left the bedroom.

I smiled and replied, "I thought you might feel that way."

Mary Ellen and I left for the store an hour later, Mary Ellen feeling the effect from every thorn prick. I didn't have the heart to tell her the scratches would probably hurt worse by morning. In this case, the snake being in the blackberry patch turned out to be a blessing. I don't know how much more abuse Mary Ellen could have endured.

"I have a whole new respect for you and your momma," Mary Ellen said as we rode along. "I had no idea picking berries could be so painful."

"You'll do better the next time," I replied cheerily.

"Virginia, there will not be a next time," Mary Ellen said. "Teach me to milk the cow and I will do that while you and your momma pick berries."

I laughed and turned the team left off Water Street onto Leavenworth Paoli road. Making a right turn a few feet later onto Main Street, I pulled up in front of the store and dropped Mary Ellen off. I then drove to the back of the store to turn Clyde and Nellie into the corral for the day.

As I entered the back of the store, I bent to pet Annie, praising her for the mouse she had caught overnight and left at the back door. As I looked about, I gasped at the sight before me. Feed bags had been cut open, their contents spilled all over the floor of the storeroom. Extra supplies that had been neatly stacked on shelves now lay strewn. Realizing someone had purposely made the mess, I hurried to the front of the store, fearing that Mary Ellen may have encountered the intruder. Walking through the doorway from the storeroom into the main part of the store I called, "Mary Ellen, you okay?"

Mary Ellen stood in stunned silence. Every item had been knocked from its shelf. There were buttons and thread everywhere, along with cat's eye marbles that had been dumped from the jars they were kept in. "Who did this?" Mary Ellen asked, finally finding her voice.

Walking to the counter to see if the gun was still under it, I answered, "I don't know, but whoever it was, they stole Papa's gun."

"So, they must have known it was hidden under the counter," Mary Ellen said.

"Yes, but just about everyone in Marengo knows Papa keeps a gun under the counter," I replied. "However, only one person has caused Papa to fire it."

"The Copperhead," Mary Ellen stated.

"Yes, and after the beating he received the last time he was here, he has motive to seek revenge," I replied.

Mary Ellen looked all around again. "What are we going to do with this mess?"

"Clean it up, I suppose. We have no other option. I probably need to go tell Papa, but I don't think it is wise to leave you here alone."

At that moment, the first customer of the day entered the store. It was Mary Wiseman, the classiest lady I knew. She lived on a 400 acre farm, just east of Marengo, in one of the three most beautiful houses in the county.

I could barely remember the houses being built, but Papa had talked about them frequently and had assisted with drafting the plans. All three houses had been built in 1853, and were made from bricks that had been formed from the red clay near Mary's house. A kiln had been built and enough bricks had been formed and fired to build three, two-story homes. The houses had fireplaces at each end and looked almost identical. The two other houses were about a quarter mile east of Mary's, but I had always liked the setting of Mary's best. It appeared to be nestled on a little knoll overlooking Whiskey Run creek, with a nice spring behind it.

"What on earth has happened here?" Mary asked, looking around at the mess.

"We don't really know," I replied, "but think it could have been an act of revenge."

"Who would want to take revenge on you, Virginia?" Mary asked.

"Not necessarily on me," I replied. "Papa fired a gun to end a fight between Kirk Schultz and a Copperhead about a month ago. The Copperhead had purposely stopped here at the general store to pick a fight, knowing that Marengo is a heavy supporter of the Union."

"Goodness, child, that man is dangerous and could certainly

come back," Mary fretted.

"Well, he probably won't. He's obviously a coward since he came to do his dirty work under the cover of darkness. However, I am afraid to leave Mary Ellen here alone so I can go get Papa," I admitted.

"I'll stay here and start cleaning up," Mary said. "I need some thread and buttons, so I'll look through the selection while I put them back on the shelf."

"Thank you, Mary," I replied. "I will hurry so you can get home before your husband begins to worry."

"Bobby's busy in the fields," Mary replied. "He's working on the second cutting of hay. He won't know I'm gone until he comes in for lunch."

"That's what Papa's doing, too. I'm sure he will quit and come to the store when I tell him what has happened."

The door of the general store opened and Delmar walked through. "Land's sakes, what happened in here?"

"We've been vandalized," Mary Ellen said, picking up and sorting buttons as she spoke.

Delmar walked closer to Mary Ellen. "Did you try to fight them off?"

"No, it happened during the night. It looked like this when we got here this morning," Mary Ellen said.

"So who did you fight to get those scratches on your hands?" Delmar asked.

"The blackberry briars," Mary Ellen said.

Delmar chuckled softly. "Mary Ellen, I believe the briars won."

Mary Ellen smiled, despite how painful the experience had been. "No, Delmar, the snake won. The briars just left a lasting reminder that no matter how delicious blackberry desserts are, they are not worth the pain!"

"Who do you think done this?" Delmar asked.

"So far, the only thing I find missing is Papa's gun he kept under the counter. It could have been the Copperhead that received such a beating a few weeks back."

"That would be my guess, Virginia. I'm sure your Papa made him quite mad by firing that gun and running him off."

"That's the only person I can think would do such a thing as this," I said, spreading my arm toward the mess. "I'm going to get

Papa now. He will want to know about this immediately."

"I'll go get your papa," Delmar said. "I think you have plenty to keep you busy."

"Why thank you Delmar. That would be quite helpful. Ollie will be so glad to see you."

"Too bad the gun was stolen," Delmar said, "or I would take it with me as a welcoming gift for your good old Ollie."

I smiled sweetly. "Momma's home, so Ollie will behave today. He just doesn't like strangers coming to our home."

"I ain't no stranger," Delmar grumped.

"Here, take him this," I said, handing Delmar some venison jerky we had in a jar on the counter. "He will be your friend for life."

Delmar took the jerky and huffed. "Ridiculous, giving that dog perfectly good jerky." Taking a bite of the jerky, Delmar stomped toward the back door to hitch Nellie and Clyde back up and head to our farm.

As each customer came in, they would put aside what they had come for and start helping us clean up. By the time Papa and Delmar returned, ten people were placing things back on shelves and putting the feed into new bags. I could never imagine anyone from our little community breaking in and making such a mess. Whoever had done this had been an outsider, someone who had no respect for his fellow man. That did not describe anyone I knew in or around Marengo.

"Virginia, I don't know who did this, but I will be staying at the store for a few nights," Papa said as we finished sweeping up the last of the mess.

"I believe it was the Copperhead, Papa, but I suppose we will never know for sure."

"One thing is for certain," Papa said, looking around at all the help, "we sure have some good friends."

"That we do, Papa."

Papa slept at the store Wednesday and Thursday night, but the intruder did not come back. He had come home on Thursday morning to work on the farm, but stayed Friday morning to wait for the mail to come. Around ten we heard Delmar hollering from the porch.

"Hey, Stephen, the stagecoach is headed this way!"

The stagecoach did not make many stops in Marengo. For it to be headed toward the general store now meant something big had happened or someone important was making a stop. Either way, none of us wanted to miss it. Papa, Mary Ellen and I all rushed out to the porch to join the other ten men already lounging around there.

"Wonder who could be on the stagecoach," Joe, Effie's father, said.

"I don't have a clue," Papa replied, watching as the stagecoach came to a stop.

The door of the coach opened and out stepped a young man in a Union uniform. He was very thin and as he turned to face us we noticed his right hand was missing all its fingers but the pointer one, and it was just a nub. The thumb was still intact but the hand was mutilated. The recognition came to Papa, Mary Ellen and me at the same time.

"Reuben," Mary Ellen whispered.

Poor Reuben was nearly knocked to the ground as the three of us encircled him. Tears streamed down our cheeks, as well as Reuben's and the men gathered on the porch. A son had come home! It was unspeakable joy. The stagecoach left his one piece of luggage and continued north toward Bloomington.

Reuben was pelted with questions from every direction. He tried to answer them all but everyone wanted to know something. "Maybe all of you should write your questions down," Reuben finally suggested. "I'll be here at the store tomorrow and will answer any of them I can."

"You better get home to see your momma," Papa said. "If I make her wait until the store closes, she will be very upset."

"Yes, you're right," Reuben said. "Mary Ellen and I will go to the farm and we'll see you and Virginia at supper."

"I'll go hitch up Clyde and Nellie," Papa said, then looked at Reuben with tears gathering in his eyes again. "It's so good to see you home, Son."

"It's good to be home, Papa."

Mary Ellen and Reuben stayed another ten minutes in town then headed home. Reuben promised to come and pick us up at the store when it closed at six, since he was taking mine and Papa's ride. Papa told him not to bother, we would just walk.

"Nonsense," Delmar said. "I'll go home and bring my wagon back. I'll take you home when the store closes."

"Thank you, Delmar," Reuben said.

"I have a better idea," I said. "Since the weather has cooled down a bit, why don't Momma, Mary Ellen and Reuben come back to the store at closing time. We could spread the word around town and have a pitch-in celebration in honor of Reuben's safe return. Mary Ellen and I could play our guitars and everyone could sing, and maybe even dance. What do you think, Papa?"

"That sounds like a wonderful idea," Papa said. "Maybe others will bring instruments, too."

"I'll start spreading the word," Delmar said, hopping out of his chair. Other men got up too, all going in opposite directions to invite people to the celebration.

"We'll be back by five," Reuben promised as he and Mary Ellen climbed up on the wagon seat. As they headed down the street, I couldn't help but wonder how soon a wedding would be taking place.

When the mail arrived later that morning, there were few men left to listen to the war reports. For this reason, Papa chose to wait a little while to read the newspapers out loud.

There had been a copy of the Corydon Democrat included in the mailbag, which contained a firsthand account of Morgan's raid. That was really the only war happenings any of the newspapers contained, other than the latest list of fallen soldiers.

I sorted the mail and waited on customers, telling each one about the pitch-in that would take place at the store that night. Papa and I were kept busy, with no time for a break until about two o'clock. Finally, the store cleared and the porch filled with men seeking shade from the heat of the day. It was then that Papa picked up the Corydon Democrat and went to the porch. I lingered near the screen door so I could hear what Papa read.

"What's in the newspaper this week, Stephen?" Delmar asked as Papa settled into a chair.

"I have a copy of the Corydon Democrat," Papa said. "The paper is a week old, but it has a report about Morgan's raid."

"Tell us what the local paper had to say about the raid," Joe said.

Papa opened the paper and scanned the article again, making sure to get the facts straight. "It explains the battle just about the same as the Louisville Daily Journal did, but it added that before Morgan crossed at Brandenburg, Kentucky, he sent some of his men east and north to confuse the Union troops as to what his plans were. Those men were captured at New Pekin, Indiana before they could rejoin Morgan. Also, a Confederate soldier who was with Morgan was tapping telegraph lines, pretending to be a Union telegrapher. The man was nicknamed Lightening Ellsworth. He kept the Union troops quite confused about Morgan's next location."

"That was actually pretty smart," Delmar said.

"Yes, it was," Papa agreed. "It states here that the Presbyterian Church in Corydon was used as a hospital for the forty wounded Confederate soldiers after the battle at Corydon."

"Well, at least they have some humanity," Pastor David said. "I'm sure the wounded Confederate soldiers will be sent to a prisoner's camp when they recover, but at least they weren't left to die."

"Where are Morgan and his raiders now?" Delmar asked.

"Still giving chase throughout southern Ohio," Papa said. "Surely they will be captured soon."

"Morgan's made quite a run of this," Joe said. "He's kept the Union soldiers chasing after him for nearly three weeks."

"Yes, he has," Papa agreed. "I'm just glad he didn't burn the first Capital building of Indiana while he was in Corydon. That surely would have been a shame."

"With everything else he has set fire to, I'm surprised he didn't," Delmar said.

The discussion continued about Corydon being Indiana's first capital and the distance Morgan's raid had covered thus far. When those topics were exhausted, the conversation changed to crops and the weather, the two most discussed things in our small, rural town. I started clearing the counter, preparing for the abundance of food and dessert that would surely show up at the store in just a few hours. There had not been much cause for celebration in our community for a while, so a good turnout was expected.

Momma, Mary Ellen and Reuben showed up at five, just as promised. Momma carried in a blackberry cobbler, still warm from the oven, among many other dishes. By the time the store closed at six, the counter was completely full of food, along with the store and porch being packed with people. We all ate our fill and Mary Ellen and I played until our fingers were sore. John Moon from up toward Piersontown had heard about the get together and brought his fiddle to add to the music. Joe had dug out his banjo and decided the strings would be good enough for now, but had ordered a new set from Louisville for the next time. The playing, singing and dancing lasted until midnight, no one wanting the good time to end.

"We should do this at least once a month," Papa decided. "It's been a long time since I've had so much fun."

"I agree, Stephen," Momma said. "It would give everyone a break from all the worry and sadness of the war."

And so it began. The third Friday evening of each month there would be a pitch-in supper, followed by music and dancing at the general store. Everyone would be welcome, and anyone who had an instrument was encouraged to bring it along. The only thing that would be forbidden would be whiskey, for drunkenness would lead to many other problems, and Papa was not going to tolerate that.

Chapter Seventeen

With Reuben home, the responsibility of the store went back to him, which was just fine with me. He seemed to have adjusted to the injury sustained to his right arm and hand, though he still experienced some pain. As we sat out on the porch of the summer kitchen after Sunday dinner, Papa discussed with us the plans for the farm and the store.

"I will take care of most of the farm work," Papa said, "if you can go to the store every day, Reuben."

"Yes, I think I can handle the store," Reuben said. "I can help on the farm, too, when you need an extra hand." Reuben laughed softly, holding up his deformed right hand, "But just one hand."

We all looked at each other, not knowing whether to laugh along or not. Reuben hadn't said much about the injury and now he was making a joke of the handicap. Reuben looked around at us and smiled, "Don't worry. I realize I will have to adjust to my injury, but I refuse to wallow in self-pity. I saw lots men with much worse injuries than mine. At least I can walk and talk and I will learn to use this arm to do what I need to do. I would have stayed in the army but I could not load a gun nor fire a cannon. I helped with the food, but all we ever ate was dried meat and hard tack. It doesn't take much to serve that. When I heard Carter had joined, I decided I would be more helpful here."

"We are so glad you're home, Son," Papa said. "I will allow you to decide what you feel you are able to handle."

Reuben looked at Mary Ellen sitting beside him and smiled. "In that case, I believe I will take a wife."

"Well, I do hope Mary Ellen is the woman you're planning to marry," Momma said with a smile.

"The one and only," Reuben said, smiling down at his soon-to-be bride.

"We will measure you for a wedding dress today," Momma said, getting up to find her measuring tape.

"Actually, we may not have to do that," Mary Ellen said. "I believe the dress my mother wore for her wedding will fit me."

"Oh, I never thought of that," Momma said. "So, have you set a date?"

"We've decided on Saturday, October 17th, when the leaves should be at their peak color," Mary Ellen said.

"Will you teach this year?" I asked.

"No, I don't think so," Mary Ellen replied. "Stephen, you might want to mention this to the rest of the men who oversee the school so they can search for a new teacher. I have someone in mind who I believe could do the job, though."

"Whom do you have in mind?" Momma asked.

"Why, Virginia, of course. I could help her with the lesson plans this first year, but she would be a fine teacher."

"Me?" I asked in disbelief. "You think I could teach school?"

"Of course, Virginia," Mary Ellen said. "Isn't that what you dream of doing?"

"Well, yes, but I didn't see it happening so soon," I admitted.

"I think it's a wonderful idea," Momma said. "Virginia, you can do this. Children love you and you love education. Mary Ellen has taken your lessons far beyond what you would ever be required to teach at the school."

"Yes, I believe Virginia is the solution," Papa said. "Elizabeth, I believe we should give the store to Reuben and Mary Ellen to run. They could live above it until they decide to build a house somewhere else. I have plenty to keep me busy on the farm, and when Carter returns, I could maybe do some drafting again to keep me busy."

"Papa, you don't have to give us the store," Reuben said.

"It was always my plan," Papa replied. "Carter always loved the farm and you loved the store. You will both do well with those things and I'm happy to give them to you."

"Thank you, Papa."

"That will keep my future grandchildren close to me, too," Momma said, causing Mary Ellen to blush.

"I will talk to the school board members tomorrow," Papa said. "I don't see anyone objecting to Virginia being the teacher, but we will discuss it. We all have to agree on who fills the position."

"So, I will open the store each day and Mary Ellen will work with me," Reuben said. "Virginia will help Momma as needed and help at the store, especially on Friday and Saturday."

"That sounds like a good plan," Papa said. "Mary Ellen can move into the upstairs of the store, if she would like, or she could stay in the teacher's cabin until you marry."

"I think I would prefer to stay in the cabin," Mary Ellen said. "Reuben and I can move into the upstairs of the store after we're married."

"Okay," Papa said. "If the school board agrees that Virginia may teach, it will be fine for you to do that. However, if they want to choose a different teacher, you will have to move. Of course, you could remain living here at the farm and Reuben move to the store."

"Actually, I believe I'll just go ahead and move to the store," Reuben said. "I wouldn't have to hitch the wagon or saddle a horse each morning."

"That's fine, Son," Papa said. "I will bring the wagon to town on days supplies are needed from Milltown and we can go together. I can make the trip to Leavenworth for supplies, too, though we don't go there often."

"I think we have everything decided," Momma announced. "Anyone for blackberry dumplings with whipped cream?"

"Yes, that sounds delicious," Mary Ellen said.

Reuben laughed softly and lifted one of Mary Ellen's hands. "By the way, please don't torture Mary Ellen in the blackberry patch anymore. She still has battle wounds."

Momma laughed and replied, "At least she didn't get snake bit."

Momma and I went to dip generous bowls of blackberry dumplings smothered in cream for everyone. As I sat down to enjoy my bowl, I couldn't help but think how much Carter loved this farm. I looked out over the fields below the house with Whiskey Run creek running through them. The big Maple stood up on the hill to the west of the house. I could hear the spring running over the rocks, creating a melody all its own. I silently whispered a prayer that Carter would get to come back to the place he loved most, and I whispered one for Angus, too. With each battle of the war bringing such mass numbers of casualties, the reality that Carter or Angus may not survive could not be denied.

****

Papa met with the other school board members the next day. They all agreed that I should be given the opportunity to take the teaching position. Teaching had been a dream, but now that it had become a reality, I was afraid I would not do the job well. When I went to the store on Friday to help out, I confessed my fear to Mary Ellen.

"Mary Ellen, are you sure I'm ready to teach school?" I asked as we straightened the bolts of fabric.

"Virginia, you're seventeen," Mary Ellen said. "I was only eighteen when I came here to teach, and your momma was only eighteen when she began to teach. You're smart and you have an adventurous spirit. Those two things will make you a wonderful teacher. You will come up with all kinds of new ways for the children to learn, and that's what makes a good teacher. Being overly strict and using a ruler every time you want a child's attention will not get you far, but being creative enough to keep their attention, well, that's where the talent really lies. Anyone can be mean and scare children into behaving, but the talent is when you keep learning interesting enough that you don't need to use a ruler very often. I'm not saying you will never have to discipline a child, but I believe it won't happen often."

"And you'll help me with the lesson preparations?" I asked softly.

"Yes, Virginia, I will help you," Mary Ellen replied, "but honestly, I don't think you will need my help for long. Once you get in the classroom, you will begin to come up with your own techniques and ideas."

"I just hope I do the job well," I fretted.

"Virginia, you will do a wonderful job. Trust me on this."

I smiled at Mary Ellen, thankful I had someone who believed in me and would help me get off to a good start. "Thank you, Mary

Ellen. Your confidence in me means a lot."

"You're welcome, Virginia."

The mail wagon pulled up in front of the store at that moment and Mary Ellen and I followed Reuben out onto the porch. Thaddeus was surprised to be met my Reuben instead of Papa. Bringing the horses to a stop, he set the brake and hopped down with the mailbag. Carrying it to the porch, he handed it to me. "You're Papa not here, Virginia?" he asked.

"No Thaddeus, Papa is at home," I replied, handing him the bag of outgoing mail. "Reuben will be running the store from now on."

Thaddeus turned to Reuben, looking him up and down. Reuben looked back and smiled, putting Thaddeus at ease. "Don't worry, Thaddeus, I can run this store just fine with one hand."

"Well, now Reuben, I didn't think you couldn't," Thaddeus stammered. "The Louisville Daily Journal has a report on John Hunt Morgan and his raiders. It seems the crazy man has finally been captured."

"Well, it's about time," Delmar boomed from his chair on the porch.

"I agree," Thaddeus replied. "Well, I'll see you next Friday, Reuben."

"I look forward to it," Reuben replied.

As the mail wagon pulled away, I opened the mailbag and handed Reuben the newspapers before heading into the store to begin sorting the mail. Reuben took the offered papers with a funny look on his face. Shrugging, he started to follow me back into the store.

"Reuben Hensley, just where do you think you're going?" Delmar asked.

"I have work to do, Delmar," Reuben replied. "I've already beaten you at checkers three times this week. How many more times do you want to lose?"

"Your Papa always reads us the important stuff from the newspapers," Delmar complained. "What do you think this porch full of men have been waiting for?"

Reuben looked questioningly at me. I shrugged and explained. "Since the war began, Papa has kept everyone up to date on the progress. He reads through the paper then tells everyone the latest news. It has become a Friday tradition. I'll explain why later, but for now, you need to read the headlines and choose the stories of interest."

Reuben stared at the bundle of newspapers in his left hand. Turning back to the porch, he discovered a chair had been vacated so he could sit down. Lowering himself into the chair, he began to sift through the papers, surprisingly turning the pages with ease with his thumb and part of an index finger on his right hand. Clearing his throat, he began to read the article about Brigadier John Hunt Morgan's capture.

"On Sunday, July 26th, Union troops finally captured…

"Um, excuse me, Reuben," Delmar interrupted, "we don't want you to read the article out loud. Just read through it and tell us what it says, in your own words."

Reuben looked at all the expectant faces on the porch of the general store. Shaking his head, he looked back down at the article and quickly read through it. Looking back up, he said, "John Hunt Morgan and his remaining 400 men were captured."

"Oh, come on, Reuben," Delmar goaded, "you can do better than that. Where was he at when he was captured and where did they cage him up?"

Sighing heavily, Reuben tried again. "John Hunt Morgan was captured in West Point, Ohio. He and his men have taken residency in Columbus at the Ohio Penitentiary, where I assume they will remain until the war is over and maybe for the rest of their lives."

"That was better," Delmar said. "Is there anything else interesting to share with us?"

"There was a battle on July 19th between the Union forces and Morgan and his men at Buffington Island, as the Confederates attempted to cross the Ohio River," Reuben said. "It was considered a Union victory, but obviously John Hunt Morgan and some of his men got away."

"That Morgan feller is like a sly old fox in a henhouse," Delmar said. "Do you think they will be able to keep him contained in the penitentiary?"

"Goodness, Delmar, I don't think the man will escape from the penitentiary," Reuben said.

"Well, he might," Delmar huffed. "Are there any other battles to report?"

"No, it appears to have been a quiet week," Reuben said. Placing the Louisville Daily Journal aside, Reuben picked up the Crisis, which was printed in Leavenworth. "This might be of interest. Bruce Kemp's pigs got out and tore up Ted Conrad's garden."

Pastor David laughed. "I bet that caused quite a raucous."

"Yep, the sheriff had to be called in. Mr. Kemp will be required to pay for the damaged plants and smooth out Mr. Conrad's yard and sow grass seed. I guess those pigs must have really tore things up," Reuben said.

I listened as Reuben warmed up to the idea of reporting all the useful information from the newspapers, if pigs getting out could be considered useful. He went all through the Crisis, reporting every tidbit printed there. There had been a fight in the tavern at Leavenworth the previous Saturday night and two tables and six chairs were broken. The Mansfield family had a new addition, making their total number of children ten now. The topic of a railroad being run from Indianapolis to Leavenworth had been brought up again, and promptly shot down. No one wanted the noisy thing running through their property, hitting their cattle and leaving bits and pieces of bovine scattered hither and yon along the tracks. Most of the men on the porch didn't know many of the people mentioned, being most were from the Leavenworth area, but it gave them something to discuss and solve there on the porch of the general store.

Two hours later, the porch began to clear and Reuben came back into the store. Mary Ellen and I had sorted all the mail and waited on customers during that time. Angus and Carter both had sent letters, and I couldn't wait for a chance to read mine from Angus. I knew it wouldn't be until I got home this evening, and I found myself reaching into my apron pocket several times to touch the envelope. Just knowing Angus and Carter were unharmed so far brought comfort. Carter had sent a letter to Effie, too, and she had come to the store to pick hers up when she saw the mail wagon leaving.

"So, Virginia, why must I report the news from the papers to the porch gatherers?" Reuben asked.

"Well, some can't read the newspaper," I began, "and the rest want the information given to them by a friend, instead of reading the cold, black and white print. You and Papa add the touch of sympathy when needed, and indignation when required."

"I see," Reuben replied. "We have now solved all of the county's problems right on the porch of the general store. Perhaps I should become a lawyer and the checker players could be my advisors."

"That might not be a bad idea," Mary Ellen said, smiling at Reuben.

As Reuben's eyes took in Mary Ellen's smiling face and laughing eyes, he knew he would be reading the newspaper to the men gathered on the porch of the general store for a very long time. If that's what it took to make her smile at him like she was now, he would do it willingly. "Maybe you should start reporting what you find interesting in the newspapers to the men," Reuben said.

"No, Reuben, that would never do," Mary Ellen said. "They want to hear things from a man's point of view. I would be too emotional for their taste."

"Sorry, Reuben, that is now your task each Friday," I said. "Don't worry, you will settle into it. I thought you did very well today, for your first time and all."

"Why, thank you, Virginia," Reuben said.

Returning home from the store that evening riding crazy Knucklehead, I hoped Momma didn't have too many things for me to help her with. Today was the last day of July, so the days were already getting shorter. I knew eventually I would be forced to read the letters from Angus in my bedroom by lamp light, but I much preferred reading them perched in the Maple. It brought a comfort I could not explain.

Momma had supper prepared by the time I arrived home. I set the table on the summer kitchen porch, and Papa came from the barn. We sat down and Papa blessed the food, asking for God's protection over Carter and Angus, as he did every meal. As we began to eat, Papa asked, "Anything interesting in the newspaper this week?"

I knew it had pained him not to be at the store when the mail arrived and be the first to peruse the newspapers upon arrival. It was a tradition he had been accustomed to for years. It was probably one of the hardest parts of giving up the store. Looking up into my father's expectant face, I replied, "Morgan and his men were finally caught. I brought all the newspapers home for you to read."

Papa smiled, "Thank you, Virginia. I believe I will sit right here and read through them after supper."

"Oh, and we received a letter from Carter," I said, reaching into my apron pocket. I had put Angus's letter in my right pocket and Carter's in my left. Pulling the letter out, I handed it to Momma. She opened it immediately and read the short missive. Carter was not much on writing, so the fact that he wrote at all was a surprise. When she finished, she handed the letter to Papa for him to read. Lastly, Papa handed the letter to me. Carter stated that they were now in Tennessee, under the command of General Rosecrans. He had been chosen for the cavalry and had been training for that position until the next battle.

When we finished eating, I cleared the table and quickly washed the dishes while Papa read points of interest to Momma from the newspapers. It wasn't like reading to all the men at the general store, but it gave Papa the opportunity to discuss the events with someone as he read them. I hurried and put the dishes in the cabinets and took the dishwater outside and dumped it. Making sure everything was put away and cleaned to my mother's strict approval, I hurried out the summer kitchen door, passing Momma and Papa who were so engrossed in the discussion of Morgan and his men that they hardly noticed me.

Hurrying across the yard past the barn and pig pen, I set my sight on the Maple. There would be just enough daylight for me to read the letter nestled in my pocket before darkness settled into our valley. Reaching up, I grabbed the lowest limb and swung myself up. Climbing as quickly as possible, I reached my new favorite limb, about half way up the tree. Settling in, my back pressed on the trunk and my legs stretched out the length of the huge limb, I reached into my pocket and removed the letter from Angus.

July 20ᵗʰ, 1863

Dear Virginia,

Carter and I are now in Tennessee and are part of the Army of the West under the command of General Rosecrans. Carter has been chosen for the cavalry, which is no surprise. He has always been able to make a horse do anything he wants, though he may meet his match here on the battlefield. So many beasts are needed that many are just green broke. I have witnessed many a good rider be thrown already.

Carter pointed out to the commander of his regiment that I have skills working with leather. Since then, I have been kept quite busy repairing saddles and making harnesses. Besides this job, when we go to battle I will be responsible for helping to find injured soldiers and bury the dead. It is certainly not something I'm looking forward to but know it must be done. How do you look a man in the eye and tell him his injuries are so severe he will not live? Pray I will do this with empathy, Virginia, whether the dying is wearing a blue or gray uniform. I could very well be the last face some of these men ever see.

Our meals consist mostly of hardtack and dried beef. I dream of my mother's cooking and pray she sends some homemade cookies or other such food to supplement our most unappetizing meals. Maybe you and your momma could send Carter some food, too. We would be sure to share with one another. If I'm forced to survive on dried beef and hardtack, I fear I will come back a much slimmer man than when I left.

Each morning we have roll call and practice marching and staying in formation. We are required to keep our guns cleaned and ready at a moment's notice. There's really not much happening at the moment as far as battles, so we spend much of our day playing cards and our evenings singing songs around the campfire. I have learned new words to the tune of "John Brown's Body", and we sing the song as we march. It is called "The Battle Hymn of the Republic." I have included the words for you on a separate sheet of paper in this letter. I know you will want to play and sing it with your guitar.

You may write to me at the address I have written at the bottom of this letter. The mail is delivered to us often, and we may buy stamps when it comes. There is nothing we men look forward to more than receiving letters from home.

I have discovered that many of the men do not know how to read or write, and I have been asked to pen letters for several soldiers. I also read letters that have been sent to the same men. I realize now that I take for granted the fact that I am educated, but I will not do that anymore. I would not like to be reliant on someone else to put my thoughts on paper.

I have run out of things to tell you for now. I look forward to hearing from you, for I know you will tell me everything from home, sparing no details. Also, in case you don't know, my favorite kind of cookie is sugar. Maybe you will find a spare moment to bake some? I know you are very busy running the store and helping your momma and I really hate to ask, but I've been in the army less than a month and the thought of hardtack already turns my stomach.

Please be careful climbing out of the Maple. I know that is where you're sitting at this very moment. Carter has demonstrated his climbing skills many times here in the camp but claims you can out climb him any day of the week! All my love,

Angus

The thought of Carter bragging about my tree climbing skills brought a smile to my face. He would have never told me he thought I climbed well but he obviously did think it. I wondered why Reuben and Carter never mentioned sending food to them in their letters. Momma and I had never thought to do such a thing but come next Friday, there would be a large box addressed to Carter and Angus leaving the general store on its way to Tennessee.

Looking to the west, I watched as the sky turned its many shades of color as the sun sank below the horizon. I wondered if Carter and Angus were watching the same sunset, dreaming of home. I knew at that moment I may travel and see many sunsets from different places during my life but none would ever be like the ones seen from home. Whispering a prayer for Angus and Carter's safety, I began my descent from the maple tree.

Chapter Eighteen

The first week of August, 1863 brought more heat and humidity. Papa claimed it was so hot he feared the field corn would turn into popped corn on the stalk.

There were no pressing chores on the farm, or none that couldn't wait until the heat passed, so Papa went to the store all week. On Tuesday, I went to the store with Papa so he and Reuben could go to Milltown for supplies that day. In the heat of the afternoon when no one was in the store, I pulled the words of the song "The Battle Hymn of the Republic" from my pocket and showed them to Mary Ellen.

Holding the paper out to Mary Ellen, I said, "Angus sent me a copy of words for a new song. It's sung to the tune of "John Brown's Body". He said the Union soldiers sing the song as they march and as they sit around the campfire at night."

Mary Ellen took the paper from my hand and studied the words. "It seems simple enough and we both already know the tune to "John Brown's Body", since it's the same melody as an old camp meeting song. Let's go grab our guitars and try to sing it."

As Mary Ellen and I sat on stools at the counter practicing the song, Delmar and three other men came in off the porch to listen. By the time we sang the second verse, the men joined in on the chorus:

Glory! glory! Hallelujah! Glory! glory! Hallelujah!

Glory! glory! Hallelujah! His truth is marching on.

We had all gotten so engrossed in the song; we did not see Papa and Reuben enter from the back of the store. As we began the chorus again after the fourth and final verse, Reuben's voice boomed over everyone else. He then continued and sang all four verses from memory again. When the song was over, Mary Ellen smiled up at him. "Reuben, you know that song very well."

"I should say so," he replied. "I have been singing it for the past year; right after Julia Ward Howe penned those new words. It is the battle song for the Union Army. How did you and Virginia get the words?"

"Angus sent them to Virginia in a letter," Mary Ellen replied. "I believe we will sing it at church Sunday morning."

"That sounds like a fine idea," Delmar said. "I like a song with a little pep to it. However, that song will give Mrs. George a whole new list of complaints."

"Well, we all have our trials," Papa said. "Mrs. George's is that she is never content."

"That may be true," Mary Ellen said, "but she did finally accept my abnormal teaching techniques. It's your turn to convince her now, Virginia."

"Oh, my," I muttered.

Mary Ellen and I put our guitars away and went to help Reuben and Papa unload the wagon. I couldn't help but whistle the tune as I went along. I felt it was one of those songs that would stand the test of time, just like "Come, Thou Fount of Every Blessing". The thought that Carter, Angus and I were singing the same song also brought a sense of connection.

"You know, Virginia, I heard the Confederates singing a couple of songs, too, as I passed hospitals that housed wounded Confederate soldiers," Reuben said. "They had very catchy tunes, even though I can't remember most of the words. One was called "Dixie" and was about wanting to go home to the South. The other was "Eatin' Goober Peas", which is a funny song about peanuts. I guess the Confederate soldiers have been forced to eat a lot of peanuts since the war began."

"I will write to Angus and see if he can get the words for them," I said. "I might use the songs when I teach."

"That's a good idea, Virginia," Mary Ellen said. "Those songs will become part of our history. See, I told you your mind is adventurous. The children are going to love you."

Smiling at Mary Ellen, soaking in her approval, I replied, "I sure hope so."

****

Momma and I spent most of Thursday preparing sweet treats to send to Carter and Angus. We baked large batches of sugar and oatmeal raisin cookies, along with a peach pie made from peaches off our fruit trees. We placed the pie in a round tin and secured the lid tightly. We were sure the peach pie would be a mess by the time it reached Angus and Carter but knew they would each grab a fork and eat it anyway.

Papa constructed a wooden box for the baked goods to be placed in for shipping. I worried that Angus and Carter would have no way to remove the nails when the box arrived but Papa assured me they would figure out a way to get into the box. I carefully wrote the address on the outside, hoping Carter and Angus would still be at that location when it reached its destination. Handing the box to Papa on Friday morning as he headed to the store, along with a letter to Angus and one for Carter, I remained at home to help Momma in the garden. With Mary Ellen, Reuben and Papa at the store, my help was needed more at home.

Taking the hoe, I went to the garden as soon as the breakfast dishes were done. I knew this would be the coolest it would be all day, though I already had sweat trickling down my face and the back of my neck. I had tied a bandanna around my head to absorb some of the moisture before it could run into my eyes.

Walking along the edge, I checked the progress of the whole garden. Noting the green beans were almost ready again, I made a mental note to pick them Monday, hoping it would be cooler. Green beans could not be picked until the dew dried off the leaves, because if any disease was present, it would be spread from plant to plant. This meant I would have to wait until late morning to begin picking.

As I reached the watermelon patch I dropped the hoe at the edge of the garden and stepped in to inspect the stems. Finding one that the stem had begun to dry on, I thumped it with my finger. Deciding the melon was ripe; I plucked it from the vine and carried it to the spring house to get cold. It would be the first watermelon of the season, and sadly, the first watermelon I had ever eaten without Carter to play the seed spitting game with me.

Walking back to the garden, I picked the hoe up again and continued looking for ripe vegetables, chopping any weeds as I went along. When I reached the tomatoes, I found several ripe. Momma had picked tomatoes the last two days and placed them on a small table that was on the summer kitchen porch. With the ones that were there, plus the ripe ones I could see this morning, I knew canning tomatoes would be at the top of the list of things to get done.

Making my way back to the house, I placed the hoe in the gardening shed and grabbed a pail to collect the tomatoes. Heading back to the garden, I was already dreading how hot it would be canning tomatoes and making juice. However, I was thankful a new invention would make the job easier. Papa had found something called a mason jar on his latest trip to Leavenworth. It was a quart jar that had a screw on zinc lid and rubber gasket. The rubber gasket sealed out any air. Tomato juice and whole tomatoes could now be canned by bringing them to a boil and placing them in the jars, along with a teaspoon of salt. There was enough acid in the tomatoes to allow them to keep in a dark, cool cellar for a long time, as long as the gasket and lid stayed securely in place. Papa said the invention had been around since 1858, but here in our rural county, new things took a while to find us.

Carrying the full pail of tomatoes back to the summer kitchen, Momma and I set to work making juice. I could almost taste the vegetable soup it would create on cold winter days, as the rich smell wafted through the hot kitchen. Filling the clean jars, we put the rubber gasket and zinc lids on, making sure to seal them well. Food not canned properly could become your last meal, or make you sick enough to believe death was surely going to come. We finished the last batch as Papa returned from the store, coming home early since Reuben could close up on his own.

"Did I receive any mail today?" I asked as soon as Papa walked onto the porch of the summer kitchen.

"Yes, you received a letter," Papa said, "and Effie received one, too. Carter didn't write to us, but he made sure to write to Effie."

"You know Carter is not a letter writer," I replied, taking the letter that Papa held out to me. Seeing the familiar script, I knew it was from Angus. Stuffing it into my apron pocket, I would wait until later to read it. The pile of letters in my dresser drawer had grown quite large and I would need to find a small, wooden box to keep them in soon.

"We find out more about Carter from Angus's letters than the ones he randomly sends," Momma said. "As long as I know he's safe, I suppose it doesn't matter how often he writes."

"I can assure you he will be glad to receive the box you and Virginia put together and mailed today," Papa said. "We all know how Carter loves to eat."

"Maybe Carter will write after he receives the box. Putting pen to paper has always been difficult for him. He would much rather be working a field than reading or writing any day," I said, defending the brother I loved and missed so much.

"Yes, maybe," Momma agreed then chuckled, "or maybe he will just tell Angus to tell us thank you."

"That is probably what will happen," Papa said, "but you know he will enjoy the goodies just the same."

Momma and I wiped everything down and I washed up the dishes from our day of canning. Momma had saved some of the tomato juice and turned it into a delicious soup. Cutting thick slices of bread, I buttered them and made grilled cheese, using the cheese we created from our Jersey's milk. As we sat out on the porch to eat our simple meal, Momma asked Papa, "Any new war reports in the newspapers today?"

"No, nothing today," Papa said. "It must be too hot to even fight a battle. I brought the *Crisis* home so you can read the local news, though. I know how you like to keep up on who's getting married and new births in the area."

"It's always nice to read some good news," Momma said. "There's certainly been enough bad news the past few years."

"Isn't that the truth," Papa muttered.

Area residents brought announcements, death notices and things they wanted advertised to the general store all written out. The information was placed in an envelope and sent to the Crisis in the outgoing mail bag, which was picked up each Friday. Each small town in the county did the same, and the Crisis would include the advertisements and announcements in the next week's newspaper. Sometimes a county resident would report something, like livestock escaping its confinement and causing damage or how crops were growing. Most of the information was pointless, but it kept us all connected and gave us something to talk about.

After finishing our meal, I washed the dishes and put them away quickly. Slipping from the summer kitchen, I silently passed Momma and Papa deep in conversation about something written in the Crisis. Making my way to the Maple, I climbed to my favorite limb. Settling in, I removed the letter from my apron pocket and began to read. Angus told of everything the soldiers did in the camp while waiting for the next battle, which would be his and Carter's first battle. Angus put things to paper so well, it was as if he were right beside me telling about his past week.

When I finished reading, I folded the letter and placed it back into my apron pocket. As I did, my hand touched the leather heart I kept there. Pulling it from my pocket, I touched the words engraved on it. There was no question that I would wait for Angus's return; I just hoped it would be soon. There had been too much blood shed; too many young lives cut short. I could not bear the thought that Carter or Angus might add to those numbers. Climbing out of the tree as darkness settled around the farm, I made my way back to the house.

****

The second week of August kept Momma and me busy with preserving the garden harvest. The grapes also ripened juicy and dark purple. We turned the fruit into juice for the upcoming winter and sweet jelly. Papa spent most of the week at the store, since the crops were growing and not ready to harvest, and the third cutting of hay would be several weeks away. When Papa returned home from the store on Friday, Momma and I gleaned information from him as we ate supper.

"Anything interesting reported in the newspapers?" Momma asked.

"The only report on the war was about a Negro troop attacking Fort Wagner in South Carolina," Papa said.

"Were there many casualties?" I asked.

"Unfortunately, yes," Papa said. "Their commander, Col. Robert Shaw, and half of the 600 men in the regiment were killed."

Momma gasped, "That's terrible!"

"Yes, a huge loss. President Lincoln has met with abolitionist Frederick Douglass," Papa added. "Douglass is pushing for full equality for the Union Negro troops."

"The Negro troops deserve the same treatment as the white troops," I said.

"I agree," Papa said, "every soldier should receive the same treatment."

"Any other news?" Momma asked.

"I brought the *Crisis* home for you to read, and here's a letter from Carter," Papa replied, holding out an envelope to Momma.

"Any letters for me?" I asked

Papa smiled and chuckled. "It took you long enough to ask. I have one for you from Angus."

Snatching the letter from Papa's hand, I stuffed it in my apron pocket. "Thanks, Papa."

"You're welcome. Effie came to the store this morning and mailed a box to Carter. He must have complained to her about the awful food, too."

"You know, I should talk to Angus's mother and Effie," Momma said. "We could take turns sending a box of food to the boys."

"That's a good idea," Papa replied. "Carter and Angus could receive a box every week, but you would only have to do the extra baking once every three weeks."

"I'll talk to them on Sunday," Momma said.

We finished our supper and Momma and Papa spent time reading and discussing the articles in the *Crisis* while I washed the dishes and put them away. When the summer kitchen was put back in order, I slipped away to my usual Friday evening spot, which was the large limb half way up the Maple. I read the letter from Angus then relaxed my back against the trunk as the sun's rays changed the sky to the brilliant colors only sunset can paint. I whispered a prayer for Angus and Carter's safety and watched the ever changing sky until there was no light left. I climbed down carefully and headed toward the house, already anticipating the next Friday's visit to my old friend.

****

The days of August passed, but by the beginning of the fourth week the heat and humidity had finally let up. Everyone was looking forward to some cooler temperatures that usually came with September. I had been working on lesson plans for the past week at the store with Mary Ellen between customers. School would start on

September 7th, just a little over a week away.

"Quit wringing your hands, Virginia," Mary Ellen scolded. "You're going to be a fine teacher. Give yourself a chance and please, relax."

"I'm trying, Mary Ellen, honest I am," I replied, "it's just I'm so afraid I'm going to fail at this."

"You will not fail," Mary Ellen said with twice the confidence in me than I had in myself. "You have me and your momma to help you if you need us."

"Yes, I know," I said, "and I am very thankful for that."

"I will help you get started," Mary Ellen said as we looked over the first week's lesson plan again, "but I want you to take over fully by the second week of school. You need to cultivate your own creativeness and not borrow from mine, though I don't mind if you use some of my techniques."

"Thank you for all your help, Mary Ellen."

"You're welcome, Virginia," Mary Ellen replied.

Just then we heard the sound of a wagon pulling up in front of the store. Grabbing the mail bag and the box Momma and I had packed for Angus and Carter, I headed toward the door. Stepping through the screen door, I reached the porch just as Thaddeus set the brake on the wagon.

"Good morning, Virginia," Thaddeus greeted.

"Good morning, Thaddeus," I replied, handing him the box and outgoing mailbag. He handed me Marengo's mailbag in return.

"So, what's in the box this time?" Thaddeus asked. "No, don't tell me. It just makes me want to open it and sample a few items throughout the day."

Smiling at Thaddeus, I reached into my apron pocket and withdrew two cookies I had wrapped in paper for him. "Here, maybe this will help."

"Gee, thanks Virginia," Thaddeus said.

Papa stepped up behind me and I reached in the mailbag to retrieve the newspapers. As I placed them in his outstretched hand, Thaddeus said, "Terrible thing has happened out in Kansas, Stephen. You might want to read that first."

"Thanks for letting me know, Thaddeus," Papa replied.

"Well, gotta go!" Thaddeus hollered as he released the brake and put the horses back in motion.

Papa made his way back to the porch, searching the newspapers for the event Thaddeus had mentioned. I carried the mailbag in and Mary Ellen offered to do the sorting. Making my way back to the screen door, I leaned against the doorframe to listen to the report Papa would give.

"Dear God," I heard Papa mutter as his eyes scanned the newspaper.

"What's happened now, Stephen?" Delmar asked, looking up from his game of checkers.

"There has been a massacre in Lawrence, Kansas," Papa replied, sinking down in the nearest chair. Today, there were only ten men on the porch of the store. Since John Hunt Morgan and his men had been stopped, the crowd had dwindled, as farmers busied themselves at home. They would always gather the latest news as they came to pick up their mail, though.

Delmar looked at Papa confused, "Lawrence, Kansas? What does Lawrence, Kansas have to do with the war?"

"Apparently, Lawrence, Kansas is full of abolitionists," Papa said. "A group of nearly 300 outlaws, led by two fellows by the names of William Quantrill and "Bloody Bill" Anderson, decided to take matters into their own hands and support the South's cause. The group attacked Lawrence at dawn on August 21st, and by nine that morning, nearly 200 men and boys lay dead and a quarter of the town was on fire."

"So, they attacked a town, not a military post?" Delmar questioned.

"It appears so," Papa answered. "By the time Union troops arrived, the outlaws were long gone."

"That's just being cowards," Delmar protested, "attacking people while they're unarmed and still asleep to boot!"

"I agree," Papa said, "however, I'm not sure I agree with the decision Union General Thomas Ewing, Jr. had for the situation."

"I hope he plans to hunt those men down!" Delmar bellowed.

"I'm sure they are trying to find the men," Papa said, "but Ewing issued what he calls General Order No.11. It's forced the evacuation of four rural counties in western Missouri, where he thinks the plan may have begun. Every person in those counties has to leave their homes and move close to a Union military post to show their support for the North. If they are not willing to do that, they must leave the area for good."

"Are you telling me four whole counties in Missouri are void of people?" Delmar asked.

"According to the article in the *Louisville Daily Journal* from yesterday, that's exactly what I'm saying," Papa replied.

"That sure don't leave a man many options," Pastor David chimed in.

"No, it sure doesn't," Papa agreed.

The men continued to discuss the bloody massacre in Kansas as I returned to the counter to help Mary Ellen finish sorting the mail. Reuben came from the storeroom and I told him and Mary Ellen what Papa had read in the newspaper. Reuben went out on the porch to join the discussion. The screen door had no sooner slapped shut when it opened again and Effie walked through.

"I just came to pick up our mail," Effie said.

"Funny how you were never overly concerned with your mail until my brother joined the Union army," I said, reaching into Effie's mailbox.

Effie giggled and blushed slightly, "Well, I never had a reason to be concerned until now."

As I gathered the pieces of mail, I recognized Carter's handwriting on an envelope addressed to Effie. "Do you think Carter received the box you sent two weeks ago?"

"That's what I'm hoping to find out," Effie said, reaching for the few pieces of mail.

"I sent another box from Momma and me today, and Angus's mother sent one last Friday. Those two will be the envy of their regiment."

"Well, it's better than starving," Mary Ellen chimed in. "Had I realized the food was so terrible, I would have sent Reuben boxes, too."

"Reuben never mentioned that he was living on hard tack and dried beef," I said, "but he was sure skinny when he returned home."

"He said he didn't want to complain," Mary Ellen said. "Reuben says that as bad as the food is for the Union soldiers, the Confederates have it much worse. Not only do they have very little to eat, there have been times when sickness has claimed many lives from Confederate troops."

"This war has brought so much sadness and heartache," Effie

said softly.

"Yes and the killings have not been limited to the battlefield," I said. "Last month there were the riots in New York where over 100 innocent lives were taken, and now nearly 200 men and boys have lost their lives just for being known supporters of the Union in the town of Lawrence, Kansas."

"I just heard the men on the porch discussing that," Effie said. "I can't believe anyone would be so cruel to drag innocent young boys from their beds and murder them. What kind of evil person could look a child in the eyes and still kill him?"

"I can't imagine," Mary Ellen said, "but I hope I never meet up with a person who could commit such acts of violence."

"The question still is how much longer will it last?" I said.

"And what if the North loses?" Mary Ellen added. "What then?"

"I don't know," Effie said, "but I do know this, our country will be changed forever, no matter who wins."

"Do you think we should still have the monthly pitch-in tonight?" I asked. "With the sad news we received today, I just wonder if we should."

"Virginia, I think we need to gather, if for no other reason than to pray for the people of Lawrence, Kansas," Mary Ellen said.

"That's true," I agreed. Turning to Effie, I asked, "Are you and your family coming to the store tonight for the monthly pitch-in?"

"Yes, we will be here," Effie said. "Momma and I already made some desserts to bring for it this morning. I have been looking forward to it all week, especially since it's cooled down and the humidity has dropped. I think you're right, Mary Ellen, we still need to gather. I need to head home now. I told Momma I would just be gone a minute."

"Okay, Effie," I said. "See you tonight."

Effie left the store, the screen door announcing her exit with a bang. Mary Ellen and I kept busy waiting on customers and retrieving people's mail. Papa and Reuben came in from the porch as the store became busy with farmers needing bags of feed for their livestock and items for various building projects some were doing. Before we knew it, it was five o'clock and items of food began appearing on the counter, as locals showed up for the monthly get together. Papa left to go home and bring Momma back to the store for the evening.

"Goodness, I believe there's more people here this time than last," Momma said as she walked into the store. "I believe we are going to need a separate table just for desserts."

"I think you're right," Reuben said, clearing off a table that held bolts of fabric. Mary Ellen and I jumped in to help, carrying the fabric to the storeroom where it could be placed safely on a shelf.

At six o'clock, Pastor David blessed the food and we all filled our plates to overflowing. I would have preferred to start at the dessert table, but I knew I would catch a good scolding from Momma. Besides, as the new school teacher, I really needed to set a good example. When everyone had eaten their fill, the instruments began to be tuned.

Pastor David stood and cleared his throat. "I think it would be fitting if we all said a prayer for the families in Lawrence, Kansas, who have been a part of this recent attack by outlaws." It was all he needed to say. Every man removed his hat and we all joined hands there in the general store and out on the porch, where the crowd had spilled over. Pastor David prayed, and afterwards we all sang hymns of comfort. As we came to the third and fourth verses of "My Faith Looks Up to Thee", I was thankful that in the midst of all the turmoil, there was always hope in Christ. We sang those last two verses, though not with perfect timing or pitch, but entirely heartfelt:

While life's dark maze I tread, And griefs around me spread,
Be Thou my Guide. Bid darkness turn to day; Wipe sorrow's tears away;
Nor let me ever stray From Thee aside!
While ends life's transient dream, When death's cold, sullen stream
Shall o'er me roll, Blest Savior, then in love Fear and distrust remove.
O bear me safe above A ransomed soul!

Though this war appeared endless and somewhat hopeless, God was in control and offered peace that passed all understanding. We just needed to put our faith in Him, for everything else would eventually let us down. Man would always have free will, for God had given him that when He created him. Sometimes man chose to use that free will to do very evil things. Our hope lay in the fact that we could choose to put our hand in His, and He would lead us through the trials of this life and safely into the next life. Without that hope, we would be a people most miserable.

<u>Chapter Nineteen</u>

Monday, September 7^{th,} 1863 dawned sunny and clear. I rose from my bed thirty minutes earlier than usual, too excited to sleep. Quickly, I changed from my nightgown into my work dress. I hurried downstairs and outside to the barn to milk the cow.

Annabelle, the cow who was now fresh, took her sweet time coming to the barn after I called. She knew good and well that it was not the normal milking time and she pinned her ears back as she shuffled into the barn.

"Come on, Annabelle, don't get cranky over a milking that's a few minutes early," I soothed as I locked her head in the stanchion. "Today is a very special day and I want to look my best. You can't blame a girl for that, now can you?"

Annabelle began to eat her grain, ignoring me all together. I washed her teats and dried them then plopped down on the stool to get the task finished. As I set a rhythm, I allowed my mind to wander to the day ahead. I rehearsed how I would greet the room full of students, telling them about all the exciting plans I had for the school year. I could see their faces in my mind's eye. They were smiling back at me, soaking in every word. This day was going to be perfect; a perfect beginning to a perfect year.

When Annabelle was empty, I placed the full bucket on a shelf in the barn. I had left the barn door open, so I released Annabelle's head and shooed her toward the barn door. "See there, old girl, that wasn't so bad, was it? A few minutes early didn't hurt either one of us."

Annabelle answered by lifting her tail and leaving a nice pile for me to scoop up before I could head to the house. "Thanks a lot. Tomorrow you get milked early with no grain." Annabelle just mooed softly and went through the door, knowing I had made an empty threat.

Grabbing a shovel, I quickly scooped up the wet pile and threw it out the barn door. Grabbing the pail of milk, I headed toward the house. As I came through the kitchen door, Momma was busy preparing breakfast. I place the pail of milk on the counter for the cream to rise and began to help her.

"Virginia, there's no need for you to help me," Momma said. "I can prepare breakfast for three people in no time. Go ahead and get ready. I know you're excited and want to look your best."

"Thanks, Momma," I said, hurrying from the kitchen. I took the stairs two at a time, entered my bedroom and closed the door. I had already picked out the dress I would wear. It was made from the fabric that had been brought back from Paoli on July 4th. Momma and I had sewed three other dresses for the upcoming school year, but the one I had chosen for today was still my favorite.

I pulled my work dress off and quickly poured water from a pitcher into a large bowl. I added lavender to the water so I would smell nice. I washed myself then slipped into clean clothes. Next, I pulled my hair into a bun at the nape of my neck, just as I had seen Mary Ellen wear hers when she first came to Marengo to teach. Looking in the mirror, I could see the excitement dancing in my eyes, along with an underlying fear. It was the fear that I needed to control.

Returning to the kitchen, I was greeted with the smell of piping hot oatmeal and toasted bread. Momma had added some molasses and cinnamon to the porridge, just the way I liked it.

Papa came in from feeding the pigs and quickly washed his hands. We joined hands and Papa blessed the food, making sure to pray for the safety of Angus and Carter, and that I enjoyed my first day as a school teacher.

"I suppose I'll ride Knucklehead," I said as we began to eat our breakfast.

"Nonsense," Papa said. "I already have the team hitched to the wagon. I'll take you to town. I'm sure there are things for me to do at the store. I'll wait until school dismisses and we can come home together."

"Thanks, Papa," I said, smiling at this kind, gentle man that was my father.

"I'm sure Delmar will enjoy playing you in a game of checkers if you can't find anything else to do," Momma said.

"Goodness woman, I can't spend all my days playing checkers with Delmar," Papa said smiling.

"Stephen, you have spent more time on the porch of the store than in it since Reuben came home," Momma chided. "Of course, I'm okay with that, since you have given the store to Reuben."

"And he is doing a fine job of running it," Papa said. "I just help when the store gets really busy."

"Well, enjoy it while it lasts," Momma said. "Next month will be very busy with a wedding and a field of corn to get picked."

Papa winked at Momma. "I plan to, Elizabeth."

Papa pulled the wagon out of the barn while I quickly cleared the table and washed the few dishes. "I'll dry those dishes and put them away, Virginia," Momma said, handing me two pails with towels covering their contents. "Here's a lunch for you and one for your father. Enjoy your first day as a teacher."

"Thank you, Momma. I just hope I do the job well."

"You will be fine, Virginia," Momma assured me. "It may take a few days to settle in, but once you do, the children will love you. Goodness, most of them you know, and they love you already."

I smiled at Momma and hurried out the door. I would reach the school a half hour before time for school to start, which would give me enough time to calm my nervous jitters. Climbing up on the wagon seat beside Papa, I placed the lunch pails at my feet. Papa clicked his tongue signaling the horses and we were off. As we pulled up in front of the school fifteen minutes later, my head felt dizzy as my heart pumped so hard and fast I could hear it in my ears.

"This is your stop, Virginia," Papa said.

"Okay," I muttered, climbing down clumsily from the wagon seat.

"Meet me at the store when you're done for the day," Papa said as he put the horses back in motion and headed for the general store.

Turning, I looked at the two doors leading into the school. I

wondered for the first time why someone chose tc
doors instead of one double door.

I looked all around the school yard where th
play later, the same place I had played for the c
attended school. There were two swings that had ‿
large limbs on opposite sides of a large white oak tree. Down the hɪɪ
toward the creek was the favorite place to play tag in the soft grass. I
could hear Whiskey Run creek bubbling out a happy tune as it ran
past the school to join in the rippling current of Brandy Branch creek
not far away. I could already see the boys skipping rocks across the
surface of the water at recess, seeing who could get the most skips
out of one rock and catching crawdads come spring.

Turning around away from the school, which was also our
local church, I looked up on the knoll where the cemetery was
located. Some of the headstones were quite grand, like the one
marking the grave of John Sloan, who had died in 1847, a year after I
was born. Others just had a small slab of rock protruding from the
ground with the person's initials carved on it.

"Are you going to stand outside all morning?"

Startled from my daydreaming, I gasped, "Goodness, Mary
Ellen, you scared a year off my life."

Mary Ellen chuckled. "I was just heading to the general store."

"If you had been outside just a few minutes sooner you could
have caught a ride with Papa," I said.

"I like to walk," Mary Ellen said. "It's so peaceful to hear the
birds singing and the water flowing in the creek."

Smiling at Mary Ellen I said, "I agree. I was just listening to the
creek a moment ago."

"You mean before you were staring at the cemetery?" Mary
Ellen asked, giving me a crooked smile.

"Well, yes, before that," I muttered. "Why do you think there
are two doors on this building?"

Mary Ellen turned to look at the school. "I wondered the same
thing when I came here to teach. I honestly have no idea, but I think
you should choose one of them and go in."

"Yes, I suppose you're right," I said, reaching for the door on
the right.

"Are you coming to the store after school?" Mary Ellen asked
before I stepped in.

"Yes, I will meet Papa there and ride home with him."

"Okay, I'll see you later then," Mary Ellen said as she waved .nd began to walk toward the general store.

Stepping into the school, I first opened the windows. I liked fresh air and I knew the children would enjoy it, too. Next, I went over my lesson plans again. I had placed them in the teacher's desk before leaving church the day before. I had included a time for music each day and my guitar was waiting in the corner ready to be called on like an old friend. Satisfied everything was in order, I walked back outside to greet the children as they arrived for the first day of school, telling each child where they would be sitting.

At eight o'clock, I walked to the front of the school. My speech was all planned out in my mind. I had rehearsed it again while I milked Annabelle, just as I had done twenty times before. I was ready for this. "G..g..good morning children." And then I went blank. Thirty pairs of eyes stared at me, waiting for me to continue. My mouth felt as if I had taken a large bite out of my favorite dress I was wearing and was now trying to talk around the mouthful of cotton. I could hear the pounding in my ears again, and then there were sixty pairs of eyes staring at me as my vision doubled. Taking deep, slow breaths, I tried to calm my nerves. How could this be going so wrong?

"Virginia, you don't look so good," little Millie Sloan chirped.

"Yeah, are ya gonna puke?" Levi Weathers asked with excitement.

My eyes, which had been closed in an attempt to clear my vision, snapped open. "No, Levi, I am not going to puke!"

"Rats," Levi said, clearly disappointed.

Gathering my wits, I tried again. "Boys and girls, my name is Virginia Hensley, but you may call me Miss Virginia."

"Aw, shucks, I've known you all my life, Virginia," Levi complained. "Why do I hafta call you Miss Virginia?"

"Because I said so, Levi," I snapped. Great! Two minutes into my new teaching position and I had already lost my patience. And what kind of answer is "because I said so?" Deciding to pitch my opening speech out the open window, I tried again. "Sorry, Levi, please call me Miss Virginia. It's only proper. Now, would you please go ring the bell to announce school has begun?"

"Yes ma'am," Levi said, jumping from his chair and running to the back of the school. As he grabbed the rope that was just in his reach and began to ring it, I realized my mistake. "Look, Miss Virginia, when I pull down the rope picks me up off my feet on its way back up!"

The bell was ringing like there was a fire or some other emergency. Running to the back of the school, I grabbed Levi from the rope on an upward ride. Reaching out, I grabbed the rope, stopping the ringing abruptly. Placing Levi on his feet, I pointed to his seat, leaving no question of what I wanted him to do. I followed after him back to the front of the school. I was gathering my words to continue when the door of the school opened.

"Everything okay, Virginia?" Pastor David asked. "I heard the bell ringing pretty good a moment ago."

"Yes, everything is fine," I assured him. "Levi just got a bit excited announcing the first day of school."

"All right," Pastor David said. "I'll just be on my way."

"Thank you," I replied, my face burning like a lighted candle.

For the next five minutes I could hear Pastor David in front of the school sending people back home that had come to see why the bell had chimed so wildly. He assured them everything was fine and that there was no emergency. I knew it would be awhile before I lived the mistake down, and I also knew Levi Weathers would never be allowed to ring the bell again.

Grabbing my lesson plan book, I read it again, though I had every detail memorized for the entire week. Taking a calming breath and telling myself to get it together, I faced the children again. "I want all of you to call me Miss Virginia," I said.

"You done did already tell us that," Levi pointed out.

"Levi, please, just let me finish," I pleaded. Gathering my thoughts I continued. "I have many fun things planned for us to do this year. I promise to do my best to teach you. Let's begin our day by quoting the Lord's Prayer. Who would like to volunteer to lead us?"

Hands shot up all over the room. Realizing that everyone wanted a chance, I quickly decided to come up with a system. "Okay, I have lots of volunteers, which is good. I will start with the oldest student today and we will work our way to the youngest. When everyone has had a turn, we will start over again."

By lunch time, I had settled down and things were running

smoothly. "It's time for lunch and you may play until one o'clock after you finish eating. We will go outside and sit at the tables to eat. Let's make a line, starting with the oldest. Pick your lunch pail up off the shelf in back as you go out the door."

The children did as instructed. As I reached the back of the room, I realized I had left my own lunch pail in the wagon. I pondered my dilemma. I could leave the children and run to the general store and get it, which was not an option, or I could take thirty children along with me to the general store, which was also not an option. Stepping out the back door, I looked up to see Papa smiling at me, my pail in his hands.

"You forgot something, Virginia," Papa said, handing me the pail of food.

Smiling back, I took the pail. "Thank you, Papa."

"Did you allow Levi to ring the bell?"

"How did you guess?"

"I didn't," Papa laughed. "Pastor David came by and told us."

"Well, I don't know if the children have learned anything today, but I have," I replied. "Don't ask Levi to ring the bell and make sure you have your lunch."

"It just proves you're never too old to learn," Papa chuckled.

"Thanks again, Papa. I'll see you in a few hours."

Joining the children at the tables beneath the shade trees, I asked a blessing on our pails of food. Noticing some of the children had brought very little to eat, I made a mental note to bring some apples the next day from our trees. I would not single anyone out; just offer them to anyone that wanted one. It seemed the right thing to do.

As I looked around the tables at the children, I felt a love for them I had never felt before, even though I had known most of them their entire lives. For seven hours a day, five days a week, and nearly eight months out of the year, these children would be mine to mold. The children were like soft clay that could be turned into beautiful sculptures, or hard, angry lumps, depending upon the influences they received throughout their childhood. I was committed to help create sculptures, to be a positive influence in these children's lives. It was a huge responsibility but one that could be very rewarding. This morning had not gone at all like I had planned, but tomorrow would be better.

As the children finished their lunch, one by one they went to play in the warm sunshine. I walked around, making sure no one was getting into mischief. I pushed the smaller children on the swings and kept track of whose turn it was. Soon it was one o'clock and time to go inside and finish the first day of school. Calling to the children, I had them form a line, youngest to oldest. I stood outside the door as the children passed, entering the school. Before stepping into the school, I looked in the direction of Mrs. George's house. She quickly disappeared from the window but I knew she had been watching the past hour. Smiling brightly, I waved in her direction and stepped inside. I knew I would receive an earful over the clanging bell at her first opportunity.

The second half of the day went much smoother than the first half. When three o'clock came, I was actually sorry the day was over. I had thoroughly enjoyed teaching the children and couldn't wait to do it again the next day.

As the children left for the day, I stood at the door and told each one goodbye, noting something each child had accomplished during the day, no matter how small. The younger children hugged my waist as they left and I willingly hugged them back. I even kept from cringing when Levi reached his filthy hands around me, leaving handprints on my favorite outfit. What had that child been doing at recess? I would have to keep a much closer eye on him in the future.

By the time the first week of school ended, I had settled into my teaching position quite well. The bell had not chimed more than three dings, and I had not experienced my heart pounding in my ears or double vision since the first day. I had brought a basket of apples the second day of school and it was now empty. As the last child left on Friday, I began to move the desks to the outer walls so the pews could be put back in place for Sunday service. Grabbing the broom, I quickly swept the wood floor. I then cleared my desk so it would be tidy and ready for Monday morning.

Effie met me outside of the school and we walked to the general store together, just like old times. "So, how was your first week as a teacher?" Effie asked.

I laughed and replied, "Monday morning didn't go too well, but the rest of the week has made up for it."

"I heard the bell ringing and of course news travels fast around here," Effie said smiling. "You should have known better than to trust Levi with any task, since trouble follows him like his shadow."

"Trust me, I've learned my lesson," I replied. "Have you been to the store to get your mail yet?"

"Yes, but I'll walk with you," Effie replied.

Effie and I talked all the way to the store. I went immediately to check our box for any mail upon arriving. Finding a letter from Angus, I slipped it into the pocket on my dress. I had sent a letter with Papa that morning to be mailed out to Angus, just like every Friday, telling him all about my first week as a teacher.

Mary Ellen came up beside me. "So, what do you think of being a teacher after your first week?"

"I love it, Mary Ellen," I replied, meaning every word.

"I knew you would," Mary Ellen said. "You have a natural gift."

"The bell chimed so many times on Monday, I thought I had died," Delmar said. "I'm sure it rang out my age."

I narrowed my eyes at Delmar as he sat in a chair near the cold wood stove. "Shouldn't you be on the porch in a heated game of checkers, Delmar?"

"Well now, Virginia, I was, but then I saw you go into the store. I followed you in to see how your day had gone."

"Thanks for being concerned," I replied, a hint of sarcasm in my voice. "I'll know who to call on if I ever need any help with the children."

"Humph, kids these days. Little whippersnappers need to be taken to the woodshed a bit more often, in my opinion" Delmar complained.

Giving Delmar my sweetest smile, I replied, "I suppose it's a good thing your opinion doesn't count."

"Got time for a game of checkers, Virginia?" Delmar asked.

"How many times have Papa and Reuben beaten you today?" I asked.

"More times than I care to admit," Delmar replied. "I need to go home on a win."

"Oh, okay," I said. "Set the board up."

Delmar lumbered out to the porch and busied himself putting the black and red playing pieces in their proper places. I asked Mary Ellen if there had been any battle reports in the newspapers. She told me there hadn't, which eased my mind about Carter and Angus. Effie followed me out to the porch to watch Delmar and I play checkers.

"What color do you want?" Delmar asked.

"I'll take black," I replied.

By my third turn to move, I knew I was beat. I just didn't possess the strategy to play checkers. It was the one game I always refused to play with Carter because he beat me so badly. As I stared at the board now contemplating my next move, I thought how I would gladly play checkers against Carter everyday if that's what it took to bring him home safely.

"Are you gonna move or not?" Delmar fumed.

"Calm down, Delmar. I'm thinking."

"Well, what's there to think about? Any move you make you're gonna get jumped."

"I realize that, Delmar," I muttered. "I just want to make sure I only get one checker jumped." Placing my finger on a checker, I slowly moved it forward. No sooner had I removed my finger, Delmar snatched up his red checker and jumped three of mine.

"I reckon you thought too long," Delmar said, grinning from ear to ear. "Sure hope you teach school better than you play checkers."

"Goodness, Virginia, you really are a bad checker player," Effie chimed in.

"Thanks Effie," I said, "that was such a nice thing to say."

Five minutes later, the game was over. I had managed to jump two of Delmar's checkers. "I only played with you so you could go home a winner," I reminded Delmar as he gloated.

"Thanks, Virginia," Delmar said, rising from the table to go home. "I'll see you at church Sunday."

"I need to get home, too," Effie said. "Are you working at the store tomorrow?"

"Probably not," I replied. "I'm sure Momma needs help at home."

"Okay," Effie said. "I'll see you on Sunday, then."

I watched Effie and Delmar leave and head toward their homes. Rising from my seat, I went into the store to find Papa and see if he was ready to head home. I was suddenly tired from my week as the town's new school teacher.

Chapter Twenty

The second week of school went smoother than the first, and I settled in to a daily routine after that. By Friday of the third week, I had made a seating chart that seemed to be working. My job was much easier when best friends were not sitting next to one another. Looking back, it would have probably helped Mary Ellen if she had separated Effie and me on the first day she taught here.

September 25th, the last Friday of the month, I walked to the general store after putting the school house in order for Sunday service. As I neared the porch, I knew the newspaper must have reported something big, for the porch was full of men who had gathered. As I stepped up amongst them I asked, "So, what's the latest news?"

All eyes turned toward me but it seemed no one wanted to speak. Finally, Papa broke the silence. "It appears the Union and Confederate armies faced off just south of Chattanooga, Tennessee along the Chickamauga creek. Something went very wrong, and a gap was left in the Union line. The Confederates took full advantage of this and the Union army was forced to retreat the 10 miles back to Chattanooga, where they are now trapped."

"Do you think Carter and Angus were part of that battle?" I asked, fear already causing my stomach to churn.

"It's a very good possibility," Papa said softly. "General Rosecrans was the commander of the fleeing forces, and their company was under his command."

"How many casualties were there?" I asked, knowing I really didn't want to know.

"The Union suffered over 16,000," Papa said, "but of that number, it's estimated over 9,000 were wounded."

"How many soldiers were killed?" I asked.

"More than 1, 500," Papa replied softly.

"Where are the other 4,000 plus soldiers?" I asked, quickly doing the math.

"They are missing. Probably captured by the Confederates," Papa replied.

I allowed this information to sink in. Even if Carter and Angus were not among the soldiers killed, they could possibly be severely wounded or in a camp set up for captured Union soldiers by the Confederates. Suddenly, I had a thought. "Did I receive a letter today?" I asked hopefully.

"Yes, Virginia, but I'm sure it was written before the battle took place," Papa said gently.

"Oh, yes, I suppose you're right," I replied. Looking around the porch at all the sad eyes, I couldn't stand it any longer. Grabbing the handle of the screen door, I mumbled, "Excuse me. I'm going to go read my letter now."

As I walked to the counter, Mary Ellen opened her arms and folded me in her embrace. It was then that I let my tears fall. How long would it be before I knew if Carter and Angus were safe?

Suddenly, something occurred to me. Slipping from Mary Ellen's embrace, I wiped my tears and went to the wall where the section of the paper was always hung that listed fallen soldiers. As I scanned the names, Mary Ellen came up behind me. "Neither of their names is on the list," she whispered to me. "I've already checked, and your papa and Reuben did, too."

"So, they must be alive," I said hopefully.

"I hope they are," Mary Ellen said, "but we both know it's too soon for all the names to be posted yet."

Nodding my head, I walked slowly to our family's mailbox. Reaching in, I retrieved the letter from Angus, perhaps the last one I would ever get. Sifting through the mail, I looked for one from Carter, too. Mary Ellen joined me behind the counter and answered my question before I formed it. "Carter sent a letter to your parents.

Your papa has it in his pocket."

"Okay," I replied. "Did Effie get a letter from Carter?"

"Yes," Mary Ellen said. "She has not been in to get it yet. She came in earlier but the mail wagon was late getting here. Her father is out on the porch now, so I'm sure he will tell her the news when he returns home."

I slipped the letter from Angus into the pocket of my dress, right next to the leather heart. I hoped Papa would be ready to leave the store soon so I could read what Angus had written.

I sank down on a stool behind the counter and ran the conversation Papa and I had just had on the porch. "Mary Ellen, if Angus or Carter have been captured by the Confederates, how will we know?"

"I honestly don't know," Mary Ellen replied softly. "I suppose if they are not listed among the wounded or dead, we could assume they are in a prisoners of war camp."

At that moment, the screen door opened and Effie walked in. As our eyes met, I knew her father had told her the news. Getting off the stool, I met her in the middle of the general store and we shed our tears on each other's shoulders. I could not remember a time when I had been so overwhelmed by sadness. In fifteen minutes, my life had crumbled around me. I knew the threat of something happening to Carter or Angus had always been there, but I had chosen not to really think about it until now. Stepping back, I looked into Effie's tear streaked face. "You have a letter from Carter."

The two of us walked to the mailboxes and I handed Effie her family's mail. She quickly found the letter from Carter. Not being able to wait to read what Carter had written, she tore the letter open and plopped down on one of the stools. Carter had written two pages, which was one more than he had probably written to us.

As Effie finished reading, she looked up at Mary Ellen and me. "Carter writes that they are heading to battle but he could not say where. He was afraid the letter might fall into the hands of a Confederate spy and give away the Union's strategy. Did you get a letter from Angus?"

I wanted to wait and read the letter from Angus while sitting on my favorite limb of the Maple but knew it would be selfish at this point to not let Effie know what Angus wrote. She had willingly opened her letter from Carter and shared the information with Mary

Ellen and me. Reaching into my pocket, I removed Angus's letter. I sat down on a stool and slowly opened it.

My dearest Virginia,

I write this letter on what will be your first day as Marengo's new school teacher. I hope the day goes smoothly for you. I know you will be an excellent teacher and the children will love your adventurous ways. You mentioned being nervous, but once you settle in, you will see you are most capable of teaching the children. I have the utmost confidence in your ability.

Carter and I are now in Chattanooga, Tennessee, as the Union has pushed General Bragg and his Confederates into Georgia. We will continue to push the Confederates south and head toward the prize of Atlanta, Georgia. We are hoping for the same success here as Rosecrans and the troops had in Murfreesboro in January. Hopefully, in a few weeks your papa can read of our victory to all those gathered on the porch of the general store.

To say I'm not nervous and a bit scared as the threat of my first battle looms before me would be a lie. I have yet to face a man and be forced to shoot him. I honestly don't know how I will do that, but I know I must. As the other soldiers around me say, "kill or be killed", I suppose my instinct to survive will take over and I will fire my weapon at another human being.

Carter has already been faced with this conflict as the cavalry rode ahead of the foot soldiers to begin Bragg's retreat from Chattanooga. He admitted it was hard at first, but then the fight to survive took over. The new Spencer repeating rifle that he was armed with has made it possible to shoot more than one time without reloading. He claims it is the best new invention of the decade but realizes it will result in many more casualties for the Confederates. None of us want to see men die but we don't know how to win this war without that happening.

Thank you for the box of food you and your mother sent. Carter and I eat like kings each time a box arrives. We are tempted to hide the box and keep all the food for ourselves but realize that would be a selfish act. Every man here is hungry for something other than hard tack and dried beef, so each soldier shares his gift of food from home. Though I have eaten sugar cookies from several different places now as the boxes of other soldiers are shared, I have yet to eat any that taste as good as yours.

I will write again as soon as I possibly can and tell you how the Union is progressing. We must win this war but I see now it takes one battle at a time.

Thanks for your continued prayers and the letters. You have no idea how much letters from home mean to me and the other soldiers. They are like the sun breaking through on a cloudy sky. We are all so far from home and our only wish

is for the war to end so we can return there.
  All my love,
  Angus

I slowly folded the letter and put it back in its cover. Looking up, I found Mary Ellen and Effie anxiously waiting to hear what Angus had written.

"Angus must have written this letter after Carter wrote his to you, Effie. The Union had just pushed the Confederates south out of Chattanooga. Angus was hopeful they could continue to push them toward Atlanta, but we know now that things didn't go as planned."

"I wonder if the Union will be able to get any supplies to Chattanooga," Mary Ellen said softly.

"I'm sure the Confederates are doing everything they possibly can to prevent any supplies from coming in, which means there will be few chances for letters to be sent out," I said. "Even if they are alive, Carter and Angus may not be able to get word to us."

"That's true," Effie said. "Has anyone checked the list to see if Carter or Angus is among the fallen?"

"Yes," Mary Ellen said, "it's been checked thoroughly. Their names are not there, but I'm sure not all the names have reached the Louisville Daily yet. We just have to pray and put this situation in God's hands."

"Yes," I agreed, knowing Mary Ellen was right but finding it hard to do just that, "Angus asked us to continue to pray for them."

"So, let's do that now," Mary Ellen said, taking mine and Effie's hands. As Mary Ellen quietly began to pray, I felt a peace I could not explain wash over me. I was still worried but I knew God was in control, just as He always was. Whatever happened, I knew He would be there to walk me through it.

****

When school ended the next Friday, I hurried to the general store. As I stepped onto the porch, Papa looked up from a checker game he was playing with Delmar. "There were no letters and the newspaper reports that Chattanooga is still under siege. I looked through the list of deceased soldiers, and thankfully, Carter or Angus's name was not among them."

"Well, at least there is still hope they are alive," I said softly.

Entering the store, I helped Mary Ellen wait on customers

until Papa was ready to go home. Keeping my hands busy allowed less time for my mind to wander. Many times over the past week I had taken up the burden of worry, forgetting to leave it in God's more than capable hands.

When the store emptied of customers, Mary Ellen picked up a box and opened the lid. "I received a package today. It's from my mother."

A smile spread across my face. Mary Ellen and Reuben's wedding was two weeks away. "Let me see!"

Mary Ellen lifted the beautiful wedding dress from the box. "I haven't shown it to Reuben yet."

"And I don't think you should. Have you tried it on?"

"No, I haven't had time. You know how busy Friday can be."

"Take it upstairs and try it on now," I encouraged. "I'll take care of any customers."

Mary Ellen smiled, "Okay. I'll call to you when I have the dress on so you can come see it."

A few minutes later, Mary Ellen called my name. I hurried up the stairs to see how the dress fit. "Oh, Mary Ellen, it's perfect." I walked around her, admiring the full length white dress. "I don't think any adjustments are needed."

Mary Ellen looked at herself in the full length mirror that was in the bedroom of the small living quarters above the general store. "I believe you're right. It seems to be made just for me."

"Your mother must have been the same size when she married your father," I said. "When will your parents and two younger sisters be here?"

"They should arrive by coach next Friday," Mary Ellen said. "Mother wants to help with preparing food for the reception."

"Momma will appreciate her help; especially since I will be busy teaching and you will be kept busy here at the store. You do plan to at least take the Friday off before the wedding, don't you?"

"Yes, if possible," Mary Ellen replied.

I smiled at Mary Ellen, knowing she was going to take Reuben's breath away when he caught a glimpse of her in the wedding dress. "We will figure out a way to make it possible. Papa and Reuben can work until school is out, and then I will come help them. We will manage somehow. All you need to worry about is getting yourself down the aisle of Big Spring church in that beautiful dress."

"Do you think Reuben will like the dress?" Mary Ellen fretted.

"Trust me, Mary Ellen, you could walk down the aisle in rags and Reuben would still gladly marry you. But when he sees you in that dress, well, he may faint dead away."

Mary Ellen began to laugh as the scene played out in her mind. "Goodness, I sure hope he doesn't faint."

"Virginia, Mary Ellen, what's so funny up there?" Reuben hollered from the bottom of the staircase.

I hurried to the stairs to keep Reuben from coming up. "Don't you worry about what's so funny, Reuben, and don't come up the stairs. I'm headed down." Turning to Mary Ellen, I whispered, "Put the dress back in the box and I'll take it with me to the farm when Papa and I leave. I can hide it in my bedroom until you need it."

"Okay, thanks Virginia."

I descended the stairs toward Reuben and he took two steps toward me. "Don't even think of going upstairs," I threatened. "Mary Ellen will be down in a minute."

"What's she doing up there?"

"You'll find out soon enough," I replied, gently pushing Reuben backwards down the two steps.

"Did I ever tell you that you and Carter are a lot alike?" Reuben asked. "You both find great pleasure in goading a person."

"I'll take that as a compliment," I spouted, loving that I had just been compared to Carter, "however, Carter would have pushed you off the steps much harder."

"That is true," Reuben agreed. Suddenly Reuben's face became serious, all teasing aside. "I sure wish he could be here for the wedding."

"Me, too, Reuben, but Carter would not want you to wait. He has already said as much in his letters. You will marry Mary Ellen in two weeks and Carter will rejoice for you."

"I know you're right," Reuben replied, "but it would sure be nice if he were home."

Tears gathered in my eyes as I thought of Carter and Angus and what might have happened to them. "Yes, it would be very nice indeed."

****

The next two weeks became a flurry of activity. Mary Ellen's family arrived from Kentucky on Friday, October 9th, and Momma and Mary Ellen's mother went to work planning the food for the reception. Papa planned to kill a pig and roast it in a pit for the occasion. To go with the pork, there would be potato salad, baked beans, rolls, pumpkin, and apple pies. The wedding would take place in the church and the reception would be at the general store.

The only report we received about the Union troops trapped in Chattanooga was that Rosecrans had not devised a plan to break the siege. President Lincoln had sent telegrams trying to encourage Rosecrans but still he did nothing.

By this time, the food supplies were running low, as telegrams coming out of Chattanooga stated. Very few supplies were getting past Confederate troops posted on the mountains around Chattanooga. Those that did make it came from sixty miles away in Bridgeport, Alabama, where Union supplies were being kept. The only good news was that Carter and Angus were still not listed among the names of the fallen soldiers.

Papa found one article of interest that stated President Lincoln had declared the fourth Thursday in November an official holiday. Lincoln stated how thankful he was for the Union victory at Gettysburg. He was quoted saying "Thanksgiving and Praise to our beneficent Father who dwelleth in the Heavens". November 26th, 1863 would be the first national holiday of Thanksgiving and would be celebrated on that day from here on out.

The morning of October 17th, 1863 dawned crisp and sunny. The leaves had not yet reached their peak color as Mary Ellen had hoped, but they had begun to show changes.

Papa had killed the pig for the meal the day before and hung it in the barn, with the help of Mary Ellen's father, Norman. The two men left the farm before dawn, taking the meat with them, to start the fire in the pit they had dug at the back of the general store. They would keep the meat turned and the fire at the correct temperature so the pig would be ready for the reception. The wedding was to take place at 5 o'clock, so the pork needed to be done in time for the men to get changed into their Sunday best for the event. Their clothes were waiting for them in the upstairs of the general store.

The store had been closed for the day and had been readied for the reception the night before. A table, laden with pumpkin and apple pies, sat off to one side. Ladies from the church had volunteered to help make pies for the occasion to take some of the burden off Momma.

The counter was ready for the food to be placed on it. Everyone attending knew to bring their own plates, glasses and silverware, for no one owned enough to provide those things for the amount of people who would be at the reception. The potato salad was in large bowls in the cold water of the springhouse and would not be removed until just before time to leave for the wedding.

Mary Ellen had spent the entire week at the farm with her family, and I had moved into the little cabin built for the school teacher. It had been strange living alone for the first time, but I had decided it was quite nice when I didn't have to start my day by milking a cow. If I was a good friend, I would have gone and helped Effie bring their cow to the barn and milk her, but so far I had not been inclined to do so. Maybe I would next week, or maybe I would enjoy the reprieve a bit longer.

I had returned to the farm the night before the wedding when Papa left the store to offer help anywhere I was needed. After hearing Papa and Mary Ellen's father leave the house, I slipped from between the warm blankets as quietly as possible, leaving Mary Ellen's younger sister, Catherine, sleeping beside me. I dressed quickly in my old clothes and went downstairs. When I entered the kitchen, I found Momma and Mary Ellen's mother, Lucille, enjoying a cup of coffee.

"Good morning," I mumbled, never being one to greet the dawn with much enthusiasm.

"Good morning, Virginia," Momma said. "There's more coffee if you would like some."

"I believe I need some," I replied with a smile. Grabbing a cup, I filled it three quarters full then added honey to sweeten it. Next, I filled the cup the rest of the way with rich cream. As I sat down at the table, Momma smiled as she looked into my cup.

"Virginia, I believe you have just made a dessert instead of a cup of coffee."

"I honestly don't care much for the taste of coffee," I admitted, "but it seems to wake me up quite well. By adding the honey and cream, the taste is pretty well masked." I took a long sip of my sweet, creamy concoction before asking, "How can I help this morning?"

"Well, it would be most helpful if you could milk for me this morning," Momma said. "Lucille and I are just getting ready to start brewing the many gallons of tea we will need for today."

I groaned inwardly, wishing I hadn't asked. After a week of not seeing me every day, Annabelle would probably give me fits. She seemed to be able to tolerate only one person at a time. "Of course, Momma," I answered, plastering on the best smile I could muster.

Finishing my coffee, I placed the cup on the counter. Grabbing the pail, I headed out the back door. Ollie greeted me on the porch, bringing me a stick to throw. I had really wanted to take him to town to live when I moved into the cabin but knew it wouldn't be fair. He had grown up here on the farm, free to run wherever he wanted. To move him into town and make him stay confined to a small area would have been cruel. Besides, Momma had grown to love him as much as I and he kept her company. He had proven himself to be a very good watchdog, keeping critters from snatching her chickens right off the roost. Momma even allowed him to come in the house on the coldest of winter nights to sleep.

"Hey, Ollie dog," I greeted, taking the stick from his mouth and tossing it. Ollie bounded after it, bringing it back before I got halfway to the barn. I threw the stick again and praised him for the good return before entering the barn. Ollie plopped down outside the barn door, knowing he was not allowed in during milking because neither Elsie nor Annabelle would tolerate him being that close.

Placing the pail on a shelf, I added feed to the trough of the milking stanchion. Walking to the back door of the barn, I unlatched the door and Annabelle barreled through. Going straight to the feed, she put her head through the boards and I locked it in place. Plopping down on the stool, I cleaned her teats thoroughly with a wet rag I had brought along. I then reached up and plucked the pail from the shelf and set my rhythm of squeeze and release, humming a song to the beat I was creating. As the milk frothed in the bucket, my mind drifted back to just a few months earlier when Carter had raced me at this very chore; the day he left for the Union army. As I squeezed the last drop of milk from Annabelle's udder, I whispered, "Where are you, Carter?" As if she understood, Annabelle mooed softly, feeling the pain of my mournful question.

Rising from the stool, I wiped the silent tears trickling down my cheeks. I vowed there would be no more tears today, for Reuben would marry his beautiful bride and we would rejoice. And hopefully, somewhere in a southern Tennessee town called Chattanooga, Carter would be smiling, too, along with Angus.

I allowed my eyes to slip closed, and I could see both their faces, smiling just as they had smiled on the day the picture was taken at Paoli on July 4th, the one Momma had framed and placed on a table in the living room of the farm house.

Placing the full pail back on the shelf, I went to open the barn door. I released Annabelle's head and shooed her toward the door. She seemed to be in no hurry, and in a rare moment of being totally submissive, she allowed me to stroke her ears. I suppose she knew it was not a day to cause trouble. She finally meandered out the door and toward the pasture. I took the full pail to the kitchen, tossing the stick again for Ollie as I went.

Papa came back to the house at four o'clock, already dressed in his Sunday clothes. Everyone scurried about, loading the food and gallons of tea into the wagon. Just before we loaded ourselves into the wagon, a beautiful enclosed buggy pulled up to the house.

"Stephen, who in the world is here in a buggy?" Momma questioned.

As Norman climbed out from the buggy, Papa announced, "Ladies, your chariot awaits. I had this built just for the occasion and bought the two fine horses to pull it. You shall ride in style and stay clean as you go to the wedding."

"Oh, Stephen," Momma exclaimed, "what a wonderful surprise! I shall never show up at church looking like a drowned rat again, even if it is raining buckets outside. But who's watching the pig roast?"

"I left Delmar in charge of it," Papa said. "He assured me he knows all about cooking a pig in the ground."

"Yes, and he also said he could handle milking a cow and collecting a few eggs while we went to Paoli," I reminded Papa.

"Maybe you better get back to the store, Stephen," Momma urged. "If that meat gets burned, we will not be able to replace it at this hour."

"Don't fret, Elizabeth," Papa soothed. "The meat will be fine. It's completely cooked already and Norman and I banked the fire beneath it to keep it warm. Delmar is really just sitting beside a pit waiting for my return. I do need to get back, though, so Reuben and I can get to the church before his bride arrives."

"Yes, and make sure Reuben stays in the church," Momma instructed. "I don't want him to see Mary Ellen until she's walking down the aisle."

"Yes, ma'am," Papa replied while pulling up and saluting. With that, he hopped on the wagon seat and headed back toward town. Lucille went back into the house and upstairs where Mary Ellen had just finished getting ready. A few minutes later, Mary Ellen and her mother came down the stairs, followed by Mary Ellen's sisters. I watched her father's eyes mist over as he looked at his oldest daughter in his wife's wedding dress.

"You are as beautiful as your mother was the day I married her," Norman said as he reached to take Mary Ellen's hand.

We all went out and climbed into the spanking new buggy. I had never ridden in such luxury and couldn't help but think how nice it would have been to ride in such style to Paoli in July. We would have certainly returned home much drier.

Norman put the fine driving horses into motion and we were off, arriving at Marengo faster than I ever had before. Norman parked the buggy in front of the little cabin I now called home and everyone exited except Mary Ellen. Norman would wait for a signal, and then walk his daughter into the church and down the aisle to Reuben.

Mary Ellen wanted music for the occasion, so I would play a song on the guitar as she walked down the aisle to get married, and again as she and Reuben walked out of the church as husband and wife for the first time.

At five o'clock, the signal was given to Norman and I began to play. The church was filled to overflowing as Marengo's beloved school teacher and the son of the owner of the general store prepared to exchange vows.

Mary Ellen floated through the left door of the church, a vision of elegance and beauty on her father's arm. I watched the emotions play across Reuben's face, his eyes finding hers as she came toward him. I had never seen my brother look happier.

Pastor David read from 1Corinthians chapter 13 and then led the couple in repeating their vows. Afterwards, Pastor David said a prayer for a long, happy and loving marriage, with Christ at the center.

As they exited the church twenty minutes later, I played

"Come, Thou Fount of Every Blessing" and everyone began to sing the song. I knew it would be the beginning of many songs to follow, as we celebrated the joining in marriage by playing instruments, singing, and possibly some dancing at the general store throughout the evening.

When the church was empty, I carried my guitar and followed the crowd to the general store, Reuben and Mary Ellen leading the way riding in the fine buggy. The food was already waiting on the counter, as Effie's mother had volunteered to get it set up when my father brought it from our house. She and Effie would take care of serving the pie and keeping the food platters filled.

As I stepped into the general store, which was packed full, Pastor David blessed the food. The bride and groom filled their plates first, and then everyone else followed.

"How did I do roasting that pig, Virginia?" Delmar asked as I took a bite of the meat.

"It's excellent, Delmar," I replied, deciding not to mention I knew he only watched it keep warm, and that was for less than an hour.

"It's tricky keeping the fire just right," Delmar said. "Too little heat and the meat don't cook through, too much heat and you end up with charred butt."

I burst out laughing. I had to admit, Delmar could be really funny sometimes. "I suppose I will know who to call if I want a pig cooked in the ground when I get married, Delmar. You are quite the expert."

"Virginia Mae, any man who would marry you and all your sassiness would be crazy," Delmar retorted. "But if you happen to find someone, I'll cook the pig."

"Why, thank you, Delmar," I replied smiling. "And by the way, I just might have already found a man to marry me."

Delmar started to make a joke of my comment but then suddenly turned serious. "Virginia, I sure wish Angus could be here today, and Carter, too. I miss those boys something awful."

"Me, too, Delmar," I replied softly, "but today, we will smile, and hope they are smiling with us. I will not ruin Reuben and Mary Ellen's wedding celebration by fretting over something that I have no evidence of. Carter and Angus may be just fine, except for being trapped in Chattanooga and unable to get word to us."

"You are absolutely right, Virginia," Delmar said. "Now, hurry up and get that plate of food ate so we can do some singing. I see the Moon family is already tuning up their instruments and Joe has his banjo on his knee just waiting to begin."

"I suppose if I hadn't been at the back of the line, I would be finished eating," I replied. "I noticed you've already eaten a plate of food and just finished dessert."

"I've had myself two plates of food," Delmar said with a grin, "but who's counting. I ate one plate before the wedding. I caught a good scolding from Effie's momma, but it was worth it."

"Goodness, Delmar, where are your manners?" I asked with a smile.

"I learnt mine from the same place you learnt yours," Delmar replied. "Now get to eatin' so we can move things along."

I played the guitar until my fingers ached and I had sung myself hoarse. Finally, at nearly eleven o'clock, everyone had gone home except for the family. I put my guitar in the storeroom and helped pack all the empty dishes out to the wagon. Papa would come to the store early on Monday and help put it back in order. Norman, Lucille, and their two younger daughters climbed into the buggy and drove off toward the farm. Momma and Papa climbed on the wagon seat and asked if I would like a ride to the cabin I now called home.

"No, I believe I'll walk," I replied. "It's a beautiful night and the stars are extra bright with no hardly any moonlight to dim them."

"Suit yourself," Papa replied. "See you at church in the morning."

"Good night," I called as Papa put the horses in motion.

Slipping back into the general store to pick up my guitar, I met Reuben and Mary Ellen at the bottom of the stairs leading to the second floor of the general store. "I'm just picking up my guitar," I explained.

"Yes, and I'm just picking up my bride to carry her upstairs," Reuben replied. Mary Ellen's face burned bright red as Reuben scooped her up in his arms. "Good night, Virginia."

I smiled at the two of them and walked toward the door with my guitar. "Good night, Reuben and Mary Ellen. See you at church in the morning."

As I headed toward my cabin, I laughed out loud. Did Reuben and Mary Ellen really believe they would be allowed to waltz upstairs to marital bliss? In an hour, many of us who had celebrated the wedding would return to give them a proper chivaree, banging pots and pans until they came outside. Reuben would be expected to give his new bride an official ride in a wheelbarrow as everyone banged their pans and cheered them on. Of course, they would be in their pajamas by this time, which would be all the better.

At least the night was cool enough that no one dared throw either of them into Whiskey Run creek, as had happened to several newlyweds in the past. I quickened my pace so I could put my guitar away and return with my own kettle and spoon.

Chapter Twenty-One

When school ended the next Friday, October 23rd, I was prepared to leave. I had asked the older boys to move the desks to clear the middle of the floor a few minutes before school dismissed. Some of the girls volunteered to sweep the floor, and I straightened my desk. When the last child left for the day, I walked briskly toward the general store. Stepping onto the porch, I was hardly noticed. The men were engrossed in discussing the latest report in the newspaper.

"I don't understand why Rosecrans did not try and figure out a way to break the siege," Pastor David said.

"Well, it's out of his hands now," Papa said. "General Ulysses S. Grant has now been given command of the entire western theater. Rosecrans had his chance and will now face humiliation for getting trapped in Chattanooga. He commanded so well at Murfreesboro. I don't know what happened."

"Grant will get the job done," Delmar chimed in. "He will figure out a way to get the Army of the Cumberland out of the mess they are in."

"I sure hope he can," Papa said. "It's been nearly a month now that they have been trapped in Chattanooga. From the reports in the newspaper, there has been a lot of rain in the area, making it even more difficult to get supplies past the Confederates on the one road they have access to. The Union supplies are being held in Bridgeport, Alabama, sixty miles across the mountains. With no railroad to bring the supplies in, they are forced to use mules and wagons."

"Stubborn, ornery critters," Delmar muttered. "It's hard enough getting one to do something in good conditions. I can't imagine trying to get a mule to cross mountains with rain and mud hampering them."

"I just hope Grant has a good plan," Pastor David said. "Those soldiers are probably just about starved to death by now."

"So, General Grant is in charge of the troops trapped in Chattanooga, now?" I asked, startling the men.

"Virginia," Papa said. "I didn't know you were here."

"I just walked up a moment ago," I replied. "I heard all of you discussing General Grant."

"Yes, President Lincoln has sent General Grant to try and break the siege in Chattanooga," Papa said. "We can only hope he does it quickly."

"Did I get any mail?" I asked, already knowing the answer.

"No, you did not receive any," Papa said. "I did send the box of food you and your momma prepared yesterday afternoon, though. When Angus and Carter finally receive mail, they will be delighted. They may get several boxes all at once, since there is one sent each week."

"After what's happened," Delmar said, "they will be ready for some good food."

I reached for the screen door handle, preparing to enter the store and help Mary Ellen. Papa stood and came toward me.

"Virginia, I'm planning a trip to Leavenworth tomorrow to get some supplies. Would you like to ride along? The leaves will be beautiful along the Ohio River."

"That sounds wonderful, Papa," I said, getting excited about the trip. "I have never been to Leavenworth."

"Yes, I know," Papa said. "I thought it would be something to take your mind off things for a little while. Your momma is going, too."

"Do you think it will be okay to leave Mary Ellen and Reuben on a Saturday? The store is usually so busy."

"They said they will manage," Papa said.

"Okay," I replied. "I will just stay all night at the farm so we can leave early. I can help Momma by doing some of the morning chores."

"I'm sure Annabelle will happy to see you," Papa said with a chuckle.

"I'm sure she will," I replied dryly.

Entering the store, I went to work straightening shelves and putting bolts of fabric back where they belonged. I could tell Mary Ellen had been kept very busy throughout the day.

A customer entered and I went to wait on them, giving Mary Ellen a much needed break. When the customer left, I turned to Mary Ellen who was busy moving stock from the storeroom to the shelves.

"Mary Ellen, go take a break," I encouraged. "I will mind the store for a little while. I can see you have been very busy today."

"Are you sure, Virginia?" Mary Ellen asked. "It's not like you haven't been busy today, too."

"Yes, I'm sure," I replied. "Your day might become hectic tomorrow since neither Papa nor I will be here to help you and Reuben. Rest while you have the chance."

Mary Ellen sank down onto one of the stools. "Your papa said he was going to invite you to ride with him to Leavenworth."

"Yes, and I'm quite excited about it. I've never been to Leavenworth."

"I have only been there a few times," Mary Ellen said. "I rode a steam boat from Louisville to Leavenworth when I came here to teach and took the stagecoach from Leavenworth to Marengo. I have also passed through the town when I returned home during the summer for a visit when I was teaching."

"I have never ridden a steam boat," I replied, "or any other kind of boat for that matter."

"It's certainly a fast way to travel," Mary Ellen said, "but I wouldn't want to do it all the time. I'm terrified of water, probably because I never learned to swim."

"Carter taught me how to swim when we were young, and Reuben had taught him. It's a good way to cool off on a hot summer day. You should have Reuben bring you to the farm and teach you to swim in the creek next summer. There are some deep places about a quarter of a mile west of the farm."

"Hmm…maybe I will," Mary Ellen said thoughtfully. She sat pondering the idea for a moment then suddenly asked, "Do you think I could go upstairs and start supper for Reuben and me?"

I laughed lightly. "I don't know how talking about learning to swim made you suddenly think of fixing supper, but yes, go upstairs. I will call if I get too busy. Otherwise, take the rest of the day off."

"Are you sure, Virginia?" Mary Ellen asked.

"Absolutely. Now go." I shooed Mary Ellen toward the storeroom where the stairs were located like I would shoo Annabelle from the barn after a milking. She started off reluctantly at first but then hurried upstairs to cook her new husband a nice supper. I decided then that I should come and work at the store in the evenings to give Mary Ellen a break. I had done that very thing when I was attending school a few years ago.

The store was not overly busy the rest of the afternoon and I did not have to call for Mary Ellen. I could smell some wonderful aromas drifting down as Mary Ellen prepared her and Reuben's food. Customers made comments when they came through the door and I would just smile and reply, "Mary Ellen is cooking supper."

Papa came in from the porch and helped me finish straightening shelves between customers. By the time the store closed at six, we had restocked and put the store in order for the next day. Reuben came in the back door and joined Papa and me at the counter.

"Gee, it smells good in here," Reuben said.

"That's your supper cooking," I replied.

"Did you get the lumber sorted and counted?" Papa asked.

"Yes and I will need to make a trip to Milltown on Monday," Reuben replied.

"Do you need to add anything to the list of items we need from Leavenworth?" Papa asked.

Reuben picked up the list and went over it. "No, I think that's all we need. I sure hope you can get ammunition because we are completely out."

"The war has made it almost impossible to buy ammunition," Papa replied. "We may have to get better with a slingshot or bow and arrow."

"Or become better trappers," I chimed in, thinking how Carter had supplied many meals by trapping.

"It takes a lot of time to keep up with trapping," Reuben said, "and I have no time to spare."

"I'll stop by in the morning on our way to Leavenworth to see if you've thought of anything else I need to pick up," Papa said.

"Okay," Reuben replied, then laughed. "Right now, all I can think about is getting a taste of whatever that is Mary Ellen is cooking."

Papa chuckled and we headed toward the back door to go home.

The next morning, Papa, Momma and I loaded up in the wagon. Papa had hitched up all four of the work horses, knowing the load coming back would be heavy.

I gazed at the beloved Maple as we headed away from the farm, dressed in its beautiful fall splendor. It never ceased to amaze me and take my breath at the sight each year.

We stopped at the general store to make sure Reuben hadn't thought of anything else. A few more items were added to the list and then we headed south. We climbed White Oak hill and then the road leveled out for a few miles, with just small hills here and there. When we topped one of the hills, Papa said, "This is called Pilot's Knob, because the riverboat captains can see it from the Ohio River."

"This must be a very high point," Momma said.

"I have heard it's the highest point in Crawford County," Papa replied, "according to the stagecoach driver."

"I would say that man would know," Momma said.

We continued south a few more miles and I pointed to a road on the right. "That's the road that goes to Curby, Momma."

"Yes, your papa and I traveled out this way one time when you were just a baby," Momma said. "The first county seat used to be at Mount Sterling, which is down that road past Curby. We were traveling to Leavenworth, though."

"Yes, I remember that," Papa said. "We were going to watch the hanging of James Fields."

"A hanging?" I asked in disbelief.

"Yes," Papa said, "a man was hung at Leavenworth, in 1846 I believe."

"Yes, 1846 was the year, and it was December," Momma confirmed. "We left Reuben and Carter with my mother and took Virginia because she was still nursing."

"I remember now," Papa said. "Your mother died of pneumonia the next spring."

"Yes and my father had been dead for three years already," Momma said, thinking back on the time.

"They hung Fields near Poison Creek in the town of Leavenworth. We watched from up on a nearby hill," Papa explained.

"Why was he hung?" I asked.

"He killed his own mother," Momma said, shaking her head at the thought that a son could do such a thing.

"Oh, my" I exclaimed. "How did he kill her?"

"He had gotten drunk and went home and demanded his mother get out of bed and fix him something to eat," Papa began. "He decided his mother was not moving fast enough to suit him, so he shot her, the bullet striking her in the thigh. She later died from complications due to that wound."

"Where did this Fields man live?" I asked.

"Milltown," Papa replied, "but hangings were to take place at the county seat, where the county jail was located and court was held. Thousands of people turned out to watch that hanging. I'll never forget that day as long as I live."

"Me neither, because when it came right down to it, I couldn't watch," Momma said.

"Well, I did watch," Papa said with a chuckle. "Sheriff Clark had never hung anyone before and he was very nervous, or excited; I actually don't know which. All I know is that when he attempted to cut the rope holding the trap door, he missed. When he finally did cut the trap door rope, the rope holding James Fields broke. Men who were gathered close to watch grabbed Fields and held him tight. The men then had to hold Fields up so the sheriff could tie the rope back together. It was the most botched up scene I have ever laid eyes on."

"Goodness," I said.

"I know that man killed his mother," Momma said, "but I just couldn't watch him die for it. It turns my stomach to think of it even now."

"I don't believe I could watch that either," I said. "Why did the county seat move to Leavenworth?"

"Well, first they moved it to Fredonia, and then Leavenworth," Papa replied. "Mount Sterling did not have a good water source and the county decided that for a place to be the county seat, it needed to have plenty of water."

"Where did the name Mount Sterling come from?" I asked.

"Most of the settlers there came from Mount Sterling, Kentucky, located in Montgomery County," Papa said. "The settlers named the area after the town they had come from."

The horses continued to plod south as I contemplated the story Papa had just told me. When we came to a place on the Leavenworth-Paoli road where it joined with two other roads, Papa turned left. "If we had gone straight at that junction, we would have been headed toward Fredonia," Papa pointed out.

"Have you ever been to Fredonia?" I asked.

"Only once," Papa said. "It's on a bluff overlooking the Ohio River, while Leavenworth is under the bluff right on the river."

"Does Leavenworth ever flood?" I asked.

"Sometimes," Papa said, "but not bad enough that anyone ever thinks of moving. Leavenworth is a happening place, and there is money to be made there."

As we rode along, the Ohio River came into view. There was a large bend in it, like a horseshoe, as we gazed down at it from the bluff. The leaves had reached their peak color, and the landscape had been painted bright reds, oranges and yellows. A person could see for miles from the bluff and the sight was like nothing I had ever seen before; absolutely breathtaking.

Papa pulled over and we all just stared in awe as we ate lunch from a picnic basket Momma had packed before we left home. On the opposite side of the river, the land lay flat and farms could be seen all down the shoreline. I recalled Angus writing about Leavenworth in his letters when he was part of the Indiana Legion, but no description could have prepared me for the sight before me cloaked in fall's splendor.

We finished our lunch and loaded back into the wagon. Papa put the horses back in motion and we descended on a winding road that eventually stopped in the town of Leavenworth.

Papa had been right; Leavenworth was a happening place. I could see steamboats on the nearly mile wide river, along with skiffs. There was a variety of businesses: a huge general store owned by a man with the last name Conrad, a mill with an enormous lumber yard owned by the Leavenworth family, a button factory, a brickyard owned by the Whitcomb family where bricks were formed and fired in a kiln, and the Lyon's Boat Manufacturing, where very fine skiffs were made, just to name a few. There was also a huge wood yard, where steamboats could purchase fuel for their engines.

"Where's the giant hay press located?" I wondered aloud. "Angus mentioned it in one of his letters."

"The press is east of town, on the Cole farm," Papa said. "Would you like to go see it?"

"Yes, if we have time," I replied.

"We'll go look at the hay press first," Papa said, "then come back into town and take care of business."

Papa guided the horses through town. We were headed east, the bluff to our left and a quarter mile wide strip of ground to our right that ended at the river's edge. We soon came to a farm on our right with a huge barn on it. Papa turned into the drive and went straight to the barn. As we stepped from the wagon to stretch our legs, a man exited the barn.

"Hello," Papa greeted. "I'm Stephen Hensley from Marengo, and my wife and daughter would like to see your hay press, if you don't mind."

The man smiled warmly at us. "Most certainly, you may see the hay press. It was built in 1850, so it's thirteen years old now. We don't have too many people come look at it much anymore, but when it was first built, a steady stream of visitors kept the road well worn."

We followed the man into the huge barn. The loft of the barn was filled with loose hay. There were a team of oxen yoked to a large, vertical beam on the lower level. The man hollered up to someone in the loft to throw hay in so he could start the press. As the loose hay was thrown into a large wooden shaft, the oxen were lead around in a circle, causing the beam to turn and a huge wooden press to come down, smashing the hay tight. When the shaft was full, the hay was tied off and the shaft lowered to ground level. The enormous bale was then dumped onto a wagon, ready to be loaded on a boat and sold somewhere along the Ohio River. It was a most amazing piece of machinery.

Papa thanked the man for the demonstration, and we made our way back to Leavenworth. Momma and I took care of picking out bolts of fabric to take back to the store while Papa bought the rest of the items on the list, except ammunition, because there was none to buy.

After everything was loaded into the wagon, Papa took us to a restaurant for supper. I had never eaten in a restaurant and was amazed that all we had to do was sit down and tell the waitress, as Papa called her, what we wanted to eat. The food was brought to the table and I didn't even have to wash the dishes when we finished eating.

The only thing I did not enjoy about the restaurant experience was the water. The waitress had encouraged us to get the sulfur water, which had come from the white sulfur well in Sulfur, which was located a few miles west of Leavenworth. The waitress claimed the well was among the finest mineral wells in the entire United States. As far as I was concerned, they could just keep their fine water. It smelled of rotten eggs and tasted just about the same.

As the horses labored to pull the loaded wagon up out of Leavenworth, I watched the busy town fade in the distance. I gazed at the river and its huge bend as we topped the bluff and headed toward home. If I had the ability to paint, I would have asked Papa to stop and let me capture the scene on canvas. As it was, I had to commit the scene to memory so I could think about the beauty for years to come.

As we neared the road that turned toward Curby, the sun was sinking low in the western sky. As I looked toward the setting sun, I was stunned for the second time that day by God's handiwork. I had never seen a more beautiful sunset, as the sun dipped below the tops of the brightly colored leaves. From the vantage point where we were on the Leavenworth-Paoli road looking toward Curby, we could see for miles off to the west. To add to the beauty, a purple haze had enveloped the landscape, blending it all into a perfect picture. Again, I wished I had the talent to recreate the scene with a brush and paint.

When we reached the general store, Papa unhitched the wagon, after the horses had backed it into the small barn at the back of the store. He then turned two of the horses into the corral and hitched Nellie and Clyde to the smaller wagon Reuben used to get supplies from Milltown. The full wagon we had brought back from Leavenworth would be unloaded Monday morning.

"I'll just walk to my cabin," I said as Momma and Papa climbed on the seat of the empty wagon. "It's not that far and I know you need to get home and take care of things."

"Okay, Virginia," Momma said, followed by a yawn. "We will see you in the morning."

Walking to the cabin, I thought back over the trip to Leavenworth. As I did, I made plans to return there again someday when the leaves were at their peak. Perhaps after the war ended and Angus and I were married, we could go there together. As my mind drifted to Angus, I whispered another prayer for his and Carter's safety, wherever they were this beautiful fall night.

****

The next week, I came to the store and worked after school dismissed for the day. Mary Ellen fussed at first, but by the end of the week looked forward to getting a break and being able to go upstairs and work in her and Reuben's home. She had already picked out some fabric from the store's supply and sewed pretty new curtains. She was now working on curtains to cover the shelves where canned goods were stored. Since no one had actually lived in the upstairs over the store for over twenty years, it was certainly in need of some sprucing up and a woman's touch. Reuben had been content to just leave it as it was, but his new wife was not so inclined.

When Friday came, I hurried to finish up at the school as quickly as possible, wanting to get the latest report the Louisville Daily Journal had on the situation in Chattanooga. As I stepped up on the porch, Delmar looked up from his checker game he was playing with Pastor David. "Hey, Virginia, did you have a good day?"

"Yes, Delmar, pretty good," I replied.

"Did you whack any fingers with your ruler?" Delmar asked.

"No, like I've told you, I have never whacked any fingers with my ruler. I only have one ruler, so I would really hate to break it. Who's winning the checker game?"

"Pastor David," Delmar muttered. "I would accuse him of cheating, but saying that about the preacher might not be a wise thing to do."

I laughed lightly, knowing full well that Pastor David was certainly not cheating at checkers. "The newspaper must not have had much to report since the porch is empty."

"Nope," Delmar replied, "just that General Grant was in Chattanooga devising a plan to end the siege."

I shivered as a cool wind blew across the porch. "You guys

may have to finish that game inside," I remarked. "It feels like cold weather might be moving in."

"Well, it is the next to last day of October," Pastor David pointed out. "It's time for some colder weather."

"Tell Reuben to get the woodstove ready," Delmar bossed. "I might need to warm up beside it when I get here tomorrow."

I smiled at Delmar and replied as I walked into the store, "I'll put in your request."

"Virginia! You have a letter from Angus!" Mary Ellen rushed toward me holding out the filthy, ragged piece of mail as I stepped inside.

Reaching out, I snatched the letter from Mary Ellen's hand. Taking the letter behind the counter, I plopped down on a stool and carefully opened it, trying not to damage it more than it already was. Unfolding the letter, I noted the date on the letter was October 8th.

Dearest Virginia,

First, Carter and I were not injured during the battle at Chickamauga Creek. I'm sure you have all been worried at home. As you probably already know, the Army of the Cumberland is trapped in Chattanooga, Tennessee by General Braxton Bragg's Army of Tennessee. The Confederates are positioned on the mountain tops of Missionary Ridge and Look Out Mountain. The chance of this letter ever reaching you is very slim, but I must try anyway.

A costly miscommunication by Captain Kellogg to General Rosecrans resulted in a gap being created in the Union line as we battled against the Confederates on September 20th near Chickamauga Creek. Kellogg couldn't see General Brannan's troops because of all the foliage. He reported that there was a gap where there really wasn't one at all. General Rosecrans sent word to Brigadier General Tomas J. Wood to fill the gap with his men. General Wood knew Brannan's men were there, but earlier Rosecrans had accused General Wood of being slow to take orders and move expediently. General Woods moved to where General Rosecrans had instructed, and the Confederates pushed through our now broken line. What resulted was a mass retreat toward Chattanooga.

As I began to flee, I noticed General George Thomas heading up onto Horseshoe Ridge with several regiments. I fell in with the men and we were able to hold the Confederates back until Rosecrans sent word that Thomas should begin a general retreat. The retreat began with the units positioned in Kelly Field leaving first. Thomas placed Granger in charge so he could begin organizing the retreat. Granger did not fully coordinate the retreat before leaving the area, leaving men to fight without ammunition. Three regiments were captured by the Confederates as a result.

We retreated to Rossville, where Rosecrans was sent a wire in Chattanooga encouraging him to come back and lead the Army of the Cumberland into battle the next day, but Rosecrans refused. He seems to have lost the will to fight.

As I mentioned, we are now trapped in Chattanooga. The Union supplies, which are in Bridgeport, Alabama, must travel sixty miles over Walden's Ridge. The trek is difficult and dangerous. A train of 800 wagons was attacked by Confederates led by General Wheeler on October first. Many wagons were set afire and the mules were killed. Adding to the difficulty is heavy rainfall, causing the mountain road to completely wash away in some places and making travel slick and even more difficult. Our food supply is very low and our horses and mules are suffering greatly from lack of nourishment.

If supplies make it through, I will hand this letter to one of the drivers and hope it reaches you. I just want to ease the worry of you not knowing whether Carter and I survived the battle. Please pray this siege ends soon, for we will not survive much longer in these deplorable conditions. A box of food from home would be most welcome right now. I know everyone is continuing to send them each week, but we have little hope of receiving one.

I will send a letter to my parents and Carter has written one to Effie, and to you and your parents. We plan to give each letter to a different wagon driver, so our eggs are not all in one basket, so to speak. Hopefully, at least one of those letters will find its way to Marengo.

I love and miss you terribly. Please continue to write, even if there is little hope of me ever receiving the letters.

All my love,
Angus

Lowering the letter, I looked up into the expectant faces of Mary Ellen, Reuben and Papa. Deciding not to try and explain the letters contents, I handed the letter to Papa for him to read aloud. Delmar and Pastor David stepped in from the porch just as Papa began to read. When he finished, everyone was silent for a moment, contemplating all Angus had written. Delmar finally broke the silence.

"Well, thank God, them boys are still alive!"

"Yes, Delmar, thank God," Pastor David chimed in. The men began to discuss the battle and the fact that few supplies were reaching the men trapped in Chattanooga. I picked up the letter Papa had placed on the counter and carefully placed it back in its filthy covering. Turning toward Mary Ellen, I asked, "Did Carter's letters get through?"

"No, Virginia, just the one letter from Angus. It must have come on angel's wings."

"Has Effie been to the store today?"

"Yes, but I didn't know yet that you had received a letter. Thaddeus handed the letter to your Papa upon his arrival. It was not in the mailbag. Your Papa had slipped it into his pocket and later brought it in to me."

"I must go tell Effie that Carter is alive," I blurted, hurrying toward the door.

"Yes, go deliver the good news," Mary Ellen said.

Rushing back toward the school and turning up the hill toward Effie's, I could not make my feet move fast enough. I had slipped the letter from Angus into my dress pocket, since I had not yet had time to pull on the apron I wore while I worked at the store. Reaching into my pocket, I touched the letter then withdrew the leather heart I always kept with me. "I'm still waiting," I whispered out loud as I trudged up the steep hill to Effie's front door. I knocked and Effie immediately opened the door.

"Virginia, what are you doing here?" Effie asked. "Did something happen to Carter?"

Trying to catch my breath, I attempted to explain. Finally, I reached into my pocket and held out the letter to Effie. She reached out with trembling fingers and took it from my hand. "Come in and sit down," Effie said. "You're completely out of breath."

I followed Effie into the house and sat down in a kitchen chair. Effie's mother handed me a glass of water, which I gulped down. The excitement of receiving the letter and the run to Effie's had completely taken my breath away. Effie slipped into the chair next to mine and slowly opened the letter. After taking a minute to read the words written on the pages, she turned to me, tears glistening in her big brown eyes.

"Oh, Virginia, they're alive!"

"Yes, Effie! It's such wonderful news!"

"Have you showed the letter to Angus's parents?" Effie asked.

"No, I just opened it," I replied. "I will head there now."

"I'll walk with you," Effie said, reaching for a sweater.

"Thank you," I said. "The company will be nice."

Effie and I walked back down the hill. Deciding to stop at my cabin first for me to get a sweater, we turned left toward the school when we reached the bottom of the hill. Pulling the sweater tight around me, we headed toward the leather shop. The shop was located just a short distance north of Marengo on the Leavenworth Paoli road. I knocked on the door and waited for someone to answer.

"Why, Virginia, what brings you here on this chilly, windy afternoon?" Angus's mother asked. "I do hope the girls did not misbehave at school today."

I smiled at this kind, gentle-hearted woman who may one day become my mother-in-law. "The girls are learning well and never cause me trouble," I assured. Holding out the letter, I said, "I have something for you to read."

I could tell her eyes recognized Angus's neat script immediately as she took the letter from my hand. "Come in out of that cold wind."

Effie and I stepped into the warm house, where the smell of leather and oils used for the trade filled the air. The shop was attached to the house and I was sure the people living there no longer noticed the pungent aroma.

Angus's two younger sisters came from the kitchen where they had been helping their mother prepare supper. "Hello Miss Virginia," Abigail, the older of the two, greeted warmly.

"Good afternoon, Abigail," I said. "Do you have that list of spelling words memorized I gave you today?"

"Not all of them," Abigail admitted, "but I will by the test next Wednesday."

"I'm sure of it," I said, smiling at the girl who looked so much like her mother.

"I read a Psalm last night for Pa," Annie chimed in, not willing to stand in the shadow of her sister's accomplishments.

"That's really good," I praised the child, who was barely eight years old.

Angus's mother folded the letter back neatly and placed it in the ragged, muddy cover. Her eyes glistened as she handed it back to me. Her voice quivered with emotion as she said, "Virginia, thank you for sharing your letter with me. At least we know Angus and

Carter are alive, and we will continue to pray they return to us, soon."

"You're welcome," I replied. "Now if General Grant can only figure out a way to break the siege and get supplies to the Army of the Cumberland."

"Yes, and push the Confederates back into Georgia," Effie added. "It seems this war is never going to end."

"One day it will end, Virginia," Angus's mother replied, "and I hope we are on the winning side."

"Yes, me too," I whispered.

Effie and I made our way back toward the general store. Papa had left for home to tell Momma the good news about Carter and Angus being unharmed. Effie stayed and chatted to Mary Ellen and me for a few minutes before heading for home, too. I sent Mary Ellen upstairs, and at six o'clock, I closed the store for the day.

Grabbing a broom, I quickly swept the floor and straightened a few shelves. Reuben came from the storeroom and collected the money box to take upstairs and count. After the store had been broken into, the money was always removed each night and put in a safe place. Papa or I used to take it to the farm each night, but now Reuben took care of the store's account book and the safe keeping of the money.

"Go home, Virginia," Reuben said as he stuffed the money box under his right arm, "we can take care of putting the store in order tomorrow."

"I will in just a bit," I replied. "I'm just going to refill the empty spots on the shelves."

"Do as you wish, Virginia, but I'm going to eat supper." Reuben walked to the back of the store and I could hear him trudging up the stairs to his and Mary Ellen's living quarters. A few minutes later, I heard his heavy footsteps coming back down.

"Mary Ellen sent this to you," Reuben said, holding out a pint jar filled with chicken and dumplings. "And this is for you too," Reuben placed a plate on the counter with a generous slice of squash pie on it. Mary Ellen knew it was my favorite and it was still warm from the oven.

"Tell her I said thank you," I said. "Do you have any cream to pour over the pie?"

"Goodness, Virginia, Mary Ellen gave you a huge piece of pie, cheating me out of extra servings," Reuben said with a smile, "and now you want me to share the cream Papa brought this morning, too?"

"Well, if it's not too much trouble," I said with a sheepish grin.

"I guess if you didn't come each afternoon so Mary Ellen would have time to fix such delicious things, I would be doing without," Reuben said with a laugh. "I'll go get a small container of cream for the pie. Would you like me to whip it for you, too?"

"No, I'll add the sugar and whip it," I said. "Thanks, Reuben."

Reuben trudged back up the stairs and came back shortly with the cream. I grabbed a small basket and placed the items inside. "I have filled the empty places on the shelves," I said. "I'll see you in the morning."

"Good night, Virginia," Reuben said as I walked through the back door.

The north wind whipped my dress around my legs as I walked toward my cabin, promising a much colder day tomorrow. A full harvest moon loomed in front of me, barely above the horizon, as I trekked east. As I stared at the huge orange globe, I wondered if Carter and Reuben were looking at it, too. The full harvest moon was always one of the most beautiful of the year, and Carter and I had watched it rise several times throughout the years while relaxing on a limb in the Maple. Again I asked the question in my mind: "How much longer will the war last?"

Chapter Twenty-Two

November blew in cold and rainy. The tables, chairs and checkers were moved off the porch of the general store and placed near the stove. As I entered the store on the first Friday of November, I knew there had been news about the war, for ten men were packed around the stove and were in deep discussion.

"What's happened?" I asked as I stepped in amongst the men.

"General Grant has opened a cracker line," Delmar said with a grin.

"A cracker line?" I asked. "What exactly is that?"

"On October 27th, General Grant floated a brigade of pontoons down the Tennessee River," Papa said. "The Union has taken Brown's Ferry back from Confederate control. By river, Bridgeport, Alabama is only thirty miles from Chattanooga. Supplies can now be sent up river by boat."

"That's good news," I said smiling. "Not only can supplies be brought in, perhaps letters will be able to be sent out."

"Yes, and when ammunition can be replenished, maybe the Army of the Cumberland can send Bragg and his Army of Tennessee south," Delmar added.

"We hope that's what happens," Joe, Effie's father, said.

The men went back to planning how the Union was going to

run the Confederates off the mountain tops around Chattanooga. I went to help Mary Wiseman pick out some new fabric for her living room curtains.

"I want something bright and cheery, Virginia," Mary said, "like irises blooming in May."

"We brought back several new patterns from Leavenworth," I offered. "We don't have room to display them all. Come to the storeroom with me and I'll show them all to you."

Mary followed me to the storeroom and finally decided on a bright yellow fabric with tiny blue flowers all over it. It was the same pattern Mary Ellen had chosen to create a quilt to cover her and Reuben's bed. She had been sewing on it in the evening and had the top about halfway finished. Momma would bring her quilting frame and help her finish it, once the top was pieced together.

"I believe that pattern will make beautiful curtains," I told Mary as I finished measuring and cutting the required amount.

"Yes, I think so too," Mary said, following me back to the counter.

I carefully wrapped the fabric in brown paper to protect it on the ride home. Mary paid for her purchase and left the store with a smile. I knew she would start creating the curtains as soon as she arrived back home.

Mary Ellen was helping Mrs. George choose some fabric, too. I watched with amusement as Mary Ellen showed her a variety of colorful prints. Each time, Mrs. George shook her head no and scowled at Mary Ellen for even suggesting such fabric. Finally, Mary Ellen came to the counter with a dull brown piece of fabric that Mrs. George had chosen.

"Are you making new curtains, too?" I asked in my most cheerful voice possible.

"Of course not, Virginia," Mrs. George said. "I'm making a skirt and shirt waist."

"For your funeral?" I wanted to ask, but instead just smiled politely and said, "That material is nice and thick. It should keep you warm this winter."

"It's sensible, Virginia, much unlike your teaching habits," Mrs. George replied.

Oh, great. Here we go. "I admit, the first week was a bit rough," I said, "but I think I have settled in quite nicely, now."

"Time will tell," Mrs. George replied curtly. "Now, tell me what I owe so I can get home before dark."

I wrapped the fabric in brown paper, thinking how one could not tell where the fabric ended and the paper began. I held back pointing out that it would not be dark for two hours yet, but there was no sense giving Mrs. George anymore reason for which to argue. Handing her the package I said, "Thank you, Mrs. George. I hope you have a nice day."

"Girl, this day is nearly over," Mrs. George grumped. Snatching up her package, she barreled toward the door of the general store. As her footsteps could be heard tromping across the porch and down the steps, I heard Delmar mutter from the checker table by the stove, "And a good day to you, too."

I turned to Mary Ellen and just shook my head. "I honestly don't know what to say to that woman."

"Obviously, neither do I," Mary Ellen said smiling, "and I certainly can't help her choose fabric."

"Just go with drab and ugly," Delmar said looking up from his checker game. "It will work every time."

The next Friday when I entered the store, Mary Ellen motioned me to the counter. "Virginia, you have a letter from Angus," she said, placing it in my hand, "and Effie received one from Carter."

I looked at the letter for a moment and decided to save it until I returned home. I placed the letter in the pocket of my dress. "Has Effie been here to pick hers up?"

"Yes. She came early and waited for the mail wagon. With the Tennessee River being opened up for supplies, she was just sure she would receive a letter."

"Virginia, aren't you going to read your letter to us?" Delmar asked from his chair near the stove.

"Not this time," I said smiling. "I'll let you know if there's anything worth sharing with you, Delmar."

"Effie wouldn't read Carter's to us, either," Delmar complained. "How we gonna know firsthand what's happening down there in Tennessee if you girls won't share the information with us."

"I'll tell you anything I believe you will find interesting when I get here tomorrow," I promised Delmar.

"Ah, well, it's just as well that you won't read it aloud," Delmar said. "I don't want to hear all that mushy stuff anyway." Delmar broke into his best feminine voice. "Oh, Virginia, I love you. Oh, Virginia, you're beautiful. Oh, Virginia, I miss you."

"Gee, Delmar, I didn't know you cared so much," I replied laughing.

Delmar scowled at me from his chair he had leaned back against the wall. Deciding to change the subject, he asked, "How about a game of checkers, Virginia?"

"Are you having a losing streak?" I asked. "You only invite me to play checkers after you have lost several games."

"I'm just trying to increase your skills, Virginia," Delmar replied. "Wouldn't you like to beat Carter at checkers when he returns?"

"Delmar, you can't even beat Carter at checkers," I retorted. "How do you plan to make me skillful enough to beat him?"

"It's because Carter cheats!" Delmar bellowed. "I bet there's not a soldier in Chattanooga who will play a game with Carter by now."

I laughed at how riled up Delmar could get over a game of checkers, becoming almost as mad over Carter cheating as Reuben used to. "Set up the board," I said. "Is it okay if I play a game of checkers with Delmar before you go upstairs, Mary Ellen?"

"Yes, Virginia, that's fine," Mary Ellen said. "I don't expect it will take long for him to beat you."

"Thanks for the vote of confidence," I said smiling. "How many games of checkers have you played Delmar, Mary Ellen?"

"Only one," Delmar chimed in. "Believe it or not, she's worse than you are."

Mary Ellen rolled her eyes. A customer walked in and she went to wait on them as Delmar and I began our very short game of checkers. I honestly did not know how men could sit and play this game for hours. The strategy of the whole thing eluded me.

"Virginia, I do believe you get worse at this game every time I play you," Delmar said.

"I hate to admit it, but I think you're right." Getting up from the table, I went to tell Mary Ellen she was free to go upstairs now. Delmar said his goodbyes and headed toward home, knowing his wife would have supper ready very soon. The store stayed busy right up to closing time, giving me little time to think about the letter in my pocket waiting to be read.

"I'm headed home now, Reuben," I called, heading toward the back door.

Reuben hollered goodbye from the front of the store. Mary Ellen called down from upstairs, "Virginia, come up here. I dipped you up a plate of supper."

Hurrying up the stairs, I was greeted with a plate of beef stew with two buttermilk biscuits on the side. "That smells wonderful," I said, picking up the plate. "I'll eat one biscuit with my stew and save the other one for dessert and add jelly to it. Thank you, Mary Ellen."

"You're welcome, Virginia. Enjoy reading your letter."

I smiled, knowing Mary Ellen understood my eagerness to read the letter from Angus. It had not been too long since she had anxiously awaited letters from Reuben. "I will," I said turning to go down the stairs.

"What's that?" Reuben asked as I passed him on the stairs. "First you take my squash pie and now you have two biscuits."

"There's plenty left for you," I said smiling. "If you eat like this every night, it won't be long before you'll need bigger clothes."

Reuben answered with a laugh. "See you tomorrow, Virginia."

"Good night, Reuben." I hurried home with my plate of food, hoping it wouldn't get too cold before I got there. Sitting down at my little kitchen table with two chairs, I bowed my head and asked a blessing on the food. I forked a mouthful of stew up then reached into my pocket and removed the letter from Angus. Opening it carefully, I pressed out the creases where it had been folded and began to read.

My Dearest Virginia,

Yes, it was a good thing I had not read the letter aloud to Delmar.

Brigadier General William "Baldy" Smith, the chief engineer for the Army of the Cumberland, devised a plan to help get supplies past the Confederates. General Grant, upon his arrival, approved the plan, agreeing that he believed it would work. Troops were sent across Moccasin Point to help secure Brown's Ferry while pontoons were used to float a brigade down the Tennessee River toward the same location. The plan went into action in the early morning hours on October 27th. Fog blanketed the region and the moon was not shining, hiding the brigade from the probing eyes of the Confederate soldiers atop Lookout Mountain. General Hooker marched from the south into Lookout Valley and met up with the other Union troops at Brown's Ferry. The Union is now in control of Brown's Ferry and supplies are coming up the Tennessee River from Bridgeport, Alabama to Kelley's Ferry then by land through the Lookout Valley. Up until this turn of events, the soldiers had been cut to a ration of four cakes of hard bread and a quarter pound of salted pork every three days. We were all near to starving before this new supply line was opened.

Countless numbers of mules have died, either trying to bring supplies across Walden's Ridge or from starvation. Horses have also perished, due to the fact they had no feed. To say the least, the Army of the Cumberland is in a sorry state. We will have to work diligently to bring ourselves and the beasts back to the strength it will take to fight.

General Grant has removed General Rosecrans from his command and replaced him with General George Thomas. Thomas has now been given the name "Rock of Chickamauga" for staying and fighting the Confederates when Rosecrans and a third of the army fled toward Chattanooga. Hopefully, General Grant and General Thomas will devise a plan to break the siege and push the Confederates from the mountains they are now looking down on us from.

I received a box and a letter from you with the first supplies that came up the Tennessee River. It was so good to hear about home. From what you wrote, half the county must have come to Reuben and Mary Ellen's wedding. Carter and I talked about how we wished we were home to see it and to fill our stomachs with the delicious food. The box I received must have contained some very delicious food too, but unfortunately, all that was left were molded items that no longer resembled anything edible. I'll admit I was quite hungry, and Carter and I debated whether or not to go ahead and eat the food. In the end, we decided against it. We could not afford taking a chance on becoming ill, especially since we had witnessed unpleasant deaths due to varying illnesses throughout the camp already.

Please, keep the letters and food boxes coming. Hopefully the next box reaches us quicker and we are able to enjoy its contents.

All my love,

Angus

Postscript: Did you happen to see the harvest moon? It was very beautiful rising above the mountains here in Chattanooga. Carter and I talked of home and all the times we had watched the harvest moon rise over Marengo throughout the years.

Folding the letter, I rose and placed it in the wooden box I kept all of Angus's letters in. I had finished eating my stew and one of the biscuits. Reaching up on a shelf, I pulled down the jar of strawberry preserves I had placed there. Sitting back down, I added a generous amount to each biscuit half I had left. The first bite brought back memories of early summer days growing up on the farm. Days that were carefree, before I knew we were part of an illegal activity called the Underground Railroad. Before that first shot was fired at Fort Sumter that started a war that had now dragged on for nearly three years, drawing two brothers and my sweet, handsome Angus into the conflict. To a time before life had become so complicated and uncertain.

****

The next Thursday, November 19th, I made several kinds of cookies and two loaves of bread when I returned to my cabin after closing the general store. Momma was making items too, and would send them in a box with Papa the next morning. Before school the next morning, I planned to take the baked goods to the store and add them with Momma's. Hopefully, the box would make it to Carter and Angus in a timely manner and they would be able to enjoy its contents.

Effie and Angus's mother planned to send boxes, too. We had all received letters stating the fact that the soldiers trapped in Chattanooga had been starving. We planned to help anyway we could.

When school dismissed on Friday, I headed to the general store. As I approached I could see several horses and wagons out front. I knew there had been a report in the newspapers worth talking about for so many people to be packed inside the general store. Opening the door and welcoming the warmth from the woodstove, I stepped into the crowded space. Papa was in the center of a group of men with a newspaper in his hand.

"What's the latest news?" I asked, not really sure if I wanted to know.

Papa looked up at me and smiled, relaxing the tension that had already formed in my shoulders. "Hello Virginia! I was just reading the speech President Lincoln made at the dedication of the National Cemetery in Gettysburg for the third time."

"When did that take place?" I asked.

"Yesterday," Papa said. "Thaddeus had heard about the great speech from a telegram sent to Leavenworth. He waited for the Louisville Daily Journal to arrive by boat so he could bring some copies along. He knew people throughout the county would want to read it."

"Is it a long speech?" I asked.

"Not at all," Delmar answered, "but it's profound. I have never heard a speech worded so nicely."

"Delmar is correct," Papa said. "There was a nearly two hour speech before President Lincoln's, but in less than three minutes, President Lincoln spoke volumes."

"I wonder what was done with all the bodies of the Confederate soldiers since that cemetery is for fallen Union soldiers," Pastor David said softly.

"They must still be there somewhere," Delmar replied. "What other choice would the ones responsible for burying the bodies possibly have had but to bury those young men, too?"

"That will be a great task trying to get the bodies of the fallen soldiers reburied on their own soil after the war ends," Pastor David said, "for the North and the South."

"Yes, it will," Papa agreed.

"May I read the speech?" I asked reaching for the newspaper.

"Actually, Thaddeus left an extra copy just for you," Papa said. "He thought you might want to read it to the children at school."

"That was quite thoughtful of Thaddeus," I replied. "Where is the copy?"

"I put it in your mailbox along with your other mail," Mary Ellen chimed in.

Hurrying behind the counter, I reached into my mailbox, which had been added after I moved to the cabin. Pulling out two letters from Angus and the newspaper, I plopped down on a stool. I stuffed the letters in my pocket for later and opened the newspaper. The speech was printed on the front page. As I scanned the article, I was sickened by the need to make a national cemetery in Gettysburg.

Since the Battle of Gettysburg had been in July, the weather had been quite warm. There had been so many men to bury the graves were dug in haste, and too shallow. As rains came, it had uncovered the bodies, creating a ghastly sight and foul odor. The government had given money to purchase seventeen acres on which to bury the men properly. The project was not completely finished, but the dedication had been scheduled just the same.

The Louisville Daily Journal had an article describing the

dedication in detail. First, a band played music and then a reverend had said a prayer, ending with the Lord's Prayer. Afterwards, a well-educated man, who had at one time been the president of Harvard University, gave a two hour discourse. President Lincoln followed with his very short but well written speech. As I read the words our 16th President had so eloquently penned and spoken, it brought tears to my eyes. I knew the first thing I would be doing Monday morning at school after we had quoted the Lord's Prayer.

When I returned home from the store that evening, I read the two letters from Angus. They mostly told of how General Grant was building morale and preparing the men for battle. The siege on Chattanooga must be completely broken, and soon. There was no way for the Union to win complete control of Tennessee without that happening.

Angus mentioned that he and Carter had received another box, and this time they could actually eat its contents, though they had shared most of it with other famished men. He also said he had received my letter telling of my trip to Leavenworth and the beauty I had seen. He stated that as pretty as Leavenworth had been when he had witnessed it cloaked in springtime splendor, he could only imagine how beautiful fall must be.

Folding the letters neatly, I placed them back into their envelopes. I bowed my head to pray for the Army of the Cumberland and that they would be successful in breaking the siege. I also prayed for Carter and Angus's safety, as I had done so many times since they had left for Tennessee. I couldn't help but wonder how many more cemeteries would be needed for the bodies of the Union and Confederate soldiers before this war ended. The thought made me shudder and again pray for a peaceful solution soon.

****

Monday morning came and I had the Gettysburg Address lying on my desk ready to read. This was the name given to President Lincoln's speech. I had cut it from the newspaper, preparing it to be hung in our school. As I stood at the front of the students preparing to read it, I found my hands trembling with the emotion the speech invoked.

"Children, I want you to listen carefully to a speech our president wrote recently," I began. "The speech was given at the dedication of the national cemetery now in Gettysburg, Pennsylvania, where so many young men lost their lives during the Battle of Gettysburg."

Four score and seven years ago our fathers brought forth, on this continent, a new nation, conceived in Liberty, and dedicated to the proposition that all men are created equal.

Now we are engaged in a great civil war, testing whether that nation, or any nation so conceived and so dedicated, can long endure. We are met on a great battlefield of that war. We have come to dedicate a portion of that field, as a final resting place for those who here gave their lives that that nation might live. It is altogether fitting and proper that we should do this.

But, in a larger sense, we cannot dedicate-we cannot consecrate-we cannot hallow this ground. The brave men, living and dead, who struggled here, have consecrated it, far above our poor power to add or detract. The world will little note, nor long remember what we say here, but it can never forget what they did here. It is for us the living, rather, to be dedicated here to the unfinished work which they who fought here have thus far so nobly advanced. It is rather for us to be here dedicated to the great task remaining before us-that from these honored dead we take increased devotion to that cause for which they here gave the last full measure of devotion-that we here highly resolve that these dead shall not have died in vain-that this nation, under God, shall have a new birth of freedom-and that government of the people, by the people, for the people, shall not perish from the earth.

"Children, I know this war has gone on much too long," I said, "and too many lives have been lost to the cause, but we cannot stop now. If we do, our nation that was formed four score and seven years ago will be lost forever. We will be divided, weakening both halves in the process."

Taking the clipping, I hung it beside the written copy of the Lord's Prayer that hung on the wall. It would remind the children, and especially me, why this war must continue until the Union won.

Chapter Twenty-Three

The last week of November was unseasonably warm. The children enjoyed the nice weather at recess, knowing it wouldn't be long before the North wind took charge and winter would set in for its season.

When recess time ended the first three days of the week, I gathered the children beneath a large oak in the school yard. The trees leaves were now brown and rustling but continued to hang to the limbs. I played the guitar and the children and I sang songs, including "The Battle Hymn of the Republic", which was quickly becoming a favorite.

If I glanced up without moving my head, I caught Mrs. George peering from her window, watching closely. When we prepared to go back into the school, I would wave toward her window and she would quickly disappear. I then smiled to myself, lined the kids up youngest to oldest and walked back into the school in an organized manner.

On Wednesday, an hour before school dismissed, I took the children outside for their history lesson. Since the next day was November 26th, the very first official Thanksgiving national holiday as set by President Lincoln, we all pretended we were Pilgrims, reenacting the very first recorded day of giving thanks in America.

I instructed the children to climb onto the picnic tables, which became our boat, the *Mayflower*. When we landed at Plymouth Rock, in Massachusetts, we all disembarked and thanked God for a safe journey across the wide Atlantic Ocean.

I explained to the children that it was December of 1620 when the *Mayflower* landed, and the Pilgrims soon realized they had not brought enough food to get them through until the next harvest. I told them how a tribe of Indians had come to their rescue.

With much reserve, I allowed Levi to become Squanto, an Indian who could speak English since he had spent some time in a prison in England, and other students became part of the Indian tribe. Levi picked up a large stick as his tomahawk and I debated if I should make him put it down. I decided to trust him not to spear anyone and hoped I had made the right choice.

We reenacted the Indians sharing food with the Pilgrims to keep them from starving and later teaching them how to plant corn and other vegetables that grew well in this new land. We ended the lesson by coming together, Indians facing Pilgrims, to give thanks for the bountiful harvest of 1621, hence the first Thanksgiving.

"And so children, you can see how the Indians played a huge role in the survival of the Pilgrims who landed at Plymouth Rock in the year of 1620," I said concluding the lesson.

"Yeah, and then you white men stole our hunting grounds and ran us from our land!" Levi hollered.

What happened next, I can hardly explain. Levi let out a war whoop and his "tribe" did the same. The girls screamed and ran as "Squanto", with his tomahawk raised high, and the men from his tribe rushed toward the "Pilgrims". The boys who were playing the role of Pilgrims saw a chance for a scuffle and headed toward the warriors. I quickly reached out and grabbed toward Levi, catching him by the hair of his head. As I pulled him back he screeched again, though probably from the pain I was inflicting and not a battle cry.

"I'm the one who's supposed to do the scalping," Levi complained as he turned to see who had hold of him.

"Give me that stick," I demanded, wondering why I had ever trusted him with the role of Squanto.

Levi begrudgingly handed me the stick. His tribe of warriors knew they had gone too far and immediately stopped in their tracks.

"Everyone please go sit at the picnic tables," I said while holding Levi's arm. As I guided him to a seat on the end close to me,

I glanced up the hill. Mrs. George's curtain fell back into place just as my eyes found her window. I made a mental note to be prepared to answer several questions as soon as the woman could get me cornered.

I had made several squash pies, and I cut a large slice for each child, even Levi; though I admit I was tempted to make him watch his classmates enjoy the dessert without him. Following the snack, I wished them all a blessed Thanksgiving as they left for the day. School would be out until the next Monday, by which time I hoped to be past my anger at the tomahawk wielding "Squanto".

The store was closed the next day for Thanksgiving. There was a special meeting at the church to give thanks and pray for the war to end, mending our country back together. The service was followed by a pitch-in meal outside on the grounds, since the weather had remained nice. There were several turkeys roasted for the meal, but they had come from tame flocks. Ammunition was in very short supply and no one had mastered a bow or sling shot well enough to take down a wild turkey.

On Friday, Papa and I worked together all day at the store, giving Reuben and Mary Ellen some much needed time off. They took full advantage of it, leaving for Corydon that morning and planning to spend the night at a hotel there. They would return late Saturday night. One thing they were quite sure of, no one from Marengo would travel all the way to Corydon to wake them up by banging on pots and pans on this their belated honeymoon.

When the mail arrived, Thaddeus handed the bag to me and I handed him two boxes just for Carter. His birthday would be December 7th, and Effie had made a special box just for him and so had Momma. I also handed him a box for Angus that his mother and I had put together, along with the rest of the outgoing mail, which included a birthday card from me to Carter and a letter for Angus.

I took the arriving mail into the store while Papa talked to Thaddeus for a moment before coming into the store to retrieve the latest copies of the Louisville Daily Journal. The men had gathered earlier, already anxiously waiting for Papa's weekly report.

"Well, Stephen, what does it say?" Delmar asked.

"Give me a minute, Delmar," Papa said.

"Yes, give the man a chance to read before you start demanding information," Pastor David said laughing.

"I never was known for having patience," Delmar muttered

"The Union is engaged in battle in Chattanooga," Papa said after reading a moment. "There's not much of a report yet, just the statement that a battle has broken out. Next week's paper should have much more in it."

"It's about time we pushed them Confederates off those mountain tops," Delmar said. "General Grant will get the job done, I'm sure of it."

"I sure hope he can," Papa said setting the Louisville Daily Journal aside and picking up the *Crisis*. "The farm report is in for the year."

"How much corn was grown this year?" Pastor David asked.

"Nearly 196,000 bushels," Papa replied, "and we grew 1,500 tons of hay."

"What were the wheat totals?" Joe asked.

"76,000 bushels," Papa replied. "Wool was up this year, too, at 15,000 pounds."

"That's a lot of sheep shearing," Delmar said. "I could never tolerate the dumb animals myself."

"I've never kept sheep either," Papa said. He continued to peruse the newspaper. "Goodness, Crawford County produced 20,000 bushels of potatoes."

"That's a lot of hilling and digging," Pastor David said with a chuckle.

"Sounds like an aching back and blistered hands to me," Delmar added.

"The report states over 8,000 pounds of maple syrup was made this year," Papa continued.

"That's no surprise," Joe said. "I tapped 100 trees myself on my farm. How many did you tap, Stephen?"

"Seventy-five," Papa replied. "The weather was good this year with several cold nights and temperatures above forty degrees during the day throughout February."

"Yeah, some years we don't get really good weather for tapping but this year was exceptional," Joe agreed.

"Now, this total does surprise me," Papa said. "Crawford County reported over 35,000 pounds of butter!"

"That's a good deal of churning," Pastor David said.

"Not to mention all the milking," Joe added.

Delmar laughed, "I believe I ate a thousand pounds of that butter myself spread over warm homemade biscuits. I say keep that good stuff coming."

The men laughed and continued to discuss all the products that had been grown in Crawford County in the year of 1863. I kept sorting the mail, enjoying the tone and cadence of the different voices chiming in on the subject. To someone from a big city, one might view the gathering at the general store as silly and the conversation useless, but it was our way of life. We gathered to share our lives, during happy times and sad times. We laughed together and cried together, and most importantly, prayed together. I may have a desire to travel and see other places, but I knew for certain home would always be right here.

The next week December rolled in and so did the first taste of winter. The nights dipped below freezing and the days warmed only into the low forties. The children ate their lunch indoors then bundled up to play outside in the crisp air. By the time recess ended, their ears and noses were red and their fingers were stinging. There was a push toward the woodstove to warm up before the afternoon lessons began.

When Friday came, I walked the short distance to the general store at a brisk pace, seeking the warmth the woodstove offered upon entering. As I rubbed my hands together and removed my coat, Delmar greeted me. "Virginia, you could have shut that door quicker. You have caused me to have a chill."

"Delmar, I know that door has been opened and closed countless times today," I said, walking behind the counter to hang my coat on a peg. "I came in it just as quickly as anyone else."

"I know you did," Delmar said, "but I'm fixing to leave here in a minute and now I have to get warm again before I can."

"Of all the crazy things to complain about, Delmar," I replied. "You're going to get cold before you get home no matter how warm you are before you leave."

"I know," Delmar said, "but I could have left sooner if you had shut the door quicker."

I rolled my eyes and looked at Mary Ellen. "Has he been this cantankerous all day?"

Mary Ellen laughed. "Yes, pretty much, and I honestly don't understand why. The Union army has had a victory in Chattanooga."

"Was it in the newspaper?" I asked looking all around for the Louisville Daily Journal.

"Yes," Mary Ellen said walking to the table Delmar was sitting at by the woodstove and snatching the paper up. "It's right here."

Taking the newspaper from Mary Ellen, I quickly read the article. The Union army had indeed caused the Confederates to retreat back into Georgia. The battles on Lookout Mountain and Missionary Ridge lasted from November 23rd until the taking of Orchard Knob on November 26th, when the Confederates retreated in two separate columns toward Dalton, Georgia. Casualties for the Union totaled nearly 6,000, with over 750 being killed and 349 missing. The Confederates reported over 6,500 casualties, with 361 killed and over 4,000 missing.

Whispering a prayer that Carter and Angus were not among the dead, I turned to Mary Ellen, "The victory was on Thanksgiving day, the day President Lincoln set aside to give thanks and praise to God for the victory at Gettysburg."

"That's the exact thing Pastor David pointed out," Mary Ellen said. "I don't believe that is a coincidence."

"I don't either," I replied.

"Well, now that you've read the good news, I'll tell you what has put me in such a foul mood," Delmar hollered from across the room.

"It usually doesn't take much to stoke your fire," I replied with a smile, "but what has happened to make you so disgruntled?"

"That crazy John Hunt Morgan and six of his officers escaped from the Ohio Penitentiary the day after Thanksgiving," Delmar bellowed. "The guards must have eaten too much turkey and fell asleep on the job."

"Are you sure?" I asked, scanning the paper for the information.

"Now, Virginia, would I make up such a story as that?" Delmar questioned. "That man must be a slithery snake and can escape from any confinement."

I shuddered at Delmar's description of the newly escaped prisoner. Finding the article stating that, yes, John Hunt Morgan had escaped with six other Confederate officers; I quickly read its contents. "I can't believe he was allowed to escape."

"He's probably already joined back up with the Army of

Tennessee by now," Delmar fumed.

"I'm sure he has," I agreed, still not able to believe John Hunt Morgan had actually escaped the prison. Folding the paper, I placed it on the counter. "Did I get any mail today, Mary Ellen?"

"Not today," Mary Ellen said. "With preparing for the battle, I doubt Angus or Carter had any time to write."

"You're right, of course," I agreed, "but I thought I would ask just in case."

The next Friday, the day could not go by quick enough. My thoughts were consumed with whether or not I had received a letter from Angus or if one had come from Carter. Just as we finished lunch, Effie walked into the school. I quickly went to her, thinking how Effie had never come before during school hours.

"Did you hear something?" I asked before Effie could utter a word.

Effie held out an envelope to me. "You received a letter from Angus but no mail came from Carter. I hate to interrupt your teaching, but I checked the time and knew it was lunch."

I reached for the envelope and gave Effie a reassuring hug. "Effie, I'm as concerned as you are. I will open the letter from Angus immediately."

Unsealing the letter, I could feel the thickness and knew it was lengthy. Even so, I was certain Angus would tell Effie and me what we longed to know in his first sentence. He would not leave me to wonder whether or not Carter was well.

As I unfolded the letter and glanced down, the answer stared back in black and white. Tears of joy filled my eyes as I looked back to Effie. "Carter is fine. He and Angus have come through the battle unharmed."

"Thank God," Effie whispered. "I will go back and tell everyone at the general store."

"Yes, thank God," I repeated. "I will read the letter tonight and give you more details tomorrow."

"Thank you, Virginia," Effie said. "I will let you get back to teaching now."

"Actually, it's time for recess, as you remember," I said with a laugh, "and how could you forget since it was your favorite subject while you were in school."

The remark put a smile on Effie's pretty face, just as I had planned for it to. She said good-bye and headed back toward the general store to share the good news. I slipped the letter into my pocket to read when I returned home after the store closed that evening.

As I entered the store after school, Mary Ellen was waiting on a customer. When the needs of the customer had been satisfied and they left with their purchase, Mary Ellen turned to me. "Have you read the letter from Angus yet?"

"No, not yet," I replied. "I will read it when I return home tonight."

"I honestly don't know how you do that," Mary Ellen said. "You remember how I was when a letter from Reuben arrived. I had to go read it immediately."

I looked at Mary Ellen for a brief moment, thinking how she looked tired. "I just like to be alone and allow each word he writes to soothe away the lines of worry I have allowed to gather on my face." Smiling, I added, "Of course, sometimes what he says causes whole new lines to form."

"At least we know for certain that he and Carter are unharmed," Mary Ellen said.

"Yes and that alone has lifted a huge burden of worry," I admitted. "The store is empty now. Why don't you go ahead upstairs and rest a while."

"Hey, the store is not empty," Delmar hollered from beside the woodstove. "Can't you see me sitting here?"

"Delmar, you're a permanent fixture," I retorted. "I meant the store is empty of paying customers."

"I buy things sometimes," Delmar defended.

"Of course you do, Delmar," I replied. "I'm sorry if I offended you."

"It's nothing a game of checkers won't solve," Delmar said with a grin. "It's been nearly a month since I've beaten you."

Mary Ellen laughed out loud. "Delmar, you are a conniver if I ever saw one." Turning to me, she said, "I believe I will head upstairs. I am feeling unusually tired."

"And I suppose I will go lose at a game of checkers," I said with a smile.

As I sat down at the table, Delmar began to divvy up the black and red pieces. After we had played for a few minutes, Delmar said softly, "Virginia, I sure was glad to hear Carter and Angus are okay."

"Me too, Delmar," I said. "I know we tease each other a lot, but down deep, you are one of my favorite people."

"I like you too, Virginia," Delmar said with a smile as he jumped four of my checkers in one move. A few moves later and I had lost the game entirely.

As closing time neared, Reuben came in from helping a customer load lumber. Papa had gone home soon after I arrived from the school, knowing with the cold weather and short days the store would not have many customers. "Virginia, did Mary Ellen go upstairs?" Reuben asked as he stepped from the storeroom.

"Yes, soon after I got here," I replied.

"I don't smell any food cooking," Reuben pointed out. "Tantalizing smells are usually drifting down from upstairs by now."

Sniffing the air, I smiled at Reuben. "You're right. Maybe she's tired of cooking you supper after less than two months of marriage."

"Don't be ridiculous," Reuben said. "Mary Ellen loves taking care of me. I should go check on her."

Just as Reuben turned to go upstairs to check on his wife, a man walked into the store asking to buy a fifty pound bag of feed. Reuben turned to me on his way to retrieve the heavy bag from the shelf. "Virginia, I'll take care of the feed. Will you go check on Mary Ellen, please?"

"Of course, Reuben," I replied, heading toward the stairs. As I reached the top step, I could see the stove did not have any food simmering on it, nor was the table set. Walking through the first room to the bedroom, I found Mary Ellen fast asleep. Not wanting to wake her, I quietly backed out of the room and went back downstairs. As I reached the counter, Reuben came back inside after loading the feed on the customer's wagon.

"Is she okay?" Reuben asked.

"She's asleep," I replied. "She looked tired when I got here today and admitted as much to me before she went upstairs. Perhaps she's coming down with something."

"Perhaps," Reuben said. "It's not like her to be sleeping at this hour of the day."

"I didn't wake her," I said. "I suppose you will have cold ham sandwiches for supper."

Reuben smiled at the thought of eating a cold ham sandwich.

"I've eaten worse, sister dear, much worse."

"I'm sure you have," I replied knowing Reuben was referring to his time in the war.

The store closed a few minutes later and I made my way home. I had grown accustomed to Mary Ellen fixing enough supper to share with me each day. I was certain I missed the good meal this evening nearly as much as Reuben. I thought over what I had at home to eat as I walked the short distance, hurrying to escape the cold.

As I entered the cabin, I was thankful I had come home and added wood to the stove before going to the store. Otherwise, I would be walking into a cold house instead of being greeted by the warm blast of heat. I removed my coat and hung it on a peg by the door. Reaching into my pocket, I removed the letter from Angus and placed it on the table.

Moving to the wood cook stove, I pulled an iron skillet onto a hot burner and added a small amount of bacon grease. As the grease went from solid to liquid, I cracked two eggs and added them to the skillet, thankful Papa always brought eggs to me from the farm. As the eggs sizzled in the pan, I buttered two thick slices of bread. When the eggs were cooked to my liking, I removed them from the pan and added the bread, grilling it to golden brown. I placed a thick slice of cheese on one slice of the bread and added the eggs on top, then added the other slice of bread. Scooping my sandwich from the skillet, I placed it on a plate and removed the skillet from the heat.

Sitting in a chair, I placed my plate on the kitchen table. I bowed my head, asking a blessing on the food. I was anxious to read the letter that lay beside my plate, but I was not willing to get grease spots on the pages. I quickly ate my sandwich and wiped my hands on a towel. I pulled the lamp across the table toward myself and unfolded the letter from Angus in its light.

Dearest Virginia,

Carter and I have come through the most recent battle unharmed. The battle began on November 23rd and ended on the 26th, though General Grant wanted to pursue the Confederates even as they retreated.

Plans for the latest battle fell to General Smith and General Thomas as we awaited the arrival of General Sherman. All of the Generals agreed upon the strategy set forth by General Smith and Thomas and we prepared for battle.

On November 23rd, Orchard Knob was taken by 14,000 Union soldiers, overrunning and capturing 600 Confederates. This caused General Bragg to reposition his Confederate soldiers from the left flank, Lookout Mountain, toward Missionary Ridge and to call back troops he had sent toward Knoxville. On November 24th, General Hooker and three divisions totaling 10,000 Union soldiers turned their attention toward Lookout Mountain. General Grant gave General Hooker the order to take the mountain only if it seemed feasible, but General Hooker gave the order to cross Lookout Creek and assault Lookout Mountain, march down the valley and sweep every Confederate from it. As the battle ensued, a thick fog settled on the mountain, making it difficult for either side to see the enemy they were firing upon. The Union army outnumbered the Confederates, and General Bragg, realizing the battle was lost, ordered the position abandoned. The fog cleared at midnight and the moon was not shining, allowing the Confederates to retreat behind Chattanooga Creek.

On November 24th, Sherman and his men crossed the Tennessee River and made it to Billy Goat Hill, where they could see the Confederates on Tunnel Hill across a deep ravine. On November 25th, Sherman and his men advanced toward Missionary Ridge from the north and General Hooker from the south. General Thomas, who was Carter's and my commander, was instructed to advance once General Sherman and his men reached Missionary Ridge. General Sherman and his men were making very little headway against the Confederates on Tunnel Hill and General Hooker and the divisions under his command had been slowed significantly by the bridges the Confederates had burned while retreating from Lookout Mountain the night before. General Grant instructed General Thomas to move forward in the center while General Sherman was fighting to the right and General Hooker was advancing to the left.

At this point I must tell you, Virginia; the Army of the Cumberland has taken quite a ribbing from General Sherman's and General Hooker's men when they joined us in Chattanooga. They have laughed and humiliated us for turning tail and running at the battle at Chickamauga Creek. Even though General Thomas regrouped a good many of us and we held the Confederates off at Horseshoe Ridge, they seemed to only remember how many ran all the way back to Chattanooga. I believe this humiliation is what caused us to do what we did next. With the first advance up Missionary Ridge, we pushed the Confederates from their rifle pits but then we found ourselves being fired upon from atop the ridge. The second advance was disorganized, but we were pushed forward by the need to avenge ourselves after the disaster at Chickamauga Creek. As we scaled the mountain waving "Old Glory", the color-bearers would be shot dead in their tracks, but another soldier would pick up the flag and we would continue. As we came over the top of the ridge, we began to yell, "Chickamauga! Chickamauga!" sending the center of the Confederate line off in a panic. General Hooker and his divisions had the Confederates from the left flank retreating toward Missionary Ridge, as well. The left and middle flanks of the Confederates joined and retreated eastward, with the right flank that had been fighting against General Sherman and his men falling in at the rear.

Unfortunately, the thrill of victory was a short-lived one for me. With the battle over, it was time to bury the dead. I was to write down each fallen soldier's home state and regiment number as we came to each body. Most of the soldiers had sewed their names and regiments into their uniforms so they could be identified, should the time come to do so.

As I began the task, I started with Union soldiers. Normally, the soldiers would be grouped and buried by which state they were from, but General Thomas had told us not to worry with that. Graves were dug and the soldiers were buried one by one. When the Union soldiers had all been placed in their final resting place, my unit moved to the Confederate soldiers. Sadly, most of the men took as little time as possible with the burial of the fallen Confederates, but I could not bring myself to be so disrespectful. These young men were someone's son, husband, brother, or father.

As I moved amongst the corpses, I was startled when a hand reached out to grab my leg. Looking down, I saw the scared eyes of a boy maybe sixteen in a Confederate uniform. As I knelt down beside him, he requested I send a last message home, as he knew he was going to die. He whispered his name and address to me and I wrote it down on a separate piece of paper. The young man then asked if I would sing "Home Sweet Home". I knew the song well, but we had been warned not to sing it in the Union camps, for it brought longing for home which led to desertion. Not being able to deny the young man's final words, I sank to the ground and softly sang the requested song, holding the young man's hand. As I got to the chorus for the last time; "Home! Home! Sweet, sweet home! There's no place like home. There's no place like home" the young man closed his eyes and took his final breath.

Virginia, I can't tell you fully the sadness that has overwhelmed me with this most dreadful task. So many young lives have been cut short on both sides and still the war goes on. Looking back, I'm sure the Confederate soldier had been watching me for quite some time as he lay on the ground with no strength to stand. He was choosing just the right man to trust with his dying words, one who would have empathy no matter what color his uniform was.

I am sorry to give you such details of the job that is required of me, but I need to tell someone who truly understands my heart as you do. How will the families of all the fallen soldiers ever find their final resting places? We charted the burial of the Union soldiers, but the Confederate soldiers are buried without a *name and sometimes without even a marker for the grave, and I'm sure the Confederates bury any fallen Union soldiers the same way. Will these bodies ever find their way back to their own home soil? I fear it will never be so.*

I must end on a good note, for I'm sure I have saddened you with my letter. Carter and I received three boxes just before we went to battle. It brought smiles to our faces and to all the other men who we shared the contents with. I must tell you, adding the copies of the newspaper, the Crisis; to your box was an excellent idea, as every soldier in the camp enjoys reading material. Our little county in Indiana has been read about by half the Army of the Cumberland by now. Please, keep the letters and the newspapers coming.

All my love,
Angus

Folding the letter, I wiped the tears from my face. The sadness of the war and all its casualties was overwhelming. I could only hope that the Confederates retreat into Georgia was a beginning to the end of this crazy war. If the Union forces could push south into Atlanta, and Richmond could be conquered, the war would surely end. The question was how many more men would give their all to see it happen?

<u>Chapter Twenty-Four</u>

On Wednesday, December 23rd, we had a Christmas program at the school. Every child had invited their family to attend. We reenacted the Christmas story, with Mary, Joseph, shepherds, angels, and the wise men. Levi begged to be Gabriel, the archangel, but after the Squanto episode, I firmly refused to allow it. I could only imagine what kind of disaster he could make of that role.

By 2:00, the school was packed. The program went well, with the exception of Levi adding donkey sounds as Mary and Joseph entered, even though he was the innkeeper. How difficult would it have been to just say "There's no room in the inn"? After the play, the children sang Christmas carols, which we had practiced with the guitar. The adults joined them in singing until we came to the last song, which the adults did not know. I had debated whether or not to use the song, but in the end decided it was time. The children had enjoyed learning the new carol and clapped along as they sang.

After the program, everyone stayed for a snack of cookies and milk. Papa had brought the milk from the farm, and several of the older girls had volunteered to make cookies. As I mingled amongst the parents and children wishing them a Merry Christmas as they left, I found myself face to face with Mrs. George.

"Where did you find that song, Virginia?" Mrs. George asked without even exchanging pleasantries first.

"What song are you referring to?" I asked, knowing full well which song she meant but was stalling to gather a good explanation.

"You know very well which song I'm referring to," Mrs.

George snapped. "Go Tell It on the Mountain" I believe is the title you gave it."

"Oh," I said nonchalantly, "I've had that song quite some time."

"I've never heard it before," Mrs. George fumed. "It's certainly not in our hymnal."

"Does it have to be in our hymnal to be a song worthy of singing?" I asked.

"Of course not," Mrs. George replied. "I was just wondering where it came from. The children were practically dancing to it."

"King David danced when the Ark of the Covenant was returned," I pointed out.

"We're not talking about King David," Mrs. George spouted. "I can see you are not going to tell me where you got that song from the way you're avoiding the subject."

"It was nice of you to come watch the children, Mrs. George," I replied. "I hope you have a Merry Christmas." I smiled at the cantankerous woman, honestly hoping that at least one day out of the year she put her rude disposition aside.

"There's nothing merry about spending Christmas alone," Mrs. George muttered.

The reply struck compassion in my heart. Mrs. George had never had children and her husband had been dead for years. Before I could stop myself, I asked, "Would you like to come to the farm for Christmas dinner?"

Mrs. George was startled silent by the question, which was a first. Considering the invitation for a moment, she finally replied tartly, "It will be much too cold to ride so far. Honestly girl, don't you realize I'm an old woman?" With that, she turned on her heel and marched out the door.

I woke up at the farm on Christmas morning 1863. Looking out my bedroom window, I was delighted to see several inches of snow covering the ground, making everything look crisp and clean. I had come to the farm the night before after the Christmas Eve service at the church so I would be able to help Momma prepare Christmas dinner. I'm sure she could have handled it on her own since there would only be five of us sitting around the table when the meal was served, so if I was honest with myself, I really just wanted to wake Christmas morning as I had in years past at the farm.

I hurried to dress and help Momma with morning chores, which of course included me milking the cow. Annabelle had been dried off, as Elsie had given birth to a little heifer in October. Elsie was now the cow to be milked until Annabelle had her calf next June. Pulling on a wool dress and grabbing a scarf for warmth, I headed down stairs. Grabbing the pail in the kitchen, I walked out into the cold morning air.

Trudging through the fresh, unmarked snow, I thought of past childhood winter days when Reuben, Carter and I would sleigh ride down the steep hill behind the barn. Carter always ended up building a ramp for the sleds to go over, sending us sailing through the air. The memory brought a smile to my face and a longing to my heart. I wondered if Carter and Angus had gotten any snow in Tennessee this Christmas.

Before I reached the barn, Ollie came bounding toward me from his warm bed. Papa had built him a little house off the side of the barn, which kept him quite cozy. Of course, Momma would allow him in the house when the weather became frigid.

Before I knew it, Ollie ran right into me, knocking me to the ground with the blow. As he covered my face with his big tongue, I couldn't help but laugh. He then ran off to find a stick and brought it back for me to throw. As he ran after it, sliding in the snow for effect, I decided to do something I hadn't done in years. I was already on the ground and covered in snow, so I lay back and created a snow angel by waving my arms up and down and my legs back and forth. Standing up, I brushed the snow from myself the best I could, knowing it would melt as I leaned into Elsie's warm flank while I milked, making me wet and cold. Ollie brought the stick back and I threw it one more time then slipped into the barn to milk the cow.

Coming back to the house, I helped Momma put breakfast on the table. As we sat down to eat, I voiced my concern for Mary Ellen immediately after Papa blessed the food. "Mary Ellen has not been feeling well. Several times in the last few weeks she has went upstairs when I arrived at the store and fell asleep."

Papa stopped eating, considering my statement. "You know, come to think of it, she has seemed worn out lately."

Mama looked at both of us then burst out laughing. I could not understand my sweet spirited mother laughing about Mary Ellen's ailment. "Momma, what's so funny?" I asked.

"I'll just wait and let Mary Ellen and Reuben explain," Momma said, a big smile lighting up her face.

Papa looked dumbfounded for a moment, and then he too was smiling. What exactly was I missing? It brought back memories of Curby Thursday and the confusion it had brought with it, until I understood that our farm was a part of the Underground Railroad. Shaking my head, I began eating my bowl of oatmeal.

Reuben and Mary Ellen arrived at the farm at noon, bringing a squash pie for dessert. The sourdough rolls were in the oven to finish baking, but the rest of the food was ready. As we sat down, Papa blessed the bountiful meal, thanking God for all his rich blessings. He ended the prayer with a plea to please keep Carter and Angus safe and that they might have a wonderful Christmas, despite their circumstances.

Bowls of food were passed and everyone ate more than their fill. I rose from the table to clear the dishes so dessert could be served. Placing the plates in the pan of hot, soapy water that remained from earlier dish washing, I cut large slices of squash pie and placed them on plates, adding some sweet whipped cream. After handing each person a plate of dessert, I picked up my own and slipped back into my chair. Just as I got a forkful of the pie to my mouth, Reuben cleared his throat.

"I have an announcement," Reuben said, staring adoringly at Mary Ellen. "We are expecting our first child."

I dropped my fork at the surprise announcement. Momma and Papa began to laugh and then so did I. Reuben and Mary Ellen stared, confusion evident upon their faces. I was sure they were wondering why the announcement of their first child brought such a reaction. Momma was the first to speak.

"That is wonderful news, Reuben and Mary Ellen," Momma said, meaning every word. "I'm sorry we laughed. It's just that Stephen and Virginia voiced their concern about Mary Ellen not feeling well while we ate breakfast. It didn't take long for me to figure out the reason why."

"Of course, Momma didn't tell me what she had figured out," I complained.

"I didn't want to ruin the surprise," Momma said still smiling. "I can't wait to be a grandmother."

Picking up my fork again, I tried to salvage the bite full of pie that had landed in my lap. I was not about to waste a piece of Mary Ellen's squash pie. As I finished the dessert, squelching the desire to pick up my plate and lick every drop of whipped cream off, I asked, "Do you know when the baby is due?"

"The baby should come sometime in August," Mary Ellen replied.

"I sure hope we don't have a hot summer," Momma said. "You will be miserable if we do."

"It will be worth it," Mary Ellen replied with a smile.

"Indeed it will," Momma agreed.

We exchanged gifts after the kitchen was put back in order. They were just homemade things but that didn't matter. The real gift had been in a manger on the first Christmas, and no one could give a better gift than that. We were all just thankful to spend the day together as a family and pray for those who did not have that luxury, including Carter and Angus.

I rode back to town with Reuben and Mary Ellen when they left the farm in late afternoon. Momma sent leftovers for me to drop off to Mrs. George. The thought of the old woman spending Christmas alone softened mine and Mary Ellen's heart toward her, even if she could be quite frustrating. Reuben pulled the wagon in behind the store and I hopped down to walk the short distance to my cabin.

"You could have taken Virginia to the cabin," Mary Ellen said.

"She'll be okay," Reuben replied. "Walking will do her good."

Making a face at Reuben, I then turned to Mary Ellen. "I'm going to stop by Mrs. George's anyway and drop off this food. I also have a small gift for her."

"That's very thoughtful," Mary Ellen said as she unsuccessfully tried to stifle a yawn.

I smiled at her, no longer worried that she may be ill. "Maybe you should go take a nap."

"I believe I will," Mary Ellen replied smiling.

Picking up the food and a small wrapped package from the wagon, I started toward Mrs. George's home. Going to the back door, I knocked softly. I waited a moment then knocked a bit harder. The door swung open and Mrs. George glared at me. "You needn't beat my door down, Virginia. I heard you the first time. I'm just old and slow, you know."

I bit back the remark that she had probably been watching me from behind the curtains. Determined to be nice no matter what, I held out the plate of food. "Momma made you a plate of food from our Christmas dinner leftovers."

Mrs. George took the plate and lifted the towel that was covering it. "Tell your mother thank you, Virginia. It looks quite delicious."

"I brought a slice of Mary Ellen's squash pie, too," I replied holding out the smaller plate in my other hand.

"I suppose I will see if the new wife can cook," Mrs. George remarked while taking the offered dessert.

"Oh, Mary Ellen makes really good squash pie," I assured her. Reaching for the package I had tucked under my arm I said, "I brought you a gift as well."

"Goodness, Virginia, can't you see my hands are full? How do you expect me to take that?"

Taking a deep breath, I forced myself to remain calm. Could this woman not muster any kindness whatsoever? "If you want, I could place the gift inside."

"If you must," Mrs. George said tartly. "You've held my door open long enough that the whole house will have a chill as it is."

Mrs. George backed up and allowed me to enter the house. I placed the gift on her kitchen table and turned to leave. I was surprised to find the old woman directly behind me. For a moment, I felt trapped between her and the table and then I noticed the moisture that had gathered at the corner of her eyes. "Thank you for your thoughtfulness, Virginia," she said so quietly I could barely hear her.

"You're welcome, Mrs. George," I replied. Stepping around her, I hurried back out the door before she could ruin the moment by adding something hateful.

1863 became 1864 on Friday, January 1st. We planned a New Year's Eve get together at the general store for anyone who dared to brave the cold weather. We spent the evening playing music and singing, and of course, eating way too much. At 11:55, we all joined hands and Pastor David prayed the old year out and the New Year in. Shortly after midnight, we all headed for home.

I was thankful I lived close to the store and Papa and Momma offered to drop me off before heading to the farm. The wind had picked up and was coming out of the north, cutting right through every piece of clothing I had on.

January remained cold all month and even longer. Everyone was tired of the frigid temperatures, especially me, as the children remained inside the school all day. Finally, half way into the month of February, the daytime temperatures climbed above freezing. I was thankful to be able to shoo everyone outside after lunch so they could run off some pent up energy.

Papa began to tap the maple trees on the farm, as the weather became perfect for the task. Reuben, Mary Ellen and I kept the store running as Papa remained on the farm to help Momma make syrup. I made sure Mary Ellen went upstairs as soon as I came to the store each afternoon. She had been quite nauseated for several weeks, along with still being tired. A small bump could be seen beneath her dress already, and the doctor thought she might have twins.

Through the winter, I received letters from Angus weekly. There were no battles for the time being, just plans in the works for when the weather cleared. Angus had spoken of all the disease and sickness that spread throughout the camp, with several young men dying daily. It seemed that being killed by the enemy had become less likely than dying from an illness. He and Carter were being careful to stay away from the tents that housed the sick men, hoping to avoid all the ailments.

March blew in, and by the middle of the month brought with it warmer weather. I had saved newspapers all winter with hopes of the children at school using them to build kites. After lunch one day, we all went for a walk to find the perfect sticks for the kite building project. Some of the children found twigs that had dropped from trees over the winter, while others preferred gathering the remains of large weeds that left hollow, woody stems behind. The next few days, we set aside a bit of time to work on the kites. By the last week of March, everyone had their kite completed.

The last Friday of March, I made an announcement right after the bell had been rung. "We will be flying our kites after lunch today," I informed all the students. "I have brought a roll of string for each kite that is exactly the same length. The first student to get to the end of their roll, with their kite still flying aloft, will be the winner of the kite flying contest."

After lunch, the school children and I walked to the large field on the opposite side of Whiskey Run creek. The field stretched the length of Water Street, which ran along one side of the general store. Starting at the east end of the field with the wind in their faces, the children lined up, leaving plenty of space between themselves. When I hollered "Go!" there was a stampede toward the opposite end of the field with thirty kites fluttering wildly behind the children. The older children were able to get their kites off the ground quickly, and then the race began to see who could get to the end of their ball of string first. If the string was unwound too quickly, the kite would get slack in the line and fall to the ground. It had to be let out just right.

As I turned to look behind me, I noticed the opposite bank of Whiskey Run creek had become crowded with onlookers. They had stepped out of the general store and their homes to watch the race. Levi hollered loudly, bringing my attention back to the race. "I'm almost to the end of my string!"

This brought on a flurry of activity. Not wanting to lose, the children began to take the risk of unwinding the string too fast. Several kites swirled around a few times then plunged to the ground. Other kites had not been built as strong and began to break apart. The younger children who had gotten their kite off the ground had now crossed each other as they ran across the field, entangling their kite's string with someone else's.

"I'm to the end!" Levi announced, followed by a wail. "Oh, no, the string slipped through my fingers!"

We all watched as Levi's kite took flight on its own. We were sure it would be found in a tree miles away. Levi hung his head and trudged toward me. As he approached, I slipped my arm around his shoulders. "It's okay Levi. You won the contest. You will just have to build another kite."

"Yes, a better kite," Levi said, with a smile lighting up his mischievous little face and bringing sparkle to his eyes.

"Yes, a better kite," I said. "Practice makes perfect. Maybe you could apply that strategy to your spelling words next week."

"Aw, shucks, why does everything come back to school work?"

"Because I'm the teacher," I replied with a smile. "One day you will be thankful you had the opportunity to learn to read, write and do arithmetic."

"I doubt it," Levi muttered then bounded off to help others

get to the end of their kite string.

I thought how interesting Levi had made my first year of teaching. Yes, he had been quite a handful at times, but I had also seen him learn, too. Honestly, the child had stolen my heart. He lived with just his father, because his mother had been lost while having her second child, and the baby had died, too. They were buried together in the cemetery on the hill by the school. I had seen Levi's father at the grave on several occasions from my cabin window. I soon realized that many of the things Levi did was to get my attention. He hungered for a mother's love.

The only news about the war reported in March was that General Ulysses S. Grant had been appointed commander of all the Union armies. This would make the fourth commander since the war began. General William T. Sherman was put in charge of the western operation.

Shortly after this news was printed in the newspaper, Angus and Carter sent letters stating that their regiments had been sent to join the Army of the Potomac, Carter in the cavalry and Angus in the infantry. It appeared that General Grant would attempt to take Richmond, Virginia while General Sherman marched toward Atlanta, Georgia. Each week, Papa looked for reports of battles in the Louisville Daily Journal. Everyone knew plans were in the works that would hopefully end the war and it was just a matter of time before fierce fighting would break out again.

School ended for the year the first week of May and I returned to the store full time. Mary Ellen, now six months along in her pregnancy, had grown quite large. The doctor was certain there would be twins born in August. For this reason, Mary Ellen worked just a few hours each day, and only if we were busy. If the store was slow, I would send her to rest her weary feet.

On Friday, May 15th, Thaddeus pulled up in front of the store and began talking before the horses came to a full halt. "It's started. General Grant has begun to push toward Richmond, though the first battle did not end well."

"Where did the battle take place?" Delmar called from the porch.

"A place called the Wilderness," Thaddeus replied. "It resulted in a huge number of casualties."

I stepped off the porch and handed Thaddeus the outgoing

mail, along with a box for Angus and Carter. Thaddeus placed the items in the wagon then handed me the mailbag for Marengo. Reaching inside, I removed all the newspapers and handed them to Papa who was standing next to Thaddeus. I hurried into the store and dumped the mailbag on the counter, frantically searching for letters from Angus and Carter.

Finding a letter to me from Angus and one to his parents, I slipped my letter into my pocket and slid the other into the proper box. Spreading the pile out and turning over envelopes, I found three letters from Carter; one to Effie, one for Momma and Papa, and one just for me. I placed Effie's letter in her box then put the other two in my pocket.

I began to sort the rest of the mail until I heard Thaddeus call to the horses and the familiar rattle of the wagon fade as he left. Scooping up the unsorted mail, I shoved it back in the bag and went to listen to the war report from the screen door as Papa shared it with the five men gathered on the porch of the general store.

"What's the paper say?" Delmar asked impatiently.

"Give me a minute, Delmar," Papa said.

After a few minutes, I heard Papa sigh loudly. "Well, men, it's not good, not good at all. The Union began the battle with 120,000 men and the Confederates with 64,000."

"So, the Union had twice as many soldiers going into the battle?" Pastor David asked.

"Yes, but the Confederates were entrenched. The Union soldiers were unprotected. They were fighting in dense forest that was very unfamiliar to them," Papa said.

"What was the outcome?" Delmar asked, tired of the chit chat.

"Neither side could claim a victory," Papa said, "but the Union suffered nearly twice the casualties of the Confederates."

"Does the paper list the numbers?" Pastor David asked.

"Yes," Papa replied and sighed heavily again. "The Union had over 18,000 and the Confederates a little over 11,000. Of those numbers, the paper doesn't state how many are dead, missing or injured."

"Goodness," Delmar said shaking his head at the unbelievable numbers.

"So, the Union is no closer to Richmond than before the battle?" Pastor David asked.

"No, and we all know that is where the Union must get to in order for this war to end," Papa said.

"Are there any reports on General Sherman and his troops?" Reuben asked.

"Just that he is pushing toward Atlanta with 100,000 men," Papa said, reading the report from the paper.

"How many soldiers do the Confederates have against Sherman?" Pastor David asked.

Papa looked at the newspaper a moment, "60,000, according to the newspaper."

"So, the Union has twice as many soldiers as the Confederates on both fronts," Delmar remarked. "Surely we can end this war soon, especially since most of the war action is now concentrated in two areas."

"I pray it will be so," Papa said softly.

I turned from the screen door, an uneasy feeling coming over me. I couldn't say exactly what it was, but I felt something had happened on that battlefield in the Wilderness that was going to bring much sadness.

I walked behind the counter to finish sorting the mail, trying desperately to shake the heaviness that had come over me. Just as I put the last piece of mail in its proper place, the door of the general store opened.

"Did I get a letter?" Effie asked before she was fully inside.

I turned from the boxes and put on my best smile. "Why, yes you did." I plucked the letter from the box and handed it to Effie.

Effie took the letter and looked intently at me, seeing right through the fake smile. "What's happened, Virginia?"

Try as I might, I could not keep tears from pooling in my eyes. "There's been a terrible battle in a place called the Wilderness in Virginia. Many lives have been lost."

The letter Effie had been holding fluttered to the floor. "That's where Angus and Carter are. They would have surely fought there."

"Yes, I know," I replied softly. "I have an awful feeling, Effie. One like I've never had before."

Effie walked around the counter and we embraced, since no words could be spoken to bring comfort. Carter or Angus, or maybe both of them, could be lying dead in a desolate place in Virginia. The reality of that fact was overwhelming.

When I returned to my cabin that evening, I didn't even take time to prepare any supper before deciding to read the letters I had received from Carter and Angus. Papa had taken his letter home to read with Momma. I sat down at the table first, and then decided to walk to the creek below the school. The sound of its rippling and gurgling would bring me comfort. Finding a soft spot in the grass under an oak tree, I carefully opened Carter's letter first.

Hello Virginia,

I know I have written very few letters to you since joining the Union army. I usually just let Angus tell you everything that's happening, for he pens a much better letter than I can. However, I feel a great need to write to you personally this night. Tomorrow we will begin to move toward our next battle against General Lee and the Confederates. It will be a risky operation, for the Confederates have had time to prepare and dig trenches. As a rider in the cavalry, I will be one of the first to meet the enemy. For some reason, one I cannot explain, I feel uneasy as I never have before. You know me well, and I would never back down from a challenge, so I will do my part as I am commanded. However, if my part is to lay down my life for the cause, then it will be so. If that happens, I want you to know I love you dearly, no matter the very few times I have ever said it aloud.

Please, don't tell Effie, or Momma and Papa what I have written unless you know for sure I am dead. I would hate to upset them unnecessarily. I just know you will understand my heart and know that I went down fighting.

Love always,

Carter

The letter just added to my grief and the sickening feeling that something had happened to Carter or Angus. I could not shake the heaviness. With hands shaking, I folded Carter's letter and put it back into the envelope. I could not bring myself to read the letter Angus had written. I felt I could keep him alive by having the unopened letter. I knew the thought was crazy, but my mind could not convince my heart.

I buried my face in my hands as great sobs came over me. This war had become endless and merciless, claiming the lives of thousands of young men on both sides, men like Carter and Angus. As my shoulders heaved and my tears drenched my face, I felt an arm encircle my shoulders and a handkerchief was pressed into my hand. Thinking it was probably Effie, I tried to gain control. I could not tell Effie what Carter had written in his letter to me. He had asked me not to, and I would honor his request. As I lifted my eyes, I found

Mrs. George knelt down beside me, with tears of her own flowing down her cheeks.

"Virginia, I heard about the battle in the Wilderness," Mrs. George said softly. "I love those boys, too, even if I don't show it very often. I watched them grow up while attending school. You know I see all that goes on at the school."

"Yes, Mrs. George, I know you do," I replied.

"I think you did a fine job teaching this year," Mrs. George continued. "The children love you, especially little Levi."

"Thank you, Mrs. George," I sniffled.

"Now, I want you to get up off this bank and pull yourself together," Mrs. George demanded. "You don't know if those boys are dead or not. Until we know for sure, we will place them in God's hands. Only He knows and sees all."

Looking into Mrs. George's stern face, I knew her moment of empathy was over. She would not allow me to wallow in my grief here on the bank of Whiskey Run creek. Life was going to go on and I best get prepared for it.

Handing the handkerchief back that smelled of lavender, I hugged the old woman with the gruff exterior, knowing to release her quickly lest I provoke a tongue lashing.

Getting up, I gently took Mrs. George's elbow and helped her back up the hill and to her house. I returned to my cabin and placed Carter's letter with all the ones I had received from Angus. The unopened letter from Angus I propped up on my dresser where I could see it every morning and every night. I would open it only after I received another letter from him, or lost hope that no more letters would ever come.

Chapter Twenty-Five

The next Friday brought more dismal war reports but no letters from Carter or Angus. When Thaddeus came with the mail, I didn't even go inside to sort it. I just sat down on the porch and handed out mail to those gathered there. The porch of the general store was full, as our little community held their breath waiting to hear from sons and grandsons who were off fighting.

"What's the latest, Stephen?" Delmar asked as Papa scanned the front page of the Louisville Daily Journal.

"There's been another battle as Grant tries to push toward Richmond," Papa said. "It was near a place called Spotsylvania."

"What was the outcome?" Pastor David asked.

"Not good," Papa muttered. "There were 30,000 casualties; 18,000 for the Union and 12,000 for the Confederates."

"Goodness," Delmar said. "The Union has lost nearly 40,000 soldiers in two weeks."

"Does the paper list the number of deaths?" I asked quietly.

"No, Virginia, it doesn't," Papa said. "Neither side claimed a victory, but the Union did not get one mile closer to Richmond."

"General Grant may have to come up with a different strategy," Joe remarked. "He cannot afford to lose nearly 20,000 men with each battle, no matter if he does have twice as many soldiers in the Union army as General Lee has fighting against them from the Confederate side."

I looked up to see Effie walking toward the store. Rising from the porch, I decided to take the mailbag in and finish sorting it. I really did not want to hear any more about the battle nor the mass casualties. As I reached for the handle of the screen door, Papa stopped me.

"Virginia, here's the list of fallen soldiers from the paper," he said, holding out the section of newspaper.

My hands trembled as I took the offered item. Walking through the doorway, I placed the mailbag on the floor behind the counter. I then opened the section of newspaper Papa had handed me and smoothed it out on the counter. Effie came in the store, and together we began to scan for familiar names. Not seeing the name of anyone we knew, we looked at each other and smiled. We both knew that the list was nowhere near complete, but for now, we still had hope that both Carter and Angus were alive.

The next two Fridays the only war reports were on General Sherman and his push toward Atlanta. The Confederate cavalry had raided the Union supplies that Sherman and his men depended on, destroying a large amount. Even so, it appeared General Sherman would take Atlanta, even if he was only advancing one mile a day.

Effie and I scanned the newspaper section set aside for the Union casualties, and were relieved not to find the names of Carter and Angus, or any names of other local men fighting in the war. There had been no letters received from any of the soldiers from our area fighting under General Grant since the battle at the Wilderness.

With the month of June came many chores at the farm. Papa stayed to work there Monday through Thursday, but came to the store on Friday and Saturday to help on our busiest days. Reuben went to the farm to help Papa with the first cutting of hay the first week of June and I kept the store running. Mary Ellen was able to only help a few hours a day without causing her feet to swell. At nearly seven months along, she appeared to waddle like a duck to balance her protruding belly.

When Thaddeus pulled up to the store on Friday, June 10th, we all knew another battle had occurred. Before the horses came to a complete stop, Thaddeus jumped from the seat with a copy of the Louisville Daily Journal in his hands. "There's been another battle,

Stephen. This time it was a definite Confederate victory."

"Good Lord have mercy," Delmar muttered, meaning every word.

Papa took the paper from Thaddeus that was already folded to the article. It was on the front page of the Monday issue. Taking his time, Papa read the entire article, shaking his head several times. Though Thaddeus was normally in a hurry, he waited for Papa to finish reading. "Cold Harbor, indeed," Papa exclaimed.

"Cold Harbor what?" Delmar demanded.

"That's where the battle took place," Thaddeus provided.

"I don't even think I want to ask this, but how many casualties this time?" Pastor David said.

"You won't find those numbers in that issue," Thaddeus said. "Check yesterday's."

"You're right, the numbers are not listed here," Papa said scanning the article again. "What it does say is that the frontline was seven miles long. It stretched from Bethesda Church to Chickahominy River."

"That's like from Marengo to Valeene," Delmar said, putting the distance into perspective.

"It's hard to imagine having enough men to stretch that far," Joe said.

I reached into the mailbag to retrieve the rest of the newspapers. Handing them to Papa, he looked until he found Thursday's copy. "The Union did not make any headway at all," Papa muttered. "There are no exact numbers, but the Union has suffered over 10,000 casualties to the Confederates 4,000. It's predicted that over 7,000 Union soldiers fell in the first thirty minutes of battle on June 3rd."

"That's devastating news," Pastor David said.

"How come there were so many?" Delmar asked.

"The Confederates were entrenched, which gave them much protection," Papa replied. "The Union soldiers were trying to break their line."

"That's about all the newspaper has to report on the war," Papa said, "but President Lincoln has been nominated to run for re-election with Andrew Johnson as his vice-president."

"With the mass numbers of casualties the Union has suffered the last month, President Lincoln may not get re-elected," Joe said.

"That's true," Papa agreed, "but what will happen if he doesn't? Will all the lives lost to put our nation back together have been in vain?"

"President Lincoln must be allowed to finish this war," Pastor David said. "I just pray it is soon and without any more loss of life."

"That is what we all pray for," Papa said. Papa removed all the sections from the newspapers listing the names of casualties and handed them to me. I headed toward the door of the store as Thaddeus put his wagon in motion to deliver the unsettling news to other small Crawford County towns. Effie stepped up behind me, and I realized then that she must have walked up while Papa had been delivering the latest bad news.

Stepping into the store, Effie took the newspaper and spread the first one on the counter. I picked up a second one and we both began to look for the names we hoped not to find. When all the names had been looked through, we posted the lists on the wall for others to view.

Dumping the mail on the counter, Effie helped me sort through it and place it in the proper boxes. We were really just looking for letters for ourselves, and were both disappointed when we placed the last piece of mail in the proper box and were both still empty handed. "Well, at least their names have not appeared in the newspaper," Effie said with a sigh.

"It would still be nice to know for certain that they are alive and well," I replied.

"Yes, it would," Effie agreed.

Standing there looking at my best friend, a thought came to me. With Mary Ellen not able to work much now, and in a few months not at all, we would be in need of help here at the store. Effie lived just up the hill from the store and would do a wonderful job. I made a mental note to mention my thought to Reuben later when we closed the store for the day.

The next Friday, Effie and I were busy straightening and stocking shelves when we heard Thaddeus call to the men on the porch of the general store. Hurrying outside, I took the mailbag and handed Thaddeus the outgoing mail, including a box Effie and I had put together for Carter and Angus. Papa came from the back of the store where he and Reuben had been stacking lumber.

"What's new today?" Papa asked Thaddeus.

"Just a long list of names in the casualties section of the newspaper," Thaddeus replied. "The Union must be attempting a new tactic that's being kept hushed up. There's not one word about where they are or what they are doing."

Taking the mailbag into the store, I listened for a moment as the men on the porch surmised about what General Grant was up to. The mass number of casualties the last three battles had resulted in surely was making him rethink his strategy. To lose nearly a third of your army in less than a month was a sure sign that a new approach to the situation was needed.

Taking the newspapers from the mailbag, I handed them to Effie so she could begin the search through the names of casualties. I continued to sort the mail, looking for the evidence I needed to assure me Carter and Angus were alive. I still could not put aside the feeling that all was not well. I sighed as I reached the last piece of mail and still had found no letters. Effie looked up, knowing full well what that sigh meant. Without saying a word, she handed me the Tuesday edition of the Louisville Daily Journal.

As Effie and I began to look through Thursday's edition, I stopped abruptly. There among the list of the injured was a familiar name; Andrew Weathers. There were several of the Weathers' boys off fighting and Andrew was the youngest of them. Effie and I finished the list, assuring that there were no other familiar names then I walked out on the porch amongst the men gathered there.

"Excuse me, Pastor David," I began. "I have found the name Andrew Weathers among the injured listed in the newspaper. I thought you would want to know."

"Of course, Virginia," Pastor David said jumping to his feet. "If you men will excuse me, I have some business to take care of." With that, Pastor David headed home to get his horse and deliver the bad news. Although Andrew was listed as injured, all of us knew how quickly infection could set in, causing death.

The last week of June dragged by and the uncertainty of what had become of loved ones made everyone who came to the store sullen. I was glad when Thursday dawned, because I knew that at least I would have Effie to talk to. She helped out at the store on Thursday, Friday and Saturday now since Mary Ellen was unable to work.

I quickly fixed myself a breakfast of oatmeal and ate it. As I prepared to dress for the day, my eyes fell on the unopened letter from Angus. Picking it up, I turned the letter over in my hand, debating on what to do. At the last moment before I tore into it, I placed it back on my dresser. I knew it contained a goodbye in case he did not survive the battle that loomed before him, just as Carter's had. I was not ready to give up hope by reading the last words Angus may have ever written.

Effie and I kept busy all day with customers. At this point in her pregnancy, Mary Ellen only came downstairs to plop on the stool behind the counter and chat with us awhile. I truly felt sorry for her, wondering if she would be able to carry the babies to term. If she wasn't pregnant with twins, she was carrying the biggest baby anyone had ever given birth to.

The next day, Effie and I could hardly stay focused on any given task as we waited for the mail to arrive. Each time a wagon would pull up one of us would go to the door and peer out. We would then sigh and go back to what we had been doing. To make matters worse, the mail wagon was running late. By the time Thaddeus finally pulled to a halt in front of the store hours after his normal time, Effie and I had nearly worn a groove in the floor.

"Papa, Thaddeus is here," I hollered toward the back of the store as I headed outside. Effie was busy cutting fabric for a customer and was forced to remain in the store.

Thaddeus hit the ground just as I stepped onto the porch. We traded mailbags and Papa came out with a box to send to Carter and Angus that Momma had prepared the night before.

"Anything new to report on the war?" Papa asked as he placed the box in the wagon.

"General Grant and the troops crossed the James River south of Richmond," Thaddeus said. "They missed an opportunity to capture Petersburg, Virginia and cut off the rail lines to the Confederates."

"How unfortunate," Delmar said.

"Petersburg is now under siege," Thaddeus added.

"Ah, I suppose the Confederates will get a taste of their own medicine," Joe chimed in. "They may find out how the Union troops in Chattanooga felt."

"They very well might," Thaddeus agreed. "I'm already late, so I must be on my way. I had a horse go lame and had to find a replacement."

"Maybe one day the railroad will go through Marengo and we won't be dependent upon such slow mail service," Delmar chided.

"That is certainly what Zebulon Leavenworth would like to see happen," Thaddeus said, "but the citizens of Crawford County continue to oppose such a thing."

"It's just a matter of time before progress comes knocking at our door as well," Papa said. "I believe a train will one day chug through our backward county, no matter what opposition."

"You are probably right, Stephen," Pastor David agreed.

Thaddeus put the horses in motion and left us eating a cloud of dust. I carried the mailbag in just as Effie finished wrapping the fabric that had been purchased. "I'll trade you this week," I said handing Effie the mailbag after removing the newspapers.

"Okay," Effie agreed, dumping the contents of the bag onto the counter.

I quickly pulled out the section of the newspapers I needed and took the remainder of the Louisville Daily Journal to Papa, along with the local paper, the Crisis. Returning to the counter, I spread out Monday's list of casualties. As I perused the names, Effie mumbled names to herself as she attempted to locate the proper box.

"You know, if these boxes were in alphabetical order it would sure help," Effie complained.

"They are in the order of the first person who set up a box to the last," I said with a laugh.

"Is there a reason it can't be changed?"

"I'll ask Reuben," I said. "You know, once you memorize the boxes, it becomes much easier."

"Alphabetical order would eliminate the need to memorize the boxes," Effie pointed out.

"This is true," I agreed, opening up the Wednesday list.

"Oh my goodness," Effie exclaimed. "You have a letter!"

Rushing to Effie's side, I took the letter from her hand. The handwriting definitely belonged to Angus. "I can't believe it," I said softly.

"Well, don't just stand there," Effie said. "Open it!"

I thought of how I really wanted to take the letter and run all the way to the farm. Once there, I would climb the Maple and savor every word written on the pages. Looking up at Effie though, I knew that would not be fair. The letter didn't just say that Angus was alive; it would also tell us about Carter. "Did you get a letter from Carter?"

Effie looked at me like I had lost my mind. "Virginia Mae Hensley, open that letter. I will finish sorting the mail while you read it first, but I need to know what it says."

"Okay," I agreed. "I'll just slip into the storeroom and read it."

"And please hurry," Effie bossed.

I plopped down on a sack of feed when I reached the storeroom. My hands trembled as I broke the seal on the letter. There was only a single piece of paper inside.

My Dearest Virginia,

By now I know you have read about the battles that have taken place in Virginia. To say they were horrific would be an understatement. The battle at the Wilderness was fought in a forest and the enemy could hardly be seen to even take aim at. The battle at Cold Harbor was even worse. I watched as thousands of men were shot down in just a few minutes time. On June 7th, General Lee allowed the Union army two hours to try and collect the wounded from the battlefield. Sadly, after five days of battle during which the soldiers were left lying where they had fallen, there were few left alive.

I abruptly stopped reading, not wanting to finish the letter. Angus had not started this letter by saying he and Carter were fine, which meant something had happened to Carter. The letter shook in my hand and the room began to spin. The next thing I knew, Papa, Reuben and Effie were standing over me.

"What happened?" I asked.

"I believe you fainted," Reuben said.

"Fainted?" I asked. "I have never swooned a day in my life. Why would I suddenly...?" And then I remembered the letter. Frantically I looked around me.

"I have the letter right here," Papa said, holding it up.

"What...what does Angus say about Carter?" I whispered.

"Carter rode in with the cavalry ahead of the infantry at the Wilderness battle," Papa began, "and he hasn't been seen since. His horse was found shot dead but Carter's body was not near it. Angus has checked all the lists of the injured and his name never appeared. He is now listed among the missing."

"Missing?" Effie asked. "Where could he be?"

"In a war camp," Reuben said quietly.

The thought of Carter being held in a war camp broke my

heart but I knew that if he was truly in one, at least he was probably still alive. I looked up at Effie and tears were streaming down her face. I stood slowly and Papa reached out to hug me and Effie at the same time. "I must go home now and tell your mother," Papa said as he pulled away.

The only July reports of the war appearing in the newspaper were of General Sherman and his quest to capture Atlanta. By the end of June, the Union army was just short of the Confederate line, causing them to pull back to the Chattahoochee River. The fall of Atlanta was inevitable; it was just a question of when. There were no Confederate reinforcements to send to Atlanta, even though the South had asked every able bodied man from seventeen to seventy to come and fight.

August arrived with its heat and humidity. Mary Ellen had been instructed to stay off her feet as much as possible. Effie and I took turns going upstairs to keep her company when the store was slow. The second week of August, Momma began to come to the store with Papa daily to cook the meals for Reuben and Mary Ellen and keep their living space tidy.

Letters from Angus arrived each week and I continued to send boxes of food and reading material to him. He apologized in each letter for not being able to find Carter's whereabouts but assured me he would continue to search. He vowed not to come home until he knew what had happened to Carter.

When Effie and I arrived at the store on Thursday, August 25th, we found Reuben in a panic. "It's Mary Ellen! It's Mary Ellen!"

"Reuben, what is Mary Ellen?" I asked, wanting to grab his shoulders and shake him.

"She's going to have a baby."

"Yes, that's quite obvious," I replied.

"No, I mean she's going to have a baby now," Reuben finally blurted.

"Oh. Oh! You mean Mary Ellen's in labor!"

"Yes," Reuben said, relieved I finally understood his rambling.

"Okay," I said. "Reuben, you go for the doctor. Effie, you open the store. I will go stay with Mary Ellen until Momma arrives."

Reuben sprang into action, not even commenting on my bossiness. Effie went to unlock the front door to the store and I took the stairs two at a time. When I reached the top, I could see Mary

Ellen lying on the bed in her nightgown. As I stepped closer, I noticed she was drenched in sweat, as the August heat had turned the upstairs into an oven. The windows were already wide open, so I grabbed an old newspaper and began to fan her.

"Should you time the contractions, Virginia?" Mary Ellen panted out.

"Um, yes, I suppose I should," I replied, having no idea what I was really supposed to do. Mary Ellen let out a groan and her face contorted in pain. I began to count the seconds off. When she relaxed again, I announced, "One minute."

"Virginia, you need to time from when a contraction stops to the beginning of the next one," Mary Ellen said with a smile.

"Well, at least I brought a smile to your face," I replied. "I'll start timing when the next one ends."

"Has Reuben calmed down any?" Mary Ellen asked.

Laughing I replied, "No, he was a rambling lunatic when Effie and I arrived. I've sent him to fetch the doctor. I just hope he remembers how to get there."

Mary Ellen laughed softly and I continued to fan her. When she groaned again, I knew another contraction was starting. I waited until her body relaxed again and began to count. When the next contraction came I had counted off four minutes.

"They're four minutes apart," I announced as Mary Ellen fell back on the bed, exhausted from the pain and heat. "How long have you been in labor?"

"My back has hurt quite a bit for two days but the labor pain didn't start until about two this morning. I didn't dare wake Reuben. I knew he would ride and get the doctor or your mother immediately."

"I've never seen my brother so rattled," I replied smiling.

Another pain gripped Mary Ellen and I began to count as it subsided. Momma topped the stairs before the next contraction began. Going straight to Mary Ellen, Momma smoothed her hair back and smiled down at her. "This will all be over soon, dear, I promise, and the pain will be worth it."

"The sooner the better," Mary Ellen replied, and then gasped as pain overwhelmed her again.

"The contractions are three and a half minutes apart now," I informed Momma as Mary Ellen gritted her teeth to keep from screaming.

"Good job, Virginia," Momma said. "Get a bucket and go to the spring for some cold water. Mary Ellen needs a cool rag to ward off some of this heat."

"Yes, Momma," I replied turning to quickly do her bidding. When I returned, I grabbed a rag and brought it and the bucket to the side of the bed. Momma had placed several towels beneath Mary Ellen and stripped the covers from the bed. Dipping the rag, I began to mop Mary Ellen's face and arms to cool her down.

"Virginia, I believe this is going to go much quicker than I originally thought. Contractions are at two minutes and coming hard. I will need your help if these babies come before the doctor gets here."

"Okay, Momma," I said, thinking back to Lucy giving birth to Joshua while hidden in the earthen room under the horse stall.

The next contraction came with such force that Mary Ellen screamed out. When it was finished, Momma pulled Mary Ellen's gown up to check for what I did not know. "Don't push yet, Mary Ellen," Momma instructed.

The next fifteen minutes brought waves of pain for Mary Ellen. As I watched, I began to question whether or not I wanted to ever give birth. I alternated between fanning and applying the cool rag to Mary Ellen. As the contractions came one on top the other, I was sure she had forgotten how hot she was and just wanted to do something to make the pain stop.

Momma looked beneath the gown again and said, "Push with the next contraction, Mary Ellen. Virginia, get a knife and place it on the stove to get hot then bring it and set it on the dresser."

I knew the knife was to cut the umbilical cord once the baby was born. I had remembered doing that when Lucy gave birth to Joshua. Locating a sharp knife, I placed it on the top of the wood cook stove, thinking how much cooler it would have been in the room if the stove had not been needed.

As the knife heated, I watched Momma hold Mary Ellen's shoulders as she pushed, allowing her to lie back down when the contraction was over. By the third time Mary Ellen pushed, I had the knife placed on the dresser, along with two clean towels.

"Virginia, hold Mary Ellen up with the contractions. She's too worn out to do it on her own," Momma instructed. As the next contraction gripped Mary Ellen, she let out a scream that made me shudder.

"Mary Ellen, we're almost there," Momma said. "One more push and we will have a baby."

Mary Ellen mustered all the strength she had left. As the next contraction overtook her, I slipped behind her for support. The next thing I heard after Mary Ellen's scream died away was the lusty cry of a baby. Jumping up, I allowed Mary Ellen to flop back on the bed as I peered at this new little life.

"Sorry, Mary Ellen," I apologized.

"It's okay," Mary Ellen smiled. "I want to see, too."

Momma wrapped the baby in a clean towel after tying off the cord and cutting it. Turning, she handed the bundle to me. "Mary Ellen, honey, you have a bit more work to do. I see a second head."

Before Momma had finished the sentence, another contraction assaulted poor Mary Ellen. This time, the delivery was much easier, as the first child had opened the door, so to speak. Momma wrapped the second baby in a towel as I handed Mary Ellen the first infant. "You have a boy and a girl," Momma announced. "Two beautiful and healthy babies and I became twice a grandmother in a matter of minutes!"

As Momma finished with the second baby, the doctor topped the stairs. "I see you didn't need me after all," he said with a chuckle.

"You can take over now," Momma said. "I need to hold my granddaughter while Mary Ellen feeds my grandson."

"You go ahead and enjoy that, Elizabeth," the doctor said. "You have assisted in many births but I believe this one will be the most rewarding."

"Yes, I believe it will," Momma agreed. "Virginia, please go share the good news with your brother and father. I will call to Reuben when the doctor is finished."

"Yes, Momma," I replied, hurrying down the stairs. I made a mental note to ask Mary Ellen later if the joy was worth the pain.

Momma hollered for Reuben to come see his son and daughter a few minutes later. Reuben stumbled and fell trying to get up the staircase. As he reached the top, he plowed into the doctor who was heading down.

"Reuben, you're going to be my next patient if you continue to be so clumsy. It's a wonder you didn't break your fool neck when you dismounted at my house earlier, not to mention the ride back to the store. My poor horse is probably still trying to catch its breath."

"Sorry, Doc," Reuben said and hurried on.

Momma came down to allow Reuben and Mary Ellen time alone with their babies. As she came into the main part of the store, I asked, "What did they name them?"

"Caleb and Clara," Momma replied.

"Well, all I can say is I'm glad all that caterwauling has stopped," Delmar fumed. "It liked to scared me to death when I heard it from the road."

"Delmar were you not around when your wife had children?" Momma asked.

"I was in the barn, where any man with good sense would have been," Delmar retorted.

"Bringing a child into the world is not easy," Momma said with a smile.

"Did you see poor Reuben?" Delmar asked. "He needed a barn far from the store this morning."

Momma laughed and shook her head. "I hate to admit it but I think you may be right about that."

Momma continued to come to the store with Papa for the next two weeks to help Mary Ellen until she recovered enough to take care of things on her own. I knew Momma was behind at home since she had been helping Mary Ellen even before the births. For this reason, I returned to the farm each evening to do what I could to help. Of course, I would reap the benefits from my labor too, as Momma always shared her canned goods with me through the winter months.

As I picked tomatoes one evening to make juice and can, I noticed a watermelon that looked ripe. Walking over, I thumped the melon and looked to see if the stem had begun to dry. Satisfied with these two tests for ripeness, I plucked the melon and took it to the springhouse to get cold. The next evening after supper, I retrieved the melon and Momma cut it into generous slices, with enough left over to take to Reuben and Mary Ellen the next morning. As we sat on the porch of the summer kitchen eating the sweet melon, I suddenly propelled a seed from my mouth, striking the porch post

"Virginia Mae Hensley," Momma scolded, "whatever are you doing?"

"Missing Carter," I replied quietly.

Momma looked at me and tears gathered in her eyes, "Me too, Virginia, me too."

Chapter Twenty-Six

School started on Monday, September 12th. Effie agreed to work at the store each day until I came in the afternoon, allowing Mary Ellen to fully recover.

When it came time for the history lesson, I couldn't help but think back to the second year Mary Ellen taught because, like this year, it was a presidential election year.

"Children, we will learn a lot about history this year," I began. "Not just history that shaped this nation into what it is today, but also about events that will become history and determine what this nation will become in the future. Today, we are going to learn about an event that is coming up that will affect our nation forever. President Abraham Lincoln has served four years. On November 8th, the United States will decide, by voting, if President Lincoln will be allowed to serve four more years."

Millie Sloan's hand shot up. "Will women get to vote for a new president?"

"No, Millie, women will not get to vote," I replied.

"Why not?" Millie demanded.

"Only men get to vote," I replied, "and I honestly don't know why that is."

"When I grow up, I plan to work to change that," Millie said defiantly.

"Maybe you'll be president one day," Levi teased.

"There will never be a woman president," an older boy chimed in.

"How about a black president?" Levi asked.

"Honestly, I don't ever see a black man being president of the United States," I said. "Right now, we're fighting a war so they are not considered someone's property. We're a long way from ever expecting them to get the respect of a white man."

"Then I plan to change that, too," Millie retorted.

"Millie Sloan, you're just planning to change the world, ain't you," Levi said.

"My momma says dream big or not at all," Millie replied with a smile.

"Okay, children, back to the lesson. President Lincoln is the Republican candidate, which means the Republican Party chose him. He will be running against George McClellan. McClellan is the Democratic candidate. Does anyone remember hearing the name George McClellan?"

One of the older boys raised his hand. "Wasn't he one of the commanders of the Union army?"

"That's correct," I said. "He was the second commander, after Winfield Scott resigned."

"So, he's running against President Lincoln because he's mad at him?" Levi asked.

"McClellan's not necessarily mad," I said. "He just has his own ideas about how the country should be run and the war we've been fighting for far too long."

"If you could vote, who would you vote for?" Millie asked, taking me by surprise.

"I would vote for President Lincoln," I said, "because if we don't finish and win this war, all the young men who died will have died in vain."

"What about the young men who died fighting for the South?" Levi asked.

"You make a good point, Levi," I said, "and I truly feel sorry for those families, too. However, if the Union wins, the slaves will gain freedom. If the Confederates win, we will be a divided nation and slavery will continue. You know, since General Sherman and his troops captured Atlanta, Georgia, last week, I feel this war will end soon and in the Union's favor."

"Papa says Petersburg, Virginia is under siege," Millie said.

"What does that mean?"

"Well, do you remember when General Bragg and the Confederates had Chattanooga under siege?"

"Yes," Millie replied.

"The Confederates kept supplies from reaching the Union army, trying to force them to surrender," I said. "The Union soldiers were starving and the horses and mules were dying from lack of food. That's what General Grant and the Union army are now doing to General Lee and the Confederates in Petersburg. They are trying to cut off supply lines and force surrender."

The discussion of the war continued and I allowed it. The youngest children were working on forming their letters of the alphabet as the older children asked questions to learn more about the history that was happening before their very eyes. Suddenly, Levi's hand shot up.

"What happens if President Lincoln dies while serving as president?"

"That's a very good question, Levi, though one I hope we never have to consider. There is always a vice-president to take over for the President, if he becomes unable to perform his job. The vice-president running with President Lincoln will be Andrew Johnson."

"Sure glad they planned ahead, just in case," Levi said.

"Me too, Levi," I replied. Checking the time, I announced, "It's time for lunch. Please line up and we will go outside to enjoy the beautiful weather."

Opening the door, I allowed the students to file past me, each child grabbing their lunch pail on the way out. It had been a good morning, much better than the first morning of school the previous year.

September flowed into October. The Union cavalry defeated Jubal Early's troops in the Shenandoah Valley by the middle of the month. Petersburg remained under siege, with General Lee still holding strong. Atlanta was under full Union control, with Sherman itching to continue south.

Papa came to the school on Friday, November 11th while I was teaching. His appearance caused alarm, since Papa did not make a habit of showing up at the school. I stopped teaching and walked to the back of the school to talk with him. "What is it, Papa?"

"I just received word from Thaddeus as he delivered the mail that Abraham Lincoln won the election," Papa said. "I thought you might want to share that with the students."

"Yes, of course," I replied. "Thank you, Papa."

I went to the front of the classroom to make the announcement. The children cheered, as most of Marengo residents were heavy Union supporters. Like most people in the United States, our little community of Marengo just wanted the war to end and the men to come home. Re-electing President Lincoln seemed the best way to get that accomplished.

As I stepped into the general store after school the third Friday in November, I knew there was something in the newspapers worth discussing. The stove was surrounded by men wanting to put their two cents worth in, and no one seemed in a hurry to leave.

"What's happened?" I asked.

"General Sherman has done went and set fire to Atlanta," Delmar informed me.

"Set fire?" I asked concerned. "Were any people injured?"

"No, the town was evacuated first," Delmar said.

"What was burned?"

"Nearly five thousand buildings," Papa said, "including all the warehouses and railroad facilities."

"Do you think homes were burned, too?" I asked.

"I'm sure there were some homes involved," Papa said.

"I know this act is considered acceptable wartime activity, but burning homes and leaving families with nothing to come back to doesn't seem quite right," I said softly.

"I agree with you, Virginia," Delmar replied.

"Yes, one would have thought a better way could have been found," Pastor David commented. "I know supplies being sent north to Richmond must be stopped but I believe that has been accomplished with the siege Grant has on Petersburg. Burning a whole town seems a bit excessive."

The discussion of Atlanta lying in ashes continued as I walked behind the counter. Reaching into my mailbox, I pulled out a letter from Angus and dropped it into my dress pocket. Effie came from the storeroom with an armload of items to restock shelves. I rushed to her side to lighten her load and we both put the items on the shelves. Afterwards, Effie left for the day and I began to tidy the shelves and finish filling them. Friday was generally busy, and I knew

Effie had been kept busy just waiting on customers.

Thursday, November 24th, we closed the store and celebrated Thanksgiving. Momma and I prepared the meal at the farm and took it to the store to share with Reuben and Mary Ellen, so they wouldn't have to travel with the babies on the chilly day. Mary Ellen provided vanilla custard and squash pie for dessert. We all found things we were thankful for, especially the two precious bundles sleeping in cradles as we ate, but the fact that Carter remained among the missing left a place of sadness in all our hearts.

November became December and 1864 would soon become another year in history. On December 7th, Carter's 21st birthday, I walked to the creek when school ended for the day. I knew I needed to hurry to the store to relieve Effie, but I needed to mark this day in some way.

Standing on the bank, I watched the water flow by. It amazed me that this little creek, that began northeast of our farm, would join other streams and rivers, the final river being the mighty Mississippi, and eventually become part of the Atlantic Ocean. The water flowing past would travel to places I would probably never see.

Bending down, I carefully selected five rocks. The first toss was a total failure, since I had not attempted to skip a rock since Carter had left. The second rewarded me with three skips. By the time I got to the final rock, I had rediscovered the perfect angle it took to make a rock leap across the surface of the water like a honeybee flitting from blossom to blossom. As I counted the skips, I reached twelve before the rock sank below the surface.

"Wow, Miss Virginia, I didn't know you had such talent," Levi said, startling me.

"Levi, you just took a year off my life," I exclaimed. "I didn't know you were behind me."

"Sorry, Miss Virginia," Levi said. "I saw you walking toward the creek instead of heading to the store. I came to see what you were doin'. I sure didn't think you would be skipping rocks."

"Want to challenge me to a duel?" I asked the adventurous little boy. It was then I realized why Levi had stolen my heart; he reminded me of Carter.

"Do you want to lose?" Levi asked smugly.

"Well, not really," I said with a smile, "but I'm willing to take the chance."

Levi and I spent the next few minutes selecting rocks. When we each had five, we stood by the creek where the water ran slow and smooth. "You may go first," I said.

Levi released his first rock. It skipped five times then sank from sight. I only got three skips with my first try. By the third toss, Levi had found the angle, and the rock skipped ten times, and mine skipped eleven. Our fourth rocks were not good choices and we both could only coax five skips from them. It came down to the final throw, with me in the lead by one skip. Levi looked at me for a moment. I could see the question in his eyes, wondering if he should do his best or not.

"Levi, if you can beat me, you do it," I said. "I won't be a sore loser."

A smile spread across his face. He eyed the surface of the water a moment then studied his rock. When he had the rock positioned in his hand just right, he drew back and threw. We both counted out loud as the rock leaped like a frog. We were at fifteen before the rock sank from sight.

"That's going to be tough to beat," I said smiling. Levi smiled back at me, feeling good about his final attempt. Looking down at the rock I had chosen, I grasped it between my thumb and pointer finger. As I released the rock, I whispered, "This one's for you, Carter. Happy birthday." The rock skimmed the surface of the water and Levi and I began to count. When Levi and I stopped counting, we were at twenty-one.

"Wow! That was amazing," Levi said. "You're quite good at this, Miss Virginia."

"I had a good teacher," I replied, holding my tears at bay. "I have to get to the store now. Thanks for playing with me."

"Anytime," Levi said, "but next time I will be practiced up."

I laughed as Levi and I headed up the bank. As we reached Water Street, I turned right to go toward the store. Levi kept going up the hill toward the farm he and his father lived on. It was nearly two miles north of Marengo on the road that ran past Effie's house. The first half mile would be the worst, since it was all uphill. The road leveled out after that, winding through forests and past fields.

I watched as he pulled his hat lower over his ears and stuffed his now cold hands into the pockets of his ragged coat. His left shoe flapped on his foot where the sole was coming loose. It made me want to order him new shoes as soon as I reached the store, but I knew that would never do. Levi's father was too proud to accept such a gift and there were too many other children at the school who needed the same thing.

I picked up my pace, knowing Papa would be wondering what had become of me. As I stepped into the store, Delmar greeted me. "Goodness, Virginia, your nose is the color of a beet."

"I've been outside for a little while," I admitted.

"Doing what?" Delmar asked, being his usual nosy self.

"Winning a game," I retorted.

"Well, I know you weren't playing checkers!"

"No, Delmar, I was not," I said. "I was skipping rocks and my rock skipped twenty-one times, I'll have you know."

"Who on earth would play against a grown woman in skipping rocks?" Delmar asked laughing.

"Levi Weathers."

Delmar burst out laughing. "Virginia, I wouldn't be telling too many people you beat an eight year old at any game, not even if it was checkers."

"Levi was quite good," I defended, "but not as good as Carter."

Delmar grew suddenly quiet. "Your papa said today is his twenty-first birthday. I do hope he is celebrating it somewhere."

"Yes, so do I."

Effie came from the store room with an armload of items to put on the shelves. I rushed to take some of the load. "Virginia, I was beginning to worry what had happened to you."

"Oh, she's just been out skipping rocks," Delmar said, leaning his cane bottom chair against the wall behind the stove.

Effie looked at me confused. "Ignore him, Effie," I replied. "You should be a master at that by now after so many months of working here."

Effie laughed and shook her head. "I did beat him at checkers today."

"She cheated!" Delmar hollered.

"Delmar, I did not cheat," Effie defended. "I beat you fair and square."

"You learned to play checkers from Carter," Delmar fumed. "Carter cheats."

"You're just a sore loser," I remarked smiling.

"It's time for me to head home," Delmar said, slamming his chair to the floor. "I'll see you ladies tomorrow."

"Be careful, Delmar," I hollered as he clamored out the door.

"Doesn't he just beat all?" Effie asked as she began to place items in their proper places.

"He beats something, that's for sure," I replied laughing. "He's just gruff around the edges, though. Inside, he has a heart of gold." I felt just a bit guilty for not warning Delmar about Effie's checker skills before he coaxed her into playing. For years, she had been the champion checker player when we attended school. I figured it would be a long time before he asked her to play again.

****

Wednesday, December 21st, was the last day of school before we broke for Christmas and New Year's. The school Christmas program took place at 2:00 that afternoon, followed by refreshments. The children did the usual reenactment of Christ's birth. As Mary and Joseph entered, I looked at the group of wise men waiting their turn and dared one of them to bray like a donkey. Levi caught me watching him and smiled, proud to be chosen as the one to carry the gold.

When everyone had taken their place at the manger scene, the song "Go, Tell It on the Mountain" rang out. The audience, enjoying the rhythm of the song, began to clap their hands and sing along. As I strummed the song on the guitar, I looked out over those gathered and caught Mrs. George tapping her foot and swaying a little. When our eyes met, I thought she would immediately become stern again, but instead, she began to clap as well. I would definitely be playing this song for the church service on Sunday, which would be Christmas Day.

On Friday, I hurried out with the mailbag when I heard Thaddeus pull up. What had started as a few flakes of snow that morning had now escalated into blinding snow conditions. I quickly made my way to the wagon and placed the outgoing mail and a box for Angus under the tarp Thaddeus had strapped across the bed of the wagon. Thaddeus handed me the mailbag for Marengo.

"Be careful, Thaddeus," I hollered as I hurried back to the porch of the general store. Thaddeus waved and put the horses into motion, pulling his hat lower to shield his face from the falling snow.

Stepping back into the store, Papa came from the storeroom. "Goodness, it's really piling up out there. Perhaps I should head to the farm before it gets much deeper."

"You may be right, Papa. We haven't been busy anyway since not many people want to brave this weather. Effie and I can handle the store and Reuben is here for any heavy lifting."

"You haven't even looked at the newspaper yet," Delmar complained, looking up from his game of checkers with Pastor David. They were the only two men at the store.

"That's true," Papa said taking the mailbag from my hands. Reaching inside he retrieved the copies and went to sit close to the checker game and the stove.

Picking the mailbag back up, I went to dump it on the counter. I found two letters from Angus, one to me and one to his parents. Placing mine in my pocket, Effie and I continued to sort the remaining mail.

"Does Angus ever mention Carter?" Effie asked quietly.

"Every letter," I said. "He says he will not quit looking until he finds him. He believes he was captured and placed in a camp."

"I hope it's warm there," Effie said as she looked outside.

"The camp is probably in the south," I assured her. "It doesn't get as cold there in the winter."

"Do you think he's treated well?" Effie asked.

"I would like to think so," I said, "but the enemy is usually not treated well, and Carter would be the enemy. Angus says some of the Union soldiers don't even treat the bodies of the Confederate men who have died in battle well. No proper burial is given to them."

"That's sad," Effie replied, "but I'm sure the Confederates do the same."

"Yes, they probably do," I murmured, not really wanting to dwell on the thousands of young men lying in mass or shallow graves, or worse, being left for animals to pick apart.

"General George Thomas has crushed the Confederate Army of Tennessee," Papa announced.

"Rock of Chickamauga strikes again," Delmar bellowed.

"That means that only General Sherman and General Grant have troops fighting," Pastor David said.

"Yes, and now General George Thomas and the 55,000 men under him can now join those efforts," Papa said continuing to read through the paper. "Oh, goodness, General Sherman has been quite busy, as well."

"What's he been up to?" Delmar asked.

"He has made it to Savannah, Georgia, leaving a 60 mile wide, 300 mile long path of destruction," Papa said.

"Oh my goodness," Pastor David said, straightening up from the checker game, all tactics forgotten. "Are you saying he burned his way from Atlanta to Savannah?"

"Yes, I'm afraid so," Papa said, "or at least according to this Thursday edition of the Louisville Daily Journal, which has been correct on the war reports up until this point."

"Surely this war will end now," Delmar said. "How can the South possibly continue to fight with no supplies and their last remaining army under siege and completely surrounded?"

"I honestly don't see how the South can hold out much longer," Papa said.

The three men continued to discuss the war for a few more minutes then decided to head home before the snow became too deep. Effie and I only had a few customers the remainder of the day, which were mostly just town folks coming to get their mail. Reuben took advantage of the rare opportunity and went upstairs to spend time with his wife and children. At three o'clock Effie left too, the snow now nearly ten inches deep. By the time I closed the store at six, I had to trudge through a foot of snow to get to my cabin.

The next morning, I was surprised to look out and see the mass amount of snow covering everything. Looking up on the hill at the graveyard, I estimated we must have nearly two feet by the fact I could not see most of the headstones. The ones I could see confirmed that my estimation was correct by how high the snow was piled around them. Thankfully, it was Christmas Eve and we had chosen not to open the store. The only place I had to go was to the church for the special service that evening, which was right next to my cabin. It was not unusual for us to have snow for Christmas, but two feet was a rarity.

Momma and Papa decided to stay all night at my cabin after the Christmas Eve service and we attended church again the next morning. Afterwards, we all went to the store for Christmas dinner, which Mary Ellen had volunteered to cook, if Momma would provide dessert. I made two side dishes to add to the meal. Mrs. George surprised us all by accepting an invitation to come for Christmas dinner, keeping her from spending the day alone.

As we gathered around the table and joined hands Papa said, "By this time next year, I hope to have Carter here with us, and perhaps a new daughter-in-law and son-in-law as well."

"We will pray that it will be so," Momma said with tears glistening in her eyes.

After the meal, Papa read the Christmas story from the second chapter in the book of Luke. We then opened our simple gifts that we had lovingly made for each other. My knitting had improved over the past year to the point that I was able to make new mittens for everyone, and they didn't look like blobs of yarn when I finished.

Of course, the best part about the day was passing around Caleb and Clara and snuggling them close. The babies had grown so much over the past four months it was hard to believe. As I stared down at little Clara in my arms, I began to reconsider my pledge to never have children after witnessing Mary Ellen give birth.

Mrs. George surprised us all by asking to hold little Caleb. As the baby lay in her arms cooing, tears gathered in the old woman's eyes. Momma reached over to pat her shoulder. "I always wanted a baby," she admitted softly. "I just never became pregnant."

"You may come hold either of the twins anytime you want," Mary Ellen offered.

Mrs. George looked up and smiled. "Do you really mean that, Mary Ellen?"

"Of course, Mrs. George," Mary Ellen replied with a smile. "There's always diapers to change, diapers to wash, diapers to hang to dry, diapers to fold; well, you get the picture. Sometimes I just need someone to hold a baby so I can tend to diapers."

We all laughed at Mary Ellen's description of having excessive diaper duty by having twins. Sometimes I wondered how she got it all done. Glancing back down at Clara, I decided that, yes, I wanted children, but hoped the Good Lord only blessed me with one at a time.

Chapter Twenty-Seven

The year 1864 rolled over to 1865, and still General Robert E. Lee and the Confederates held on. On January 31st, 1865, Congress approved and added the 13th amendment to the U.S. Constitution. This amendment abolished slavery in the entire United States of America. The amendment was then sent to the states for ratification. I shared this fact with the school children as part of the history lesson.

"Miss Virginia, what does abolish mean?" Levi asked, beginning a long line of questions to follow.

"It means that something has been stopped," I replied. "In this case, it means that no one in the United States is allowed to own slaves."

"What is ratification?" an older boy asked.

"Ratification means that you confirm or approve. In this case, the states have to approve adding another amendment to the U.S. Constitution."

"I ratification the abolishment of slavery," Levi piped up, causing the rest of the students to laugh. I started to correct the grammar, but finally just laughed along.

"Why do the states have to confirm a new amendment?" Millie asked.

"Our government is set up with checks and balances," I explained. "This means that our President can't just add amendments or change laws without getting approval from other branches of government. The United States is a democracy, which means the government is run by the people."

"Oh, that's what President Lincoln meant in the Gettysburg Address," Millie said.

"Yes, that this nation, under God, shall have a new birth of freedom-and that government of the people, by the people, for the people, shall not perish from the earth," I said, quoting the last line of the Gettysburg Address. "You have a very good memory, Millie. It's been over a year since I read that speech to you."

"Thank you. But honestly, I have read it several times from the clipping on the wall," Millie replied, pointing to the wall behind me.

"I knew you ain't that smart," Levi said rudely.

"Levi Weathers, that was not nice," I scolded.

Levi hung his head in shame. Softly, he muttered, "Sorry, Millie."

"Levi, it's good that you apologized, but I also want you to pack Millie's books home for her each day after school for a week."

"Aw, shucks," Levi grumbled, "me and my big mouth."

I turned around so Levi could not see the smile on my face. I knew he had only been jealous of the praise I had given Millie and had not intended to hurt Millie's feelings. But I also knew I could not allow him to say mean things, no matter what the reason. The child's father was gruff, with no time for affection for the blond haired blue eyed child. It wasn't that he didn't love Levi; he just couldn't find a way to show it. For this reason, Levi soaked up every ounce of affection I showed him and resented when I showed any to the other children.

Checking the time while I was turned around, I turned back and announced, "It's lunchtime. Please line up and get your pails. You may play marbles, checkers or other inside games when you have finished eating."

The children made a line and began to gather lunch pails. I sat down at my desk and picked up my own. As the children sat back down, I blessed the food and we began to eat. As lunches were finished and pails put away, games began all around the school house. As Levi sat playing marbles with a group of children, I patted his shoulder softly, letting him know that even when he got into trouble, I still loved him.

****

The Louisville Daily Journal reported that President Lincoln met with Confederate Vice President Alexander Stephens on February 3rd. A peaceful solution to the war was discussed, but in the end, the meeting failed. The war would continue.

We had thought that the Confederate troops in Georgia had been defeated, but they moved north into North Carolina and continued to fight. The Union army was now 280,000 strong and even General Robert E. Lee would be a fool not to realize that the South was doomed to lose the war at this point. They had fought well and hard, but it appeared the nation would be mended and the slaves would be freed.

****

"It's over!" Papa announced as he came bursting through the doors of the school on Monday, April 3rd. "General Grant and the Union troops have taken Richmond. A telegram came to the Crisis newspaper office in Leavenworth and Thaddeus just stopped to inform us."

"Praise be to God!" were the only words I could muster. Looking around at all the children, and though it was only 10 in the morning, I announced, "School's dismissed! Go home and celebrate this victory with your families!"

As the children clamored out the door before I could have a chance to change my mind, I sank into my chair in the front of the school. Papa came to stand beside me. "This victory has been a long time coming," he said softly.

"Yes, Papa, it has," I agreed, "but now there will be no need for an Underground Railroad and Angus and Carter can come home!"

"Virginia, you know Carter may not…"

"Please, Papa, don't say it," I begged. "I will hope until there is absolutely no reason to hope any longer."

"Yes, Virginia, I understand," Papa said. "Let's go celebrate with the rest of the town."

Papa and I walked to the general store watching as one by one the residents of Marengo learned of the war's end. There was hollering and singing breaking out all around us. If ammunition hadn't been so scarce, I'm sure there would have been gun shots going off, too.

As we reached the general store, we had to cut through the crowd to get to the door. As we stepped in, Effie came running and nearly knocked me flat as she hugged me.

"It's finally over, Virginia!" Effie exclaimed.

"Yes, Effie, finally," I replied, smiling through my tears.

The next hour was filled with hugs and happy tears. Papa went home and brought Momma to town to celebrate. As everyone crowded on the porch and yard of the general store, Delmar hollered out, "Virginia, Mary Ellen, go get your guitars! Joe, go get that banjo! It's time to celebrate!"

"I have to get mine from the school," I said, starting in that direction. When I reached the Y in the road where going straight continued to the school and turning left headed up the hill toward Effie's, I heard my name being called. As I looked up the hill, I could see a small boy running toward me at full speed. Realizing it was Levi, I started toward him. As we closed the distance between each other, I could see he was covered in blood. Thinking he was injured, I broke into a full run.

"Miss Virginia…tried to help…Papa…the horses bolted…the disc…"

Even though Levi could not form a complete sentence in his distressed and out of breath state, he had said enough to paint a picture of horror. Farming accidents were not uncommon, and I was sure he had just witnessed one that had taken his father's life. Grabbing the child, I held him close. "Levi, let's go to the store. I will send someone to check on your father."

"He's …he's dead Miss Virginia," Levi hiccupped then continued the story in more detail. "He was disking down last year's corn stalks and got off the disc to check something. I had come home to tell him the good news but I waited until he stopped what he was doing. I hollered to him and he looked up at me. Miss Virginia, I don't know why, but the horses took off and Pa was in front of the disc. It ran right over him. I ran to help, but all he could mutter was, "I love you Son, and now I'm going to see your mother."

I held the child close as he sobbed out the story of his father's last moments on this earth. When he had calmed a bit, I looked down at him. "Levi, let's go to my cabin and I will get a rag so you can clean the blood off yourself. Then, we'll go to the store and I'll send Pastor David and my papa to your farm."

"Okay," Levi agreed.

A few minutes later, Levi and I returned to the store. A hush fell over the crowd as they realized the child's clothes were covered in blood. I could clean his hands, arms, and face, but there was nothing I could do about the clothes. Papa broke from the crowd and came to me. "Virginia, what has happened?"

"Levi's father has had an accident," I said softly. "The disc has run over him."

Papa gasped, knowing that few men lived to tell about such an accident. Pastor David stepped beside Papa and the men looked at each other, speaking without words. "We will go check on him," Pastor David said.

"He's dead," Levi muttered.

"I'm so sorry, Son," Papa said, touching Levi's shoulder. "You stay here with Miss Virginia, and Pastor David and I will tend to your father."

"Okay," Levi whispered.

Walking to the back of the store, I opened the door and took Levi up to Reuben and Mary Ellen's living space. Sitting him at the table, I went to get a glass of cool water from the crock. Momma came up the stairs as I sank into a chair next to him. Taking one look at Levi, Momma said to me, "Virginia, did you tell your papa to bring Levi some clean clothes?"

Jumping from the table, I hurried toward the staircase. "Will you stay with Levi until I get back?"

"Of course," Momma said, pulling a chair next to the shocked child.

Hurrying to catch Papa before he could get far, I ran out the back door. Papa and Pastor David were just leaving with the wagon. I called to them as I ran to catch up. "Papa, please bring Levi back some clean clothes."

"Of course, Virginia," Papa said.

When I returned upstairs, Momma had stripped the blood-stained shirt and pants from Levi's small body and placed one of Reuben's night shirts on him. The shirt reached to the floor but Levi didn't seem to mind. I hugged the child again, not knowing what else to do for him. Momma's voice came soft from behind me.

"Levi, would you like to lie down a moment?"

Levi shook his head yes, and Momma and I helped him into Reuben and Mary Ellen's bed. He shivered and Momma pulled a quilt up around him. Sitting on the edge of the bed, Momma stroked Levi's hair back and began to sing softly. A few minutes later, the child's eyes closed and his breathing leveled out.

"Stay here in case he awakes," Momma instructed me. "I'll go tell everyone what's happened."

"Thank you, Momma," I said quietly.

I sat down in a kitchen chair to wait for Levi to wake up. I could hear it grow very quiet downstairs and then footsteps thudding on the wood floor as the crowd began to leave. There would be no singing and guitar playing on this day. Our celebration had been cut short by tragedy.

School would be closed the next day, as the church would be needed for a funeral. I would ask Reuben to please go move the desks to the edge of the room and put the pews in place. As far as I knew, Levi had no other family. It would need to be decided where the child would live and who would care for him.

Levi awoke two hours later. Papa had brought back the body and a pine box was now being built. He had also brought back all the clothes he could find that belonged to Levi, consisting of two shirts, one pair of pants, two pairs of underwear, the ragged winter coat, and two pairs of socks.

Momma and I helped Levi dress in his own clothes. I could see Momma sizing his small frame as she did so and knew Levi would have new clothes by the week's end, if not sooner.

"What do we do now?" I asked Momma as we headed downstairs with Levi.

"Bring him to the farm," Momma said. "He can have his own room there and you can stay there with him. He has no one else, Virginia."

Reaching the bottom step, I bent down and looked into Levi's eyes. "Is that okay, Levi? Do you want to go live at the farm I grew up on?"

Levi nodded his head yes. I had never seen the child so quiet before. Holding out my hand to him, I led him out the back door of the store and to Papa's wagon. We climbed on the back and sat with our feet dangling off, just like I used to do when I was younger. Papa and Momma climbed on the seat and we were off.

We stopped by my cabin so I could get a few clothes. When we reached the farm, I took Levi upstairs to Reuben's room.

"This room is yours," I said.

"Okay," Levi said softly, sinking down on the bed.

"Hey, why don't we go outside?" I encouraged.

Levi slid off the bed and followed me back downstairs. As we walked out the back door and toward the barn, Ollie came running with a stick. I greeted the loveable dog then took the stick from his mouth.

"Watch this, Levi." I threw the stick as hard as I could. Ollie bounded after it, making sure to slide past it then run back to pick it up. Running at full speed, Ollie brought the stick back, crashing into my legs and knocking me flat. Levi looked at me with surprise for a moment then burst out laughing. It was the sweetest music I had ever heard.

"Here," I said handing Levi the stick "you try."

Levi tossed the stick with all his might. Ollie took off again, repeating the same action. As he bounded back, he stopped just short of knocking Levi flat. Ollie had shown his intelligence yet again, knowing not to knock the child down. Dropping the stick at Levi's feet, Ollie begged him to throw it again.

For the next thirty minutes, Levi played with the dog. We then walked down to the creek to skip rocks. I knew it was just a small reprieve from the grief that would come in full force the next day as we lay Levi's father to rest, but the joy of seeing him smile again brought great comfort.

That night when it was bedtime, Momma helped Levi into one of Carter's old nightshirts. As he crawled under the covers, I came in with one of my favorite childhood books. Sitting close to the oil lamp, I began to read. An hour later, Levi was still awake, so I continued another thirty minutes. When I looked up, Levi was still staring at me.

"Levi, it's time to go to sleep," I said.

"I know, but my eyes just won't close."

"Maybe a glass of warm milk would help," I suggested.

"Yes, maybe," Levi said thoughtfully, "and maybe if Ollie came to sleep on that pretty rug on the floor, too."

"Levi Weathers, my momma is not going to allow that big dog

upstairs. Sometimes she feels sorry for him and allows him to sleep in the mud room on really cold nights, but that's as far as she lets him come in."

"Maybe I could ask her," Levi suggested.

"If you think you must," I said, pulling the covers back so Levi could get up.

I followed Levi downstairs to warm him a cup of milk. Momma was sitting in the living room sewing Levi a new pair of pants to wear to his father's funeral the next day. I listened intently to see how Momma would graciously turn down this grieving child's request.

"Mrs. Hensley," Levi began, "would you allow Ollie to sleep on the rug beside my bed?"

"Bless your heart child, of course I will," Momma replied softly. The pan I had been holding full of milk slipped from my hand and crashed to the floor. Levi ran to the kitchen to see what had happened.

"Gee, Virginia, you sure made a mess," Levi scolded.

"Why don't you just let Ollie in to clean it up?" I replied smartly.

"Okay!" Levi said, thinking it a grand idea. Running to the back door, Levi threw it open and called for my dog. Ollie bounded in but stopped abruptly before entering the kitchen.

"Come on, Ollie," I called, "your confinement to just the mud room has miraculously been lifted."

Momma stood in the doorway between the kitchen and living room shaking her head. "He can sleep in your room tomorrow night, Virginia," she said smiling. "Come on Ollie, clean the milk off the floor."

At the sound of Momma's voice, the dog came bounding into the kitchen and licked up every last drop. I washed the pan and started to fill it with milk again.

"That's okay, Miss Virginia," Levi said, "I don't think I will need the warm milk now."

With that, Levi called to Ollie and the two of them headed back upstairs. By the time I mopped the floor and ascended the stairs myself, the child was sound asleep, and Ollie was obediently lying on the rug keeping watch.

"Traitor," I whispered to Ollie then bent to kiss Levi's

forehead. I patted Ollie's head on my way out, just to let him know all was forgiven.

The next morning, Momma had Levi try on his new pants. They fit perfectly. Next, she handed him a pair of boots. "These belonged to Carter as a child and I just never throw anything away," she told Levi as he tried them on. Those too fit well. Next, he slipped into the better of the two shirts he owned.

"How do I look, Miss Virginia?" he asked.

"Very nice, Levi," I replied. "We will have to leave soon. The funeral is scheduled for ten this morning."

"Okay," Levi said softly.

As we sat down on the front pew of the church, Levi slipped his hand into mine. I looked down at him and squeezed his hand a little. The bell began to toll just before the service began. I counted to myself. When it reached thirty chimes, it stopped. Pastor David stood and opened with prayer. When the service ended, everyone present followed the coffin to a dug grave on the hill. The pine box was lowered into the ground and Calvin Weathers' body was in its final resting place. Leading Levi away before the dirt was thrown back into the hole; we climbed back into the fine buggy Papa had bought when Reuben got married.

The rest of the week I rode to town with Papa, and Levi stayed with Momma at the farm. Levi would not be attending school until Monday, a week after his father's death. Levi had suggested it might be best if he didn't return until fall, since there was only a few weeks left of school, but that idea didn't get too far with Momma or me.

As I stepped down from the wagon on Friday, Papa said, "Happy 19th birthday, Virginia."

"It is my birthday," I said thoughtfully. "I had forgotten with everything that's happened this week."

"I thought you had," Papa said smiling. "I'm sure Levi and your mother will make you a cake today."

"I sure hope it's an oatmeal cake," I replied. "That's my favorite."

"After nineteen years, I'm sure your mother knows what your favorite cake is," Papa said with a smile. "I'll see you at the store later." With that, Papa put the wagon in motion and I headed into the school to get prepared for the children who would start arriving soon.

When school ended for the day, I hurried to the store to read the latest newspaper report. I wanted to see it in black and white that the war was finally over. Stepping up on the porch, Delmar looked up at me. "Did you have a good day at school, Virginia?"

"Yes, I did," I replied. "I see it finally got warm enough to move the checker games back outside. Have you won any games?"

"Everyone I've played today," Delmar said with a grin.

"In that case, I'll send Effie out to play you," I said smiling.

"Oh, no you don't," Delmar said. "She cheats."

"That's what you say about everyone who beats you," I said. Changing the subject, I asked, "Did the Louisville Daily Journal have a report on the fall of Richmond?"

"Yes indeed," Delmar said. "The Confederates set fire to their own capital as the Union army pushed in, causing mass destruction."

"Why would they burn their own capital?" I asked in disbelief.

"I don't know," Delmar replied, "but maybe because the Confederate President Jefferson Davis fled the city."

"The South's president ran off?" I asked.

"Yep, and nobody has found him yet," Delmar replied.

"Well, I'm sure he will turn up somewhere," I said opening the door and walking into the store.

I found Effie busy helping Mrs. George choose a fabric color and print. I wanted to pull her aside and tell her to save some time and just cut black or brown, but refrained. Instead, I walked behind the counter to check my mailbox. Finding a letter from Angus, I stuffed it into the pocket of my dress. With no other customers in the store, I started to go upstairs and say hello to Mary Ellen when Mrs. George called out to me. "Virginia, do you think this color would make a nice dress for spring?"

I slowly turned around, prepared to tell her that, "Yes, brown makes a lovely dress for all seasons." To my surprise, she was holding the pale yellow fabric dotted with small blue flowers. "Why yes, Mrs. George, that will make a beautiful dress," I said, truly meaning it.

"Fine," Mrs. George said. "Effie, please cut me off six yards of this fabric."

Walking to the counter, I cut paper from the roll, preparing to wrap the pretty fabric. I tried to imagine Mrs. George wearing such a print, but I could not conjure the image in my mind's eye. A few minutes later, Mrs. George left the store with a smile on her face, something I had never seen happen in my life.

"What's gotten into her?" I asked Effie as the door banged shut.

"I have no idea," Effie said, "but I hope it stays!"

"Do you think helping Mary Ellen with the twins has softened her?"

"That could be the reason for the change," Effie agreed. "Like I said, whatever it is, I hope it stays."

Chapter Twenty-Eight

The newspapers reported the official surrender of General Robert E. Lee to General Ulysses S. Grant on April 9th, 1865. They met at the village of Appomattox Court House in Virginia. Celebrations broke out in Washington as the four year war officially ended. All of these reports came with the mail delivered on Thursday, April 13th, being the next day was Good Friday.

Saturday morning, I opened the store and Papa stayed at the farm. He claimed Reuben, Effie and I could handle things and he would just spend time with Momma and Levi. Thaddeus rode up in front of the store a few minutes later. I knew he must have a telegram, since he was on horseback and not driving the wagon. Dismounting, he slowly stepped toward me as I came out onto the porch. The look on his face said volumes. Something terrible had happened. My first thoughts were of Carter and Angus. I was tempted to cover my ears and run back inside, not wanting to hear what Thaddeus was about to say.

"Virginia, I have really sad news," Thaddeus began. "President Lincoln has been assassinated."

At first I was relieved that the name Carter or Angus had not come out of his mouth. But as the truth of his words sank in, I realized our country had just lost the greatest leader it had ever had. Reuben came out on the porch behind me and I turned to him.

"Someone has killed President Lincoln," I whispered.

Reuben gasped. "Dear God," was all he could murmur.

Our little town of Marengo mourned the death of our 16th President, along with the rest of the North. We found out later he had been shot in the back of the head on Good Friday, April 14[th,] while watching a play. He had died early the next morning without ever regaining consciousness. He had gotten to see the Stars and Stripes raised over Fort Sumter earlier that day, signifying that the nation was once again whole. His mission had been completed, though his life was cut short.

By May, all Confederate forces surrendered, though the war had been decided when the Union army took Richmond. After that, I began to watch for Angus and Carter daily. There had not been a letter from Angus since the fall of Richmond on April 2nd. With all the destruction and food shortage that city had experienced, I was sure he was quite busy.

School concluded for the year after the second week of May. Levi and I had continued to live at the farm after his father's funeral. Momma had grown quite attached to Levi, and he to her. There was no one to contest him staying with Momma and Papa, so they claimed him as their own. I now had a new little brother, which was fine with me.

On Tuesday, May 16th, the stagecoach pulled up in front of the general store. This had happened several times the last two weeks, as soldiers returned home. Each time, Effie and I would rush out to see who got off. This time was no different. As the door of the stagecoach opened, I held my breath. Suddenly, standing before me was Angus. Scooping me up in his arms, he twirled me around until I became dizzy. Placing me on the ground, he bent down and kissed me right on the lips.

"Angus Zink," Delmar hollered from the porch, "you best be making your intentions known if you're going to kiss a girl on the lips right here in front of God and everybody!"

"It's good to see you too, Delmar," Angus hollered back.

"It's all just fine," a familiar voice spoke from behind Angus. "All I've heard on the way home is how he can't wait to get home and marry my sister."

Pushing Angus aside, I found myself face to face with Carter. He looked terrible. Reuben had appeared well fed upon his return from the war compared to the skeleton my brother had become, but I hardly noticed. I hugged him so hard he yelped out in pain. As soon as I stepped back, Effie took over. Reuben and Papa stood in line waiting their turn to hug him, also.

"Where did you find him?" I asked Angus.

"I didn't," Angus replied. "He found me. He's been in Andersonville, Georgia, in a camp since the Wilderness battle. When he was released after the fall of Richmond, he knew where to find me, if I was still among the living. He showed up in a food line in Richmond where I was serving."

"Thank you for bringing him home like you promised me you would," I said, tears flooding my eyes.

"I keep my promises, Virginia," Angus said, suddenly dropping to one knee. "And may I get a promise from you? Will you be my wife, Virginia Mae Hensley?"

"Yes!" I squealed.

"Oh, for goodness sakes, take that mushy stuff somewhere else," Delmar complained.

"Hey, Delmar, you have a pig to cook," I replied with a smile.

****

The newspaper reported at the end of June that an estimated 620,000 men had died during the war, and of that number, disease had claimed the lives of over half of them. Carter read the report out loud on the porch of the general store.

"It doesn't surprise me that so many died from illness" Carter said after reading the astonishing number. I watched men die daily in the camp at Andersonville."

"That's awful," Delmar said.

"Yes, it was," Carter agreed. "At one point, there were 30,000 men being kept in Andersonville prison and it was designed to hold no more than 10,000. I won't go into great detail, but Papa's pig pen smells better than Andersonville prison camp did."

I listened from inside the store as Carter talked of his time in the camp in Andersonville, Georgia. He mentioned that when General Sherman was setting fire to Atlanta, the men in the camp had hoped they would be rescued. Instead, many of the men were moved to other camps in South Carolina and on the coastline of Georgia. Carter had remained at Andersonville, but no rescue came until April.

Marengo planned a huge celebration on July 4th, 1865, to welcome back all the soldiers. The event started inside the Big Spring's Church, followed by a pitch-in outside beneath the oak trees.

Mary Ellen and I played our guitars and everyone sang "The Battle Hymn of the Republic" as the returning soldiers lined the front of the church. Many limped to the front while others, like Reuben, had missing fingers and arms. The time in the war had also changed many of them inwardly, like Carter who was now much more subdued. To those of us honoring them, it did not matter. We were just thankful they were home and the war had ended.

It had been reported that 20,000 of the Union soldiers who fought in the war had come from Indiana, and the young men from Marengo standing before us were proud to have contributed to the cause.

At the close of the ceremony, we all stood and sang "The Star-spangled Banner". As the last line of the first verse echoed off the walls of the church, "O'er the land of the free and the home of the brave", I couldn't help but think how true those words were now more than ever. Each person who called the United States home, no matter what their skin color, was now free; and every soldier, no matter which side of the Mason-Dixon Line they called home, was definitely brave.

Epilogue

The wedding took place on Saturday, September 23rd, after the weather had cooled down but the leaves were still green. Carter and Effie decided to get married the same day and make it a double wedding. Effie and I helped each other get dressed in my bedroom at the farm.

"I can't believe you talked me into getting married under that stupid maple tree," Effie fussed.

"That was the only thing I asked for," I reminded her. "At least Carter and I aren't making you and Angus race with us to the top of it to say the vows."

"I have never climbed a tree in my life and I don't plan to start now," Effie said.

"But there's so much to see from up there," I replied.

"I see enough with my feet on the ground," Effie retorted. "Are you ready?"

"I've been ready for a long time," I said, heading toward the door.

Papa, and Effie's father, Joe, were waiting in the kitchen. They would walk Effie and me to the maple tree and give us away. As we stepped out of the house, I could smell the pig roasting for the meal after the wedding. Delmar was standing watch over it up on the hill where it cooked in the ground.

We continued past the barn and toward the Maple. Family and

friends sat on wagons that had been pulled under the tree. I could see Mrs. George perched beside Momma in that pretty yellow dress, and they each had a baby in their arms. Levi sat beside Momma and waved as I walked by. Mary Ellen played her guitar as Effie and I approached.

I smiled as I neared Angus and Carter. As Papa placed my hand in Angus's, I glanced down so I wouldn't trip on the tree's roots. As I did, my eyes fell on the rock Carter had placed over the grave of the little girl who had died as her family sought freedom in Canada. I was shocked to see it engraved with "Rosie 1860". Glancing at Carter, he smiled that contagious smile, and I knew he had come out that morning to take care of a detail left undone for far too long.

The wedding vows were said, and before I knew it, I became the wife of Angus Zink. As he bent to seal the vows with a kiss, I heard Delmar holler from up on the hill, "Save that for later, Angus Zink! It's time to eat!"

About the Author

Beca Sue makes her home on an organic farm in Southern Indiana with her husband, daughter and son. She also has a grown son who makes his home in a neighboring county. She is a homemaker and enjoys helping out on the farm.

Beca Sue began her career by writing Vacation Bible Schools and has completed six different VBS programs, many of which have been used by churches throughout the region. She has also been involved with several elementary schools as a physical education instructor, director of music, and Christmas Program director.

If you have comments or questions, please contact Beca Sue at becasuebooks@gmail.com

Thank you so much for choosing this book. Please look for other books and EBooks by Beca Sue on the web.

Words of Thanks

I am grateful for the ones inspired to pen the hymns that are included in this book. Although they are all public domain at this point in time, I still would like to give the writers credit for these wonderful songs that are still enjoyed today.

Come, Thou Fount of Every Blessing-Robert Robinson, 1758
Amazing Grace-John Newton, 1779
The Battle Hymn of the Republic-Julia Ward Howe, 1862
My Faith Looks Up to Thee-Ray Palmer, 1830

Also, thank you to my husband and family who have encouraged me along the way and the many friends who have taken the time to read and critique manuscripts. You have been a blessing.

Thank you, God, for sending your Son to give his life's blood for the sin of the world.

If you have not accepted the free gift of salvation, don't wait another minute. Please, do it today.